THE FUTURE
FALLS

THE FUTURE FALLS

TANYA HUFF

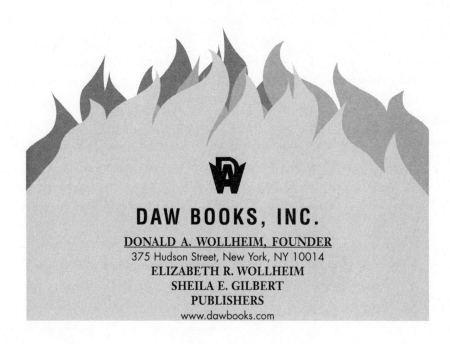

DAW BOOKS, INC.

DONALD A. WOLLHEIM, FOUNDER

375 Hudson Street, New York, NY 10014

ELIZABETH R. WOLLHEIM

SHEILA E. GILBERT

PUBLISHERS

www.dawbooks.com

First Printing, November 2014
1   2   3   4   5   6   7   8   9

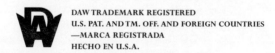

For Gary and Sheryl,
who trusted me a TRULY TERRIFYING AMOUNT to get it right.
Thank you.

ACKNOWLEDGMENTS

With thanks to Vicki Farmer, who brought JPL to life, to Alex Potter, who did the same for Vermont, and to John Chew, who helped with two plus two. Any deviation from reality is on me.

ONE

SHE LAY STRETCHED OUT under a beach umbrella, long silver braid coiled on top of her head, the fingers of one hand wrapped around a piña colada—made with real island rum and fresh coconut milk—the fingers of the other drumming against the broad teak arm of the lounge chair. She'd been watching a beach volleyball game and she hadn't appreciated having her view of half-naked, athletic young men bounding about on the sand interrupted by the Sight of a falling rock.

Usually, what she Saw was as open to speculation as an election promise. She Saw fire burning in the center of Calgary, and her granddaughter holding a double handful of water, ready to put it out. She saw discarded antlers on an empty throne, and knew the bloodline had been both challenged and changed. Granted, the Elder God rising up from a rift in the ocean bed off Nova Scotia had turned out to be more literal than she'd anticipated, but, usually, what she Saw was the metaphysical equivalent of interpretive dance. She got out of it only what she put into it.

Usually.

She wasn't in the habit of making the family a gift of what she'd Seen. A firm believer in anything free was worth the price paid, she usually arranged it so that the family worked for the information while providing her with weeks, or even months, of amusement. This time, however, she thought she might have to make an exception.

Having been banished from Calgary by her granddaughter, who was strong enough to enforce the banishment—pride warred with annoyance and occasionally won—she'd have to return to the family home in Ontario. To the old farmhouse where she'd raised her children and arranged for her grandchildren. In Ontario. In October. When the weather was seldom pleasant even with September barely out of sight.

Ontario meant Jane.

Who was less likely to be pleasant than the weather.

A warm breeze wafted past, bringing with it the scent of coconut oil and sweat, the sound of laughing young men willing to be charmed.

She had to be crazy to leave this behind.

Except . . .

It had been a *very* large rock.

Still, it wasn't as if a few more days of lovely weather and obliging young men would make any significant difference in the end.

". . . turns out that 2007 AG5 had masked the other asteroid."

Pam Yorlem noted that Dr. Grayson's voice had remained admirably steady throughout his report. The Director of JPL had dark circles under both eyes and his hands had been shaking slightly before he shoved them into his jacket pockets, but, considering that he'd spent the night on the red-eye from LAX then taken a taxi directly to NASA HQ after landing at Dulles, that was hardly surprising. Dr. Mehta, one of the scientists involved with the Near-Earth Object Program, looked significantly less affected, but she was twenty years younger than both Dr. Grayson and, Pam allowed, herself. Perhaps that made her more hopeful.

No, she seemed too smart for that.

Drawing in a deep breath, Pam released it slowly and said, "Let me see if I've got this. Sixteen months ago, LaSagra in southern Spain, determined that 2007 AG5, an M-class approximately 45 meters in diameter, will pass within about 3.5 Earth radii of the Earth's surface inside the geosynchronous satellite ring. Seventeen hours ago, you, Dr. Mehta . . ." Pam nodded toward the astrophysicist on the other side of her desk. ". . . discovered that 2007 AG5 was hiding another asteroid. A larger asteroid. An asteroid over a kilometer in diameter, masked by the metal content of AG5, including, but not limited to, the brightness of reflected light from its polished surface. You determined the existence of this second asteroid mathematically while killing time waiting for Vesta data to run rather than by actually finding another bright spot in the sky."

Dr. Mehta's brows rose, but before she could speak, Pam raised a hand.

"My apologies; that was uncalled for." Blaming the messenger was not the response of a person with her training and experience. "I'm not doubting your math. I'd like to, given that we apparently have twenty-one months before impact, but I'm not." At least not right now. It seemed a safe assumption that after discovering an NEO on its way to becoming slightly more than *near*, everyone would check and then recheck the math. "How long before the trajectories of the two asteroids diverge to the point where there'll be too many sightings of the second for us to keep . . ." She glanced down at the screen of her tablet, frowned, and looked up. "Seriously, Dr. Grayson? The Armageddon Asteroid? You're naming a large chunk of rock that will destroy a significant proportion of life on this planet unless we pull off the Hail Mary Pass to end all Hail Mary Passes after a Michael Bay movie?"

"Subsurface nuclear explosives are one of the listed diversion options," Dr. Grayson pointed out. He covered a yawn with the back of his hand. "Sorry, I can't sleep on planes. And technically, subsurface nukes are possible. Sort of."

"Maybe Bruce Willis can save us," Dr. Mehta offered, rolling her eyes.

"Let's not rule it out. All right . . ." Pam rewound the conversation back to before the distraction of a scientifically ludicrous movie. ". . . how long before there's too many sightings worldwide for us to keep this secret? And when I say secret, I mean out of the media, off the blog-sphere, public panic delayed?"

"Given the way the budgets have been cut for the big scopes and that amateurs tend to ignore asteroids once they've been listed . . ." Dr. Mehta tucked a strand of short dark hair behind her ear and shrugged. ". . . with luck, six months."

"Or someone could stumble over it tomorrow the way Kiren did. Or we could luck out and it'll be another 2012 LZ1—unseen until Siding Springs spotted it before the flyby." Dr. Grayson shrugged. "It's a crap shoot, Chief." He spread his hands. "And we're screwed either way. Twenty-one months, big hunk of rock, bam, extinction event."

"Bam?"

"Scientifically speaking."

"No." Pam squared her shoulders. She was a Brigadier General in the United States Air Force. She'd logged over 5,000 hours flight time in over 50 different aircraft and over 38 days in space. She was the second woman to command a shuttle mission and the first to command the International Space Station. She was the first woman to be in charge at NASA and she didn't do *bam*. "We stop it."

"How?"

"I have at NASA, Dr. Grayson, the best and the brightest minds in the world—and I include the two of you in that assessment. That's neither hyperbole nor flattery, that's fact. I'm sure that in the six months before the panic starts, you and your colleagues, here and internationally, will come up with a solution."

Dr. Grayson stared at her for a long moment, then all the tension left his body at once and he sagged down in his chair. "You really believe that."

"I do." She had to because *when in danger or in doubt, run in circles scream and shout* was no way to live. Or die, if it came to it. "I'll inform the president. I'm sure he'll want to speak with both of you, and I'll advise him to lock down both this information and what we plan to do about it at the highest security level. Thank you for bringing this to my attention. I'm sure I don't have to tell you to mention this discovery to no one else."

"It was why we got on a plane." Dr. Grayson covered another yawn. "You can't hack wetware. Well, you can, but it's not usually where they start. I hear everyone breaks on the third day."

"Dr. Grayson . . ."

Another yawn. "Sorry. Free associating."

"Before you got on the plane, did you mention this discovery to anyone?"

"I told the wife we were heading east for another budget discussion."

"What about Houston?"

"I thought we should see you first."

"Dr. Mehta?"

She shook her head. "I told Dr. Grayson . . ."

"Of course." Dr. Mehta had begun to look drawn, shocky if Pam was any judge. It seemed the younger scientist had held it together until she'd passed the buck upstairs and now reaction had begun to set in. "Talk to my assistant on your way out. She'll see that you have a place to stay until we know when you're heading back to the west coast. Get some sleep. Get ready for questions. In my experience, the joint chiefs appreciate PowerPoint."

"And small words," Dr. Grayson muttered under his breath. Given that she wasn't intended to hear it, Pam decided she hadn't. And he wasn't entirely wrong.

"Thank you for this." She gestured with the tablet. "You've given us a chance, however slight. I'll let you know what else we'll need from you as soon as I find out."

She'd started making notes before they were completely out of the office. The heads of equivalent organizations internationally would have to be informed. Media Relations could spin any leaks—and there would be leaks, there always were—on the conspiracy websites the government assisted the deluded to maintain.

Only nine million dollars of NASA's yearly budget went toward searching for NEOs, the majority of it supporting the operations of several observatories, and a significantly smaller portion into finding ways to protect the Earth from a potential collision. That would have to change.

While waiting for the president's office to get back to her, Pam started running the numbers, lips pulled back off her teeth as she imagined bringing this before the House Committee on Appropriations. "Let's see if *this* is enough to free up more than not quite half of one percent of the budget . . ."

With Dr. Grayson dozing beside her, Kiren stared out the window of the taxi, watched the rain, and wondered if she should have protested General Yorlem's interruption. The military might consider an assumption by a brigadier general to be fact, but she was a scientist and she knew better. Would have known better even had this particular assumption by the general not so personally concerned her.

Dr. Grayson had been the only person connected with NASA she'd told, but before she'd spoken to him, right after she'd checked the math for the sixth time, she'd called her oldest friend—fingers trembling so violently it had taken her three tries to make the call. She'd known Gary since third grade when his parents bought the house next door to hers. They'd gone through middle school and high school together—double-dated at both junior and senior prom—and headed off to MIT together, science nerds and proud. Their ways had started to diverge then; he'd headed into engineering and she'd gone into space science and data analysis, but they'd stayed friends. Accomplices when possible.

She'd stood for him at his wedding to a wonderful woman, her red sari a burst of color by their canopy.

"He's like my brother," Kiren always said when it came up. Actually, Gary was closer to her than her brother who was five years older and a bit of an ass. She hadn't called her brother when she'd worked out the mathematical possibility of the world ending.

Gary had listened to her babble, taken a deep breath, and said, "Are you sure?"

"Yes."

"Twenty-one months?"

"Yes." She chewed her lip while he thought. He might not have access to all the details, but he had information enough to draw the correct conclusions.

"Even if they free up the money, there's no way we—you, NASA—can stop an asteroid that size . . ."

"It's not so much the size, it's how close it is."

"All right. There's no way you can stop an asteroid already that close in twenty-one months."

"No." Oh, they'd try—the entire international community of space scientists would try—but, realistically, no. Unrealistically, no. Actually, no. Deflection efforts required years of warning. They had less than two. NASA had compiled a list of options back in 2007, but time had passed and Congress had never approved the funds necessary to begin developing them.

"But you're not going to give up." It wasn't a question.

She almost managed a smile at the certainty in his voice. "No."

"Well, then, I guess we'd better make the next twenty-one months count . . ."

Charlie loved Red Dirt music. It had a raw power that sang under her skin and buzzed through blood and along bone. More than merely a distraction, it was a cleanse and she desperately needed a few things washed away. It wasn't always pretty music, but she'd take power over pretty any day and she much preferred music meant for kitchens or cabins or smoky bars where her shoes stuck to the floor than music trapped by the engineered pattern of acoustic tiles.

If the family in Calgary wanted to believe she'd run from the occasionally cloying domesticity of Allie and her babies, well, Charlie was good with that. The actual reason was no one's business. Cloaked in their useful belief that *musician* meant *irresponsible*, she'd stepped out the back door and into the Wood and followed the music to Norman, Oklahoma, where she spent Wednesday night listening to the Damn Quails at Libby's, Thursday night at the Deli with Camilla Harp, and Friday in Oklahoma City at the Blue Door.

John Fullbright's concert, his first back at the Blue Door for a while, had been sold out for weeks, but Charlie was a Gale girl and a ticket returned in time for her to make use of it. Fullbright was amazing. His voice was a soft burr, a rough prayer, or shared laugh as required, and his roots were sunk so deep in Southwest Oklahoma he had almost a Gale connection to the place.

He wasn't so young that he reminded Charlie of why she was on the road, but he was young enough the words "old soul" were tossed about the room between songs. He wasn't an old soul, at least not so old it was obvious in his voice—Charlie would have been able to hear an internal age beyond Human norm—but he was undeniably talented.

"If you're Canadian . . ."

Charlie stared across the table at the burly redneck she was sharing with; she hadn't thought her nationality was up for debate.

". . . you should hear John's cover of 'Hallelujah.' "

"Leonard Cohen's 'Hallelujah'?"

"No, Handel's 'The Hallelujah Chorus.' Of course Cohen." He erased his frown with another swallow from a root beer can full of bourbon. "That boy and that song'll strip the meat right off your bones. Closest thing to a religious experience you'll ever get in a place where your shoes stick to the floor."

Hearing her own qualifier thrown back at her, Charlie grinned and hummed a quick charm onto his tattooed forearm, the sound slipping through pauses in the room's ambient noise. There were powers that respected a Gale charm, even this far south, and this man, who understood what music meant, needed a little luck in his life. From the moment he'd sat down beside her, she'd been half afraid of a lightning strike from the metaphysical black cloud hanging over his head.

A few days later, the music led her to a campground on a river, emptied of the summer tourists and filled with family in all but blood. Although the days were still pleasant enough, the nights nudged freezing. Charlie barely noticed the chill as she jammed until dawn with old women and young men and old men and young women and banjos and mandolins and fiddles and a dozen guitars. There was even a set of pipes and although the piper got pelted with bottle caps every time he began to play, he was clearly a familiar and loved part of the circle. Charlie had to fight to keep her power from rising with the music. She let it go once, after midnight had safely passed and let her creation hang in the air for a moment after the last note had been played.

"Well, damn," breathed the piper as wings and scales and fire dissolved into the night.

Then one of the banjo players picked out the opening bars of "Talking Dust Bowl Blues."

And they were off again.

The next day Charlie stopped off at a coin laundromat in Austin—even Gale girls needed clean underwear—then stepped out of the world, back into the Wood, and listened for where the music would take her next.

Allie's song wove through a stand of rowan, berries formed in the Wood's perpetual late summer but never getting a chance to ripen. She could follow Allie's song home, only Charlie wasn't ready to go home yet—and not only because Allie's song sounded a little sharp. Allie wanted Charlie to stop wandering. To stay home for more than a few months at a time. To allow herself to be gathered in under Allie's newly maternal wing.

Jack's song moved through the crowns of the birches, never settling, skirting the line between the Wood and what passed for sky in a place that ended where the trees ended. Like Allie's song, Jack's song had always been separate from the family symphony—hardly surprising given the unique combination of Dragon Prince, sorcerer, and Wild Power. Charlie stood for a moment, wrapped in what was almost a symphony on its own, well aware that with very little encouragement, Jack's song would fill the Wood until it was the only song she could hear. "Oh, no, you don't." Hands clenched so tightly her knuckles ached, she concentrated on not hearing him, not veering toward him, pulled by the power of his song.

Fortunately, Charlie had been walking the Wood for almost as long as Jack had been alive.

"Unfortunately," she muttered, following a fiddle through the maples, "I've been walking the Wood for almost as long as Jack's been alive." Irony was a bitch.

The fiddle joined a drum and led into the shadows under the oldest oaks where she lost the melody. Drums often led back to the aunties and she really wasn't in the mood to deal with that. Them. They'd poke and they'd pry and, while misdirection was possible, she'd pay for it later. Where the aunties were concerned, *later* was a guarantee. Avoidance had been working for her so far, so avoidance remained her best bet.

Spanish guitars. An accordion. A pipe organ that made the leaves on the alders quiver.

Curiosity almost sent her after a marching band, but the memory of the 2011 Rose Parade stopped her. Who knew massed potted roses would be enough greenery to give her an exit from the Wood? Or that the Rose Queen would be so high-strung? Although the screaming and the flailing *had* provided an opportunity for Charlie to slip away.

Power prickling under her skin, she cocked her head to catch something that sounded like a bluegrass mandolin. Richer. Fuller. A little like a cittern . . . No, a bouzouki. Flat picking "Snug in a Blanket," interwoven around a bass guitar, a fiddle, and a bodhran. Irish then, not Greek.

Now *that* was a worthy distraction.

Grinning, Charlie followed the song in and around the willows and out of the Wood, humming a countermelody as she stepped out from between two browning verbena and down off a concrete planter. Fortunately, at 9:10, the optometrist behind the planter was closed, and although there were a fair number of people still out on the old, red-brick sidewalks, no one seemed to have noticed her arrival. The surrounding buzz said fairly large city, the traffic told her she was in the US, and the license plates of the passing cars declared specifically for Maryland. To be on the safe side—not that stepping out of a planter was even close to the weirdest thing she'd ever been spotted doing—Charlie sang out a quick charm to erase her arrival from the memory of anyone who might have seen her.

Then "Mama Mia"—from the Abba Gold album, not the Meryl Streep movie version—rang out from the gig bag on Charlie's back, demanding attention and re-attracting every eye for blocks.

"Family," she sighed to the couple who stared at her as they passed. The nearer woman nodded in understanding. Slipping her gig bag off her shoulders, she dropped her butt down on the edge of the planter as she rummaged for her phone. She'd tossed it into a washing machine on her way out of the laundromat in Austin after fifteen minutes of her mother complaining about her twin sisters, twenty minutes of Auntie Meredith telling her about the weather in southern Ontario, and five minutes of her sisters declaring it wasn't their fault—where *it* remained mercifully undefined. Unfortunately, Gale family phones were hard to lose.

Not so much *smart* as *scary* after the aunties finished messing with the basics, these days the phones were handed out to every member of the family as soon as they turned fifteen. Although the general consensus was that the aunties used the phones in ways that would make James Bond shit jealous bricks, no one refused the gift—cheap, reliable cell service was far from the default on the Canadian side of the border.

"Okay, you've had three weeks to play around. Come home."

"You sound stressed, Allie-cat." Phone clamped between her shoulder and ear, Charlie tucked her guitar safely away and zipped the bag up.

"You know what would make me less stressed? If you came home. I know, I know, you're Wild—outside the family, beyond the laws . . ."

"Actually, I think that's Torchwood."

"Charlie! I have something to tell you."

"Okay." Charlie slid her voice into a soothing register, not quite a charm, but intended to calm. "I'm listening. Tell me now."

"Not over the phone."

Ah. Allie didn't want the aunties to overhear and, being Allie, didn't care if the aunties knew it. Odds were high there'd been more problems between Auntie Bea and Auntie Trisha. Auntie Trisha's initiating first circle ritual as an auntie had been in Calgary with David, so her ties to the original branch of the family back in southern Ontario were significantly less deep than Auntie Bea's—or Auntie Carmen's or even Auntie Gwen's. As the heart of the family in Calgary, Allie constantly had to play peacemaker between the dominant personalities. Not that *dominant personality* wasn't essentially a redundant description when referring to the aunties.

A door opened across the alley next to the optometrist's and the bouzouki music Charlie'd followed from the Wood spilled out onto the sidewalk, lifting her onto to her feet. "I'm chasing a piece of music right now, Allie, but I promise I'll be home later tonight."

A red sign over the scarred wooden door identified the bar as Nick O'Connell's. A sign taped to one of the three big vertical windows announced that the bands started at nine-thirty and there was no cover. Gales didn't pay cover charges, but Charlie appreciated the thought. Slinging her gig bag over one shoulder, she opened the door . . .

"Charlie, are you going into a bar?"

. . . and hung up the phone, allowing the music to draw her into a narrow room; a long wooden bar along one wall, tiny tables along the other. The clientele seemed younger than she often saw in these kind of quasi pubs and the number of sweating bodies already in place defeated the cooler air that entered with her. The fans hanging from the high, pale ceiling merely pushed the warm air around.

The pass-through at the far end of the bar showed part of a second room. Specifically, a stage and musicians. The music pulled her forward.

As much dining room as bar, the inner room was twice the width of the outer, the ceiling half as high. The stage had been tucked into the front corner by the bar, the walls were lined with booth seating, and the rest of the room filled with small round tables. This room was significantly less crowded and two of the three tables closest to the stage were empty. Charlie'd seen enough girlfriends, boyfriends, techs, and roadies to know that the occupants of the third table were with the band.

The bouzouki player was a slender man in his late thirties, early forties, with brown hair that curled around his ears and brown eyes behind wire-rimmed aviator-style glasses. He wore jeans and sneakers topped by a blue flannel shirt over a dark gray T-shirt. A ten-string Irish bouzouki hung from his shoulder by an embroidered strap—it was the wrong angle for Charlie to get a good look at the headstock—and the finish had the kind of small nicks and scratches that told her it was both well loved and well played.

Most people preferred to sit where the band couldn't see their reactions, but Charlie wasn't most people. She tucked her guitar under one of the open tables by the stage, caught the waitress' eye and ordered a Fat Tire as the song ended and the bouzouki player moved to the front microphone.

"I want to thank you all for coming out tonight, we're Four Men Down . . ."

There were five of them. The fifth was a woman with blue streaks in her hair and a smile that could probably be seen from space.

". . . and we call Baltimore home."

He waited until the crowd's cheering died down a bit before continuing. "I'd like to take a moment now to introduce the band. On guitar, Dave Anders. On electric bass, Mike Carter. On fiddle, our mistress of the bow, Tara McAllister. On drums, Paul Stephens. And I'm Gary Ehrlich on bouzouki."

"Can you do that in public?" someone yelled from the back.

"We can't get him to stop," the bass player responded.

Gary dipped his head and grinned, adjusting his tuning pegs as the room filled with laughter and innuendo. When he drew a fingernail across the strings, Charlie set her beer down and took notice. He'd re-tuned to FCDG, one tone below standard, in a noisy bar, by ear. Not too shabby. Bouzoukis usually played an interwoven accompaniment—a mix of open-string drones, two-note intervals, bass lines and melodic play—but Gary took the lead, fingers flying into "Boys of Blue Hill," a popular Irish session tune, familiar, given the reaction, to many of the people listening.

He played a double drop style, two adjacent strings struck simultaneously, one with a flat pick and the other with his first fingernail. More importantly, at least as far as Charlie was concerned, he played like he was exactly where he wanted to be, doing exactly what he wanted to be doing. She drank her beer and drew petty, inconsequential charms in the condensation. Charms that said, *I want what he has* and were wiped away again before they could take.

Damn, he was *good*. This music didn't cleanse, it moved in and made itself at home, leaving little room for anything else and that made it totally worth the crap she'd catch from Allie when she finally got back to Calgary.

By quarter to one, the three tables by the stage had been pulled together and O'Connell's had emptied but for Charlie, the band, the band's extended family, and Brian and Kevin Trang-Murphy who'd kept the original name when they bought the bar. No one remembered or cared that Charlie was a stranger—the universe arranging itself to fit the needs of a Gale girl.

"Specials didn't do so well tonight." Brian set two platters of wontons stuffed with cheese and potato down on the tables then dropped into an empty chair. "We might as well eat them, they won't keep."

"No bacon this week?" Dave asked. When Brian assured him they were as close to kosher as Vietnamese/Irish bar food got, he smacked Tara's fingers away from the wonton closest to him and popped it in his mouth. Tara cradled her hand and declared she'd never play the piano again. Someone pointed out she was a fiddler. Someone else said violinist and all fourteen of them got into a discussion about the difference, arguments tumbling over and wrapping around each other like puppies.

Charlie kept at least part of her attention on Gary, who sat drinking a coffee and eating his share of the wontons. When he spoke, she heard so many layers in his voice it took her four wontons and half a beer before she managed to separate the parts. Granted, less beer earlier on might have made the separation a bit easier, but since the beer also blunted a few other edges, screw it.

She heard contentment. As when he was playing, he was, right now, exactly where he wanted to be.

She heard love. For these people, these friends in general, and for Sheryl, his wife, in particular. When he spoke to Sheryl, that layer overwhelmed the others, obvious to anyone with working ears and half a brain.

She heard sadness. It sounded as though he were counting down the days to loss. Half of what he said had good-bye as the subtext.

He had a secret, Charlie realized with a sudden sense of kinship. He'd made his peace with keeping whatever it was to himself, but every now and then he wondered if he'd made the right choice. Every now and then, he'd shift his shoulders as though he were shifting the weight of the world.

He wasn't dying. Charlie'd heard Death join in every conversation she'd had with Auntie Grace last spring—they'd buried her in June—but Death didn't lurk behind Gary's laughter. Although death did. It was a subtle difference that seemed a bit emo for the bouzouki; it wasn't an instrument that lent itself to eyeliner and studded wrist bands.

She heard fear and anticipation. Doubt and joy.

"So, Charlie, got any advice about the whole itinerant musician gig?"

"Learn to depend on the kindness of strangers." Charlie snatched the last wonton out from under Mike's fingers and saluted him with it. "Why? You planning on trying it?"

"Not likely," Mike's wife Rhianna snorted. "And speaking of the kids . . ." She pushed her chair out and stood, one hand smacking her husband's shoulder. ". . . we should get back to them before my brother sells them for scientific experiments."

"Nothing's open this late," Mike told her, then turned back to Charlie as he got to his feet. "I'm not trying it, Gary is. Well, Gary and Sheryl. They sold the townhouse, bought an RV, loaded the cats, and are heading off to see the world."

"Or as much of it as you can reach in an RV with a cat," Paul added.

"This was in the manner of a good-bye gig," Kevin said, stacking the empty platters. "Next week at this time, they'll be hell and gone away from here."

"You can't get to hell in an RV," Dave pointed out. "Even with cats."

"I have a few gigs lined up." Gary ducked his head, adjusting and readjusting his glasses. "We'll be fine."

"We have savings," Sheryl added.

While that wasn't his secret, quitting a secure job for the road certainly explained the fear, anticipation, and doubt as well as the undercurrent of good-bye. Charlie helped sort cables and listened as Gary talked about finding their wedding DVD when they packed up the townhouse.

"We have no idea how it ended up behind the hot water tank."

"I suspect the cats," Sheryl sighed.

Charlie'd already bought both the band's CDs and when Gary tried to give her a copy of his EP, she paid for that, too. "This is your living now, dude. Don't give it away."

Half an hour later, they all stood out on the sidewalk in front of the bar as Kevin locked the door and Brian waved good-bye from inside the nearer front window. There were hugs and some tears and promises to stay in touch then, as Dave and Tara headed south, Charlie fell into step on Sheryl's right, heading north.

"My ride's this way," she explained, glancing up at the sky. It looked as though the clouds were resting on top of the streetlights and, as little as she wanted to be caught out when the storm finally broke, she could feel a small park or a large yard a block or two away—either less likely to attract attention than waving good-bye and jumping back into the planter outside the optometrist's.

"So, Charlie . . ." Gary shifted his case to his left hand and put his right arm around Sheryl's shoulders. ". . . *do* you have any words of wisdom about the whole itinerant musician gig?"

Her itinerant musician gig wasn't exactly typical, but most of her friends walked the same road without her advantages. And some things were universal. "Getting called for three months' session work in Vancouver while your cousin's twins are teething is a godsend." In more ways than one. She'd even managed to slip away before Jack could beg to go with her. Deciding to drive rather than drag half a dozen instruments through the Wood had meant she hadn't been able to use her inability to shift his scaled size as an excuse to leave him behind.

"Uh . . . Teething's not really an option. Anything a little less specific?"

Charlie waited for her phone to ring with one of Auntie Carmen's random bits of advice about clean underwear. When it didn't, although Auntie Carmen seldom missed so obvious a cue, she said, "Like anything else, music can be as much who you know as what. You'll have to work your contacts."

"Contacts? He was an engineer until two weeks ago," Sheryl laughed. The theme from *Jaws* ran under her words.

Ever since that summer in Cape Breton, Charlie had picked up a personal, albeit intermittent, soundtrack. Background music for the inside of her head. It had started as fiddle music, specifically Cape Breton fiddle music, but had branched out into multiple instruments and genres. Usually, although sometimes obliquely, pertinent to the matter at hand. Movie themes were new. "So you're thinking you might need a bigger boat?"

"I guess . . ."

Charlie could hear the worry behind Sheryl's confusion and suspected Gary could hear it, too.

"It's just," he began without prompting, "that this . . ." He patted his bouzouki case with his free hand. ". . . is something I've always wanted to do. I finally realized I had no good reason not to do it. This is my chance, my one chance to let music have its place in my life, and I'm taking it."

There was the joy.

Only the secret left.

"Fortunately," he bent and kissed the top of Sheryl's head, "my wife loves me enough to give up heated tile floors in the bathroom."

"I gave up the entire bathroom," Sheryl reminded him with a laugh.

Charlie considered bluntly asking what his secret was. Not the secret of why Sheryl loved him more than heated tile floors—less impressive in Maryland than in Alberta where it sometimes snowed in July—but why he'd decided to finally give music a chance. He'd tell her, Charlie could make sure of that, but, bottom line, his secret had added music to the world—which Charlie was all in favor of—and they were all—Gary, Sheryl, and the secret—thousands of miles and an international border away from her family. That made it none of her business. She suspected the whole not telling his wife thing would come back and bite him on the ass, but that was even less of her business and, as she was quite possibly the worst person she could currently think of in regard to relationship advice, all she said was, "Good for you."

He frowned. "Good for me?"

"Hey, Sheryl gave up heated floors. Good for both of you."

"Most people think we're crazy."

"First, I know *crazy*." Auntie Ruby had been insisting the chickens were flying monkeys for long enough even the chickens had begun to believe her. "Second, I'm not most people. Me, I'm all about people following their dreams. My family is a big believer in dreams." And, occasionally, in reading entrails. "I don't know of any bands looking to sign on a bouzouki, and I haven't heard about anyone who might need one for session work, but I do know someone who pays more attention to that sort of thing than me." When Gary and Sheryl stopped to wait for a red light, Charlie looked up and down the empty street, shrugged, and waited with them. She pulled a pen from the front pocket on her gig bag, and, after a little digging, managed to find a crumpled receipt. "If anyone's recording or gigging folk or Irish in North America, Dave Clement will know about it. Actually," she added thoughtfully, scrawling his number, "he's got a decent line on what's happening in the UK, too. Tell him I told you to call and he'll know you're worth his time."

Sheryl began to protest, but Gary stopped her.

"And this . . ." Charlie paused, decided she might as well go big since she still hadn't gone home, and wrote another line of numbers. ". . . is my cell. Call if you need me. If you're ever in the Calgary area, maybe we can throw a band together for a couple of local gigs." She couldn't promise more than that. A band would tie her to a place, and she needed to be free to run.

"Calgary, Alberta?" Gary shook his head. "Canada? That's a bit of a distance. What are you doing in Maryland?"

Charlie grinned. "Being itinerant."

Sheryl turned the receipt over, twisting it so it caught the spill of light from the streetlamp. "The Derby Girls?"

"My youngest sisters are on a team in the local roller derby league," Charlie told her as the light changed. She flashed a smile at a very pissed-off cabbie trapped behind the red, the only car in sight, and started across the street. "Gale Force Eleven and Gale Force Twelve. Our last name is Gale," Charlie added as both Gary and Sheryl looked confused. "Gale force eleven is a violent storm, twelve is a hurricane."

"Isn't Roller Derby a little . . . dangerous?"

Not as much as staking vampires in the Paris catacombs. Or beheading zombies in New Orleans. Or whatever the hell they'd been up to in Peru before Auntie Jane got a call from an old friend and sent Charlie to haul their butts home.

"Please," she snorted, "it's Canadian Roller Derby. It's all 'sorry about the kidney shot and excuse me, coming through.'"

"Really?"

"No."

"Okay, then. This is where we turn." Gary pointed west at the barely visible sign for a public parking lot. "You're . . ."

"Still heading north." She could feel trees on the other side of the big brick church. "Best of luck following the dream." As there'd been enough beer and music for hugs, Charlie took the opportunity to trace a charm on the bouzouki case, protecting the instrument within from rough handling, sudden changes in the weather, and cat urine.

"If we're in Calgary . . ." Gary grinned, all of them aware of how unlikely that would be. ". . . we'll be sure to . . ."

"Brush Up Your Shakespeare" rang out from Charlie's pocket. "It was gangster Shakespeare or Katy Perry," she explained, pulling out the phone.

Gary laughed. "Good choice." They waved as she unlocked it, Gary's arm around Sheryl's shoulders as they walked away.

Charlie half expected the overture from *Man of La Mancha* to follow them down the street, but when the silence remained unbroken except for a squeal of tires from the passing cab, she turned her attention to her phone. "Katie?"

Katie sighed with enough force Charlie almost felt it. "You hung up on Allie."

"I was . . ."

"Don't care. Every stoplight in Calgary has been red for the last four hours."

Charlie checked her watch—2:15 AM EST—and rounded back. "It's 11 PM in Calgary."

"Yes, and four hours ago it was 7 PM and traffic's been a complete bitch. I'm only grateful you waited until after the evening commute. Do you know why all the stoplights have been red for the last four hours? Why I've been here instead of spending the evening in the park with David? Because you hung up on Allie."

"Graham . . ."

"Graham got threatened with an ice cream scoop, decided discretion was the better part of valor, and spent the evening down in the store."

"An ice cream scoop?"

"She couldn't find the melon baller; not the point. The point is, you hung up on her."

"About four hours ago. Why'd it take you so long to call?"

"We tried. What did you do to your phone?"

"Nothing."

"I don't believe you."

"Why would I lie about that? Trust me, if I actually figured out a way to block calls, I'd tell you all about it." But her phone hadn't rung once while she was in O'Connell's or while she was walking with Gary and Sheryl, at least not until it was time for them to separate. In the last four hours, Charlie hadn't considered flushing her phone down a toilet, tossing it through the open window of a passing cab, or mailing it to Argentina to get a temporary reprieve from family.

She watched Gary and Sheryl turn into the parking lot. Someone or something had really wanted her to spend that time with them. If Charlie ever found out who or what it was, she'd have to thank them. "Is Allie okay?"

"What part of all the lights have been red for four hours sounds like okay to you?"

"I'm on my way."

"On your way where?"

Okay, maybe she deserved that. "Home."

"Aim for yesterday."

She couldn't make yesterday, but it sounded like Allie's reaction had been strong enough Charlie could have followed it back to the moment right after she'd hung up. "It won't change anything. The lights will still be red, and you'll still be pissed off when you call."

"Fucking Schrödinger's future," Katie muttered.

"You're the one who opened the box." Because the past had already happened, Charlie couldn't know what she was trying to change. If she were going to change it, she already had. If Katie had called and told her to go home to the moment right after she'd hung up, and nothing more, Charlie would have been able to follow the *oom pah pah* of Allie's reaction out of the Wood. Later, Katie would have told her to do something she'd already done and, for approximately four hours, Charlie would have been in both Calgary and Baltimore.

Once Charlie knew she hadn't been with Allie while she was also at O'Connell's, she couldn't go and *be* with Allie.

Being able to exit the Wood at different times had seemed like a kick-ass travel option until it became obvious that fulfilling the parameters was an absolute bitch. Once she'd realized that, Charlie'd let the family know she'd be happy to help with any do-overs, but the person making the request had to work out the details. So far, no one had taken her up on her offer although Auntie Gwen had spent the last three years working on an elaborate plan involving Joss Whedon and a shot-but-never-shown, second season of *Firefly*.

Having passed the church, Charlie rocked to a stop, stared into the shadows under the trees, and sighed. "It's not a park, it's a cemetery."

"What?"

"I need to concentrate now, Katie."

"Straight home, Charlie. No detours. She refuses to talk about it until you're here."

"Talk about what?"

"I don't know, do I? You decided to go bar hopping."

"One bar," Charlie began, but Katie'd hung up.

One bar was not bar hopping. Charlie shoved her phone into her pocket. It was *hop*, at best.

The cemetery was old. Historic even. Shadowed by the church and the office building across from it, the graveyard was distinctly darker than the sidewalk she'd left. Sycamore trees whispered overhead. The storm seemed more imminent here.

Modern cemeteries weren't so much cities of the dead as parks filled with inconvenient stone slabs and they usually attracted nothing more dangerous than joggers and dog walkers. The possibility of witnesses—mourners, caretakers, the recently dead—tended to keep thrill seekers and the terminally stupid away. Historic cemeteries, however, with their gnarled trees and high iron fences, time-darkened crypts and worn tombstones, attracted the sort of person who thought burning a few candles and scribbling chalk notations found in musty books bought at library yard sales would have no unforeseen consequences.

It was possible that this particular historic cemetery, enclosed, private, and urban, had, over the long years of its existence, escaped being visited by those sorts of people. Anything was possible; Charlie knew that better than most people. It was possible that the shadows wrapped around the worn stones were the result of a solid object blocking both starlight and streetlights. It was possible. But it wasn't very likely.

She actually didn't need to go into the cemetery to get home. If she didn't want to return to the planter—and she didn't—Baltimore had plenty of other ways into the Wood. Not so long ago, she'd have sketched a charm on the gate to keep people out and figured she'd done her bit to keep the accumulated malevolence from screwing up too many lives. Those who avoided the gates, clambering up and over the wrought iron, would have been looking for trouble so, hey, not her problem if they found it. Making them even less her problem, they wouldn't have been family. Or a threat to her family.

Not so long ago, that would've been enough. But not-so-long-ago was back before a troll had helped her discover that being a Wild Power in the Gale family meant more than charming strangers and collecting metaphysical frequent flyer miles by taking shortcuts through the Wood. Where *helped* meant *holy fucking shit that hurts.*

As the shadows shifted beyond the gate, Auntie Gwen's voice rose up out of memory. *"With great power comes great responsibility, a responsibility someone decided generations ago that not everyone in this family can be trusted with. You, Charlotte Gale, are a free electron, able to affect what you will. A warm body between this world and all the metaphysical shit that comes down the pike."*

"Because I'm responsible enough to handle it?"

"Because until you were put in a position where you needed to use it, you had no interest in it."

"Yeah, still not interested," Charlie sighed. It was possible this was the reason she'd been drawn to follow the bouzouki, but she doubted it. That had been all about Gary. This felt more like serendipity—in the universe's favor. "What a happy accident that Charlie Gale ended up where she can be made use of," she muttered, pushed her hair back off her face, and hummed a charm to open the heavy lock. The shadows shifted again. The wrought iron gate swung open so quietly, she could hear the trees rustling.

Although there was no wind.

Not rustling. A warning. *"Go back. Go back. Go back."*

"Chill, guys. I've got this." She caught the clang as the gate closed and sang it silent. When she turned, she could barely see the cemetery through the gathered dark.

Gordon Lightfoot's "Shadow" started up in the background. "Seriously? Lightfoot?" It switched to Britney Spears and Charlie shuddered. "I can see it's a shadow. Is Shadow. Shut up." Tucking her thumbs under the straps of her gig bag, and wishing she'd taken out her guitar if only to have something to do with her hands, she took one long step forward.

The world dimmed; the blurred and indistinct surroundings a cross between Corey Hart and Tolkien, between sunglasses at night and the one ring. She felt the shadow prod for weaknesses it could use, knew what it would find, and braced herself.

less human than you . . . half dragon, half Gale . . . rules for Gales don't apply . . . how can they apply . . . you know how you feel . . . you'd take care of him . . . see that he isn't hurt . . . you've been trusted with great power but not with this . . . damned for feelings . . . it's like they think you'd deliberately hurt him . . . you know you won't . . . you know you won't . . . they tell you your feelings don't matter . . . they don't trust you . . . all that power and they still don't trust you . . . he could be everything if you only had the courage . . . do it . . . do it . . . do it . . . show them they're wrong . . . do you want to be alone all your life . . . he'd go with you . . . why live in pain . . .

"Because it's the right thing to do," Charlie muttered. Salt in open wounds; so much fun. And that had only been the first verse. Those who dared the cemetery after dark—to hide, to sulk, to shit disturb—would be poked and manipulated and shamed and convinced they deserved to have what they wanted. Regardless of consequence. Had the shadow been able to hold a beer, it would have been indistinguishable from the assholes who finished the night with "Where's your phone, man? We got to put this on Facebook."

Charlie was deeply in favor of expending the least amount of effort necessary, but this sort of thing, this *deserved* a rousing rendition of "The Sun Will Come Out Tomorrow." Eyes squinted shut against the sudden flare of light, she finished a final irritatingly perky run-through of the chorus as the cemetery came back into focus. Show tunes, one. Gathered malevolence, zero.

That said, it took her a moment to unlock her fingers.

Remaining shadows were nothing more than a temporary absence of light. The sounds of a city in the very early morning—distant traffic, the hum of transformers on the power lines—pushed in from both sides, met in the middle and smoothed out to normalcy.

"Thank you, you've been a great crowd . . ." Names and dates on the gravestones moved in and out of focus as Charlie walked away from the gate. ". . . but it's time to go home."

In a cemetery this old, it was unlikely she'd pick up any hitchhikers, an annoyance in newer cemeteries where some of the recently dead seem to believe that being incorporeal was an excuse to cling. Given the situation, arriving with a haunt in tow would only put her further into Allie's bad books.

Although, it would also be a distraction . . .

No. Allie'd be distracting enough all on her own. She shouldn't have hung up. She was thirty years old, for gods' sake, and Gale girls learned young what happened to those stupid enough or unlucky enough to make a Gale girl angry. Younger members of the family reported that the boys' washroom at the Darsden East Public School still smelled like cordite and cinnamon.

"Now *that*," Charlie told Honor Brown, 1871 to 1907, Beloved Wife and Mother, "had been effective use of a muffin."

She stepped past a weathered obelisk, between two ancient white oaks, and into the Wood.

Two AM in Baltimore. Midafternoon in the Wood. October replaced by perpetual late summer. The smell of asphalt and lingering car exhaust and six hundred thousand sweaty people replaced by the scent of damp earth and growing things with the faintest hint of autumn on the breeze. In all honesty, Charlie had no objection to the smell of civilization—civilization gave her coffee and beer and the Mesa/Boogie Mark Five—but the Wood was like a member of the family.

After a quick check that she remained alone—Baltimore's aged dead evidently preferred the grave to travel—Charlie took a deep breath and sagged against the smooth bark of the closest birch. The moment she stepped out of the Wood, it had to be business as usual, so it was best she take a moment to regain the joy Gary's music had given her and to make sure nothing the Shadow had poked was seeping past the Charlie everyone expected to see.

The songs of family and friends wrapped around the bouzouki. Steadying. Comforting. Right up until Jack's song pushed its way to the foreground.

"Emotional scab picking. You're a class act, Charlie Gale." The complex harmonies of Dragon Prince, sorcerer, Gale boy wrapped around her, and in the Wood, where no one would judge, she could . . .

Shit. If Katie'd mentioned the cemetery, Allie would worry.

Worried on top of angry; not good.

Charlie slipped out of the Wood in the enclosed courtyard behind The Enchantment Emporium, the Calgary junk shop Allie had inherited from her grandmother—Charlie's Auntie Catherine and the oldest of the family's three Wild Powers. The shrubs in the small center planting were in full bloom even though, given the season, they should've been completely dormant. "Okay, that's weird."

She twisted around. The lights were on in Auntie Gwen's loft over the garage, but neither Auntie Gwen nor Joe were in the window, even though both of them would have felt her emerge. Joe wasn't family, as such, and while he might be a little tall for a Leprechaun, he *was* fullblood Fey with all the sensitivity and proclivity to angst that included. They had to have known she was the reason for Allie's mood and Auntie Gwen, at least, wouldn't want to miss the finale.

"I guess she's got her hands on his Lucky Charms."

The rim shot from her backing band was one of its few inarguable perks.

Facing the store again, Charlie noted that no one looked down from the apartment windows either. The lights were on in the kitchen/living room. The twins' bedroom, the bedroom that used to be Jack's, was dark.

She didn't look up at the sky. Didn't listen for the sound of wings.

The back door was unlocked. As the door could be only be accessed from the courtyard and the only way into the courtyard was through the Wood by way of the shrubbery or through the garage, the door was always unlocked. The last kid to try and break in through the garage had found himself in culinary school. The one before that still hadn't been found.

In the hall behind the store, Charlie turned left toward the stairs leading up to the apartment and paused in front of the large, rectangular mirror that dominated the space. The mirror needed no external light source to cast a reflection and although the background was a familiar expanse of Jack's golden scales to scale, it had, to Charlie's surprise, not changed a thing about her Docs, cargo pants, and leather jacket. Even her *Dresden Dolls* T-shirt had made an appearance.

Her eyes were still Gale gray, her hair dark blonde and barely long enough again to tie back. She'd gotten the small scar through her eyebrow when she was seven and pitched headfirst out of the treehouse. Had her Uncle Tomas, Allie's father, not made an impossible catch, she'd have probably broken her neck. The shiny, quarter-sized scar on her jaw had been a burn last year and to this day Charlie had no idea if Auntie Gwen's *and now you know what happens when you get too close to a dragon* had been a comment on only the flame.

She'd shut down "Ring of Fire" hard enough to hear strings snap.

Allie, who had a degree in Art History she'd actually got to use for a while before the grant paying her salary had run out, had declared the mirror to be an 1870s Renaissance Victorian original. Charlie, who almost had a degree in Sociology, Music, Drama, and/or English depending on how *almost* ended up being defined, considered it more a friend. Auntie Catherine, as willing as any auntie to take credit where credit may or may not have been due, had found it and hung it but denied having anything to do with its working.

As she watched, a red-brown stain spread out over the fabric covering her reflection's heart.

"It wasn't that bad. I'm fine."

The stain split to show a gaping wound with a fleck of gold in its depths.

"You're a romantic. I swear, it wasn't that bad." One hand on the heavy walnut frame, Charlie leaned in and rested her forehead against the glass. The mirror knew because the mirror always knew. She didn't know why it had chosen to keep her secret, but she was grateful. Considering the shit she'd given Allie about the angsting she'd done over her entirely unrequited and borderline cliché feelings for Michael, her gay best friend, Charlie was fully aware that payback would be a bitch.

At least she wasn't angsting. Running, sure. Angsting, no.

"So, any idea what's up with Allie?"

When she leaned back, her reflection wore a hazmat suit and stood knee-deep in dirty diapers.

"Did Jack try to feed the twins raw liver again?"

The pile grew.

"I'd ask if you knew something I didn't, but since you usually do, I'm going to go upstairs and take my lumps."

Her reflection held a shield.

"Thanks."

A line of charms to keep the twins away from the edge of the landing had been added to the standard protections around the apartment door. It seemed they'd figured out the doorknob while she'd been gone.

"And the lock?" Charlie wondered. "And the charms?" She hadn't been gone *that* long.

She fumbled out her key. Graham, for all that being a seventh son of a seventh son made him a special snowflake, couldn't charm his way in and out, so the rest of the family had gotten out of the habit. Show time. A deep breath and a reminder that Allie loved her, and she slowly pushed open the door.

"Hi, honey, I'm home."

A piece of pie splattered against the wall beside her head.

TWO

CHARLIE WIPED AWAY FLAKES OF PASTRY, opened her mouth to apologize, and snapped it closed again.

With two years and dozens of other cousins separating them, she hadn't been particularly close to Allie until she'd taken that first Walk in the Wood at fifteen and gotten hopelessly lost. Literally, lost without hope. She'd wandered for about two days; no food, no water, no idea of how to get out and then, in amongst the cacophony of sound slamming against her from all sides, she'd heard a simple and familiar melody that said, *this way home.* Allie's song had not only kept Charlie's first Walk in the Wood from being her last Walk in the Wood, but had taught her how to separate the sound into paths she could follow. That alone would have been reason enough for Charlie to believe Allie was something special, but after feeding her, her younger cousin had all but carried her upstairs, put her to bed, and stood guard outside the door to the room, refusing the aunties entry until Charlie'd recovered enough to cope with their interrogation.

While they hadn't exactly been attached at the hip ever since, their lives had been entwined. And if Charlie had come second in Allie's life to Michael and then Graham, she'd never minded because Allie had always come second to the music.

As it turned out, Charlie'd been right all along and Allie really was something special, objectively speaking. Powerful enough to have defeated *a* or possibly *the* Dragon Queen, she'd claimed and held Calgary, Alberta; all one million, two hundred and fourteen thousand, eight hundred and thirty-nine people, one million, two hundred and fourteen thousand, eight hundred and thirty-eight souls plus assorted Fey and family. For the most part, the city rocked on as it always had, but, when push came to shove, it didn't have to.

Now, Allie sat on the nearer of the two sofas, wiping her hand with a paper towel, an empty plate in front of her on the coffee table, tendrils of power extended far enough to lift the hair off the back of Charlie's neck and trail a heated touch up her spine. The only other time Allie'd ever been so overt, she'd been . . .

"Holy crap, you're pregnant again."

Katie, sitting on Allie's right, moved her plate and half-eaten piece of pie out of reach. Graham, on Allie's left, wasn't quite fast enough. Fortunately, he'd nearly finished.

Charlie swiped this second splattered bit of pie off her cheek and sucked the sticky pastry off her fingers. Apple. Auntie Mary's if she wasn't mistaken. Allie's mother made amazing apple pie—not too juicy, not too sweet, and barely charmed. Get enough sleep. Eat properly. Use the potty.

She frowned. Use the potty? "Aren't the twins a little young for pie?"

"You've been gone for three weeks," Allie reminded her.

"I know, but . . ."

"Mom's just trying to help."

"I get that." Allie anchored second circle and couldn't leave Calgary, and Auntie Mary was still disentangling herself from Darsden East where she'd anchored second circle before crossing to first. It was weird thinking of her as an auntie, but it happened to all Gale girls in time. Technically, first circle, like third, could go where they wanted, but with Allie's brother David in antlers in Calgary, the older aunties had decided Auntie Mary needed to be more connected to Uncle Arthur in Ontario before she risked it. And they'd all ignored Auntie Ruby muttering about the insipid morality of the masses and how they should have shot the balloon out of the sky the moment the damned thing appeared. When the twins were a little older, Charlie'd promised to run them back east to meet their grandmother and the rest of the family, but for now, all Auntie Mary could do was bake. "Does she know about the . . ." The expression on Allie's face cut off potential teasing before it reached Charlie's mouth. ". . . new pregnancy."

"No. I wanted to tell you first."

That wasn't it. Or that wasn't all of it, at least. Allie's pique drowned out the rest of the reason. It was, Charlie acknowledged, impressively loud pique.

"But you hung up on me."

The lights flickered.

"Is that the twins?" Katie jumped to her feet, head cocked toward the smaller bedroom and the sound of silence from two peacefully sleeping babies. "I should check on them."

Graham shot her a look as he stood, suggesting that, as they were his peacefully sleeping babies, he should have dibs on using them as an excuse to flee. "I think I . . . I left my laptop in the store. I'll just go down and check."

Later, Charlie had every intention of calling them both out on their cowardice. Right now, she let them run—exchanging a quick kiss with Graham as he passed her on his way to the door. When it was just the two of them, she crossed to sit beside Allie on the sofa, sliding into Katie's spot because Graham's wasn't hers to take.

Half-dismantled wooden train tracks made a figure eight between the overstuffed sofas. Plush animals had been piled high on one of the two matching chairs, folded laundry on the other. Four loaves of zucchini bread cooled on a rack on the kitchen counter and a pile of zucchini still to be dealt with had been stacked on the enormous dining room table. Kitchen, living room, dining room, all one big room with nowhere to hide. Although, in fairness, if Allie were really angry, there was nowhere in Calgary to hide.

Bare feet on the edge of the coffee table, Allie grabbed a throw cushion and clutched it to her stomach. "I'm not mad," she said, fingers picking at a bit of scorched fabric.

"You threw a piece of apple pie at my head. Sorry, two pieces."

"I'm not mad anymore." She flicked a bit of charred fluff out from under her fingernails. "But that doesn't mean I don't want an explanation."

"For?"

"Hanging up. Blowing me off to go to a bar. For not being there when I needed you."

"Allie . . ."

"A better explanation than *I'm Wild,* Charlie, because that's not an explanation, that's an excuse!"

She hadn't been ready to come home. She hadn't wanted Allie to talk her into it. If she was to go home, she'd go because it was her choice because she *was* Wild, damn it. And yes, she had other reasons, but they were her reasons and none of Allie's business.

Charlie searched for an explanation Allie would accept and found, "I had to banish a shadow from a cemetery."

Gray eyes narrowed. Well, technically gray eye because Charlie was looking at Allie's profile, but she assumed they still worked as a pair. "You were already on your way home, then. Go back to hanging up on me and try again."

"There was bouzouki music."

"I don't know what that means."

"It's like a mandolin on steroids."

"What is?"

"A bouzouki."

"I still don't know what that means, but go on."

Before Charlie could explain, or even work out what exactly the explanation was beyond *I heard bouzouki music and I followed it,* her phone rang.

"That's a classic ring," Allie pointed out as Charlie ran for the gig bag she'd hung by the door and rummaged in the outer pockets. "No appropriate, ironic, and/or sarcastic music?"

"About two weeks ago, every auntie switched to "We Are Family." So when I hit my limit on Sister Sledge, I locked the classic ring in."

"You can do that?"

"I was desperate."

"How do you know which auntie it is?"

"Does it matter?" Charlie sighed. "Hel . . ."

"So you're there," Auntie Bea sniffed. Auntie Bea was the senior of the four aunties now living in Calgary. The aunties themselves would say they had no hierarchy, but then the aunties themselves said a lot of things the rest of the family couldn't get away with. "Good."

"Actually, I'm in Baltimore, Auntie Bea. It's two-thirty in the morning, and you woke me out of a sound sleep."

"Don't be ridiculous, Charlotte; you're clearly in Calgary."

"Because I answered the phone?"

"Because the stoplights are working again. As you seem to have returned from where the wild things are . . ."

Charlie buried a yawn in her forearm. Aunties being clever. Just what the world needed.

". . . you could make an effort to think of someone other than yourself and be there for your cousin."

"I *am* here for my cousin."

"I was referring to emotional support, rather than the soothing balm of your mere presence."

"I got that."

"We offered our support, singly and collectively, but Alysha . . ."

Refused them entry to the apartment, Charlie figured, since none of them were there.

". . . wanted you."

"I know."

Charlie could practically hear Auntie Bea forcing her teeth to unclench. "So what was the problem?"

"I'm not sure you actually want to know . . ."

"Charlotte, we're her family. We want to help."

"It's a sex thing, Auntie Bea. It seems that while I was gone, Graham just couldn't match my practiced ability at . . ." Charlie snickered as Auntie Bea hung up. Some aunties would have wanted the details. And then offered advice. The trick, as with most performances, was knowing the audience.

Allie snorted. "They can tell when you're lying, you know."

"Unless Graham got in some serious practicing while I was gone, it wasn't a lie."

"Wanting to talk to you about the pregnancy before I made it common knowledge does not make my emotional state your responsibility."

After giving serious thought to throwing her phone out the window, Charlie tossed it on the coffee table and sat back down. "I know."

"I'm fully capable of being responsible for myself, this branch of the family, two babies, these new babies, the last zucchini out of Auntie Carmen's cold frame, and as much of Calgary as needs me at any given time."

The pique shifted and Charlie almost heard . . . No. Gone again. "I know."

"Stop saying that!" Allie took a deep breath and clutched the cushion a little tighter. "Okay, let's go back to when you heard bouzouki music."

"And I followed it." She raised a hand before Allie could protest. "I'm not being facetious, Allie-cat. I was supposed to talk to that bouzouki player. I might not have known that for sure when I walked in, but it was hard to miss by the end of the evening."

"Why?"

"No one called while I was with him."

"Yes, that's impressive, but I meant why were you supposed to talk to him?"

"He needed my help. Maybe even my blessing for the road."

Allie shifted on the sofa, turning to stare at her for a long moment. "Your *blessing?*" she said at last. The lights flickered again.

"I'm not ruling out this being a setup for some shit still to come, but, yeah, my blessing. In a musical sense. And a couple of phone numbers."

The noise Allie made in response was almost a growl. "He isn't family, Charlie, I am, and I needed . . ."

"You wanted," Charlie cut her off. "Not the same . . . Hang on." Frowning, she teased out a piece of information that had nearly slipped by. "*These* new babies? Twins again? Boys?" she asked when Allie nodded.

"Yes."

"You're sure?"

"Not something I'd make a mistake about."

"Because Uncle Arthur is failing to hold just like Uncle Evan did, and when the center of the family is weak, more boys are born to raise the odds of one with strength enough for the job." There'd been no Hunt called for over thirty years, but the aunties had called for two in the three years since Allie'd transplanted a new branch of the family to Calgary. Charlie swung her feet up onto the coffee table and slumped down against the sofa cushions. In a family that ran five to one, girls over boys, Allie and Graham's twin sons were already proof of the shifting powers at the center of the family. A second set of twin boys? The aunties would be smug and Uncle Arthur would get at least a year's reprieve. "Weren't you going to wait until the boys were older?"

To her surprise, Allie laughed. "Remember back when Graham was an assassin for Jonathon Samuel Gale and he never missed? Well, we just found another way his seventh son of a seventh son thing manifests."

"Through his dick?"

"Through not missing! Sperm. Egg. Bam. His dick is incidental. Not to me," she added hurriedly while Charlie cursed that last beer and the two times zones between Baltimore and Calgary that slowed her response, because incidental dicks were comedy gold. "He's a little freaked about it because he feels like he made some kind of unilateral decision even though I explained, again, the difference between using power—like a Gale—and controlling power—like a sorcerer—and I just talked him down from that, so please don't tease him about it."

"Would I?"

"Yes. The aunties are going to be bad enough and that's why I had to talk to you before they found out. We have to present a united front in this. Besides, now that we know, it's easy enough to deal with."

"You want me to neuter your husband?"

"Don't be ridiculous." Allie reached past the cushion to pat Charlie's knee. "I'm second circle, I could neuter him myself. I'm referring to condoms. Later. When they're not entirely redundant."

"Are you're sure they'll block the seventh sperm of a seventh scrotum?"

In fairness, getting smacked in the face with the cushion came as no surprise.

"Oh, good. You've made up."

Charlie emerged from behind the pillow in time to see Katie cross from the twins' bedroom to the window and peer down 13th Avenue.

"Auntie Carmen just called me. Apparently the . . . yes, the stoplight's working again. Did Allie tell you her theory about Graham's boys getting a little boost from his ancestry?"

She perched on the sofa arm and Charlie stretched up to give her a kiss before saying, "The seven sperm of a seventh scrot . . . Ow!" Again, not a surprise.

"Stop saying that."

"Stop saying what? The seventh sperm of a . . ." This time Charlie took the cushion away. "Okay, my brain is still on Baltimore time, so just to be sure I've got this . . ." She pointed at Allie. "You're pregnant again because Graham's the seventh son of a seventh son and that gives him gnarly, albeit unintentional, procreation prowess. I needed an advanced heads up before you tell the aunties—and nice job on keeping it from them, by the way, since I noticed the moment I saw you."

"You noticed because I wasn't hiding anything," Allie told her smugly. "You didn't notice before you left and I'm seven weeks along."

"Good point. So in case the aunties, who've been angling for the seventh son of a seventh son of a seventh son of a Gale, say something that infuriates Graham . . ."

"Odds are high," Graham muttered from the doorway.

". . . I'm to throw myself in the line of fire because you're pregnant . . ." She pointed first at Allie and then at Katie. ". . . and you're a chicken shit."

"I'm not sleeping with them," Katie snorted.

"Valid point. Okay, so the aunties need to be told soon before they find out on their own and get pissed off because, although you hid it from them, you told me and Katie . . ."

"I only found out tonight because you hung up on her."

". . . and Graham."

"I think my right to know supersedes theirs."

Charlie stared at him until he opened his mouth. Then she said, "It's like you don't even know them."

"Jack knows, too," Allie broke in before Graham could speak. "Apparently, I smell different."

"Where . . ." The word got out before Charlie could stop it. She closed her teeth on the rest of the question.

"And David knows because he's David." Allie hadn't noticed her slip. "And Kenny in the coffee shop knows because I switched to herbal tea. I'd have told the aunties sooner, but you were away."

"You should've called."

"I did call." Allie snatched the cushion back, her fingers white where they dug into the worn velvet. "You hung up on me! I gave you a chance to be Wild and then I called and then you hung up on me and I don't have any sisters and now I won't have any daughters!"

"There it is," Charlie murmured as Allie began to sob. She tugged the cushion away and gathered Allie up in her arms as Katie slid down onto the sofa with them. When Graham stepped forward, she caught his eye and jerked her head toward the twins' room.

Graham was sitting in the rocking chair, one of the boys tucked up against his chest, his cheek resting on the soft cap of chestnut hair. Standing in the doorway, Charlie grinned when she realized he was humming Burton Cummings' "Rocket Launcher" as he rocked. He'd been remarkably understanding about the boys being Gales, only insisting they carry Buchanan as a middle name. Charlie'd assumed Allie had charmed him, but she insisted she hadn't.

When he looked up, she softened her expression although, with only the night light on, he probably wouldn't be able to see much detail. "We put her to bed. Katie's with her until you go in."

"Is she . . ." Graham kissed his son on the top of the head and stood. Tried again. "Is she all right?"

"Mostly." Charlie moved over to the crib and stroked Evan's cheek. No, Edward, it was definitely . . . probably Edward still in the crib. "It's complicated. We have sisters. And daughters. And she's . . . different."

"So are you." Evan fussed a little as Graham set him down beside his brother.

The difference was, Charlie liked being different. "Hanging up on her worked out for the best. Katie's always been more of a sister to her than I have."

Hand rubbing his son's back, Graham huffed out a soft laugh. "I should hope so." Fingers lingering, he straightened. "Are you coming in?"

"Not tonight. Katie and I will sleep in my room. At the risk of sounding all tree of life tote bag, you two need to . . ." Charlie waved a hand. ". . . connect."

"If you're sure."

"Since neither of us are fifteen and all oh-my-God insecure about where we stand in her life, yes, I'm sure. Go."

He got halfway to the door, stopped, came back, and kissed her sweetly. Forehead resting against hers, he whispered, "It'll be okay."

Charlie was pretty sure that was supposed to be her line, but, hey, he was second circle and she wasn't, so she managed to make her *I know* sound not quite so much like *and you don't* as usual. "If you need me in the night," she whispered, leaning close enough to brush her lips over first Edward then Evan's forehead, "just yell. You know where I am."

The apartment upstairs over the Emporium only had two bedrooms, so when the twins were old enough to move into Jack's old room, Jack had moved to a bedroom in the renovated apartment over the coffee shop. Thanks to a Fabergé egg found in a box of ancient Easter decorations down in the basement . . .

"What is that smell?"

Charlie pulled a flattened mass of fur and bone and rattan out of the box. "I don't think you want to know. The Peeps still look good, though."

. . . they'd been able to buy the building next door and gut the second floor, turning a one-bedroom apartment into three bedrooms and a bathroom, now attached to the original apartment by a short hall. Jack had one bedroom, Charlie had the second, although she wasn't often in it, and she expected that once these new babies were born, Evan and Edward would be moved over to the third. Michael and his husband Brian had designed the renovation and had spent a couple of weeks working on the construction with the cousins—Brian complaining the whole time that they were architects not tradesmen as he took over the tiling in order for it to be done *right*.

Allie'd hit month seven just before the renovation began and had gotten a little moody. Sure, sometimes Calgary had snow in July. But it didn't usually need to be shoveled.

The telephone poles leafing out had been new for everyone.

Auntie Trisha had arrived the same day Michael and Brian had. The aunties believed that's what had settled things down—this sort of hormonal carrying on didn't happen back east where there were plenty of aunties—but Charlie knew it was Michael. He'd been Allie's touchstone since they were five.

"And let's hope Uncle Michael has been banking his vacation time," Charlie murmured as she tucked the tiny stuffed minotaur, a present from Boris, back under Edward's chubby arm. "So Mama doesn't make life quite so interesting for the rest of us while we're waiting for your new brothers."

Although, personally, she wouldn't complain about interesting. Interesting would not only keep her distracted enough to stay around, but keep the family's focus locked on Allie.

Jack had seen Charlie come home.

He'd been flying too high—high enough to be mistaken for a night bird should anyone look up—for Charlie to have seen him. Except, she hadn't looked up.

Why hadn't she looked up?

Allie and Graham had spoken for him, but he knew Charlie'd been the main reason the aunties had let him stay in the MidRealm when he turned fifteen. Charlie'd planted her feet, folded her arms, swept a disdainful gaze around a full circle of twelve aunties, and pointed out that the three Calgary aunties had as much as declared him Wild when they let him go east with her. *However,* she'd continued, *as nine of you weren't there at the time . . .* She then reminded them that while there'd occasionally been sorcerers—hunted down and destroyed when discovered—there'd never been a Dragon Prince in the family before. That made him unique. Unique, Charlie'd insisted, had always meant Wild, so unless they were going to start changing the way the family functioned, that meant Jack was Wild.

At that point Allie'd muttered something about all cats not being named Socrates. That had seemed so obvious Jack had ignored her, his attention on Charlie. He still wasn't sure if it had been her argument or her power that had finally convinced them—only Auntie Gwen had been overtly on his side—but after two days and three hundred and forty-seven cups of tea and sixteen pies—dragons liked to keep track of things—they'd decided he could stay. With the understanding that should he become a sorcerer instead of merely using sorcery, they'd hunt him down like any other Gale male and then he'd wish they'd sent him back to the UnderRealm. Jack had recognized a sincere threat when he heard one; he'd had plenty of practice. His uncles, the Dragon Lords, had never made a threat they didn't fully intend to carry out. They didn't always succeed; he was still alive after all, but they took their shot.

He'd expected that once he'd been recognized as an adult Gale that he and Charlie would be a . . . thing. Team. That he'd travel with her when she left. That hadn't happened. She'd traveled alone, like always. When he'd asked to go with her, she'd looked at him like she'd never seen him before and said no.

Well, actually, she'd said, *"I'm a musician, Jack, I travel for gigs. What would you do if you came with me?"*

But when the ashes were sifted, she meant no.

He'd tried to learn to play the bass. According to the internet, a bass player and a guitar player could form a band. A small band, but a band. Unfortunately, it turned out dragons had zero musical ability. Or maybe it was just him. He wasn't feeling quite bummed enough to go back to his uncles and ask.

So he watched her leave and come home and leave more often and he didn't know what to do to make her want him like she used to, so he'd gone out on *his* own and done a little exploring up north. It had been interesting, but it would have been better with Charlie. He kept turning to talk to her about things and she wasn't there. Since sometimes he turned to talk to her in midair, her absence seemed like it should've been obvious, but it took him by surprise every time.

His one trip back to see the family in Ontario had been entirely too full of Auntie Jane.

Mostly, though, he stayed close to home because that's what Gales did and he was trying to be a Gale first. And because as often as she left, Charlie always came home.

As an adult, he'd been expected to take part in ritual. He hadn't, too afraid he'd be unable to control the change to be able to perform the duties required. At least that was the way Allie'd explained it to the aunties. Their original conversation had been more along the lines of: "*You try and get it up when all you can think about is barbequing a cousin.*"

"*You've got more control than . . .*"

"*And thinking of how good she'd taste!*"

"*Okay, then.*"

He couldn't tell if the cousins he would have joined in ritual had been relieved or disappointed. Cameron did his best, but he was still the only third circle Gale boy the aunties had allowed to go west and it would be another year before the first of the boys who'd moved west as children grew up. Cameron's entire list of potential breeding partners had moved west with him and, in ritual, he was responsible for the rest of the third circle as well. He'd been talking about choosing his way into second circle just to get some rest.

"*Step up, Jack, I could use a little help.*"

When Jack had explained the problem, Cameron had hissed as he settled flesh rubbed raw into an ice-water bath, antlers still evident, and muttered, "*So eat a couple. It's not like there aren't plenty of them.*"

Jack didn't know if the aunties had a list for him. He hadn't asked and no one had offered to tell him. And there was always the species problem. Would the result be a baby or an egg?

Charlie stayed out of ritual, too, joining him as a fourth circle of protection around the rest of the family. Maybe if Charlie took part . . .

Pulled from his thoughts by the sudden roar of a jet, Jack realized he'd drifted into the approach path of the Calgary airport. Dropping a wing, he slipped sideways, careful to cause as little turbulence as possible. Even at only half his full size, an impact would destroy the plane.

The thought of imminent destruction reminded him of flying in the same sky as his uncles, and feeling slightly nostalgic about the adrenaline rush— less so about the blood loss—he circled back around toward the city.

As he passed over Nose Hill Park, a stag broke from cover and raced across the open ground on the top of the hill. Jack always had kind of a mixed reaction when he saw David running on hooves. He'd eaten a lot of deer since he'd come to this world.

Throwing a glamour on as he circled lower, he changed just before his feet touched the ground to drop the final few centimeters in skin. Normally, he'd create clothing out of whatever he could find around him, but as David wouldn't dress within the boundary of the park, he didn't bother. Neither of them would feel the cold.

David circled him half a dozen times before finally rearing up on two feet and becoming Human—or Human appearing, at least. The Gales didn't talk much about what they actually were, but taking his mother into account, it was clear Jack's father had needed more than mere sorcery to survive his conception.

"Jack."

"David." Unlike the girls, all so similar in appearance to someone who'd grown up with the brilliant variations of the Dragon Lords that half the time he still needed scent to tell them apart, Gale boys had a broader choice of coloring. David was tall and muscular with dark hair and dark eyes—rim-to-rim dark when he forgot to change all the way, the physical manifestation of the power he channeled. The aunties and Charlie did it too sometimes, reminding Jack, somewhat uncomfortably, of his Uncle Adam. On the dragon side.

"Problem?"

The anchor to the land, David was the conduit for this branch of the family's power. As far as Jack could tell, he had a pretty raw deal. Allie couldn't leave the city until she crossed to first circle, but David would never be able to spend much time away from the park. Plus, he had to deal with the aunties during ritual. "No, I just . . . I mean I saw you and . . ." He dragged a hand through his hair, pushing it back off his face. "Charlie's back."

"I know."

Of course he did.

Jack sighed and dug his toes into frozen bits of grass as the breeze blew the smoke away. "She's home because of Allie."

"Yes. You want her to come home because of you."

"Well, yeah, but . . ." When he glanced over, David wasn't smiling. "What?"

"On this land, Jack, I can touch your heart. I know you don't understand, but we have the seven-year splits for a reason—seven years older or seven years younger, no one chooses outside those parameters. Gale girls get more powerful as they age, and we're all attracted to power. That's a potential for abuse the family's chosen to guard against. We haven't always been so civilized."

"This from a man with antlers," Jack muttered rolling his eyes. He hadn't known he was a Gale until he was fourteen, so he got a lot of lectures on family dynamics his cousins had practically been born knowing.

David spread his hands, the calluses and dirt making them darker than his forearms. "This from a man with a tail."

"And wings," Jack pointed out. "Everyone loves the wings." He might—or might not—have a list, but he had no shortage of cousins pleading for rides. Although that had an age limit now, too; adults only. It wasn't as if Jennifer and Wendy had hit the ground. And he'd managed to gather up all the butterflies and change them back. He had a feeling at least some of the requests were for rides of a different sort, but while his cousins were blunt with each other, they weren't entirely sure of him. "Charlie's Wild," he said, not entirely certain why.

"And you're seventeen. Which is why you're stating the obvious. Charlie's thirty. Wild doesn't change that."

"I'm Wild."

"I repeat, Wild doesn't change that. It's not going to happen." Antlers arced up from David's brow.

"Just to be clear, when you say it's not going to happen, you mean me and Charlie? Happening? Like Allie and Graham happening?"

"Allie and Graham are second circle. You and Charlie are . . ."

Suddenly finding himself trapped by the weight of David's regard, Jack stared back as calmly as he could. Within the park, in spite of what their other forms suggested, David was the apex predator. Or at the very least, the greater power—which to the dragon part of him meant the same thing.

After a long moment, David allowed him to look away. "Yes, like Allie and Graham."

"Oh."

"Oh? You hadn't . . ."

"I thought it was a Wild thing." It seemed obvious—he didn't feel that way about anyone else in the family and no one else in the family was Wild. Except Auntie Catherine. Jack hadn't spent much time with her, but it had been enough that he felt confident in saying she didn't make him feel like Charlie did. Charlie made him feel like he belonged.

"It's that, too. But, mostly, it's that ritual is calling and you can't . . ." David actually hesitated. He took a deep breath and let it out slowly, his breath pluming like smoke in the cold. "Ritual is calling," he repeated, "and there's no one powerful enough to be safe with you."

"The way Allie is safe with Graham?"

"Yes."

That sounded more like a *sure, why not* to Jack. "Except for Charlie." It always came back to Charlie.

"Yes, except for . . . Jack."

Steam rose where the damp air touched his skin and, when Jack looked down, he realized he stood in an irregular circle of charred grass about two meters across. The edge of the char stopped at the edge of David's feet. "Sorry."

"Ritual's unanswered call makes you restless. That's all this is."

"This?"

"This," David repeated solemnly. "What you feel for Charlie."

"Oh." Was that what they were talking about, what he felt for Charlie? While ritual, or at least what happened during ritual, definitely had something to do with it, Jack admitted, it certainly didn't explain everything. But it was what David wanted him to think, and it was no skin off his tail if pretending he agreed made David happy. Appeasing the powerful was a basic survival skill. "Okay."

They stood together in silence for a moment, more aware of the city around them and the land under them than the rest of the family. Except for maybe Allie, Jack amended silently.

"Don't you ever want to leave?" he asked at last.

"It's not what I am."

"Who."

David snorted, sounding as much stag as man. "That, too."

"Cha Cha!"

"Edward!" Charlie scooped the toddler up out of the crib, balanced him on one hip, then reached for his brother. She never had trouble telling the twins apart when they were awake. Edward's speaking voice was pitched a little higher than Evan's, although Evan could hit a higher pitch while shrieking, and they were seldom quiet at the same time unless they were asleep. They both had brown hair and blue eyes like their daddy and a sprinkle of freckles like their mama. Katie insisted she could tell them apart by the pattern of the freckles. While not entirely willing to call her a liar, Charlie couldn't.

At just over eighteen months, they still mostly shared a personality.

The moment she reached the living room, they demanded to be put down, so she settled on the floor with them.

The oldest aunties—essentially Auntie Ruby who was two years older than God, well, some gods—believed that the family's identical twins shared a soul. The remaining aunties agreed that was a remnant of the old beliefs and Gale twins were no more likely to be short a soul than non-Gale twins. The rest of the family pretended not to notice that the aunties had hedged their bets with a distinctly nondefinitive statement. Charlie thought of her younger sisters and wasn't entirely certain Auntie Ruby was wrong.

"Your daddy says you'll become more individual as you get older." Charlie grunted as Edward threw himself off the sofa into her arms, squirming free of her grip in time for her to catch Evan who followed the identical flight path. "Your daddy thinks because he's a boy and you're boys, he knows what he's talking about. But your daddy isn't a Gale, and Gale boys are in a league of their own, aren't they?"

Evan burbled what Charlie took as agreement. Edward crawled under the coffee table, emerging a moment later holding a stuffed sheep. He stared at it, as though he'd never seen it before, then threw it across the living room. Evan took off after it—four running steps before he fell and decided crawling was faster.

"Dog!" Edward handed her a piece of a wooden train.

"Not even close, kiddo. Train."

He shrugged, grabbed it back, and threw it. Evan dropped the sheep and beetled after the train.

It was possible that *dog* had been in reference to his brother who had apparently learned to fetch while Charlie was gone.

Given that most Gale boys had between fifteen and twenty girls on their lists, most Gale girls moved straight from third circle to first without stopping at stretch marks and cracked nipples and that weird let's be connected to everything second circle got into. Charlie watched Edward run after Evan, bare feet slapping against the floor, plastic cover on his diaper crinkling with every step, and realized, given the impossible place her interest had fallen, that this might be as close to having children of her own as she'd ever get.

She was good with that.

Both boys looked up as the door into the hall opened, then returned to racing the train and the sheep across the floor when they saw it was only Jack.

Charlie kept most of her attention on the boys because that was the responsible thing to do, but she saved enough to watch Jack shuffle toward the fridge, eyes half closed, one leg of his worn sweat pants torn and trailing on the floor, the other halfway up his calf. The sleeves had been ripped off his Calgary Stampede T-shirt—given his effect on livestock, he never actually got to go to the Stampede—and his golden-blond hair appeared to be sticking up in seven or eight different directions. Fridge open, he tipped back the milk carton, swallowed half a dozen times, put the carton back in the fridge, pulled out a piece of bread, tucked a jar of peanut butter under his arm, and finally closed the fridge.

There were times when he made it easy for her to remember the relationship they were supposed to have, when he made it easy for her to show him the Charlie he thought he knew. It was, she had to admit, the best performance she'd ever given. Okay, maybe second best. She'd once done such a kickass cover of the Cowboy Junkies' "I Did It All For You" that when they finished the gig the drummer'd walked off stage and become a Trappist monk in New Brunswick. It might've been a coincidence, but Charlie didn't think so.

She waited until he'd started to toast the bread before saying, "Morning, Jack."

His huff of surprise fed the flame. "I knew you were there," he muttered as ash and a few black bits of bread still holding their structural integrity fell to the floor. He rubbed the smudge of soot off his thumb and forefinger and swept his hand over the scorch mark on the upper cabinet door, paint smoothing out behind the motion.

"That's new. When did you become so comfortable with interior decorating?"

"When you weren't here."

That might've been fraught, except for the petulance. "Jack . . ."

He sighed. "Allie doesn't like the burn marks so, if I'm alone, I get rid of them before she sees them. If anyone's there when it happens, I just take the shit."

"Not so much comfortable as sneaky." Charlie nodded and grinned. "I like that I'm not anyone."

He blinked at her, confused. "Yeah, sure."

He *had* known she was there. In that he'd known she was home and that made *there* limited and he'd scented her in her room over in the other side of the apartment and her scent permeated this part of the apartment so it was like he'd known she was sitting on the floor by one of the sofas. Right? Why was she watching him like she'd never seen him burn the toast before? And what did she mean, she liked not being anyone? She was the most *someone* he knew.

David hadn't helped. If anything, David had made him more confused. It was still all questions when it came to Charlie.

The whole time she'd been gone, Jack had kept mental lists of stuff he wanted to tell her when she got back, but he couldn't remember any of it, so he said, "You're up early."

"So are you."

"Couldn't sleep." He kept thinking she'd leave before he saw her. She did that; showed up, did laundry, left. Left without saying good-bye, like by wanting her to stay he'd done something to drive her away. "Allie?"

"Still asleep."

"Katie's in your room." He didn't bother toasting the two new slices of bread he pulled from the fridge. Charlie'd probably think it was funny to see if she could make him burn them again. "She's here a lot when you're not."

"Katie fills in for the sisters Allie doesn't have. I'm not her sister."

"Duh. You know Allie's going to . . ." He waved at the twins, who turned in unison to stare at him, but when he didn't burn anything down, they went back to running the train over with the sheep. "You here to have Graham knock you up?"

"What!"

Yeah, that broke the whole *too cool for the living room* thing she had going. Jack gave himself a mental high five and wished he had a way to record Charlie's expression. "If Allie's actually going to produce the seventh son of a seventh son of a seventh son of a Gale, you might have come home to help."

Charlie raised both hands, like she was shoving the idea away. "I didn't."

"The aunties think it'd be a good idea."

"I don't."

"Me either."

"Wasn't that one too many sevenths?"

He'd mumbled his protest into the cabinet while grabbing the peanut butter, so he wasn't surprised she hadn't heard it. Although Charlie usually heard everything. "Graham's a seventh son of a seventh son," he said as he turned, "so his seventh son will be the seventh son of a seventh son of a seventh son. And Allie's a Gale. So, seventh son of a seventh son of a seventh son of a Gale. Dragons are all about keeping bloodlines straight." It was one of the nonlethal ways they reminded him of the aunties.

"I thought there only was one bloodline."

"Sure. Now." Licking peanut butter off the side of one hand, Jack balanced his two pieces of bread on the other and collapsed onto the end of a sofa. From deep between the cushions, he pulled up two fluff-covered cookies, one infant Iron Man shoe, and finally the remote. He flicked the TV on, hit the mute, and started surfing. He wasn't ignoring Charlie because she kept leaving and he wasn't ignoring her because David had as much as told him to. He was seventeen not six. He was channel surfing while eating and besides, even if Charlie was doing that *I'm not watching you even though I'm really watching you* thing she'd started lately, she wasn't exactly keeping up her side of the conversation.

When Edward face-planted into the cushion next to him, Jack hauled him up onto the sofa by his diaper. At Edward's age, unable to defend himself from his uncles' attacks, he'd never left his mother's side. So far, no one had attacked the twins and, given Allie's reaction to a misunderstanding with a customer when the twins were napping down in the shop, that was a good thing. Graham had to call Michael and find out how to replace a whole section of the floor. Auntie Gwen had replaced the guy's memory. And his hair. Weirdly, she'd left his eyebrows to grow back on their own.

Half his attention on the past, and half on Charlie walking scales—musical scales, not his kind—up Evan's belly, Jack was a little too slow when Edward climbed into his lap and grabbed the remote. "Hey, not for larva!"

"Go!" Edward yelled and threw it across the room. Evan squirmed out from under Charlie's grip and tottered after it. Instead of bringing it back, he sat down and gnawed on one end.

So much for surfing. *Calgary Morning Live* started in on the weather and Jack turned his attention back to Charlie.

"You feed them?" he asked as Edward tried to pick a scale off his arm. He shifted the rest of the way into skin and ignored Edward's dirty look.

"Not yet." Charlie leaned back on her arms and stretched her legs out. They were tanned, even though the sun hadn't been out in Calgary for days. Jack wondered whose boxers she had on and hurriedly patted out a bit of smoldering upholstery on the arm of the sofa, hoping she hadn't noticed. "But Katie told me if they couldn't wait until Allie got up, I should give them some dry cereal."

"They need more meat," he muttered.

"They're not dragons."

"Duh. Dragons at that age *are* meat." He wondered, given the twins had no sense of smell to speak of, if they ever got Charlie and Allie confused. Charlie's hair was shorter, but nearly the same honey color. "Why'd you stop dyeing it?"

"What?"

"Your hair. When I first got here, it was all colorful." Dragons wore their personal colors like warnings. "Now it's bland and . . ."

". . . on the morning drive."

They turned together as Evan waved the damp remote, having gnawed the sound on.

"And now . . ." The anchor smiled at the camera. ". . . a story about our own local Doomsday Dan."

"Come on, Evan. Give the remote to Charlie."

"No, Cha Cha!"

"Wait!" Jack leaned forward and Charlie paused, one hand on the re-mote, the other holding Evan away from it. "I want to watch this. I know Dan. When he won't go to a shelter, I make sure he doesn't freeze."

On the television, in a familiar corner of the park by the zoo, a familiar ragged figure faced the camera.

"It's just down the road," Jack added, aware Charlie's attention was on him, not the television even if she was trying to pretend otherwise. "And that makes Dan . . ."

"One of yours?"

"That's not . . ." Except it was. "Yeah. Fine."

"It's a Dragon Prince thing; you find subjects." Charlie reached out, grabbed his leg, and shook it. Where most of the family would have looked condescending, she looked almost proud. "Go you." As she turned her atten-tion to the television, Jack patted out another small fire. "He's really into that end is nigh thing, isn't he?"

Dan had his toque in his hand, waving it wildly, the long gray tangle of his hair flapping around his face like greasy wings as he jumped up and down and shouted, "Bam! Bam! Bam! That's how it ends! Bam! Bam! Bam! All the king's horses! Bam! Bam! Bam! All the king's men! Bam! Bam! Bam! Can't put the sky together again!"

"You could rap that," Charlie murmured, fingers tapping her thigh.

"Recently someone posted Dan's . . ." The anchor's smile broadened in the pause. Jack growled in reaction to all the teeth and gave Edward a hug as the larva growled with him. ". . . *warning* online, and in a very short time it went viral. We sent Kelly Ahenakew down to talk to Dan."

Kelly had clearly explained the situation off camera—Jack doubted Dan knew what the internet was. When she pushed the microphone toward him, she said only, "So Dan, what do you think of your sudden notoriety?"

He snorted and Jack gave Kelly credit for not jerking back even though the spray was thick enough for the camera to catch. "I think we're all going to die."

"Because the sky is falling?"

Dan glanced up, took one long step to the left, and said, "Yes."

"The actual sky?"

Dan nodded. "The sky," he said solemnly, "is heavy."

And that was the last thing Kelly could get him to say. This time, Jack didn't protest when Charlie turned the sound off.

"How crazy is he?" she asked thoughtfully.

Jack shrugged. "He's Human. It's hard for me to tell."

"Good point. Thing is, the way I heard it, he believed what he was saying."

Jack shrugged again. "Belief doesn't make something true."

"I know, but . . ."

She waved it off, but Jack could hear her humming, mouth pressed against the top of Evan's head. Charlie trusted her ears the way most people trusted their eyes, and she couldn't seem to think without making noise.

"There's a lot of things up there," she said after a minute. "A whole bunch of junk, not to mention a space station, and beyond that asteroids, comets . . . You fly high, Jack. What do you see?"

He snorted. Edward reached up for the swirls of smoke. "Nothing falling."

"If there was a factual basis to Dan's claim, don't you think one of the scientists on that space station you listed might have mentioned it?" Graham pointed out, closing the bedroom door behind him. "They've got the best view."

"Daddy!"

Jack grunted as Edward launched himself off his lap.

Charlie stood as Evan joined his brother's charge across the living room. "Scientists don't know everything," she said as Graham lifted his sons into his arms. "They'd struggle to explain either of us and they wouldn't have the faintest idea of how to explain Jack."

"They'd have a go at explaining all of us," Graham muttered, "if they could get us onto a dissection table."

"Dissection!" the twins chorused in unison.

"Oh, sure . . ." Charlie tossed Jack a smile he couldn't stop himself from returning. ". . . I get Cha Cha, but they can manage dissection." She leaned between the boys and gave Graham a kiss. Jack bit back a growl. "Maybe Doomsday Dan is just ahead of the curve. Don't scientists say an asteroid is bound to hit in the next million years or so?"

"In the next million years or so pigs could fly." Katie hadn't exactly snuck up on him. Jack had heard her crossing the apartment; he'd just ignored her because she posed no danger. Well, no more danger than most Gale girls.

Jack swatted her hand as she ruffled his hair. "I could do that. Make pigs fly." Although he wasn't sure he could get them to fly under their own power or if it would be more of a controlled fall when dropped.

"Jack."

He looked up in time to catch Evan as Graham dropped him into his arms.

"Don't make pigs fly."

Allie woke up as Graham got out of bed. She kept her breathing steady, listened to him dress, heard the short burst of sound as he opened the bedroom door into the living room, and relaxed back into the only real quiet time she'd get all day. Reaching out, she checked on the boys, checked on the family in the city, checked on David and was thrilled to find him out of the park and eating breakfast with Auntie Carmen and Auntie Bea. With any luck, his presence would mute their smugness at her news.

It looked like they were getting their seven sons.

Given the Gale ratio of sons to daughters, she and Graham and Charlie had laughed about the thirty-five girls they'd have to get through for seven boys. The only thing keeping the aunties from putting Graham out to stud was that cursory research on blended families suggested the seven boys had to be full siblings.

She could still draw the line at four.

"And if a condom can't stop your daddy, there's always more permanent solutions," she murmured as she stroked the slight curve of her stomach—a curve that had nothing to do with this set of twins and everything to do with the last set. And possibly all the pie her mother had been sending. The permanent solution would mean she and Graham would no longer be anchoring second circle, fertility being nonoptional, but there were enough second circle Gales out here now . . .

Of course none of them had the benefit of their grandmother's meddling, the need to defeat the Dragon Queen making them strong enough to hold the entire city.

They could take turns so no one would have to hold it for more than the space between rituals, but with Calgary changing so quickly on its own, they'd have to scramble to keep up.

"Looks like we're doing this, babies." She sat up and threw off the covers. "So let's do it right."

After she broke the news to the aunties, she'd call Peggi and talk her into moving west. Her son would horn by next ritual and Cameron needed backup. The city could always use another pharmacist and her husband could return to school for the master's degree he always talked about. Both her older daughters were already third circle so, if they didn't want leave Darsden East in their last years of high school, there was plenty of family to take them in. Peggi wouldn't be hard to convince; Allie'd heard she hadn't spoken to Auntie Jane since the Hunt for Uncle Evan.

"The aunties won't like losing Steve," she told the babies, "but I don't really care what those aunties won't like. We have more than enough aunties of our own."

But no sisters.

She pulled on a pair of Katie's yoga pants and grabbed one of Charlie's band sweatshirts from the pile of clean laundry on top of the dresser. Judith had given her Richard's old crib, Rayne and Lucy had passed on about three dozen onesies, and there were tiny overalls that had been circling the family for generations.

She could manage without sisters; she'd done it her whole life.

But now there'd be no daughters either.

Just six sons and then the seventh son of a seventh son of a seventh son of a Gale.

So she'd love her sons like she would have loved her daughters.

Flinging open the bedroom doors, she stood and looked and listened . . .

Jack and Graham were arguing over porcine aerodynamics. Given the cloud of smoke up near the ceiling the debate had gotten heated. Evan was chasing Edward around waving a stuffed sheep, both of them yelling, "Bam! Bam! Bam!" Charlie and Katie stood shoulder to shoulder at the long counter dealing with the last of the zucchini. Charlie seemed to be weaving complaints about grating off her calluses into an explanation of the differences between a bouzouki and a guitar.

French toast this morning, Allie decided as the boys spotted her and charged across the room. Harder to charm than pancakes so she'd be less tempted to . . . fix some things.

*   *   *

"Jack, do not let Evan drink the syrup out of the bottle!"

"I didn't exactly let him." Jack grabbed the bottle with one hand and shoved half a banana toward his cousin with the other. "He's fast."

"Graham! Incoming!"

"Charlie, don't throw the eggs!"

"He can't miss, remember?"

Allie dropped a fresh loaf of bread on the counter and turned as the apartment door opened. "Auntie Gwen, have you got any . . ."

"Cinnamon." Auntie Gwen held up a spice container as Joe grabbed Edward on his way out the door.

"He's fast."

"See?" Jack demanded. "It's not my fault."

"Oh, for pity's sake, Jack, if he's running circles around you now . . ." Auntie Gwen's voice trailed off, the sudden silence so weighted it squashed all other conversations. She stared at Allie, dark eyes wide. "You're expecting again."

"I am."

"Twins."

"Yes."

"Boys."

"So it seems."

"You've been hiding it."

"Yes, I have."

To Allie's surprise, Auntie Gwen nodded. "I can't say as I blame you. Once Bea finds out, she'll go right to Jane and none of us will get any peace." She crossed the room and wrapped Allie in a hug. "Congratulations, at least now I know what we're celebrating."

"This isn't a celebration, it's breakfast."

"So it is."

Five adults, a Leprechaun, a Dragon Prince, and two toddlers required a lot of French toast, but with Allie on one grill and Katie on the other, Graham beating the eggs, Charlie pouring juice, Auntie Gwen setting the table, Joe dealing with the coffee maker, and Jack watching the twins, breakfast got made.

This was what she needed, Allie realized. When Charlie was home, then her family was home and family could deal with anything life threw at it.

Even near noon, the sunlight felt thin and the wind was cold and damp. As Catherine tucked her chin down in the collar of her down jacket, she thought of all the reasons why she'd left Ontario and put the weather at the top of the list. She hadn't been back since Edward's Hunt; he'd fathered her children, she'd owed him for that. She hadn't been the one to take him down, that honor had gone to their eldest daughter, newly changed, but she'd been there at the end. When she'd left, she'd assumed it was for the last time.

Second last, she'd be back when her time came.

Fine, third. She'd be back for Jane's time, too.

Her eldest sister had wanted her to be her good right hand—a desire she'd have been less insulted by had Jane not been left-handed. She'd Seen how it would be; Jane, already armed with both power and personality—and fully aware of how to wield them both—would use the Sight to nudge the family, then to steer the family, then to command the family, then it would have spread outside the family, then it would've been poisoned apples all around and no one wanted to go there again, least of all, if she were honest, Jane. It always took months to sort out the pies.

With the wind trailing chill fingers across the back of her neck, she watched Jane stand on the back porch for a long moment before descending to cross the yard, sighed, and revised her list. The weather now came a close second to her sister.

Dressed in boots and jeans and one of her late husband's jackets, Jane had begun to look old. To anyone else, she appeared to stride across the field much as she ever had, but Catherine could see how she placed each foot with care. The frailties of age might come late to the Gales, but they came. Of course, anyone who assumed those frailties lessened the danger was an idiot.

Catherine was no idiot. Which was why she'd walked out of the Wood at the edge of the woods and stayed there. It didn't matter that she couldn't See any charms of Jane's on the house. The ones she couldn't See would be the problem.

"You're so Wild you can't come in for a cup of tea like a civilized woman?"

"The tea would be charmed and we'd spend the entire time jostling for position." She'd stepped outside those petty power struggles a long time ago and she had no intention of stepping back in.

"You've Seen that?"

"I know you."

Jane clicked her tongue against the roof of her mouth. "Fair enough. Why are you here, then? Or more precisely, what have you Seen that's brought you home?"

"I've Seen Ruby's death."

"Please, we've all seen Ruby's death. Ruby's seen Ruby's death, she's just too loopy to recognize it." Steel-gray brows drew in. "While I think of it, Meredith says if you're not coming home for pickling next summer, she wants Auntie Martha's recipe for bread and butter pickles. She's given up trying to replicate it."

"Auntie Martha left the recipe to me."

"That's why I'm asking you, Catherine."

And just like that she was fifteen again, at her first ritual, watching Jane, already in second circle, blazing like a comet across the night sky.

Which reminded her of why she was there.

It must've shown on her face because Jane sighed, shoved her hands deeper into her jacket pockets, and said, "Out with it."

Because she'd never been about making it easy for Jane, she smiled and said, "The sky is falling."

THREE

AUNTIE GWEN PUT THE LAST FORK AWAY, closed the drawer, and turned with enough deliberation in the movement that Charlie dropped Evan into the curl of Jack's tail with his brother and stepped in front of them. Jack shoved her out of the way with his muzzle.

"Call your mother, Alysha." Auntie Gwen sighed as she pushed Jack's wing aside with her foot—even at a fraction of his full size, he took up most of the floor space in the apartment. "You have sixty seconds, then I'm calling Bea. You don't want your mother to find out from Jane, and Bea will waste no time calling Jane to gloat."

"Auntie Bea has nothing to gloat about."

"Do you honestly believe that will matter?"

Allie picked up her phone. "I should open the store . . ."

"Joe's got it. Call your mother."

Charlie thought of the likely fallout should Auntie Bea be the one to spread the news and shuddered. "She's right, Allie."

"And your acknowledgment of that has made my day, Charlotte. Don't chew on the dragon, Edward." She reached down and pulled the tip of Jack's tail out of Edward's mouth. "You don't want him to chew on you. Fifty seconds, Alysha."

When the door closed behind her with Allie still staring at her phone, Charlie crossed to the kitchen, plucked the phone from Allie's hand, and dialed. "Hey, Aun . . . tie Mary." Even two years after Aunt Mary's eyes had darkened and she'd crossed to first circle, Charlie still screwed that up. "Allie has something she needs to tell you. We'll be downstairs," she added as Allie snatched her phone back. "Jack, you'll need arms. Grab a twin."

"Mama?"

"Mama's busy right now, Edlet." Charlie lifted him from Jack's hold. "Let's go down to the store and see what Joe's doing."

"Yoyo!"

"Probably."

At the bottom of the stairs, she paused in front of the mirror and let the baby dive toward the glass, playing patty cake with himself. Her reflection looked up toward the ceiling, her face in shadow. Beside her, Evan hung from two enormous claws in front of a gleaming gold background. Except for the fact that the claws were unattached—Jack's forefeet would have engulfed Evan, Edward, and Charlie completely, taking up the entire reflection—they appeared to be to scale.

"Are you looking up at me?" Jack bounced Evan who shrieked with laughter.

Given their relative sizes and how little of Jack's reflection she could see, it was hard to work out the eye lines, but Charlie shook her head. Looking up, yes. Looking up at Jack . . . "No, I don't think so." With Edward balanced on her right hip, she lifted her left hand and stroked a line of blue into her hair.

Jack grinned, the mirror adjusting his reflection's size until his teeth were visible. "Did you do that for me? Because I said it was bland?"

"No, I did it for me."

"Why?"

"None of your damned business."

His grin broadened. "You did it for me."

She hadn't, not consciously. She'd just thought a little color might be less domestic. Less . . . bland. Yes, fine, she'd done it for Jack. Done it so he'd smile at her exactly the way he had. But he didn't need to know that. "Sure I did." Nothing sent up a smokescreen quite like the truth. "Because you're the arbitrator of all my fashion choices."

"Yeah? Then you might want to give the cowboy boots a rest."

"Bite me."

A burst of laughter pulled them away from the glass and into the store in time to see a pair of girls dressed in purple and black head out the door. A tattered lace shawl and trailing ends of a purple scarf became black wings on the other side of the clear-sight charm etched into the glass of the door.

"Corbies," Joe said as Charlie set Edward down on the counter. "They emptied their box. Seems they're moving on."

Charlie glanced behind the counter at the mailboxes the store provided for the local Fey. A surprising number of them got government checks, a few had magazine subscriptions—the water-based had trouble with personal electronics—and Boris regularly got the latest Victoria's Secret catalog. Charlie really hoped it was for the obvious reason because the thought of the minotaur in drag hurt her head. Bad enough that every time she saw him she had to squash the probably suicidal urge to say, *"Don't have a cow."*

"Corbies never stay in one place for long," Jack pointed out, setting Evan beside his brother.

"Yeah, but the whole flock's leaving." Joe pulled the royal blue, classic wooden yoyo from Evan's hand just before he bit down. "I wouldn't, kiddo. Your Auntie Catherine left these behind and they're likely to bite back. A flock of Corbies," he continued, moving the box of yoyos out of reach, "can't agree on what day it is, most days. Granted, they don't care, but that's not the point. For a whole flock to move on . . ." Dragging a hand back through ginger hair, he frowned at Jack. "You haven't heard about anything that might've spooked them?"

"Not a thing."

"If you caught up, think they'd talk to you?"

"They'd most likely shout insults at me." Jack caught Evan as he threw himself off the counter and set him down on the floor by a basket of toy cars.

"Even though you're you?" Charlie asked, pitching her voice to carry over Edward's scream of *"Down, down, down!"* As she understood it, the whole Dragon Prince thing had as much to do with being the meanest SOB in the immediate area as it did with politics and, excluding the aunties, that certainly carried over to the MidRealm.

"Corbies don't care. Not here, not in the UnderRealm. Just after I hatched, a couple used to come by and talk to my mother sometimes, but my uncles told me you couldn't trust anything they said."

"Could you trust anything your uncles said?"

"Not usually," Jack admitted. He turned back to Joe and waved at the door. "You want me to catch up."

He didn't look thrilled by the idea, not that Charlie blamed him. The Corbies never bothered with volume control, and their insults had a way of turning both nasty and personal. "I'll go," she said before Joe could answer. "They'll talk to me."

"You can make them talk to you, sure, but I don't think even you can make a Corbie tell the truth if they don't want to and if they think you're laying down a geis . . ."

"It's not a geis," Charlie protested. "It's just asking questions the right way." When both Jack and Joe looked dubious, she sighed. "Whatever. Call it what you want. Bottom line, it's Corbie business, not ours."

"If it's enough to spook a Corbie, we'll hear about it sooner or later," Jack pointed out, nudging a fire truck back toward Edward with his foot. "Probably sooner."

Charlie didn't find that exactly reassuring and, from the way Joe's brows nearly touched his nose, neither did he.

"They could have been lying about leaving," Jack reminded them after a long moment where the only noise came from plastic wheels on worn hardwood.

"True enough." Joe reached into the cash box and pulled out a twenty. Charlie wondered if it had been fairy gold the night before, changed to Canadian currency by Auntie Catherine's charm on the cash box, or if it had come from the slightly less mythological community the store also serviced. It never ceased to amaze her how many people needed mismatched saucers. "And now you've reassured us, Highness, go get coffee. When you get back, I need you to sort through a couple of boxes of old magazines. Last time we put a box out without checking, there were three that hadn't been published yet."

"It's like a bad episode of *Warehouse 13* in here some days," Jack sighed, waved the smoke away, and took the twenty. "Charlie, coffee?"

He said coffee. The subtext said, *at least you'll have to stick around long enough to drink it.* Fort Minor's "Where'd You Go" played in the background. She knew Jack didn't understand why life couldn't be a constant loop of that summer together down east, but the thought of sitting down and explaining things to him gave her hives. She valued their friendship even if a good part of it had become smoke and mirrors.

"Charlie?"

"Why not." It wasn't like she could leave before the aunties descended on Allie—not unless she wanted to find new living arrangements.

Over the next half hour, she drank a very good coffee and told her mother that, yes, she'd known Allie was expecting. Built a fairly decent reproduction of the Saddledome with the twins out of old wooden blocks while she told Auntie Meredith that, yes, she'd known Allie was expecting. Watched without watching the muscles in Jack's back and arms shift as he lifted boxes of magazines up on the counter to be sorted while she told Auntie Esther that, yes, she'd known Allie was expecting. Dragged Evan out from under a set of shelves while telling Auntie Ruth that, yes, she'd known Allie was expecting. Rescued Edward from the top of a set of shelves while she told Auntie Trisha that, yes, she'd known Allie was expecting.

When she came back from cleaning the grime off both boys, Joe had sold a yoyo.

"Mama!"

Charlie turned from the ledger in time to see Allie enter the store and stagger slightly, tackled by her sons.

Shuffling forward, a toddler around each leg, she smiled tightly at Charlie. "I'm about to ask Jack to eat Auntie Carmen."

"Did you want me to stop you or get Jack some condiments?"

"Good question." Allie gave up on the smile. "Mom's bearing the brunt of Auntie Jane, but Auntie Carmen's in tears because she was the last to know. Translation, she found out after Auntie Bea."

"They live in the same house."

"Auntie Bea answered the phone when Auntie Gwen called. While Auntie Bea was on the phone with Auntie Jane, Auntie Carmen called me and wailed for . . ." She checked her watch. ". . . just over twenty minutes. Auntie Bea wouldn't get in a taxi with her as long as she kept crying which is why they're still not here. Mixed blessings. Where *is* Jack?"

"Taking the mugs back to Kenny's. You weren't seriously considering . . . ?" Charlie waved her hands in the universal gesture for *going to ask Jack to eat an auntie?* Perhaps not *universal*, she acknowledged silently, but it came up surprisingly often.

"No, but they're on their way over now and he might need to singe them slightly."

Before Charlie could point out that would probably just make them angry "Will the Future Blame Us" rang out from her pocket. "I should take this, it's Auntie Catherine."

"She still gets her own ringtone?"

"It seemed safest. Do you think your mother called her?"

"Maybe. Maybe Auntie Jane called her to brag. My plans are working," Allie cackled, rubbing her hands together. Edward stared up at her wide-eyed. Evan sat down and put his thumb in his mouth. "Even though I'm thousands of kilometers away, I'm directly responsible for a seventh son of a seventh son of a seventh son of a Gale!"

Charlie paused, finger over the phone. "That's your impression of Auntie Jane?"

"What's wrong with it?"

"She doesn't usually sound like she's about to toss a fireball at the Scarecrow."

"Neither did . . ." Lips pressed into a thin line, Allie bent and scooped Evan up off the floor. "Answer your phone, Charlie."

That seemed like the best option. "Hello, Auntie Catherine. Yes, I did know that Allie was expecting."

On the other end of the phone, Auntie Catherine snorted. "Oh, for pity's sake, Charlotte, who asked? I Saw my granddaughter's condition months ago and it doesn't take a Seer to realize you'd be one of the first to know that she was about to present the family with yet another set of male twins."

"You Saw it and you didn't think to mention it?" *Saw the babies,* she mouthed at Allie.

"You'd be astonished at what I See and never pass on to the family. Half of it they wouldn't believe and the other half they don't need to know. You may still be all about sharing and caring, but I live in hope that you'll stop diving to my granddaughter's lure when you've been Wild a little longer."

"If you already know about the babies, then why did you call, Auntie Catherine?"

"I can't call just to talk?"

"You don't."

"True. There's a Calgary . . . What is the politically correct label for bums now? Economically disabled? Never mind," she continued before Charlie could answer. "Let's go with *personality.* There's a Calgary personality known as Doomsday Dan."

Charlie felt a cold touch along her spine. The odds of it being a coincidence that she'd seen Dan on the same day Auntie Catherine called and mentioned him were slim to none. The universe didn't work that way, not for Gales. "What about him?"

"He's right."

"What's he right ab . . . Auntie Catherine?"

"She hung up."

It wasn't a question, but Charlie answered anyway. "Yeah."

"And you're leaving."

"How did you get that from *yeah?*"

With Evan on her hip, Allie couldn't fold her arms, but her entire posture screamed that, had she been able, they'd have been crossed with extreme prejudice. "Are you?"

"Well, yeah." Although she still didn't get how Allie'd figured it out. "There was a crazy street dude on television this morning before you got up, ranting about . . ." Charlie edited *the end of the world* out of her explanation. Since the babies, even joking about death and disaster had been taken off the table. ". . . all sorts of weird shit. Your grandmother just called to say he was right."

Allie's left foot began to tap. Edward watched it, fascinated. "She's Seen a crazy street dude talking about weird shit?"

"Apparently."

"*Crazy street dude talking about weird shit?* Really, Charlie? You're thirty, not thirteen."

"And thank you for reminding me." But, yes, it sounded idiotic repeated over and over. "Mentally unstable homeless person making obscure prophecies about the future."

"Was that so hard?" As Edward grabbed two handfuls of Allie's jeans and began to haul himself up onto his feet, she shifted position and even Charlie, third circle though she was, felt her anchor herself in the city. Her gaze blanked for a moment—checking on the rest of the family, Charlie assumed—then refocused on Charlie's face. "Why did she call you about it?"

Because I'm Wild and she's Wild and we're not like you. We don't dig in and wrap ourselves in family to the exclusion of all else. But we're still Gales and we still need family . . .

"Charlie? Charlie, are you having an epiphany in front of my children?"

"What?" She shook herself free to find Allie and both boys grinning at her. "No. No epiphanies. Not with minors in the room." Allie's grin broadened, Evan blew a spit bubble, Edward climbed onto Allie's foot, and Charlie felt like she'd dodged a bullet. The last thing she needed was for Allie to think she'd ever take Auntie Catherine's side. Not after what had gone down with the Dragon Queen. "And I don't know why Auntie Catherine called me," she continued as if there hadn't been both an epiphany and a lie about it. "That's why I need to talk to her and find out what she's actually Seen."

"Maybe she's just messing with you. You know how she hates not being the center of attention."

Actually, Charlie knew how Auntie Catherine had created a new life for herself in Calgary away from the family and then left that life to Allie when she was banished. Later, she'd set in motion a plan to stop one of the old gods from rising and while the plan had been high-handed and bordering on downright nasty, the family wouldn't have known about the rising *or* the plan had it not overlapped with Charlie's music. In Charlie's opinion, Auntie Catherine had no interest at all in being the center of attention. But this was not the time to address Allie's issues with her grandmother, so Charlie let it go.

"How do you know she'll talk to you?"

Charlie shrugged. "She called me."

"That doesn't necessarily mean . . ."

"Precedent suggests it does. Okay, you two, take care of your mama. And you," she leaned in and kissed Allie softly, "I'm sorry I won't be here when the aunties arrive. If you want to distract them, why not feed them your grandmother."

"Oh, I wish," Allie sighed.

"Metaphorically."

"Sure. Be like that."

Charlie dropped her hand to the slight curve of Allie's belly. "She knows they're boys."

"Of course she does."

Warm enough in a T-shirt in spite of the damp cold, Jack paused outside the door of the Emporium and wondered what the clear-sight charm would show if it worked both ways. From inside the store, the charm gave the family advance warning on the true form of their customers—a precaution Jack heartily approved of even if none of the customers were a threat to him. From outside, it was just glass. Watching Allie watch the twins build a fort out of old goalie equipment, Jack doubted he and David were the only Gales with another form. Distracted by the family/food scents of flesh and blood, he hadn't noticed it at first, but nose to any Gale and he could smell damp earth and ancient trees. Nose to Allie, he could smell earth and trees plus asphalt and car exhaust and people. Pancakes and livestock during the stampede. Nose to Charlie, the trees were stronger and sometimes she smelled like cheap beer and new guitar strings; under that a scent unique to Charlie. He'd sniffed a lot of stuff trying to figure out what it was but had never been able to. If she ever got lost, he knew he'd be able to find her.

Of course Charlie would never get lost, so that was pretty useless.

Thing was, after four years working off and on in the store—more off than on, but still—he'd never managed to see a Gale through the charm.

Allie glanced up, frowned, and beckoned him in.

"Where's Joe?" he asked.

"Down in the basement."

That explained the noises coming from under the floor. This time. "And Charlie?"

"My grandmother called and . . ."

He snorted, remembering at the last instant to turn his head away from the twins. "She's gone. That figures."

"What figures?"

"Like it matters if she says good-bye or fuck off or even acknowledges I might give a flying fuck."

"Flying!" Evan chorused.

"Fuck!" Edward agreed.

"Sorry." He cut off Allie's rebuke before it began, shoved his hands in his pockets, and headed for the back door. Charlie'd taken him with her once, but that didn't mean she'd ever need or want him with her again. "I'm going hunting."

Once in the Wood, it didn't take Charlie long to tease Auntie Catherine's song from the aunties' chorus and that meant Auntie Catherine wanted to be found. Convenient, sure, but not exactly comforting. Humming along under her breath, Charlie let the song draw her forward. One step. Two.

Slammed back on her heels by a burst of percussion, she fought for breath against the sudden pressure on her chest.

Jack.

Anger. Confusion. The drum solo wasn't merely a place holder for the teenage petulance he'd almost outgrown, Charlie could hear an undertone of pain. The beat resonated under the arc of her ribs, reverberating through the bone. Her heart skipped a beat until it matched Jack's rhythm.

She half turned.

Then turned again.

Jack had Allie, and Graham, and Joe, and four aunties more than willing to interfere in his emotional well-being, but Auntie Catherine wouldn't wait. If Charlie ignored the window of opportunity provided, there might not be a second chance. Charlie could no more lose Jack's song than she could lose Allie's, but Auntie Catherine could go to ground like a ninja.

Mixed amid the crazy and the phlegm, Doomsday Dan had said, *"I think we're all going to die."*

Auntie Catherine had said, *"He's right."*

Murmuring an apology Jack would never hear, Charlie took up Aunt Catherine's song again . . .

. . . and emerged between two enormous ferns outside Caesar's Palace. Given that she was by no means the weirdest thing that had ever happened in Vegas, she headed inside without bothering to charm her sudden appearance away. The lack of crowds midmorning in the casino should have made it easier to find an older woman with a three-foot silver braid and a fondness for lime-green clothing, but the layout had been designed to confuse and confine. It was a maze of bright lights and noise with a five-star steak house at its center instead of a minotaur. Charlie finally closed her eyes, cocked her head, and headed for the sound of a consistently winning slot machine.

When she bounced off the first three bars of "Mandy," she opened her eyes to see a middle-aged man holding a beer in one hand and his phone in the other. He stood frowning at her, a polyester-covered barrier preventing her from covering the last few feet to the Lucky Seven slot machine with the good luck charm gleaming on the glass.

"You're carrying a guitar."

"Wow." Charlie's lip curled. "It's like you can actually . . . see."

Unwashed hair flopped over his forehead as he shook off her tone and said, "Why do you have a guitar?"

In spite of the hour, that wasn't his first beer. "Go eat something healthy."

"I should go eat something healthy," he muttered, and wandered away.

"You've lost your edge." Silver bracelets chiming, Auntie Catherine entered her bets. "You should have told him to go get a tattoo. Or a hooker."

"Or a tattoo of a hooker?"

"Don't be ridiculous, Charlotte." She touched the icon to double up, then leaned back waiting for the machine to run through half a dozen complicated patterns before settling on an enormous flashing seven and what sounded like a midi version of six bars from around the middle of Tchaikovsky's *1812 Overture*. "I think that'll do it for now." The number on the strip of white paper was pleasantly, but not impossibly, high. Auntie Catherine had learned that lesson some years ago and Auntie Jane still brought it up whenever she wanted to stress the irresponsibility of her youngest sister. Rubbing the charm off the glass as she stood, Auntie Catherine caught up Charlie's hand and tucked it in the crook of her arm, holding it in place. "We'll talk while we walk."

Given the rarity of one-handed guitarists, Charlie walked. "Where are we going?"

"The cashiers' cages, of course." The wide legs of her black linen trousers whispered secrets as they crossed the casino.

"Of course." Away from the slot machines and cutting through the closed section that catered to the more serious weekend gamblers, it became obvious Auntie Catherine wasn't going to begin the conversation. "So, Doomsday Dan is right?"

"Has all that loud music damaged your hearing?" Silver hoop earrings glittered as Auntie Catherine shook her head with exaggerated sympathy. "Did you come all this way to have me repeat myself?"

"Fine. Dan's right. He thinks we're all going to die because the sky is heavy." Charlie matched the annoyingly artless tone. "Now, what did you See?"

"Besides Doomsday Dan?" Auntie Catherine turned her head far enough to meet Charlie's gaze and, between one blink and the next, her eyes flashed black; a warning, Charlie assumed, to take her next words seriously. "I Saw an asteroid in the night sky."

That was serious. *"The sky is heavy. I think we're all going to die."*

"What," she demanded a moment later, "did you think I Saw?"

"No idea." Charlie sang in cowboy bars. She knew how to sound like it didn't matter. "Dan was a little less than specific." Auntie Catherine offered nothing else and Charlie considered her next question while they passed the high stakes blackjack tables, closed now given the hour. Her free hand felt damp enough to smudge the felt should she reach out and touch it. The hand Auntie Catherine held in the bend of her elbow seemed to know better than to stain the lime-green silk. *I think we're all going to die.* Jack was right, belief wasn't truth, but Auntie Catherine Saw an asteroid in the sky. "I don't suppose you Saw a date?"

"No. I didn't."

"How big was the asteroid?"

"Big enough that if it's not stopped, we'll be the dinosaurs."

"Really? That big?" The sudden flush of relief was so intense, goose bumps rose on Charlie's arms. Dan was right about the sky being heavy. About the sky falling. He was wrong about the dying. And this had nothing to do with the Corbies leaving. "It's not going to just hit Calgary, then?"

"What part of 'this was a very large rock' are you having trouble understanding, Charlotte?"

"Dan said we and you said he was right and I assumed that meant your asteroid was going to land right on Calgary."

"It's not my asteroid, and I have no idea where it's going to land." Auntie Catherine sighed. "But it's large enough that the impact will definitely affect more than merely Calgary. Or Alberta. Or Canada for that matter."

"Then we've got years."

Charlie stopped because Auntie Catherine did. When an auntie refused to be moved, she became both the immovable object and the irresistible force. Charlie saw practiced pique in the thinned lips and the dipped brows. "Years?" But she *heard* hope. "How do you figure that, Charlotte?"

"NASA."

The grip on Charlie's hand tightened. "Now you're being a little nonspecific."

"Okay." She took a deep breath and let it out slowly. "I'm a musician. Most of what I know about NASA, I learned from the Discovery Channel . . ."

"Where a show called *Ice Road Truckers* is apparently science."

". . . and I know," Charlie continued, ignoring the interruption, "that if there was an asteroid, a big asteroid, heading for impact in the near future, NASA would know about it and it would be all over the news. I mean, that meteor that hit in Russia and ended up recorded on half a hundred cell phones and all over the internet, it fell off an asteroid NASA'd been monitoring for years. Years. There's telescopes all over the world pointed into space, Auntie Catherine. There's scientists on a space station *in* space watching for this very thing." Graham's observation aside, she didn't know that they were *watching* in the station, but they'd have definitely noticed an asteroid that big and that close or what the hell were they doing up there. "You just See farther than NASA does."

Steel-gray brows rose. "Just?" The aunties never did well with qualifiers.

"Did you See the impact?"

"No, Charlotte . . ." She started walking again and, as she still held Charlie's hand captive, Charlie fell into step beside her. ". . . I did not."

"Then we're good, right? No impact means we stopped it. It's like that summer when you saw one of the old gods rise, but you didn't see Jack deal with it."

"It's not like that at all. By the time you became involved, I'd already implemented a plan to prevent the rising."

"And cause an environmental disaster."

"A *potential* environmental disaster, and still preferable to having the Maritimes fall into soulless chaos."

Charlie's personal soundtrack managed the beginning of "Farewell to Nova Scotia" before she shut it down. Distracted, she missed the step as the casino dropped to a lower level and would have fallen but for Auntie Catherine's grip on her arm. "Thanks."

"I didn't want anyone to assume I'd pushed you." She shrugged and the corners of her mouth twitched into the shadow of a smile. "Not if I hadn't pushed you."

"Of course." Charlie found herself smiling as well and they walked in what seemed very like companionable silence for a moment or two.

"Can I assume your minimal reaction to the warning of a cataclysmic event, however distant, means you have a solution?"

"NASA."

"Charlotte . . ."

"It's a falling rock, Auntie Catherine." They skirted three muscular young men in appreciatively tight T-shirts arguing about tickets to Celine Dion. "All I have to do is give NASA a shove in the right direction and they'll do the rest."

"Can it be that easy?"

Something in the timbre of the question told Charlie that Auntie Catherine had also been hearing *I think we're all going to die* and for longer than Charlie had. That Doomsday Dan had confirmed what she'd feared since she'd Seen the asteroid. Although the question had been asked more to the world at large than Charlie specifically, Charlie answered it. "Piece of cake."

"Well . . ." Auntie Catherine tossed her head. ". . . if I'd known this was going end up as such a nonevent, I wouldn't have mentioned it. But, as you're here, just how are you planning to shove NASA in the right direction?"

"They have these things called bars," she said, wondering when she'd started talking to Auntie Catherine like she was talking to Allie. "I go where NASA is . . ."

"And that's where?"

"No idea. Thus the internet."

"Thus?"

"Perfectly good word. And NASA has a Twitter account, for crying out loud."

"There's toothpaste with a Twitter account," Auntie Catherine snorted. "So that doesn't fill me with confidence."

"The point is, they're not a secret organization. I find out where NASA's located, I find a group of scientists out for a few after work, and I motivate them."

"Sounds like fun."

That response was a pale shadow of the entendre Charlie'd been expecting. *Motivate*, in that context, should've been irresistible. Auntie Catherine's profile gave nothing away. She didn't seem relieved that it wasn't the end of the world. She didn't seem to be calculating a way to turn the situation to her advantage. She didn't seem pleased the solution could be left to the rest of the world with minimal Gale involvement. She seemed thoughtful. Contemplative. Small hairs lifted off the back of Charlie's neck.

As they arrived at the velvet ropes separating the cashiers from the rest of the casino, Auntie Catherine tightened her grip for an instant, then dropped Charlie's hand and turned to face her. "Before you motivate NASA, talk to Doomsday Dan."

It was a suggestion, not a command. It almost sounded as though she were talking to an equal. Lost in the implications, Charlie missed the next few words.

". . . already knew about the asteroid, and certainly have no need for corroboration, he must have another part to play."

"You'd mentioned him to me," Charlie pointed out. "And I came to Vegas."

"You came because I called you. Surprise, it's not all about *you*. He's not a Gale . . . although I suppose he could be one of the Courts' accidents." Bracelets chimed as she dismissed the Courts, waving off practically immortal, ethereally beautiful, magical beings from another reality as if they were the neighbor's annoying teenagers. "Honestly, live for thousands of years and can't figure out how to use a condom."

"Jack says Dan's Human. And he sounds Human."

"Then how does he know that the sky is falling?"

"Good drugs. No, *bad* drugs." Charlie exaggerated a frown. "Conversation with Chicken Little over beer and nachos?"

Auntie Catherine sighed, the worry that had weighted her voice replaced by more familiar and infinitely less disturbing irritation. "Oh, for pity's sake, Charlotte, just go ask him. Find out how he knows. Find out what he knows. Find out why he thinks we're all going to die. Find out why I Saw him."

Ignoring the bouzouki music in the distance—although sitting in on a session with Gary seemed like it'd be a lot more fun than trying to get anything coherent out of Doomsday Dan—Charlie followed Jack's song out of the Wood and back to . . .

. . . the badlands outside Drumheller. Crouched with his wings tight to his back, an overcast sky almost but not quite blending his gold into the soft cream rock of the ridge, Jack didn't react as Charlie emerged from a clump of sagebrush. His eyes locked on the distant horizon, he might not have seen her. Taking advantage of this rare chance to really look at him at full size—he was significantly less than full size and somewhat less majestic curled up in the living room covered in babies—she began at the slightly paler gold of his muzzle, swept her gaze up over the sweep of his horns—flesh, not the bone the other Gale boys sported—down past the shimmering folds of his wings, and finally out along the sinuous curl of his tail. He was gorgeous. Magnificent.

Charlie flinched as Johnny Diaz's "Fool for Love" blared out so loudly it was hard to believe Jack hadn't heard it—actually, it was hard to believe Allie hadn't heard it back in Calgary and Charlie wasn't going to discount Auntie Jane's radar ears until she'd gone a good half hour without a phone call. Before she could shut it off, it faded out to a smug silence, point made.

Yes, the standing and staring *was* getting a bit creepy.

Shoving everything she felt back down out of sight where it belonged, Charlie dialed the cousin/friend/Wild up to eleven and called Jack's name.

He didn't react.

He'd told her once that he could hear a rabbit fart from thirty meters up, so while he might have missed her arrival, he'd definitely heard her. Conclusion: he was deliberately ignoring her. Sometimes, he was so much more than what he seemed, he overwhelmed her. Sometimes, he was so seventeen she couldn't believe she'd gotten herself into this mess.

He didn't react as she climbed up the ridge toward him. As the ratio of her foot to his side was about the same as a mouse kicking a moose, it wasn't entirely surprising when he ignored the toe of her boot jabbed into his armpit.

Clearly, she was supposed to know what she'd done wrong and open with an apology. Shifting her guitar over toward her right shoulder, she pushed her left side into Jack's bulk, warming her hands on his scales. Tucked in under his front legs, they were like snake scales, soft and almost hot from the fires banked inside. "So, you want to help me save the world?"

Even expecting the change, she toppled sideways as thousands of pounds of dragon disappeared. *Conservation of mass, my Aunt Fanny.* Aunt Fanny taught grade eight physics.

Jack caught her before she hit the ground. One hand wrapped around her upper arm, he hauled her back onto her feet with no apparent effort. "Seriously? We need to save the world? Is it another old one rising?"

"Nope, big rock falling."

"Big rock?"

"Auntie Catherine's Seen an incoming asteroid. She says it's big."

His eyes flared gold. "Dan said the sky was heavy."

"And Auntie Catherine said Dan was right."

"How will we stop it?"

"We won't. NASA will. But since they haven't seen it yet," she continued before he could ask another question, "that means it has to be years away, giving them plenty of time to get their shit together once I point them in the right direction."

"So you don't actually need me." Releasing her arm, he stepped back, smoking heavily. Clearly, he wanted to continue sulking and just as clearly figured he couldn't do it since he'd both changed and spoken.

Charlie waited, tucking her chin down into the collar of her jacket. Without Jack blocking the wind, it was cold and smelled of snow.

"You left without saying anything," he muttered at last.

"Allie knew . . ."

"To me!" His cheeks darkened and he turned away. "You left without saying anything to me."

About to point out that she often left Calgary without telling him, Charlie remembered the pain she'd heard in the Wood and closed her teeth on the words. She'd done that. Her leaving had really upset him. "I'm sorry."

"For what?" he growled.

"Hurting you?"

"I wasn't *hurt,* I was angry!"

Yeah, they'd go with that. "Auntie Catherine called to tell me Doomsday Dan was right," she said. "Since one of the things he'd said was that we're all going to die, I thought I'd best pry a few more details from Auntie Catherine ASAP."

A line of scales rippled up his spine, glistening against the creamier gold of his tan, and he turned back around to face her. "*Are* we all going to die?"

"No. It's an asteroid. A falling rock. Plain old everyday physics." Charlie paused to consider that for a second. "Or possibly geology. Either way, NASA will deal with it. But Auntie Catherine wants me to talk to Doomsday Dan."

"To find out why he thinks we're all going to die?"

"That'd be good, yeah. She also thinks we should find out how he knows the sky is falling. Turns out talking with Chicken Little is not an acceptable answer. Chicken Little," she continued as Jack frowned, "is a story about . . ."

"I know. It's one of the kids' favorite books."

Charlie had a sudden vision of Jack reading to the twins; his hair in his eyes, Edward on his lap, Evan nestled in the curve of his tail. Over the last year, his voice had deepened into a smooth baritone that made her think of a cross between Michael Bublé and Stan Rogers. Charlie cut the thought short. "I do need you, Jack; you know where to find him."

"Chicken Little?"

"Doomsday Dan."

Brows drawn in, he folded his arms. "If he's in the city, Allie could find him for you."

"Yeah, I don't really want to talk about big falling rocks and crazy people announcing we're all going to die with Allie. Ever since the twins, she's been a bit . . ."

"Scarily overprotective?"

"I was thinking insanely overreactive, but yours is good, too."

Jack scratched at the small patch of scales in the center of his chest. "Dan's not really coherent at the best of times and today didn't sound like the best of times. I think he freaked when he realized people were listening to him."

"We still have to try." Charlie couldn't stop herself from looking up. "The sky is falling."

"It's not . . ."

"Well, not all of it," she cut him off. "But when an auntie is that insistent about something, it's best to pay attention. Or run," she added after a moment.

"Allie doesn't think Auntie Catherine can be trusted." He met her gaze. "What do you think?"

"Honestly . . ."

"That'd be good."

". . . I don't know." Hands in her pockets, she rubbed a guitar pick between thumb and forefinger and heard Auntie Catherine speaking to her Wild to Wild. The gulf between first circle and third was definitely wider than any gulf between her and Jack, but Auntie Catherine had crossed it. "I think that if I noticed she was relieved when I told her why it wasn't a problem, then she had to be damn near panicked going in. She knew this wasn't something she could deal with; she's all about manipulation and you can't manipulate a falling rock. It was also the most straightforward conversation we've ever had, so I think she's realized that if she's not the only Wild Power . . ."

"And she's not."

". . . then she's not alone anymore."

He folded his arms. "So why wasn't I there, if I'm Wild? I was just at the coffee shop, you could've waited for me."

"And done what? I can't haul your ass through the Wood—you're too heavy. If we take the car, we need to know we have room to stick the dismount . . ." The car picked up a lot of momentum crossing the Wood and a Dragon Prince on board extended the room necessary for a full stop by a significant margin. ". . . which we can't know if we don't know where we're going."

"And because you'd already spent the whole morning in the same room with me and you figured that was plenty."

Maybe because very similar words had run through her head as she headed out to meet Auntie Catherine, she was sharper than she'd ever been with him. "Surprise, Jack, it's not all about you!" He had no choice but to believe her. She hated herself a little, but she let it stand.

They stood for a moment, listening to the wind howl through the badlands.

Then Jack said, "I'm sorry."

Charlie swallowed her second apology. "For what?"

He shrugged, scales rippling down his torso. "Making the end of the world about me."

"It won't be the end of the world."

"Okay." They watched sparks trail behind his bare foot as he rubbed the side of it against a rock. "We good?"

"Always." She may have put a different power behind that. With any luck, Jack was still young enough he couldn't tell them apart.

"Right." He smiled a little sheepishly. "So do you trust Auntie Catherine?"

"Not entirely."

Jack snorted, changed, and glided down off the ridge to stomp out a burning bush.

"And that," Charlie called down to him, "is also why we need to talk to Dan."

Resting up on his hind legs, tail stretched behind him for balance, Jack adjusted his size until his head was level with hers. "He has a flop down by the water."

"The Loireag . . ."

"Leaves him alone." Jack smiled.

Dragons had a lot of very sharp teeth. The Loireag may have been chronically depressed, but she wasn't stupid. "Will he talk to me if you're there?"

"I don't know how much sense he'll make." The tips of Jack's wings stirred up dust devils when he shrugged. "But he'll talk. Fly with me?"

As Jack spread his wings, Charlie took a step back. He'd never asked her before. She thought about climbing onto his shoulders, settling with the smooth, gleaming curve of his neck between her legs, gathering up a double handful of the flexible strands of flesh that made up his mane, her heart pounding as he rose into the sky . . . "I don't think that's a good idea."

"Afraid?" He'd gone nearly cross-eyed trying to look down his muzzle at her.

"Hell, yes." Although not of flying.

"Your loss." Spread out like golden sails, his wings blocked what sun there was. He leaped skyward with the first downstroke.

"Wait! You didn't wipe out your footprints!"

He circled around, grinning as he swooped in close enough Charlie had to brace herself against the wind, eyes squinted almost closed. "I know. Drives the dinosaur guys crazy. Funniest thing ever!"

Charlie was there waiting as he landed on the Fort side of the river, in behind a bank of dogwood, out of sight of the road.

"How long have you been here?" he asked, back on two legs.

She shoved her hands into her jacket pockets. "Well, I went to Mexico for a couple of days to shake off October in Alberta, but after that, only a few minutes."

Jack stared at her for a long moment, nostrils flared. "Liar. You don't smell like tequila."

"I can go to Mexico and not smell like tequila."

"You smell like tequila when you go to Taco Bell."

"Ow!" She clasped her hands over her heart. "Brutal! Get dressed and let's find Dan."

He made his T-shirt from late leaves, golden brown and skin tight. His jeans and shoes and jacket were brown as well, probably from the darker mud by the water. Although he usually stayed on the Gale side of the line between Gale and Fey, the colors he'd chosen made him seem otherworldly. Exotic. Momentarily less like himself than when he wore gold scales and wings.

"Okay, so Dan . . ." Rubbing a hand over the back of his neck, Jack looked past her toward the fort. "At this time of day Dan's probably out by the parking lot, trying to decide where to go for lunch."

"Nice he has choices," Charlie muttered, stepping off the narrow path so Jack could lead the way.

"The Chinese place on the corner of 9th and 8th sometimes feeds him and so does the diner on 13th. If there's something on at the stadium, he'll dumpster dive and the stadium Brownies know they're to save stuff for him."

"There's Brownies at the Saddledome?"

"It's a prime holding." Jack paused at the edge of the parking lot and Charlie moved up beside him. "There he is."

Toque holding his hair in place, hands shoved deep into the pockets of an oversized trench coat, Dan shuffled along the graveled path that led to Fort Calgary.

"He knows you," Charlie began, and stopped when a plain black sedan drove into the lot and parked as close to Dan as possible. The man and woman who got out might as well have had police stamped on their foreheads. Carefully looking at nothing in particular, Charlie whistled an eavesdropping charm at them.

"What does the FBI want with this guy anyway?" the driver asked, circling around to join his partner.

She twitched her collar into place. "Why would I know if you don't?"

He shrugged. "You might have heard something."

"If I knew more, I'd have told you while we were driving over here to pick up the crazy person who's going to stink up the backseat of our car."

"He's not going to go quietly either. There's going to be yelling and he'll piss himself and then there'll be more yelling. We should wait until that school group gets in their bus and goes; I don't want to traumatize the kids."

"Is Dan an American?" Charlie asked Jack as both cops smiled and nodded at the gaggle of preteens leaving the Fort. The kids collectively rolled their eyes.

"Don't know." Jack glared across the parking lot. "You think they're after him because he was going on about the world ending?"

"I think it's more likely YouTube dredged Dan's past and something nasty floated up."

"If he's like Auntie Catherine . . ."

"If he was female, clean, and significantly less hairy," Charlie muttered.

"If he sees the future, like Auntie Catherine," Jack specified, "he could have escaped the American government. One of their experiments where they're trying to make super soldiers with psionic powers."

"One of?"

"And before you say it's all comic books," he continued ignoring her question, "why does it keep coming up? Books, movies, comics, TV . . . You know what they say where I come from?" He folded his arms. "Where there's smoke, there's lunch."

"You know what they say where I come from? Don't be a dumbass. Unless the question is who's dumbing down the electorate, government conspiracy is never the answer." Charlie frowned as the kids began piling into the bus, the arguments over seating arrangements needing no amplification. "You distract the police. I'll take Dan into the Wood and out again across the river by the zoo. That should be close enough, he won't freak out too badly. You meet me there."

Jack grabbed the gig bag as she stepped forward, rocking her back on her heels. "Why distract them? Why can't you just tell the cops to go away? It's not like they could refuse."

"Removing choice is a slippery slope, Jack."

"Tell that to the aunties."

"You first." Hypocrite she might be, but she sure as hell wasn't going to give the aunties that kind of an opening. As the bus pulled out onto 9th and merged with traffic, she shoved him toward the parking lot. "Distract."

"Fine."

Flames shot out of the garbage can farthest from Dan. The smoke smelled like pot.

The pot smell was a nice touch, Charlie acknowledged racing across the crushed gravel, humming "You Don't See Me" as she ran.

Between the smoke and the yelling for backup and the digging for the fire extinguisher buried under dry cleaning in the trunk, neither cop noticed as Charlie hooked Dan under the arms and dragged him toward the trees at the edge of the path.

He yelled, "Depress handle!"

It had been a long time since Dan or his clothing had been in contact with soap and water. Grateful for the cold, but still breathing as shallowly as possible, Charlie hit an A and wrapped it around Dan.

Dan yelled, "Damn kids!"

They stumbled between two sycamores and into the Wood. Dan stiffened, then relaxed in Charlie's grip. She heard him draw in a deep breath and let it out slowly. A moment later they were in the copse of trees next to the zoo's south parking lot.

"Six pounds of oranges!" Dan's volume was impressive and, while the sound of sirens approaching from across the river meant the police were still busy, attracting their attention would be a bad idea.

She grabbed his wrist as he twisted out of her hold. Dug in her heels as he tried to get away. He was stronger than he looked.

"Four sixty-nine a dozen? Who the hell can afford that?"

"Dan, be quiet."

Yellowed whites showing all the way around his eyes, he flailed his free hand in the general direction of the zoo. "I don't want to hurt him!"

"Then don't!" Hand poised to go over Dan's mouth, Charlie let it drop as Jack stepped out of a familiar pillar of flame. "Jack, tell him to be quiet."

"Why don't you *tell* him?"

"Second verse, same as the first. Choice. Slippery slope. Also, he's broken." She could hear the pieces rattling around in his voice. "I'm afraid that if I tell him to stop, there's no guarantee I can get him to start again."

"Why even have power if you never use it?" Jack muttered, crossing to take Dan's face in his hands. "Come on, dude, you know me. Calm down."

"I didn't get his name!"

"Whose name?"

"Still two hundred short!"

"Dan."

"Polycarbonate!"

"Okay." Jack stepped back, rubbing his palms on his thighs. "I've never seen him this bad. You might as well let him go, Charlie. He's too fried to tell us anything."

"If we let him go . . ." Charlie jerked her head toward the river. The sirens had gone quiet, the fire dealt with. It wouldn't take long for the police to find him. They clearly had a fairly good idea of his natural habitat.

"Fucking elephant shit!"

Jack coughed out a small cloud of smoke and shifted upwind. "So we stash him somewhere until he's chilled."

No longer fighting to get free, Dan maintained a constant pull against her grip, tendons corded under her fingers. He'd been cranked tighter than Auntie Jane's sphincter since she'd grabbed him.

Wait . . .

"While we were crossing through the Wood, he relaxed."

"You were in there for like five seconds," Jack pointed out. "How's that time to relax?"

"I've shifted plenty of drunks, I know limp. I'll bring him out in the park, wait for us there." Maintaining her grip on Dan's wrists, Charlie charged toward him. Eyes wide enough she could see the bloodshot, yellowish whites all the way around, he stumbled backward, mumbling about being late. "Tell David we're coming."

Kicking up faded cedar mulch, they crashed between junipers in a parody of a two-step and out into the Wood where sunlight spilled through a canopy of birch and ash and alder, drawing lines of gold from sky to earth. There were no paths through the underbrush. No birds. No insects.

Dan froze, drew in a deep breath, and closed his eyes. "So quiet," he said after a moment.

Allie's song, Jack's song, her mother, her sisters, the aunties . . . Charlie thought she even heard Gary's bouzouki taking the lead on "The Mist Covered Mountain." When Dan opened his eyes and tugged against her hold, she let him go. He couldn't get anywhere without her, and she was curious about what he'd do.

Hands out to either side, he walked slowly forward, placing each duct-tape-wrapped rubber boot carefully on the leaf litter, grimy fingertips lightly caressing bark and leaves. "My head is empty." He spun around suddenly and fixed Charlie with a remarkably sane stare. "I can't hear you."

"I'm not talking."

"No. I can hear you here." Fingers tapped his ears. "But not here." Tapped his forehead. "You're not in my head. No one is in my head but me. I'm all alone."

"And you're usually . . ."

"Not. Not alone. Not ever alone."

"You're not usually alone in your head." That was the sort of statement that needed considering. Charlie listened to the staccato, neo-punk rhythms of her younger sisters for a moment, then let them fade. "You hear what people think?"

"Think. Think. Think. All the damned time. People never stop thinking. So noisy. So shattered. Think. Think. Think." His mouth was open, his eyes wide, his chest heaving. He spun around in a circle, first to the right. Then to the left.

"It's okay. Calm down." Here in the Wood it was harder to keep it a suggestion. Charlie did the best she could.

Dan stared out from inside a mismatched collection of twitches and visibly forced himself to calm. He closed his eyes. Nodded. Opened his eyes. "I think I should sit."

"Not a bad idea." Charlie held out her hand. He glanced down at it, then up at her, eyes narrowed suspiciously. "Your choice," she told him, "but you'll find it easier to move if we're in contact." The dirt and callus on his hand made it feel more as though it were covered in bark than skin. It felt almost familiar, almost like Uncle Edward's hand near the end, thirty odd years on hooves having left its mark. Resolutely not thinking about the likely composition of Dan's dirt, Charlie led him through the Wood to where memory placed a tree that would serve as a bench.

The fallen tree was exactly where she remembered it. Exactly how she remembered first seeing it fifteen years before. The Wood untouched by time, the tree untouched by rot. They could stay here as long as Dan needed, the only time brought in with them.

Dan clutched his chest as he collapsed down onto the log, and Charlie gave him a moment to catch his breath. She'd taken family as well as Jack's

Uncle Ryan through the Wood, but that had always been on a direct path in and out; walking within the Wood was an entirely different matter and she had no idea how far Dan thought they'd traveled.

He concentrated on breathing for a moment; then, when he sounded less like he was sucking air through a hookah, he unbuttoned his trench coat with shaking fingers. Then the coat below that. As the top two layers folded back like stained flower petals, he reached into the next layer—Charlie thought it might be a pinstriped suit jacket—and pulled out a plastic water bottle. Given the color of the liquid half filling it, she really hoped it wasn't water.

Dan unscrewed the blue plastic cap and titled the bottle toward her. "Drink?"

"Thanks, but no."

Outlined in dirt, his Adam's apple rose and fell and rose and fell and rose and fell again. Half the liquid was gone when he lowered the bottle. "Smoother than I remembered."

"So." Charlie shrugged out of the gig bag. "You're a telepath."

"No." Still clutching the bottle in one hand, Dan reached up under his toque with the other for a good scratch. "I just hear shit."

Well, that answered Auntie Catherine's question. He knew because he heard shit.

Human mutations happened all the time, although they were usually less comic book and more in need of minor surgery.

New question. Who had he heard this particular shit from? Who else knew about the asteroid? Of course there was always a chance he'd heard Auntie Catherine's thoughts. Which meant nothing good in a whole different way. Eavesdropping on the aunties had destroyed stronger men than Dan.

When she asked, Dan stared at her like she was crazy. "How the fuck should I know?"

"You can't identify the voice in your head?"

"Voice? I wish I had a fucking *voice* in my head." His laugh bordered on hysterics. "I have two-legged radio stations playing in my head 24/7, and I can't shut them the fuck off."

"Was it a woman?"

"Was what a woman?"

"The voice that said the sky was falling."

"No women. No men. Just thoughts." Dan stared at the ground between his feet with such intensity, Charlie leaned forward to see what he was staring at, but all she could see was grass. And a stick. "Thoughts have no gender. No pink. No blue. But I can tell you that the sky fell in English. It wasn't French or Spanish or any of the First Nations languages. It wasn't in Chinese. Or Japanese. Or Hindu. Or Portuguese. Or Farsi. Or Ukrainian. Or Gaelic. Or Italian. Or . . ."

"I believe you." Charlie had no idea how many languages there were in the world. Nor did she want to find out. "You heard the thought in English. That doesn't really narrow it down." As neither the grass nor the stick seemed to have any answers, she straightened and tried to come up with a question that would actually get them somewhere. "You hear thoughts from all over the world?"

"North America. Melting pot. Mosaic. North part of Mexico. Siberia once or twice. Sometimes I can pull in Brazil." He shrugged inside the cocoon of his clothing. "Depends on the weather; needs the right cloud cover, atmospheric conditions, ducks."

"Ducks?"

"They tell you geese'll do. But they're wrong."

"Okay." She frowned. "So if you were shouting things you heard, and you hear in all these other languages, why do you only shout in English?"

"Because I don't speak French or Spanish or any of the First Nations languages, or Chinese or Japanese or Hindu or . . ."

Charlie raised a hand and cut him off. "Got it. So when you heard about the asteroid . . ."

"About the sky falling."

". . . what exactly did you hear?"

The look he shot her had actual substance. "The sky is falling."

"Those exact words?"

"How the hell should I know. Too many thoughts. Needle in a haystack. Haystack of fucking needles." He took another drink.

"Were there other thoughts around it?"

"Do you ever listen, girl? Too. Many. Thoughts."

"I need you to remember them." Given a little more to work with, Charlie was certain she could tell if he'd overhead Auntie Catherine.

"I need to stop hearing shit. We don't always get what we need, do we?"

There was that slippery slope again, but Charlie didn't see as *she* had much choice right now. "Dan, you have to remember."

"You have black eyes. Not punched black, that's purple. Really black. Inside."

"I know." The breeze had stilled, but leaves on the surrounding trees continued to whisper. "Remember the thoughts you heard around the same time you heard about the sky falling."

". . . can't tell people the sky is falling, millions will die in the panic. . . . damn dog on the bed again. . . . said it was cancer. . . . don't find a solution in six months, millions will die in the panic anyway. . . . You lying, cheating, bastard! . . . looks more like an Argentinian than a Brazilian. . . . take natural disasters for a thousand, Alex."

Millions will die in the panic was so specific a phrase, the two thoughts had to be connected. "That's a wrap, Dan. Thank you."

Dan shrugged, tipped his head back, and poured the liquid remaining in the bottle down his throat.

Too bad. She could use a drink.

He hadn't overheard Auntie Catherine. Someone else knew. And that someone thought they had six months to find a solution or millions would die in the panic. Overwrought much? Would the asteroid be visible to NASA in six months? Would they have to publish the news because they were government funded? Who'd already seen it and how? Had the government seen it and was that why they were pulling Dan in, before people started listening to him?

Too many questions. Not enough answers.

"Damn it, Jim, I'm a musician not an astrophysicist."

"Dan."

"What?"

"Dan, my name is Dan." He sighed and slumped forward, elbows on his thighs. "First time in a shitload of time I tried to do something about what I heard. All anyone did was laugh. Started calling me Doomsday Dan. Assholes."

"I'm not laughing."

He turned his head and stared at her through narrowed eyes. "No, you're not."

"I have an auntie who sees the future. She saw the same piece of the sky falling."

Dan snorted. It was slightly less damp than his snort on camera. "And I'm the crazy one."

"You're sitting in a Wood that doesn't exist." Charlie's gesture took in the trees and the . . . well, trees. The landscape was all variation on a theme. "That didn't cue you in that something unusual was up?"

"This is real?"

"It is."

"Damn. I thought it was another hallucination. Like the big yellow dragon."

"He's gold. Golden. And he's real, too."

"The gray lady in the river?"

"Real."

"The raccoon in the hockey sweater?"

"That one's on you."

"So, what're you going to do about it, now you know?"

"Nothing."

He cocked his head and narrowed his eyes. "How do you figure?"

"If there was an asteroid heading for impact in the next year or two, and it was big enough to do a lot of damage, it'd be all over the news by now. There's hundreds of telescopes looking for that sort of thing." Seriously, was she the only one who ever watched *Daily Planet*? "Since it isn't, there's lots of time for NASA to deal with it."

"No." Even confined by the hat, his hair slapped against his shoulders as Dan shook his head. "The voice said six months. Then we're all going to die."

"They didn't say we're all going to die."

"Millions."

"Dan," she tried for soothing rather than impatient. "That doesn't mean we don't have years to stop it. The person you overheard saw the asteroid, somehow, and overreacted."

"How do you know?"

"If the asteroid was close enough that millions would die in six months, it would be really, *really* close. We'd be able to see it. You and me." She waved a hand between them. "Without a telescope. Okay, not from here," she allowed when he glanced up. "From out in the real world. We can't see it, so it isn't close enough for anything to happen in six months. Okay?"

"You should ask them."

"Them? The person you heard?"

He nodded. "Them. Gender neutral not plural people."

"All right. How do I find them?"

He snorted, a gentle, dry snort. "We're sitting in a wood that doesn't exist. You tell me."

"I wish I could." She stood and looked down at Dan, who'd closed his eyes, the deep creases across his brow smoothed out enough that she could see clean lines of skin. Damn. Taking Dan back to Calgary meant taking him back to the cacophony of overheard thought. He wasn't family, so it shouldn't matter, but Charlie couldn't just drop him back into crazy.

Not when she could help. Great power. Great responsibility. Pain in the ass.

"When this is over, will I be able to play the piano?" he asked as she dropped to one knee and freed her guitar.

"Can you play it now?"

"The joke doesn't work if you step on my line."

"Sorry." Standing and running her fingers lightly over the strings, Charlie watched him lean into the notes and wondered if the voices he heard in his head counted as sound. Did a voice falling in the overgrown area between Dan's ears make a sound if there was only Dan to hear it? She frowned at the strain on the homily and fiddled with her tuning pegs even though everything seemed fine. Usually, she'd be all over a charm about sound, but right now, next to a man who certainly knew every dirty crack in the sidewalk, the only thing in her head was George Canyon's cover of "Rhinestone Cowboy" and once that got in, good luck getting it . . .

She smiled. "Do you know what an earworm is, Dan?"

He scratched up under the edge of his toque again. "Crawls in your ear, lays eggs, lots of screaming?"

"No, I think that was an episode from one of those retro TV shows." She really didn't want to know what he was studying under his fingernails. "An earworm is what they call a piece of a song you can't get out of your head."

"No room in my head."

"Not out there, no." Humming softly, she ran G F E up the fretboard. "But I'm going to give you an earworm that'll write a charm on the *inside* of your head, and that charm will block all the thoughts that aren't your own."

"So, no screaming?"

"Not unless you want to."

He shrugged. "Sometimes it helps."

"Used be in a punk band," Charlie told him. C, Cmaj7, G. "I get that."

Dan held up his hand before she could touch the strings again. "You're telling me all this because I'm crazy, right? Because if I tell people about sitting in the forest with a girl writing a song on the inside of my head, no one will believe me."

"Pretty much."

"Okay, then."

FOUR

"I DON'T SUPPOSE IT OCCURRED TO YOU to ask if Dan might be wanted by the FBI for reasons pertaining to actual criminal activity?"

Charlie shoved her hands into her jacket pockets and stared out over the city skyline. Naked and horned, David sounded more like the old David, the David with the doctorate in criminal psychology, than he had at any time since the change. Which would have been a good thing had he not been sounding like the old David at her. The old David had been a pedantic know-it-all and she'd always been glad they were too close to be listed.

"Charlie?"

"That would be a no."

"That would be because?"

"Because it doesn't matter. Dan hears thoughts and most of the family thinks. If he overhears a member of the family thinking and repeats what he heard, we could be playing *clean up in aisle three* for months even if he never makes it back on YouTube. Better an ounce of prevention." Here and now, Charlie saw no reason to mention the incoming asteroid to David. While she still had faith in NASA's ability to save the day, her conversation with Dan had raised a couple of questions she wanted answered before she spread the word the sky was falling. Dan hadn't overheard Auntie Catherine, so who else knew? And what was up with their belief that millions were going to die? If she told David what his grandmother had Seen while those dead millions were still on the table out of context, he'd pass the information straight to Allie and send Calgary into a lockdown that'd make the last NHL strike seem like a pleasant memory in comparison. "Besides," she added when the silence stretched a little too long, "Jack likes him."

"Jack's feelings in this case are irrelevant."

"Not to me."

David's brows rose until they disappeared under the shaggy fall of his hair.

"Wild Powers stick together, right?" A laugh would oversell it, so she let the words stand alone and hoped they had enough weight to counterbalance the response she'd snapped out without thinking.

After a long moment, David made an indeterminate sound—a little worrying; there weren't a lot of indeterminate sounds left in Charlie's world. "If Dan's going to be protected by the family, we need to know the extent of his criminal background, if only to determine how much effort the FBI is going to put into retrieving him."

"Big words."

"Charlie . . ."

"Fine." She started down the hill, her tone a mix of annoyed and re-signed, the relief carefully buried. "If it makes you happy, I'll ask."

"*Ask.* Don't let him lie to you."

"Hey!" Turning to face him, she walked backward, arms out to keep her balance, one finger up on each hand. "You don't tell me how to do what I do, I don't tell you how to do what you do."

David snorted, sounding significantly less doctoral. "You'll be first circle soon enough."

The hell she would; she was thirty. "Twenty-five years, and that's a low-ball estimate."

Facing downhill again, she could hear the future in his voice. "Twenty-five years, then. I'll be waiting."

She found Jack and Dan about halfway down the hill, sitting out of the wind with their backs to a charred slab of granite. Lichen sacrificed to Jack's flame, the stone radiated heat enough to keep the chill away. Charlie'd ex-pected Dan to look relaxed, pleased the silence of the Wood had carried over into the world. The dirt made it difficult, but, if Charlie had to hazard a guess, she'd say Dan looked pissed.

". . . because it's not where I live!"

"If you go back to your flop by the river, the police will pick you up."

Jack's hands were clenched. Charlie figured he'd gone over this a few times already. "If you go to a shelter, the police will pick you up. If you just wander around, the police will pick you up."

"They have granola bars."

"Who do?"

"The police."

Two streams of smoke rose from Jack's nose. "This isn't like spending a cold night in the drunk tank. You get picked up now and the cops will hand you over to the FBI."

Dan's eyes narrowed. "Smoking will stunt your growth."

Jack pinched his nostrils closed. "Do you want the FBI to pick you up?"

"Efrem Zimbalist, Jr.?"

"What?"

"Marvin Miller?"

"Dude . . ."

"Why's the FBI want me?"

As Jack opened his mouth, Charlie cut him off. "You tell us, Dan. Have you done anything in the US terrible enough they'd want to haul your ass across the border?"

"I went to North Dakota once."

"That doesn't sound so terrible," Jack muttered.

"You ever been to North Dakota, golden boy? I don't go to shelters, though." Hands over his ears, Dan shook his head. "Too noisy. It's like a murmur, here. The sea in the distance. Wind in the trees. Background noise."

"Partly that's the park," Charlie allowed. Then repeated it when Dan lifted his hands. "It's muting the city. I couldn't make the earworm a complete block, not and leave you functional."

"The worm in my ear sings to me."

"Yeah, sort of." Functional was, after all, variable. She reached for compulsion because David had a point. They needed to know if the FBI was going to be a problem so someone—probably Auntie Bea, she had the most experience—could deal with it. "Dan, you need to tell me if you've done anything that would make the FBI want you."

He thought about it for a moment. "I hear what people think."

"Does the FBI know that? That you hear what people think?"

"I didn't tell them."

"And there's no other way they might know?"

"The internet told them."

"Any other way?"

"No. I don't know why they want me."

"Truth," Charlie said for David's ears. Within the park, it was safest to assume he was always listening.

"Don't let them take me to America." Dan grabbed Jack's sleeve. "They'll make me watch NASCAR. I don't want to watch NASCAR."

"No one's taking you anywhere."

"Except you." He released Jack and pointed at Charlie. "And her."

He had a point. "If you stay with us, you're safe."

"From the FBI?"

"Yes."

Dan folded his arms although it wasn't a particularly definitive gesture given the bulk of three coats and whatever he had on under them. Dirt cracked and flaked off the outermost layer with the movement. "Then I want my stuff."

"I'll get it." Jack bounded to his feet, wings visible on his shadow. "The aunties—not Auntie Gwen, but the rest—are on their way up from the parking lot."

"And I want Chinese food. Noodles!" he added, squinting against the backwash as Jack left the ground. "Not rice!"

Charlie could hear Auntie Carmen complaining about her shoes as she climbed.

"Charlotte Marie Gale." Auntie Bea's voice carried. Charlie gouged a quick charm in the dirt and stepped over it, putting the charm between her and Dan. As long as he stayed put, he wouldn't hear what the aunties had to say. Better safe than sorry was a given around the aunties. "It isn't enough Alysha brings in strays," Auntie Bea continued, "now you have to start? Is that him?"

"No, I'm standing in front of a random vagrant."

"And I doubt it's the first time." An arm's length away, Auntie Bea mirrored Charlie's position; feet planted a shoulder's width apart, hands in her pockets. It might have been a sign of respect, but Charlie suspected mockery. "You're sure he's hearing actual thoughts?"

"Positive."

"Well, that's not something we want wandering around. Particularly not now he's gained some notoriety. You say you've blocked what's coming in?"

"I've blocked most of it. I can't block it all and still leave him functional."

"Of course you can't." Auntie Bea sighed. "I miss the old days."

Auntie Trisha leaned out to peer around Charlie at Dan, one hand patting her hair back into place, the curves of her cheeks a windblown pink. "I think it's fascinating that he knows what people are thinking."

"Really?" Auntie Bea pinched the bridge of her nose. "Well, I know exactly what *you're* thinking. You're thinking Gwen got the Leprechaun, you should be able to have this one."

Unrepentant, Auntie Trisha smiled. "He's not bad looking under the dirt."

"How the hell do you know that?" Waving off her answer, Auntie Bea muttered, "Never mind, I don't care."

"Have you determined why he's wanted by the FBI?" Auntie Carmen asked.

Charlie shrugged. "Does it matter?"

"It does not." Auntie Bea's smile suggested the FBI wouldn't know what hit it should they attempt to remove Dan from her protection. Which was, Charlie acknowledged, completely accurate. "Get out of the way, Charlotte."

Charlie stepped aside, but turned as she did. "Dan, these are my aunties. They're going to help keep you safe."

"They look like hot baths and vegetables."

"Yes, they do."

"That's not necessarily a bad thing," Dan admitted.

"So, that's Dan taken care of."

"It is." Charlie had retreated to David's side as the aunties escorted Dan out of the park. Someone had to tell Jack where to take his stuff and David couldn't be counted on to remain on two legs. "Jack thinks he's part of a secret government experiment, got spotted by the wrong people when his rant went viral, and now they want him back."

"Possible."

"Seriously?"

"All governments keep secrets, Charlie."

She could hear sirens in the distance—ambulance, given the distinctive *out of my way, out of my way* sound. Not like David was saying anything she didn't know, although the secrets governments kept were generally about money wasted on dumbass ideas while social services held bake sales.

"Do you want him?"

After a brief and unsuccessful attempt to breathe spit, Charlie managed a mangled, "Who?"

"Dan."

"What? No."

"After he's been cleaned up a bit?"

"No!" Wanting Dan was the farthest thing from Charlie's mind. She shoved both hands back through her hair, walked three steps out, three back, and snarled, "For fucksake, David, we're standing on sacred ground. On your ground. You feel what I feel. Why would you even say something like that?"

He tossed his head, the antlers suddenly much more physical than they had been.

Oh, shit. They were standing on sacred ground. He felt what she felt, and he'd prodded her into feeling it strongly enough that he couldn't mistake it.

"Jack's thirteen years younger than you."

"I know!" She took a deep breath and let it out slowly. Yelling at David wouldn't help. "Trust me, I *know*."

"You would never take advantage."

"Of course I wouldn't!" As it happened, yelling at David wouldn't hurt either. "What kind of person do you think I am? He's seventeen. He's Wild, I'm Wild, and he thinks I'm cool because, frankly, I am, but what I feel for him is irrelevant because I'm an adult and am fully able to recognize I can't always have what I want. So do you know what I do?" David opened his mouth, but Charlie cut him off. "I'll tell you what I do, I put on my big girl pants and I suck it up and I live my life knowing I will always have a dragon-sized, empty hole in my heart and, in the finest tradition of crappy ballads, I'll never let it show. So don't patronize me, you overgrown billy goat."

"You done?"

"Yes." The October wind had made her eyes water. She swiped at her cheeks.

"That's not all you do."

"What?"

"You run."

"Fine, and I run. Hello! Wild. I don't have to stick around, it's in the rules."

"Jack feels the same way."

"As what?"

"As you do. You fill that same place in his heart."

And now she knew how the dinosaurs had felt when *their* asteroid hit. "Oh, that's just fucking wonderful," she growled when she got her breath back.

"I tried to convince him it was the pressure of ritual."

She could hear a dog barking off to the northeast, a siren to the south. "Why?"

"For comfort. It seemed like the logical solution; I had no idea you felt the same way until I saw the two of you together."

"You didn't see . . ."

"Felt," David amended, eyes black from rim to rim.

"Right. Fine. Whatever." Charlie knew a warning when she saw one. "I'm sure you were trying to help. You want to keep helping. Tell me how the hell am I supposed to look at him now and not see him looking back?"

"You two need to talk."

"Talk to each other? No, we don't."

"He doesn't know why you keep running away, he thinks it's about him and . . ."

"It is about him. I know, I know," she continued before David could respond, "he assumes he's done something wrong or that I suddenly don't like him." Positions reversed, him thirty, her seventeen it was what she would've thought.

"So talk to him."

Eyes narrowed, Charlie folded her arms. David had made no effort to hide the threat. "Or?"

"Or you can continue living your lives at cross purposes, trapped in a bad romance novel, until it goes beyond misunderstandings and one of you lashes out—which is likely to cause irreparable damage to the relationship you already have, the family, and very probably the city, given who and what you two are . . ."

"You make it sound like Godzilla versus Mothra," Charlie muttered under her breath.

". . . or you can talk to each other. Now. When the aunties find out, they're not likely to give you that option."

"They're not likely to be quiet about it long enough for us to have the opportunity."

"That's what I said." His eyes flashed black again, he dropped to hooves, and shoved her shoulder with his nose.

She didn't fall over, but it was close. "You're a little hard to argue with in that form." Probably why he'd changed. Arms around his neck, Charlie rested her cheek on his shoulder. There were times when a world-destroying asteroid didn't sound like an entirely terrible prospect.

Her backup band usually took a break while she was in the park, so there was a distinct lack of hurtin' music happening. She kind of missed it.

"I'm not running away from you because I don't like you. I'm running because I like you too much."

Jack stared up at her, opened and closed his mouth a couple of times, and finally said, "What?"

Perched on the rock Jack and Dan had been leaning against, taking advantage of the residual warmth, Charlie picked at a bit of charred lichen. "The seven-year rule is there for a reason. Gales are all attracted to power and that attraction opens up a terrifying potential for abuse."

"Yeah, that's what David said." Head cocked, he studied her face for a moment, then stepped closer as a patch of dead brush and a medium-sized hunk of stone disappeared to become gray jeans and gray shoes and a beige, corduroy jacket. "So . . . you like me too much because I'm powerful?"

Easy out. She sighed and wished she could take it. "No. I like you too much because I like you too much. The power has something to do with it, sure, but you're funny, you're smart, you're unique, you're attractive, you laugh at my jokes. Who knows why someone likes someone too much? They just do."

He looked intrigued. "How much is too much?"

"It's too much when certain people bring up the seven-year rule." Certain people were certainly listening.

Jack nodded, hair falling into his eyes. "Oh. Okay." When he looked up, the line of his shoulders had changed just enough Charlie realized he'd relaxed—which made her wonder how long he'd been tense and why hadn't she noticed it. "Then I like you too much, too." There was gentle mockery behind his repetition of her phrase. Before Charlie could call him on it, before she was even sure she was going to call him on it because she'd certainly tossed around a little self-mockery back when she'd first realized her feelings, he added, his tone matter-of-fact, "I want to be with you all the time and it drives me nuts when you just take off like I don't matter."

Charlie was reminded that dragons weren't raised to indulge in the emotional constipation of seventeen-year-old boys. "You matter."

"Great." His attempt at looking lecherous was funnier than it was sexy. She managed not to laugh. "Let's . . ."

"Talk."

"But . . ."

"No."

Eyes flaring gold, Jack rocked back on his heels. "It's a stupid rule and it shouldn't matter."

"No, it shouldn't. Do you know why?" she added, cutting him off before he could get all excited about her agreeing with him. "Because I am thirteen years older than you and nothing is going to happen. Rule or no rule."

"But we're Wild." He climbed up and sat beside her.

"You're seventeen, Jack." Staring down at their dangling feet, she bumped the toe of her boot against the toe of his sneakers.

"I've been an adult for two years!"

"I've been an adult for fifteen. The numbers aren't really helping your case."

"But in ritual . . ."

"Ritual's different." Slate-gray clouds had started to pack into the arc of the sky and the temperature had dropped. She wished she could lean into the warmth Jack radiated even in skin. "I'm probably the only third circle who could handle you—maybe Katie, maybe not—but I don't go into the circle where age doesn't count because I don't want to drive myself crazy with what I can't have outside the circle."

"What about what I want?"

Charlie shrugged. "I don't want to drive you crazy with what you can't have outside the circle either."

"Think highly of yourself."

"No complaints so far."

Jack snorted. Charlie had to lean back out of the cloud of smoke. They sat in silence for a few minutes until it dissipated, then he said, "You said I'm unique."

"I did."

"So the situation is unique."

"Not arguing."

"So the age thing . . ."

"Matters."

"If you were a dragon . . ."

Charlie waited, but Jack didn't finish. The only female dragon he'd ever known was his mother and that probably made it a little hard to extrapolate relationship cues.

"If I was thirty and you were forty-three?" he asked at last.

"Then the seven-year rule would apply."

She could hear the heels of his sneakers impacting against the rock as he kicked his feet. *Thud thud. Thud thud. Thud thud.* After a moment, she realized he'd matched her heartbeat. Sitting up, she cocked her head and listened, shifting through the ambient noise.

His head swiveled around until he was staring back over his right shoulder. "What?"

"Nothing." Their hearts were beating in time—a cardiopulmonary twist on happily never after. Had they been synced since she'd matched his rhythm in the Wood? Had she moved them one double step closer to the point of no return?

Nothing she could hear offered an answer. *Thanks, world.*

"So what do we do?" he asked after a long, quiet moment.

"We suck it up. We spend more time apart than together. You'll know that when I leave it's not you, it's me." She'd never hear that cry of pain in the Wood again. "When we're together, we enjoy what we have and try not to think about what we can't have. We don't let misunderstandings destroy Tokyo."

"What?"

"Godzilla versus Mothra." When he continued to stare at her like she was speaking Urdu, she shook her head. "Not important. We accept that the universe occasionally acts like a dick and we make the best of it."

"I thought we weren't allowed the best of it."

"Fine. We make the second best of it. Honesty. Friendship." Heels and fingertips, she tapped out random rhythms, trying unsuccessfully to break the pull of his heartbeat. "The smug and sanctimonious feeling that comes from knowing you're doing what's right, not what you want."

"Yeah, that sounds like so much fun." He twisted around on the rock to face her, spine curving in a way Human spines did not. "Charlie, Gale boys choose. What would happen if I chose you?"

I chose you. She was wet-wired to respond to the words and, given the feelings involved, the *if* out in front almost wasn't enough. It took a silent recitation of the chromatic scale before she could trust her voice. "Okay, you didn't grow up with this so, first, you know that whole no one says no to a Gale boy thing? It's kind of the way no one says no to kittens or puppies. They're . . . you're indulged because there's so few of you. And second, by the time a Gale boy makes a choice, no one says no because it's pretty much a done deal. And third, the aunties wouldn't allow it."

"They'd take away the one power that Gale boys have in this family?"

"Sucks to be you."

"And if I don't choose?"

"Then they won't take your choice away." And some day, in the future, when the Gale girls now concentrating on soccer and Justin Bieber grew up, he'd still have the chance to choose. Maybe he never would, not if he was as fucked up about this as she was, but if he did, she'd be happy for him. She'd go live in Nashville and have sex with fake cowboys and drink too much and only come home to annoy Allie and spoil her kids, but she'd be happy for him. And really pathetic. Screw that. It couldn't hurt any more than not having him now and while she *would* be happy for him, she'd resent the hell out of the situation, pour that resentment into an album, and continue the fine musical tradition of making a fortune off a broken heart. Maybe she'd have tea with Adele circa 2011.

"What'll the aunties do if they find out? Would they keep us apart?"

"No. They wouldn't need to because, and this is me repeating the chorus, I'm not going to do anything."

Golden brows drew in. "What if I do something?"

It actually hurt to grin at him, but hey, thirteen years, that's why she got the big bucks. "You think I can't stop you?"

He didn't return the grin and Charlie could see how hard he fought to hold his current form, scales slipping across his face and hands like drops of liquid gold. "I know you can't." Matter-of-fact. Fact.

Matched. "Then I'll go where the Wild things are and the aunties will tell you over and over that you're young, you'll find someone else, as though what you're feeling right now doesn't matter. Worse, Allie will drown you in sympathy until *you* boot. You may be able to track me . . ."

"I can."

". . . but I can move faster than you. We won't have family. We won't have each other. I'm banking on you being too smart to start something where nobody wins."

"It's not fair."

And hello seventeen. "Fair has nothing to do with this. But at least we know why we're hurting."

"Joy," Jack muttered. "I still think you being old shouldn't matter, if we want each other."

"You can't always get what you want."

His shrug was more Dragon Prince than Gale. "But sometimes you get what you need."

Her smile felt like it fit on her face for the first time since breakfast. "Seriously, you're quoting the Stones?"

This shrug was all nonchalance. "They're old, too."

She'd almost managed to push him off the rock when her phone rang and she called a time out. "What's up, Allie-cat?"

"Do I even want to know why you're breathing heavily?"

"I'm old." She flipped Jack off when he snickered.

"But you act like you're seventeen, so it doesn't matter."

Charlie's breath caught in her throat. Had Allie been there, she'd have noticed the reaction to her word choice, but Allie was on the phone and by the time Jack glanced her way, Charlie'd forced herself to breathe.

"Did Jack not ask if you guys were coming home for lunch? I'm just about to take the corn bread out of the oven."

"We're on our way." Charlie carefully said good-bye and waited for Allie's response before she hung up. She drummed out "Luke's Theme" against her thigh. "Lunch will be the test. Allie's sensed a disturbance in the Force."

"I don't know what you're talking about half the time," Jack muttered jumping down off the rock.

"Yeah, but you love me anyway." The words dropped out of her mouth into silence. No, not silence—she could hear the wind rubbing tree branches together. She could hear two crows arguing just out of sight. She could hear traffic in the distance. She could hear her own heart beating.

Jack turned to stare up at her, his eyes gold from rim to rim. "I do, you know."

"I know." He was waiting so she sighed and said, "I do, too."

"Like me too much?"

"Jack . . ."

"Okay, then." He disappeared in a tower of flame. Reappeared, spreading his wings. "Fly with me?"

"No thanks, I'll Walk." She could use a few minutes alone in the Wood. It would give her a chance to beat her head against a tree.

Allie watched Charlie butter a piece of corn bread, and frowned. Barring the piece of bark in her hair, she looked much like she always did. Acted like she always did. She added hot sauce to her chowder, she laughed with the twins, and she pretended nothing was wrong. She pretended so well that had Allie not known Charlie inside and out, she might have even believed it. Charlie felt like guilt and concern.

It had nothing to do with the street person Charlie'd thrust into the protection of the family so he didn't repeat thoughts he shouldn't have heard—not that he *should* hear thoughts at all. No, Allie knew that if something was wrong it could be traced back to her grandmother's call because anything off in the Gale family in the last thirty years could be traced back to her grandmother.

"It was a Wild thing, Allie-cat, don't worry about it. The crazy street people prophecies are being dealt with."

She anchored second circle. Charlie would have to tell her if she pushed. Allie didn't know if Charlie could lie to her or how she'd be able to tell if Charlie had. She knew she never wanted to doubt her, not the way she doubted her grandmother, so for now she'd let it go.

Jack, who was clearly a part of the Wild need-to-know excuse, still ate like he'd missed his last six meals, but since nothing affected his appetite, that wasn't as reassuring as it might have been. Allie frowned as she studied the side of his face; he felt like resentment and relief and . . . "Are you two keeping secrets?"

"Secrets?" Charlie winked. "You make it sound so dirty, Allie-cat."

That explained the guilt, Allie reasoned as Jack spit soup across the table. But if it also explained Jack's resentment, it could be . . . She lost track of the thought as the twins shrieked with glee and added to the mess.

"You hiding up here?"

Stretched out on an elderly teak chaise, Charlie watched the pigeons who'd been perched on the edge of the roof take flight, and muttered, "Why would I be hiding from you?"

The matching chaise protested as Jack dropped onto it, but held together. "I didn't ask if you were hiding from me, I just asked if you were hiding."

"Not hiding. Thinking."

"Yeah, I could smell the smoke. You're going to get wet."

She transferred her gaze to the sky. Pure October in Calgary, the clouds they'd watched moving in while they were in the park now hung so low it looked as though she could reach up and touch them. "Please, it's barely spitting."

"We could go inside. . . ."

"No one's stopping you, princess." She nodded toward the door.

"Oh, yeah," Jack snorted. "You're tough."

The roof deck had been added during the renovation of the apartments; built by Michael so Jack would have a place to land out of Auntie Gwen's direct line of sight. Charlie had no idea how often he used it, but after Allie'd grown too large to maneuver her bulk around the turns of the spiral staircase, she'd found it an excellent place to get a little alone time. She was well aware of the irony of looking for alone time in a place built for Jack.

"So at lunch . . ."

"Come on, you hunt. You've got to understand the whole leaving a false trail thing."

"With dragons, it's not so much hunting as it's swooping and devouring."

"What's the difference?"

"Hunting implies a chance of failure."

"Right."

"So, what're you thinking about?"

He didn't add, *Us?* Charlie heard it anyway. "Dan." A raised hand held him silent while she sang out a subtler anti-eavesdropping charm than she usually used. *Piss off, this is private!* occasionally backfired and attracted more attention than it prevented. She hadn't had a chance to tell Jack what Dan had told her in the Wood; not with David able to hear every word. David could keep personal secrets as long as Allie or the aunties didn't ask a direct question, but if there was the slightest chance the family was in danger, he'd raise the alarm without considering that they might need more information. It was part of his function to be crazy overprotective and part of hers as a Wild Power to make an end run around him.

"He could've heard Auntie Catherine?" Jack said thoughtfully when she finished filling him in.

"Millions are going to die? I'm positive that wasn't Auntie Catherine overreacting."

"Yeah, because the aunties never overreact."

"The aunties can make *Game of Thrones* look like *Dora the Explorer*, but that's not the point. The point is, out of all the millions of people tossing their thoughts into Dan's head like it was some kind of mental dumpster, how do we find the other person who knows about the asteroid?"

"You don't know it's only one person." When Charlie turned to glare at him, Jack shrugged. "You think Dan heard one person, but there could be more people Dan didn't hear. He doesn't hear everyone."

"Stop helping."

"We should check Dan's Facebook page. He didn't set it up," Jack continued, before Charlie managed to move past the stunned surprise of her initial response. "It's the bam bam video and reactions. Maybe the person Dan overheard posted a '*dude, you know the sky is falling, I know the sky is falling, too*' comment."

"Yeah . . ." Charlie shook her head. "I bet there's a bunch of those and they're probably as useful as most things on Facebook."

"How would you know? You're still on MySpace."

"It's an indie music site now!"

"Uh-huh."Tipping his head back, Jack let out a short burst of flame. "And now it's snowing."

"Three flakes hardly count as snow."

"Four."

Charlie held out her hand and watched as the fourth flake, grayer than the rest, drifted down onto her palm. "I think that's ash."

Jack stared down at it. "What did I burn?"

"No idea." She scrubbed her palm clean against her jeans and wished everything that fell from the sky could be dealt with so easily. "Count the pigeons."

He snickered instead of protesting; an adult's response not a child's. Not adult enough, unfortunately.

After a moment, Charlie sighed and said, "I suppose I could just go looking for people having random panic attacks. That might narrow it down a bit." Panic seemed like a reasonable response to believing millions of people only had six months left. "First you panic, then you go a little crazy and do all the things you always . . ."

Her personal soundtrack played the *Jeopardy* theme as the pieces fell into place.

"I'm an idiot."

She expected a smartass remark. When all she got was silence, she turned to see Jack staring at her, his expression pure dragon.

"You're leaving again."

"I have to see a man about a bouzouki." She sang the anti-eavesdropping charm away as she stood—an auntie stumbling over it would lead to an exploration of the entirely incorrect statement that *"In this family we don't keep secrets."* The aunties kept plenty of secrets. Charlie was just the only non-auntie who could manage it, and reminding them of that never ended well. When she reached the door alone, she assumed Jack planned to stay on the roof. Then she heard the chaise fall over, and he joined her on the stairs.

"Does bouzouki mean you're going to have sex?"

Her boot slid past the last step. The dance across the hall to keep her balance was not one of her more graceful moments. "No. Not sex. Bouzouki means there's no such thing as a coincidence in this family." Dropping her voice as they moved through the apartment, she told him about the sudden decision of an engineer to lead the life of an itinerant musician.

She'd left her guitar leaning against the wall by the mirror. A glance at her watch, certain it was near four or five, informed her it was only just past two. They'd had a busy morning.

"Take me with you."

Weren't they past this? "I can't."

"I know you can't take me through the Wood, but if we flew . . ."

The warm strength of Jack below her, the sky roads open and infinite. Charlie shook her head to dump the overwrought anthem she could feel building. "There's nowhere for you to fly to. I don't know where I'm going until I leave the Wood and get there."

"Yeah, I get that, but . . ." He stared at the floor for a moment, then squared his shoulders, folded his arms, and looked her in the eye. "Like I said in the park, I don't like it when you're not here."

Charlie wrapped both hands around the gig bag's straps so she didn't reach out and press her palm against his chest over his heart. When did he grow taller than her? She didn't remember that happening. "If it helps, it's not just you; it's a Gale thing."

"It's not a Gale thing."

"Yeah, it is." Even after four years, there was still a lot about the family he didn't know. Things the rest of them had internalized so thoroughly, they were never mentioned until minor disasters brought them up. If she could make Jack believe that at least part of what he felt was no more than family feelings, that would be best all around. Convince. Not make. Never that. Charlie glanced toward the stairs. "Allie freaks out when I leave because she wants to tuck everyone she cares about close around her and keep them safe. Classic second circle. But don't mention that makes you think of her as a giant chicken because she really doesn't appreciate it." When Jack didn't share her smile, she let it drop. "David, well, David doesn't exactly freak out, he never did, but he's not happy when his people are outside his sphere of influence. And the aunties freak when I leave because I'm Wild, and they figure sometime I won't come back."

"You won't."

"Sure I will." But she could hear the lie. Charlie had no idea why Auntie Catherine had finally left, had put herself definitively outside the family's influence, but Charlie knew, deep down where she knew the way into the Wood, that someday she, too, would slip the family leash. And after her, Jack.

Who'd filled the hall with smoke.

"Oh, that's mature." Waving a hand in front of her face, she crossed the hall and opened the back door.

When she turned to face him again, his eyes flashed gold. "It's *not* a Gale thing," he growled. "You said the aunties would tell me what I felt didn't matter; isn't that what you're doing?"

The mirror usually chose to show Jack as a dragon. Not this time. His shoulders were broad and his arms well muscled—probably from all the flying—and although his nose was still a little big, all the individual parts of his face had begun to match up and settle into an attractive whole. His eyes—his reflection's eyes—were a warm amber and his hair a little paler gold than his scales. A trace of gold glinted along his jaw and his upper lip. His reflection played a set of bongos, two beats on one skin, two on the other.

His heartbeat.

Her heartbeat.

Fingers tight around the straps of her gig bag, Charlie took a deep breath. Fortunately, most of the smoke had dissipated because nothing added to the sincerity of an apology like hacking up a lung. "I'm sorry. I shouldn't have done that. But you have to admit, it was pretty indicative of that whole *significantly older than you* problem."

"I don't have to admit anything and it's your problem." He was still smoking a little. "You need to get over it."

She needed to get over him, but as that was unlikely to happen . . .

Given the way his expression changed from challenging to resigned, he'd read that off her face. "What if the bouzouki guy isn't who we're looking for?" he asked, chin rising, challenging her to comment on the abrupt subject change.

Yeah. Like that was going to happen. "Gary used to be an engineer, then all at once, bam, he gave up everything to follow a dream. And he had a secret."

"And he's the guy because there's no such thing as coincidence in this family."

"That, too."

There was a faint smell of scorched fabric as Jack shoved his hands into his pockets. "Weren't you leaving?"

"Can you do me a favor?"

"You want me to tell Allie you've gone." His smile showed teeth. "Coward."

"You betcha."

In the Wood, Jack's song sounded grumpy but not pained. Allie's sounded fussy but not suspicious. Charlie couldn't hear the bouzouki.

"Seriously? *Now* you decided to be coy?"

She checked her tuning, then played "Boys of Blue Hill," pausing after each measure to listen. Gary'd played it so beautifully in Baltimore it was clearly a signature piece for him.

Nothing.

She played his love for his wife. His decision to follow his dream. The secret that convinced him he had nothing to lose. The cats; singly and collectively.

And more nothing.

"Well, fuck you. We'll do it the old-fashioned way."

Charlie stepped out of the Wood at the Forks in Winnipeg and called Dave Clement.

"Gary Ehrlich? Yeah, he gave me a call yesterday. I sent him to Vermont. George Frost's band has a line of gigs at small fall fairs through New England and his bouzouki player broke his wrist teaching parkour in Jersey City. Frost's playing Art on the Street tonight and tomorrow in Carter, Vermont, then I think he's heading into Connecticut. Give me a minute and I'll find the list of where he's heading after that."

"Thanks, Dave, no need. I'll catch him in Vermont."

Charlie came out of the Wood in a cemetery, near a section of Civil War graves surrounded by trees large enough to have been planted at the same time as the dead soldiers. Many of the graves, even those so worn the names could no longer be read, had the sticks of paper flags pushed into the earth by the stones. Those who'd left the flags hadn't intended their offering to stake the dead in place, but, fortunately, the dead were beyond intent. As a result, Carter had one of the most peaceful cemeteries Charlie'd ever been in.

The sky was clear and the temperature was about fifteen degrees warmer than it had been in Calgary. After tucking the guitar back in the gig bag, she unzipped her jacket, shook the damp out of her hair, and checked to make sure the charm etched into the glass had set her watch to local time.

She could hear "Ashokan Farewell" playing as she made her way toward the street, and it took a moment to realize the music wasn't inside her head but coming from a stage down the road to the right.

Art in the Street was just that. Art. In the street. To Charlie's eye some of the art looked more like craft and some of the craft looked more like kitsch, but Auntie Kay made corn husk dolls she sold for a stupid amount of money to tourists, so Charlie had to admit that her idea of art was fairly basic to begin with. The dolls, Auntie Kay explained, were perfectly safe as the tourists had no idea who the dolls represented. In that instance, intent counted. Auntie Kay's intent had always been to take as much money from the tourists as possible.

Carter had few cross streets. Large frame houses, so familiar in the New England states, lined the road through town, their faded paint and vaguely shabby air giving them a look of genteel poverty. The B&B/general store combination across the street from the church, however, had clearly been recently bought by someone with money, its red-and-green trim fresh and gleaming. From the way the nearer displays of carvings, paintings, and quilts seemed to be funneling people into the store, Charlie suspected the owners were the driving force behind the fair.

Charlie turned right, toward the music. And froze.

The three-story, gray frame house was classic Vermont. The windows full of teddy bears, not so much. Little plush faces stared out from every window on all three floors, their eyes locked on Charlie.

"Optical illusion," she muttered, heading for the stage. She didn't have time for this. A dozen steps later, when she glanced toward the house again, the bears were still staring. And not only the bears facing the front of the house, but the bears who'd been facing the graveyard a moment before. "Oh, come on, guys. I'm here to talk to Gary. That's all."

Polyester fur faded from the sun, noses pressed against grubby glass, the bears stared. A large powder-blue-and-white bear, slumped on the sill in the third-floor dormer, looked almost exactly like a plush toy Charlie'd owned

as a child. It also looked depressed, but there was always a chance she was
reading too much into its expression.

"Ashokan Farewell" ended, and she could hear a bouzouki laying in a harmony line to "The Factory Girl." Gary's sure touch was nearly drowned out as
her personal soundtrack played "Cardiac Arrest" by the Teddybears. Odds
were high *shake your bonemaker* was meant to be more metaphysical in this case
as the windows full of depressed teddy bears were full-out disturbing.

It was the Baltimore cemetery all over again. Only with more polyester.

The bears weren't Gales, it therefore wasn't Gale business. Walking past,
leaving the bears staring out at the world, would not result in large-scale
death and destruction by the Dragon Queen and it would not assist one of
the old gods to rise. Walking past would take her to the man who had the
answers she needed in order to put the phrase *millions will die* into context
because those millions would definitely include Gales. Standing at the point
where the front path met the sidewalk, ready to walk past, Charlie could see
the small crowd watching in front of the stage, the pole lights shining
down . . .

The bears stared down at her.

The hair lifted off the back of Charlie's neck.

"If we start cleaning up the crap people get into, where does it stop?" the aunties
snapped when the young inevitably asked why the family didn't help if it
could. *"Best we keep our own house clean, treat them like adults, and let them make
their own choices. Why would we want to fill the world with dependent children when
we already have a surfeit of purple-haired smart-asses who play their music too loud,
and if you want to know what tragically hip really means, you take a look at your
Auntie Rose from behind. There are articles of clothing that should not come in a Two
X, but does she listen to me? No."* Specifically, that had been the answer Charlie'd
gotten when she'd asked.

Influenced by too much television, her younger sisters occasionally
hunted in the world's darker and nastier places. Hunted, Charlie corrected
silently, having been corrected significantly less silently by the twins. The
word required a capital H. Her sisters were pretentious maniacs with a
slightly scary Joss Whedon obsession, but, as Allie pointed out, better they
got that out of their system when they were away from home.

Charlie'd played in some of the world's darker and nastier bars, but that wasn't quite the same. She considered calling the twins in, but aside from the bears, Carter seemed like too nice a place to deserve them.

Her arrival had been delayed by the need to make a phone call. That usually meant something. It was possible, it meant she'd spend less time waiting for Gary to finish playing before they could talk. Possible. But it wasn't looking very likely.

"There's no one home right now, is there?" she asked the bears, and wasn't even a little upset when they didn't answer. The person or persons responsible were probably spending a lovely fall afternoon with their neighbors enjoying Art in the Street. With a locally sourced candy apple in one hand, they'd probably gotten caught up discussing the merits of scrollwork over lathe work and wouldn't be back for hours.

"It looks like they're silently screaming '*help me*,' doesn't it?"

She glanced over at the man who'd paused beside her, and sighed. "Yeah. It does."

He shoved his hands into his jacket pockets and grinned sheepishly, his teeth a pale curve within his beard. "Of course they aren't really."

"Of course they aren't," Charlie muttered as he crossed the street to greet a woman selling fabric art. As the band finished up with "The Factory Girl," the crowd applauded with polite enthusiasm. "Fine," she told the bears, wondering what part of Wild Power meant being at the beck and call of stuffed toys. "It's not like I can drag him off the stage before the show ends. I might as well spend the time dealing with you."

She was absolutely not going to acknowledge the feeling that Jack, who brokered agreements between feuding Brownies and made sure Dan didn't freeze, would have been disappointed in her had she refused to help.

A sign on the front lawn declared the house a B&B called The Teddy Bears' Picnic.

"Of course it is."

On the way up the walk, Charlie pulled her guitar out of the bag and reflected on how the 2010 Teddybears album containing the song "Cardiac Arrest" had been called Devil's Music. "Foreshadowing," she sighed. "The sign of quality metaphysical fuckups." No one answered her knock, or, after she discovered it, the ringing of the brass doorbell.

A simple charm popped the door open.

Too easy?

"Don't even start," she muttered.

Given the bears in the windows, Charlie had expected to there to be bears all over the house. While she couldn't guarantee it was the same in every room, the four she could see from the large foyer had bears *only* in the windows. She wasn't sure if that was better, or worse.

The furniture looked old and shabby, but comfortable. The walls in the sitting room to the left were covered in red flocked wallpaper. The scuffed hardwood floors were covered in worn rugs. The banister on the stairs leading up to the second and third floors had been painted black and the stairs themselves were covered in red-and-black paisley carpet. Nothing about the house said evil lived there.

Nothing but the bears, and they wouldn't shut up about it.

Charlie half thought she could smell the lingering scent of homemade chocolate chip cookies.

Yeah, well, baking was not a character reference. The aunties baked. The younger members of the family learned to stay away when the breeze carried the scent of gingerbread.

The teddy bears knew she'd entered the house. She could feel their awareness like pop rocks fizzing against her tongue . . . only she felt it all over. It wasn't an entirely unpleasant feeling.

Standing quietly, fingers resting lightly on the strings, she took a moment to figure out what to do next. The bears were pressed against the windows, staring out. Free the bears. Break the windows. Break the windows from the *inside*.

"All of a sudden, I miss my Orange Thunderverb 200." Cranking the big old amp up to eleven would certainly make what she was about to do easier. Humming "Teddy Bears' Picnic," she reached into the watch pocket of her jeans and swapped out her flat pick for a thumb pick. While her hands played the song, Charlie built a charm with her voice. She didn't *know* that all the windows had to be broken at the same time, but better safe than sorry. The charm fought to fly free. She fought to hold it while building it larger, stronger.

A small part of her attention pointed out that she was standing with her back to the front door and someone was hurrying up the walk. So much for the standing around holding a candy apple scenario. She should've charmed the door locked, but it was too late for that.

Without David to pull the power and Allie to feed it to her, she needed time.

If you go down to the woods today . . .

The skin between her shoulder blades crawled as the door opened.

. . . safer to stay at home.

Fingers grabbed at her gig bag.

Jerking forward, she released the charm.

The house filled with sound—although the charm itself made no noise. The windows shattered.

For every bear that ever was there . . .

The grip on her gig bag fell away and Charlie spun around in time to see a totally innocuous looking old man fall to the floor. A bit of powder blue fuzz clung to the grizzled stubble on his upper lip. He looked Human—although that didn't mean much, David and Jack both looked Human at least half . . . a quarter of the time.

Her skin had stopped sizzling.

The teddy bears slumped on the sills of broken windows or flung out on the lawn with the glass were no more than grubby, stuffed toys.

While people outside loudly argued about the possibility of a second, larger explosion, Charlie headed for the back door. The kitchen, with its faded linoleum floor and painted plywood cabinets, smelled *interesting* but she didn't pause to find out why because she honestly didn't want to know—many of the aunties' kitchens had faded linoleum and painted plywood cabinets and *interesting* smells. In her experience *interesting* was just a little too general a description to be safe. The bears were free, the rest could be left to the good people of Vermont.

She reached for the back door to the sound of "Footsteps" by the English doom metal band Warning.

A warning about footsteps.

Footsteps?

"Technically, they're foot*prints* and I don't think we have to worry about CSI Vermont," she muttered, glancing back to make sure she hadn't left a trail. Tucking her hand up into the sleeve of her jacket, she opened the door and slipped outside. Somehow, she managed to get across the yard and back into the cemetery without slicing her boots on pieces of broken glass or leaving too obvious a trail and, fortunately, the loud speculation from the crowd now inside the house and gathered around the old man covered any noise she might have made.

She barely heard her phone ring.

"Well, you've been a little busy, haven't you, Charlotte." Auntie Jane, however, came through loud and clear.

The fieldstone wall around the cemetery was about hip-high. Charlie planted her ass on a spot free of moss and lichen and swung her legs over. "You felt that?"

"Did I feel you poking into things that were none of your business, releasing certain energies without discovering if those energies were vicious or benign, not to mention being directly responsible for the snuffing out of a power without ever considering if that power might possibly be a guardian protecting the people you profess to be so concerned about rather than a jailor illicitly confining the innocent?"

"He was a guardian?"

"Don't be ridiculous, Charlotte; he was a nasty piece of work. Once his sort's started on stuffed toys, the world is a better place without them. But he was neither family nor bothering family and should have been left alone. Why are you in Vermont?"

"I'm here to see a friend who's playing at a street fair."

"You're in Vermont for the music?"

"Have you met me? It's why I go anywhere."

"Only for the music?"

"And, apparently, the teddy bears."

"I see. So given this was clearly a case of a Wild Power assuming she knew best . . ." When Auntie Jane hesitated, Charlie frowned. The aunties liked to pause and allow their listeners a chance to really realize just how much trouble they were in. This didn't sound like that kind of a pause. It sounded, strangely enough, like Auntie Jane was unsure. ". . . have you spoken with Catherine recently?"

"Auntie Catherine?" Charlie couldn't see a clear path from teddy bears to Auntie Catherine, but that didn't mean Auntie Jane couldn't. "This morning in Vegas. Why?"

"Vegas again." As disapproving snorts went, Auntie Jane could give Dan a run for his money. "Of course. Drink some tea with honey, Charlotte, your voice sounds like you've been gargling glass."

"Funny that," Charlie muttered. Given the emphatic click as Auntie Jane hung up, she'd either called from one of the farmhouse's old rotary phones or Auntie Phyllis had created a new app.

Auntie Jane and Auntie Catherine didn't get along, although, Charlie realized, being able to see random bits of the future would put a strain on most relationships, and Auntie Jane's expectations had never been particularly flexible. That said, this was the first time Auntie Jane had ever assumed that Charlie and Auntie Catherine were in contact because they were Wild. Did Auntie Jane want Auntie Catherine to call home? Was Charlie supposed to pass on the message?

"A little less obscure in my life would help," she pointed out to a squirrel watching her from the top of a gravestone. "So I need to ask Gary what specifically sent him out on the road and I need to ask Auntie Catherine to call home and I need to ask Jack to be less . . . Jack."

The squirrel's response sounded distinctly rude.

"You're right. My problem, not Jack's. I will try to own my own shit. Because who else would want it," she added as the squirrel bounded away. "Okay, we're here for Gary. Focus."

Safely behind the church, out of sight from the road and what seemed like the entire population of Carter gathered out in front of the ex house of bears—minus those who'd managed to cram inside—Charlie settled her guitar strap and decided she really needed to learn more songs on the penny whistle. A penny whistle weighed next to nothing, it could be used as a splint should the circumstances demand, and a simple thing like freeing a couple of hundred teddy bears wouldn't throw it out of tune. As she worked to bring her B and G back, she swallowed and realized gargling glass had been an accurate observation.

Fortunately, she didn't have to sing in the immediate future.

A moment later, she walked out of the graveyard like it was the first time she'd done it, fingerpicking Dan Mangan's "Not What You Think It Is." The bearded man who'd spoken to her before she'd gone inside to free the bears still stood by the fabric art stall, so she hummed a little reinforcement toward him.

People had begun to pick the fallen bears up off the lawn, clearly believing they weren't disturbing a crime scene and that they, personally, were immune to shards of glass. Charlie could hear multiple sirens coming from the south. Given the number of nicks and cuts she could already see on the people posing for cell phone pictures, not to mention the loud argument about the proper way to perform CPR coming from inside the house, emergency responders would be too busy to immediately worry about what exactly had gone on.

Once she broke out onto the open road, Charlie stopped playing, shook her thumb pick off into her pocket and tucked her guitar back into her gig bag. She'd always thought that approaching a stage with an instrument out reeked of desperation.

The band, tethered to the stage by their instruments, were watching the crowd, not her, and she was watching Gary, not the rest of the band, so she was less prepared than she might have been when the keyboard player launched himself off the stage.

"Charlie? Charlie Gale?"

"Toby! Toby Sum . . ." Before she could finish, Charlie found herself caught up in a hug that drove the air out of her lungs. She'd hooked up with Toby Summers while they were playing in Further Demented, a Montreal band with delusions of punk revival. He was tall, talented, and he made her laugh, but when the band broke up seven years ago, so had they. No regrets.

"What are you doing in Vermont?" Toby demanded, steadying her when she wobbled upon release.

"Passing through," she gasped. "As one does."

Gary waved from the stage, his smile managing to express *small world* and *the hell?* simultaneously. Not a bad trick.

"I see you got some blues back." One arm around her shoulders, Toby ruffled his other hand through her hair. "Last pics you posted, you were au natural again."

Given Auntie Catherine, Dan, falling rocks, millions who might or might not be dying, and Jack, Charlie'd forgotten all about the color she'd streaked into her hair. "Something, something about swearing a blue streak; I can't be arsed to find the clever."

"Well, if you're heading back to the hard stuff, for God's sake, take me with you. I love Frosty like a brother, but he thinks "Whiskey in the Jar" is rock and roll. Do you know what keyboards involve in a folk/Celtic/roots/ trad band, Charlie?" They'd reached the edge of the stage, and Toby nodded toward the Excalibur Double Crown tucked up against the side of his amp stack. "I am white America's worst nightmare; a big black man with an accordion. The only way it could be worse was if I was also Muslim and played the banjo. Hey, Frosty!"

An older, heavyset man with the ubiquitous gray ponytail and a Fender bass turned toward them.

"George Frost, of Frost on the Windows, Charlie Gale just passing through. Charlie plays killer lead, doesn't suck on vocals, and when she was twenty-two, she drank Benji Cheung under the table."

"In fairness," Charlie pointed out. "Benji was stoned at the time."

"When wasn't he?" George snorted. "You looking for a job, Charles?"

"No, like Toby says, I'm just passing through. Heard the music, thought I'd come see what was up." Gary had knelt to put his bouzouki in the case. He was listening, but he hadn't come any closer. Charlie couldn't figure out a graceful way of blowing Toby off or, more significantly, blowing George off to go talk to him. Burning bridges with someone who actually managed to put a band together and find paying gigs in the current economy would be beyond a stupid idea.

"You know what pulled our audience?"

She shrugged, shoulders moving under Toby's arm. "Looks like all the windows blew out on an old house."

"Gas leak?"

"How should I know? Freaky thing is, there's teddy bears all over the lawn."

"Freakier when they were in the windows," Toby muttered.

"True that," George allowed. He checked his watch. "Well, we were supposed to go to four and then on again at eight for the street party—looks like that's fucked. I think I'd better go find Morris Winchester and find out what's what. Toby, you're with me."

"Should I bring the accordion?"

"Dear lord, man, no; we're just going to talk to him." George set down his bass, sat on the edge of the stage, and pushed off. "I don't need you to go all Sam Jackson on his ass."

"Okay, first, Sam?" Toby gave Charlie's shoulder's one last squeeze and murmured, "Do not leave without saying good-bye. And second," he continued, raising his voice as he fell into step beside George, "Samuel Jackson has never been in a movie with an accordion."

"On the plane . . ."

"That was an anaconda."

"So . . ." Charlie turned to Gary as the argument shifted to background noise. ". . . fancy meeting you here."

"I'm working." He smiled as he came closer and dropped to sit on the edge of the stage. "Looks like you haven't made it home yet."

"It's complicated." Charlie grinned. "This is me not telling you the road is my home. So, where's Sheryl?"

"She was at the art fair, so I expect she's trying to find out what happened at the house. You know, when it blew . . ." He swung his legs and rubbed one hand over the back of his neck. ". . . I thought I heard the last few bars of 'The Teddy Bears' Picnic.'"

"That's weird." Charlie'd stopped playing when the windows blew, so Gary'd heard the music continuing on its own. As a rule, she had no problem with music taking on a life of its own—it happened often enough even without her help—but the memory of the bears' awareness sizzling over her skin added a little emphasis to her reply.

"Yeah." They considered *weird* together for a moment, then Gary shook his head and said, "Listen, I want to thank you for giving me Dave's number. I've barely been on the road for twenty-four hours and I've got work for the next month." Brows dipping in, he waved a hand at the crowd ignoring the stage. "Hopefully. Anyway, I owe you."

"Good." She hadn't decided how she was going to do this, but, now he'd admitted he owed her, blunt and to the point seemed like the best idea. She'd had a long day and she just wanted it to be over. "Want a chance to pay me back?"

"Sure."

"Tell me why you think that millions are going to die?"

"What?"

Oh, yeah. It was Gary. She could hear both the initial panic and the *gone a little bit crazy* in his voice.

"Specifically, you thought . . ." Charlie tapped her fingers against her thigh, the rhythm jogging free the exact words Dan had overheard. ". . . can't tell people the sky is falling, millions will die in the panic. Then you thought: . . . don't find a solution in six months, millions will die in the panic anyway."

His eyes wide, he licked his lips and leaned away. "I don't know what you're talking about."

He was such a terrible liar it was kind of cute. "You've got a secret that's big enough it pushed you away from your old life, convincing you there was no reason not to follow a dream. It's so big, you can't tell anyone, not even Sheryl, about it. So, why do you think that millions are going to die?"

"I can't . . ." Fingers clutching the arms of his glasses, he shook his head. "I gave my word."

Choice, she reminded herself. "And I bet it would take something pretty extraordinary to convince you to break it." One of the things Charlie loved about Vermont was the number of trees. National, state, and town forests aside, even new builds were careful of old growth. The Wood was as close in Vermont as it had been back in Darsden East where the family had been settled for over a century. "Walk with me."

"No."

"I guarantee that what I have to show you is extraordinary enough you'll want to tell me everything."

"No."

His head shaking had gotten a little frantic, so Charlie said the magic word. "Please."

Releasing his glasses, he took a deep breath and ran the fingers of his right hand through the hair over his ear, repeating the motion over and over. "Walk where?"

"That's a little hard to explain, but I swear on my mother's cherry pie that you'll be back before you know you're gone."

"You swear on your mother's cherry pie?" Gary's laugh wobbled a little as he slid off the stage. "Must be one amazing cherry pie."

"You have no idea," Charlie told him, getting out her guitar.

"Should I bring the bouzouki?"

She could hear the unease under every word. "No, we're good. But bring a jacket . . ." She nodded toward one end of Gary's instrument case and the clothing in question. ". . . just in case."

"In case of what?" he asked, reaching back.

"Weather."

After a dubious glance at the brilliant pinks and oranges the sunset had seared across the sky, he shrugged into his jacket and fell into step beside her.

FIVE

THE STAGE FOR THE STREET FAIR had been built just before the corner of Adam's Crescent and Main, so Charlie led Gary across the street to the trees at the east side of the T-junction—enough behind the stage they wouldn't be seen, close enough to the stage that Gary wouldn't balk. She played a soft arpeggio, using the guitar to carry them forward rather than her voice in case Gary needed reassurance. "Put your hand on my shoulder."

"Is this . . ." He let the question trail off as Charlie started to play. His grip tightened. He jerked forward as she stepped between two chestnuts, nearly treading on her heels. When she stopped playing, he gasped, "Where are we?"

"In the Wood."

"I can see that, where . . ."

"Between."

"Between *what?*"

"B and C on the chromatic scale." Charlie spread her hands, allowing the guitar to hang by the strap. "Or E and F."

"There isn't anything between B and C or E and F."

"That's what they want you to think."

He let go of her shoulder, made a sound that stopped just short of being a whimper, and grabbed hold again. "This can't be real."

"Real is subjective."

"No, it really isn't!"

"That's the engineer talking, not the musician." A fiddle started up in the distance, and Charlie grinned. She couldn't take him to either Calgary or Darsden East; it wouldn't be safe. "Come on." Two steps. Three. Four. And . . .

The gray of the sky reached down to touch the gray of Northumberland Strait, Port Hood Island barely visible in the distance like a floating Brigadoon. A strong breeze ruffled the tops of the waves, and half a dozen gulls banked and dipped and screamed insults at each other in the last of the light. Charlie's knee sank into damp sand as she dropped down to slide her guitar into the gig bag out of the damp. Another hour east of Vermont, it was almost dark and not quite raining.

"This," Gary said, his voice free of doubt, "is real."

"You seem very sure. Not that that's a bad thing," she added, twisting to face him as she closed the zipper. "What convinced you?"

He snorted. "The smell of dead fish."

"Welcome to Nova Scotia."

"Canada?"

Charlie stood and waved a hand. "Specifically, Cape Breton, just outside Port Hudson. You can see the end of the pier if you look to the right."

"This is nuts." He looked to the right. "Completely insane." Back at her. "What *are* you?"

"That's a long story. And not particularly relevant."

"I disagree. While I'm willing to grant this as being extraordinary enough to break my word, I'll tell you what you want to know if you tell me what I need to know, because if you think you can change my perception of the world, then . . ." Both hands up, he stepped back, stumbling as the sand shifted. "You're not going to kill me after I tell you what I know, are you? In order to keep *your* secret?"

Why would he think that? "If I say yes, that's pretty poor motivation."

"You didn't answer my question."

"No, I'm not going to kill you. Nor," she added when he opened his mouth, "am I going to dump you in Antarctica where the climate will kill you for me. Nor, off the top of my head, into a nest of rattlesnakes where you technically die of snake bite. Nor in the middle of the north Atlantic where your bones can drift down to rest by the remains of the *Titanic*. Nor . . ."

"I get it. You're not going to kill me. Also, the top of your head is a little terrifying." He sat down heavily on a log, the upper curve polished smooth by countless pairs of jeans. "Okay. The secret. There's an asteroid . . ."

"I know about the asteroid." Charlie cut him off. "What I need to know is how you know and why you think millions are going to die."

Gary stared at her for a long moment. "How do you know about the asteroid?"

"I have an auntie who can see the future."

"Okay." He pushed damp sand into a pile with one foot. "All things considered, it seems a little pointless to argue about that. So, why *don't* you think millions are going to die?"

Charlie sighed. This was the third, no, fourth time today she'd sung the ballad of NASA and the asteroid. She felt like an episode of *Schoolhouse Rock*. "If it's big enough to do extinction type damage in six months, it's either big enough to see—and no one's talking about it—or it's still so far away NASA will have plenty of time to deal with it."

"That's . . ." He shook his head and laughed. "That's actually a smarter observation than about eighty percent of the general population and a hundred percent of Hollywood could make. Unfortunately, in this particular case, you're wrong."

"I'm what?"

"I have a friend," Gary said so softly that Charlie had to strain to hear him over the seagulls, "Dr. Kiren Mehta. We grew up together. She works at NASA, at JPL in California, and she was killing time waiting for Vesta data to run. She mathematically discovered that a NEO, Near Earth Object, that everyone's seen and knows will miss us by a significant margin, has been masking another NEO that won't. Won't miss us," he added, in case Charlie hadn't understood.

She indicated he should continue, fairly certain that the roaring in her ears was the surf.

"The paths of these asteroids have already begun to diverge. Within six months, six months being the happy fun estimate, someone with a telescope will catch sight of two points of light where there should only be one and break the news. One of the big observatories, some guy in his backyard; there's a Defense Research sky-monitoring project called SpaceView that uses amateur astronomers to track space debris and I'm banking on them, but in the end, it doesn't matter." The rock he threw skipped through the curl of a wave before sinking. "In six months, panic. In twenty-two months, impact. The Armageddon Asteroid . . ."

"I'm sorry?"

"Yeah." He shrugged. "I didn't name it. It's bigger than the one that may or may not—depending on your belief in science or rhetoric—have wiped out the dinosaurs. Only this time, we're the dinosaurs."

Three steps forward and the waves of Northumberland Strait lapped against the toes of Charlie's boots. When she turned to face inland, she realized it was dark enough now and they were far enough apart that Gary's face was a pale expressionless oval. Charlie didn't have to see his expression; she could hear the truth in his voice. "Twenty-two months?"

"Until impact. Six months until millions die in worldwide panic. Panics. Probably plural."

"Wait . . ." She shuffled through everything he'd told her. "You said your friend discovered it mathematically. Maybe she was wrong. Maybe she forgot to carry a two or something."

He sounded a lot more amused than the situation called for. "You have an auntie who can see the future."

"Crap." Two long steps back and the log rocked as she dropped down beside him. "NASA can stop it. Right?"

"In twenty-two months?" Charlie felt the shrug as much as saw it. "Figure out a way to stop it, probably. Work out how to implement the solution—research, financing, engineering, construction—and get it into space before the asteroid gets too close all in twenty-two months, from a zero start? Life isn't a Michael Bay movie."

"Usually, that's a good thing."

"Usually."

"Is it money? Is that why they can't . . ." She took a deep breath and stopped leaning toward him before she pushed him off the damned log. "You'd think the world's governments would be falling over themselves to throw money at not dying."

"You'd think. But you've clearly never had to apply for government funding." Gary picked up another rock and tossed it into the water. "I'm sure you can understand why I haven't told anyone; not Sheryl, not my parents, not even my rabbi. The panic will start soon enough; they might as well enjoy those last few months of peace."

"You've come to terms with the end of the world."

His turn to shrug. "There's no way to stop it."

"NASA . . ."

"Yeah, well . . ." He rubbed sand off his fingers against his jeans, the soft *shunk shunk* almost comforting. ". . . some of the smartest, most motivated people in the world are at NASA, but they can't stop time and they can't work miracles."

Charlie sagged forward, hands dangling between her knees. "I feel like I've been betrayed by the Discovery Channel."

"Actually, it's hard to imagine science having much to do with your . . . with your life." There was light enough she saw him spin around toward her and she definitely felt it when he grabbed her arm. "You can stop it."

"I sing."

"And take half a dozen steps through an imaginary forest to cover the distance between Vermont and Nova Scotia. You can't tell me that all you do is sing."

"I can." Charlie could taste salt on her lips. "I can tell you whatever I want." And make him believe it. "But you're right, it's more complicated than that."

"Complicated enough to save the world?"

"I don't know." Heart pounding, she thought about it. About a Dragon Queen in Calgary and an old god across the province from where she sat with a bouzouki player who had a friend who'd mathematically discovered the end of the world. The end of the world by falling rock. She'd Sung the seabed. How different was that from a falling rock? She could skip the research, financing, engineering, and construction, so how hard could it be? This was what it was about. Auntie Catherine hadn't needed to talk to her because she needed contact with family. Gary hadn't needed her blessing for the road.

This.

It was about stopping a falling rock from ending the world in twenty-two months.

Twenty-two.

Seven years had turned out to be forever. Twenty-two months might as well be tomorrow.

She needed to know the details.

"Charlie?"

"It's just a falling rock, right?"

Gary's mouth opened. Closed again. Finally, he offered a tentative, "Essentially."

"All right, then." She could do this. "Did your friend tell you where the rock was coming in from?"

"The angle of approach? No. Does it matter?" Resignation had been replaced by hope.

"It might." If it was heading straight for one of the family's anchors, for David or for Uncle Arthur, *they* could probably stop it. Possibly stop it. Maybe. "Does she know where it's going to hit?"

"There'll be multiple points of impact; that part the movies get right. As soon as it gets close enough, gravitational stresses will begin breaking pieces off. How many and what size they are will depend on the composition of the asteroid."

"So if it breaks into a billion little tiny pieces?"

Gary waved that off. "Small enough pieces will burn up in the atmosphere, but that's unlikely to happen, not when it's held together this long—although they can't get a good read on its composition until it clears the metal heavy asteroid in front of it. And remember, the damage from multiple impacts could be as bad as from one big one. Which is why once it's close enough to use nukes with the delivery systems already available, nukes are a bad idea."

Nukes are a bad idea had to be one of the most redundant things Charlie'd ever heard. "What's a good idea, then?"

"NASA's probably working on deflection, planning to use Orion—it's the new capsule, nearly ready to go up and the propulsion is basically old-school Saturn tech. They've probably talked about suicide missions by now." His mouth twisted up into an almost smile. "Of course, they've probably also talked about discovery missions, gathering as much information as possible about the rock before it kills us just for the sake of having it. They're kind of crazy in a good way at NASA."

"Crazy in a good way is good."

They sat quietly for a moment. Charlie listened to her fiddler play "Whiskey" and agreed that a drink wasn't a terrible idea.

Gary played with the left earpiece of his glasses. "Can you move the asteroid somewhere else?" he asked at last. "Like you moved me?"

"Somehow I doubt there's a connection to the Wood in space. I need growing things, and space is kind of an absence of that." Although, the Discovery Channel *had* been wrong about NASA. "It is, right? An absence of life?"

"As we know it, yeah."

She stretched out her legs, her jeans beginning to damp up from the mist. "So tell me everything about your doctor friend."

"Kiren Mehta? Why?"

"I need the details you don't have and I'll need her song to get to her."

"You'll need her what now? Wait, never mind." Charlie could hear him breathing a little heavily but, all in all, Gary was dealing with the sudden change in his worldview remarkably well. Of course, he'd already dealt with the end of the world, so dealing with the Gales' world was not that big a step, relatively speaking. "Promise me you won't hurt her."

"Why would I hurt her?"

"Vermont." He waved a hand. "Creepy forest." He waved the other hand. "Nova Scotia. You can see why I might be concerned."

If a short trip concerned him, it was a good thing she hadn't taken him home. The aunties would have sent him into full-fledged fight or flight. Although, in fairness, they had that effect on a lot of people. On purpose. "I won't hurt her, but I suspect she'll be more willing to share if I tell her you sent me."

"Why can't you take her through the Wood? It's . . ." Words were considered and discarded in the pause. ". . . convincing."

"Yeah, but you and I have history, however short, and she doesn't know me. A hysterical reaction won't produce anything worth listening to."

"So tell her you found out from whoever you found out from. You know, your auntie who sees the future."

"And a telepath being driven crazy by the voices in his head who lives on the street and is being hunted by the FBI."

Two branches rubbed together with a sound between a creak and a groan. A car with a bad muffler drove by on the other side of the trees. A dog barked in the distance.

"Really?" Gary asked at last.

"Yeah."

"Fine. Tell her it was me. There's the music connection; that should help. She already thinks my choosing the bouzouki is kind of crazy." He took his glasses off and tugged his shirttail out from under his jacket to clean them. "I've known Kiren since the third grade when her family moved next to mine . . ."

Charlie listened, blocking out the wind and the waves and the Selkies making rude noises out past the breakwater, and built Kiren's song, adding layers and harmonies until, when Gary finally stopped talking, she knew she could find her. Or find the exit from the Wood nearest her. "Thank you," she said.

Gary nodded. They sat quietly for a moment.

"It's a heavy secret to carry," Charlie said at last. "I admire your strength."

He shrugged. "Most of the time it's easy enough to forget. I mean, there's nothing visible in the sky and the end of the world is a little hard to get your head around. Sheryl thinks I quit before I got fired . . . Sheryl!" He flung himself to his feet with enough force he stumbled and nearly fell. "We've been here for hours! She's going to be going nuts wondering where I am!"

Charlie stood a little more slowly, rolling her shoulders. "Don't worry, I'll take you back to just after the moment you left."

"Time travel, now? You move through space and time?" After a moment's consideration, he added, "You're not the . . ."

She wished. "I'm not."

"Time travel," Gary prodded.

"Every entrance into the Wood leaves a mark." She gouged a line in the sand with her heel. "You've only gone in once. One mark. Easy to find. No possibility of error."

"And the guitar?" he asked, as she slid it out of the gig bag.

"It's . . ." Auntie Jane had called it a crutch. ". . . comforting." The damp had flattened her six.

"Comforting? Okay." Gary watched her tune for a minute than said, "I've told you what you need to know, but still you haven't told me what you are." He folded his arms. "I'm not going with you until you do."

She should have known he wouldn't forget; engineers were all about the details. "A long, long time ago a woman went into the woods and met a god. Rumor has it, she had a bit of an antler kink, so she kicked his feet out from under him and beat him to the loam." Out in the water, one of the Selkies said something very rude. "Nine months later, she had twin daughters."

"That's it?"

Charlie shrugged. "She was horny. He was horny. Best I've got."

On the way back to Vermont, she added a charm to the end of the song.

It was one of the oldest charms in the family, although Charlie gentled the aunties' blunt force trauma version.

When Sheryl arrived at the stage to tell Gary about the gas leak and the glass and the bears and the old man who'd had a heart attack when faced with the destruction, she was as surprised to see Charlie as Gary had been. Exactly that surprised. As far as Gary knew, there'd been no more surprises.

"Why has your hair gotten so curly? And why is your jacket damp?" Sheryl leaned forward and sniffed. "And why do you smell like fish?"

Gary lifted his sleeve to his nose. "I have no idea."

Charlie spread her hands and grinned. "Vermont, eh."

When she left to find Toby, they were laughing and making cat noises at each other. They sounded happy. Gary had secrets enough to carry. He didn't need to carry hers as well.

Allie answered on the first ring. "Seeing a man about a bouzouki, Charlie?"

She sounded more exasperated than annoyed, and Charlie found herself smiling although she couldn't name the emotion that prompted the smile. Relief, maybe. How could a world with Allie in it end? "Remember how I told you I thought it was important? The time I spent with the bouzouki player?"

"I remember."

"Well, it's important."

"You want to tell me about it?"

Yes. Charlie stared up at the stars and wondered which of them was falling. Evan, Edward, two more babies on the way; Allie didn't need to know. "No, it's . . ."

"A Wild thing."

"Close enough." She stepped aside as a small pack of teenagers sped by on skateboards. "I don't know when I'll be home. I'm heading to the west coast, so it might be later tonight, might not."

"Same old, same old."

"Is Jack there?"

"No, he's out flying. Did you want to leave a message, or am I not Wild enough to pass it on?"

"No message. I just . . ." The question had slipped out on its own. Charlie had no idea of what she'd intended to say to Jack. *Hey, I found out why the guy Dan heard thought millions were going to die.* Might be better to say that in person, after she had more information.

Allie rolled her eyes, the motion present in the tone of her voice. "Don't forget to eat."

"Good thing I'm at a street fair with ribs and corn on the cob."

"A street fair? That sounds very important."

"The important isn't about where, Allie-cat, it's about what."

"Right. And, apparently, it's about ribs and corn on the cob."

Charlie stopped at the edge of the crowd watching the EMTs roll the old man out of the house. Strapped onto the stretcher, he didn't look like a nasty piece of work, he looked like what he'd been pretending to be. An elderly man. Only, dead.

Turning, she realized death as street theater hadn't slowed the women setting out the food. She could hear what they were thinking from the sound the platters made as they hit the tables.

We've worked all day preparing this food and it is going to be eaten!

They weren't aunties, but they were close enough to be frightening.

"Charlie . . ." Exasperated had become impatient.

Meanwhile, in Vermont, Toby beckoned to her from behind a display of pies. "I'll be home as soon as I can."

"You always say that."

"I always am."

Charlie waited for the pause after good-bye before she hung up. Waited until after the ambulance cleared the road with a brief burst of siren, then headed south before she crossed the road to join Toby. Given the high-tech security around Dr. Mehta's job, she'd be unreachable until she left work. Guards, Charlie could get around. Scanners, not so much. Given the time difference, she had six to eight hours to kill.

Twenty-two months minus six to eight hours . . .

Seven years minus twenty-two months? No. That wasn't how it worked.

She dropped down on the picnic table bench and leaned against Toby. "Distract me."

He shifted so his arm wrapped around her shoulders. "Bad day?"

"Might be. Won't know for sure until later."

"How distracted did you need to be?" he grinned. Willing. "I've got ninety minutes before I have to be back on stage. We're doing two shorter sets this evening to make up for the cluster-fuck this afternoon."

Sex would help. Sex always helped. Her stomach growled. On the other hand, a dozen local women had spent all day preparing food. "Tell me about George Frost while we eat."

As the evening progressed, bears began appearing propped up on tables or laps or cradled in arms. They looked a lot happier.

"Hey look, a falling star!" Sounded like a teenage girl, looking up at the sky while others watched the band. "Make a wish."

"Make a billion of them," Charlie said softly.

Kiren shoved her chair away from the desk, adjusting her weight automatically to compensate for the jammed caster. She hadn't been quite fast enough during the last personnel shuffle to swap out her old chair for a newer model and office furniture wasn't exactly a budget priority at JPL. The padding on the seat had long since compacted, and it felt as though even her gel pad had surrendered to the constant pressure of her ass. Since returning to California, she'd been part of two conference calls so highly classified she'd half expected a follow-up visit from Nick Fury. After the second call, she'd returned immediately to her desk to begin compiling data. In order to have a snowflake's chance in hell of preventing impact, they needed accurate computer modeling; achieving that had kept her butt in the chair.

Pushing her glasses up onto her head, she rubbed her eyes and wondered who'd come up with the phrase *snowflake's chance in hell*. Cold was as likely to be a part of narakam as not, and the Christian hell had a whole frozen sinners section. Not to mention that she couldn't remember the last time she'd seen a snowflake, so why use one in her mental dialogue?

"I think," she said, carefully forming each word out loud, "that I need to get some sleep before we all die."

The only response was the omnipresent hum of the machines.

Replacing her glasses on her nose, she glanced up at the old analog clocks that had probably been hung back when the building was new. Three twenty in Washington. Two twenty in Houston. Twelve twenty at JPL. Her office—

the outer of a double suite, originally intended for the secretary of the person in the inner office—had no window so it was easy to lose track of time. It wasn't so much that the hour was late, as it was the second time she'd seen it since arriving from the airport.

And she had a horrible feeling the smell lingering closest to the desk was her.

On her left monitor, every piece of information she'd been able to pull—right down to an email to Spaceguard from an eleven-year-old girl in New Mexico with a rooftop telescope—was being used to image 2007 AG5. It was an elongated, irregularly-shaped object, high in metal, rotating slowly around the narrow axis once every three or four days. On the right, similar equations to those that had allowed her to find the second, hidden asteroid, stripped out any incongruous data in an attempt to image Armageddon. Engineers worked better with even an incomplete visual than they did with a purely mathematical representation, and Kiren was all for giving the engineers as much assistance as possible.

"Because when physicists see the solution is obvious," she muttered, checking the remaining run time, "they go back to bed."

Bed sounded like an amazing idea. Bed, a shower, and a change of clothes, not necessarily in that order. The "Come to the nerd side; we have pi." T-shirt she currently wore didn't exactly go with her gray dress pants, but twenty-four hours ago it had been all she could find. It looked as though trying to prevent the end of the world as known meant she needed to start keeping a change of clothes at the office. Maybe two.

The center monitor showed only the image of Jupiter she used as a wallpaper. She noted the point where Shoemaker-Levy 9 had struck. Jupiter had survived the impact although any aliens—she had gaseous clouds of communal intelligence in the office pool—had probably not been happy. But Jupiter provided a softer landing site than Earth would. Drop a marble into pudding, the pudding survived, closing in and over the entry point. Drop a marble into crème brûlée and the crust shattered.

"We're living on the crust of a crème brûlée," she told the empty office. "And I'm starving. And more than a little sleep deprived."

After ensuring that new information as well as revealed anomalies, no matter how small, would ping her phone, she turned off the monitors, slipped her feet back into her pumps, and stood. Her backpack seemed to have gained about twenty pounds sitting by her desk, but she swung it over one shoulder and made her way, wobbling slightly, out past the cubicle wall that created a narrow walkway to the inner office.

The door to the hall stuck a little. She jiggled the handle until it turned, then applied a hip bump to get the door closed again. Only every fourth light remained on in the corridors after nine and, walking through an artificial twilight, her heels tapped out an urgent Morse code against linoleum old enough to have been trod on by Wernher Von Braun. As she passed, Kiren glanced toward the viewing room that overlooked the Spacecraft Assembly Facility. Their lights were still on and she knew that somewhere down in that gymnasium-sized room, people in clean room garb were working to complete the Dusk spacecraft—a follow-up to Dawn now out on Vesta—and muttering amongst themselves as they wondered what the hell was suddenly so urgent.

They were smart people. They'd have floated half a dozen hypotheses by now. One or two would have hit close to the mark.

Sooner or later—sooner rather than later—they'd have to be told.

The men and women in the aerospace industry were good at keeping secrets. NASA employees and the employees of NASA-like organizations in other countries signed confidentiality forms, and NASA's media relations department walked a fine line between keeping the public informed of how their tax dollars were being spent and keeping the public from being bored and/or terrified.

But this secret . . .

Kiren wondered who'd break first. Who'd tell the wrong person. Who'd tweet *OBTW, we're all going to die.*

She'd told Gary and she couldn't really expect him to be stronger than she'd been. Although he probably would be. When they were kids, he'd always been able to keep a secret. To this day, Mrs. Bowen had no idea who'd released the class bullfrog into the wild. Which was, she supposed, why she'd told him. One of the reasons . . .

Eventually the number of people who knew would reach a tipping point, and the secret would be a secret no longer. There were social science equations to determine that exact number, although Kiren didn't find the math as comforting as usual.

The shuttle bus that ran around the Lab, to and from the east side parking lot, ran only from 7AM to 6PM. At this point, she wasn't so much late for the last bus as early for the first one. Her office to the gate was a little better than three quarters of a mile and her pumps weren't exactly walking shoes. One hand wrapped around her lanyard, she stared up the hill and weighed hot water and her mattress against distance and sore feet.

Hot water and her mattress won.

"So much for Dhruv's belief I put my research before everything," she muttered, beginning the long walk. Her ex-husband had been astounded when she hadn't miraculously become a traditional wife immediately after marriage. His second wife, Adrika, had produced three children and stayed home to raise them. As they all attended the Shri Lakshmi Narayan Mandir temple in Riverside, Kiren had come to know Adrika and the children and, quite frankly, liked them all better than Dhruv. Those three beautiful children, grown to be astounding young adults, were the future and she couldn't stand to think of them dying because of something she'd discovered.

"You're not responsible, you idiot." Kiren scrubbed the palm of her hand over her cheeks. "Your discovery may have given them a chance to survive." Which was all very logical and accurate and didn't seem to matter in the slightest. All at once, she couldn't stop crying.

So she walked and wept.

She should've put her jacket on.

It was easy to forget, tucked away in front of her computer, that JPL was the size of a small town. It had its own clinic, its own fire department, and an extensive support staff that kept the buildings clean and the grounds landscaped. It was, at 1AM, a small ghost town, the streets deserted and the only sounds coming from the Angeles National Forest pressed up against the perimeter fence.

Night birds. Raccoons probably. Coyotes definitely. There hadn't been a mountain lion sighting in years and . . .

She stumbled to a stop, head cocked, almost certain she could hear "My Hero, Zero" from the old *Schoolhouse Rock* videos.

A young woman holding a guitar suddenly appeared between two eucalyptus trees and paused in the circle of light under a lamppost. She pushed blue-streaked hair back off her face, glanced around, spotted Kiren, and walked toward her.

Kiren stumbled back a step, caught her heel on the curb, and nearly fell.

"Who," she demanded, rubbing her nose over the back of her hand, "are you?" She fumbled for her phone, ready to call security, fully aware it would take them a minimum of ten to fifteen minutes to arrive.

The young woman stopped and held up both hands, the guitar hanging from the brightly patterned strap around her neck. "Dr. Mehta? Dr. Kiren Mehta?"

"What if I am?"

"Gary Ehrlich sent me. We have to talk about an asteroid impact." She grinned suddenly and gestured toward Kiren's chest. "I like the shirt."

The sun was pretty much up by the time Jack returned to the roof, making it somewhere between seven thirty and eight o'clock. He'd taken wing right after he'd told Allie that Charlie'd left, slipping away while she muttered about how Charlie needed to start thinking about other people once in a while. He'd wanted to leap to Charlie's defense, but he knew that under the full force of Allie's attention, he'd spill like a gutted boar and tell her what Auntie Catherine had Seen and what Dan had heard and what Charlie was trying to do about it. Wild to Wild, Charlie'd said. Not Wild to Wild to the whole family. So he'd left while Allie was still muttering about musicians and headed north to check the nearest wood bison herd—although at the last minute he'd decided not to hunt in case Charlie needed him.

A whole bison would need a couple of days to digest before he could change.

He dove out of the sun and snickered as the line of pigeons roosting on the edge of the roof exploded into the air, all wings and panic, instincts screaming hawk even though the only thing remotely hawklike about him was his current size. And that he'd be perfectly willing to eat pigeon had Allie not declared the birds on the roof off limits.

Cameron had finally explained all the sniggering around Allie's instructions on who he was allowed to eat and why. He didn't know a lot about the sex lives of dragons, his mother was the only female he'd ever met, but he knew it wasn't something dragons did. When a dragon said eat, they meant chew and swallow.

The last thing he expected to see as he came in for a landing was a person-shaped bundle wrapped in an old quilt on one of the chairs, the fabric lightly frosted. He changed and had to take an extra moment to twitch the new body parts into place, his skin fitting less comfortably than scales lately. Looking back, he realized he'd been twitchy in his skin for about as long as he'd been setting fires thinking of Charlie. It was like his Gale half knew what he couldn't have while his dragon half insisted it was a stupid rule and dragons took what they wanted. Actually, both halves were in agreement that it was a stupid rule and that taking wouldn't end well. For anyone. But mostly for him.

His bare feet left steaming footprints as he crossed the deck toward the bundle. The quilt reeked of charms, a tangle of dos and don'ts, protections and warnings that made his nose itch and blocked the scent of the sleeper.

"Poke me again and you'll lose the fucking finger."

Charlie. No mistaking her cheerful good morning.

"Aren't you cold?" he asked as she sat up, her scent released when the quilt fell to drape around her shoulders. He didn't think she noticed him inhaling, but even if she did, he doubted inhaling had been covered by the stupid seven-year rule.

Her teeth when she yawned were . . . pretty pathetic really, but teeth were one of the hardest comparisons to drop. "The quilt's charmed."

"Yeah, I know. There's . . ." Half of them, he didn't recognize so he settled on, ". . . lots."

"Gale girls used to make charm quilts to give their daughters." She shifted around until she could free her arms but remain mostly covered. "My mother made this."

It was fabric, but he still didn't understand how fabric came together without sorcery. Knitting, he understood. Enough of the aunties wielded needles to make figuring it out a matter of self-defense. "Have you made one?"

"I'm no one's mother nor do I want to be." Her hair spilled through her fingers as she tugged both hands back through it, and her laugh sounded broken. "And in twenty-two months, what I want or don't want may be moot."

"A cow's opinion?"

She looked at him then, and when she laughed this time the shards fell into place, making her laugh whole again. Jack relaxed, pleased with himself.

"I thought Dan heard six months and millions of people?"

"That's merely the intro, and there's one hell of a downbeat dropping in." Charlie waved a hand. "Sit. Make some clothes or you'll freeze your ass on the chair."

"I won't." But he made some clothes anyway, careful not to pull the rare bits of uncharmed fabric from the quilt. The wooden slats on the other lounge sizzled when he made contact, the frost evaporating. "You went to see the bouzouki guy," he prodded when Charlie sat silently and ran her thumb over a pink patch covered in purple polar bears.

"Gary. Good news is, he *was* the guy Dan overheard. Bad news, he has a friend at NASA who told him about the asteroid Auntie Catherine Saw. Impact in twenty-two months."

Jack shook his head. "But Dan heard millions will die in six months."

"Because six months is the outside estimate before someone else spots it and *hello, worldwide panic*."

"Why would people panic if NASA can stop it?"

"NASA can't stop it."

"But you said . . ."

"I was wrong, okay?" She shot him a narrow-eyed glare that reminded him of Auntie Bea—and he was not going to mention that. Not to anyone. Ever. "It doesn't happen often, but it does happen. I went and talked to Gary's NASA friend and the rock that's going to hit us has been masked by a bigger metal heavy rock—totally different than heavy metal rock."

"Annihilator." Jack knew this game.

"Black Moor."

"Coney Hatch."

"Death Cartel. And you're going to lose when we get to J because there's no Canadian metal band that starts with J. So, moving on. The masking rock is how the following rock got so close without anyone seeing it. Masking rock will slide on by, following rock will . . ." Charlie whistled as she dove a hand toward the ground. ". . . blam. Just like Dan said. It's too close for NASA to stop. Although, credit where it's due, they're trying. Shut up."

"I didn't say anything."

"Not you." Both hands drove back through her hair again. "If I have to listen to 'End of the World as We Know It' one more time, I'm going to hit myself in the head with a brick."

Jack could hear traffic. He could hear Charlie breathing. Charlie's heart beating. The pigeons gossiping. And, about a block away, a guy yelling, "Way to strut it, baby!" out of a truck window. He couldn't hear music. "Are you okay?"

"Not really. I told Gary I could stop it. I Sang the seabed, right? What's a big rock? Oh, sure, maybe you and me and Auntie Catherine would have to gang up on NASA to get me on the Orion capsule thing to get me close enough, but between sorcery and singing and, well, an auntie, that shouldn't be a problem, right? We could probably even manage it and make the six-month deadline. Except," she continued before Jack could answer, "do you know what I realized, lying here? In space, no one can hear you sing."

She sounded serious. But it sounded like a joke. "I don't know what that means."

"Right. Okay. First, space is a vacuum. Sound doesn't happen in a vacuum. Second, we're raiding Roland's DVD collection and you're watching *Alien*. It's a haunted house movie in space with a monster even you, Your Dragon Prince-iness, will think is fucking terrifying, a kickass Sigourney Weaver and an orange cat."

Jack knew whistling in the dark when he heard it. Charlie was slammed. He could almost see her control cracking and he half wished she'd lose it, break down, and need him to comfort her. On the other hand, he didn't ever want to see Charlie break down because that would be wrong. So wrong. Charlie was strong and she didn't give up. Ever. "So, what do we do? About the rock. Not the movie."

"Do? Dr. Mehta, Gary's friend, showed me computer simulations of what's going to happen. If the rock isn't stopped, we die. If not all of us, most of us."

"So we stop it." It seemed like a simple solution to him.

"How high can you fly?"

When he was very young, when he was a Dragon Prince but not yet a Gale, he'd gone to the edge of the sky where the air was thin. His vision had grayed, his wings had folded, and he'd almost died. "Not that high. Not as far as the darkness."

Charlie'd shrugged, like that was the answer she'd expected. "Then we learn to play the bouzouki."

"What?"

"And we make a good-looking corpse."

"Charlie!"

Her shoulders slumped and she sighed, her breath pluming out so thickly he was almost homesick for other dragons. "I don't know what we do, Jack. I can't sing rock a-buh-bye baby in space. You can't get there to devour it."

He didn't think he needed to point out that he didn't actually eat rock.

"At least we know for sure why the FBI wanted Dan."

"We do?"

"The longer the asteroid stays secret, the longer the world has before someone hits the panic button. Dan spilled that secret all over the internet and while Doomsday Dan the crazy street person can be ignored, the FBI's going to want to find out who told him and plug that leak."

"But no one told him. He heard a random thought."

"Yeah . . ." Charlie paused to yawn. ". . . not a big stretch to assume that won't go well for Dan. At least he can live out the last few months of his life clean and well fed."

Sliding over, Jack bumped his knees against hers and thought about moving to sit beside her and offering a more physical comfort and . . . His thought process kind of hit a slipstream there and he wondered what more physical comfort could entail. How physical? How comforting? If the world had twenty-two months, how much more stupidly irrelevant could seven years get?

"Jack, the chair."

"Shit." He brushed the scorch marks out of the wood and lifted his head to see Charlie staring at him. "What?"

"Sorcery."

"Okay."

"You can use sorcery on the asteroid! You could . . . turn it into butterflies!"

The family was never going to let that go. "You turn your cousins into butterflies once and suddenly it's always butterflies?"

"Pay attention!" Charlie's freezing cold fingers closed on his jaw and she shook his head back and forth. "You can turn the *asteroid* into *butterflies*. Or, if not butterflies, then something else. Something *harmless*."

"Oh."

"Yeah, oh." One final shake and she released him. He rubbed his jaw, stopped when he saw her eyes following the movement of his hand, and said, "I can't."

"You can't? Of course you can't," she continued before he could explain. "It's too far away. Okay, we get you into the Orion capsule . . . no, that's too dangerous. If it was me, I could nudge. I'd have to bludgeon to make them believe you belong, and then what happens if I've overwritten crucial information? Not a problem. You can take the asteroid out when it appears in the atmosphere. It's there! It's not!" She raised both arms, then grabbed for the quilt as it fell. "It's a miracle! And, okay, we'll still have the panic in the streets, but that's better than the worst case scenario. We'll call the family home and hunker down. I'm not saying enforced close proximity won't take out a few of us, but that, that we can live with."

She looked so pleased—and manic—Jack wished he could let her have the moment. "That's not what I meant. I meant, I can't—no matter how close it is. I don't . . ." Admitting a weakness went against everything he'd been taught for the first thirteen years of his life. Admitting a weakness was like exposing the softer scales on his belly to his uncles' claws. But this was Charlie and exposing the softer scales on his belly was right up near the top of his list of things he wanted to do. Metaphorically. Sort of. "My sorcery is instinctive. The butterfly thing—I just reacted before they hit the ground. I didn't do it on purpose. I can't do it on purpose."

"Fixing the scorch marks . . ."

He shrugged. "I don't like it when Allie's mad at me."

"Allie's going to be pretty pissed about being part of a mass extinction."

"Yeah, but she's not going to be pissed at me."

Charlie stared at him for a long minute, then she laughed. "It's like I don't even listen to myself. This is the argument Allie and I made to the aunties about you being a Gale. You don't do sorcery, you use it." To Jack's surprise, she actually sounded amused. "Okay, not so funny when weighed against the end of the world and since there isn't anyone around to train you, it looks like the family habit of killing sorcerers is about to bite us on the ass." Her smile softened and, just for a moment, Jack saw exactly what she'd meant by *I like you too much*. He'd been raised in fire, yet her smile still burned. "At least you'll be safe."

"I what?" The roaring in his ears had nearly drowned her out. At least he hoped the roaring was in his ears; he half thought he'd changed and given the pressure in his chest a voice. As Charlie seemed neither deaf nor singed, he congratulated himself on his self-control.

"You can go back to the UnderRealm."

"The UnderRealm?" That was it. He could save her. Them. Save the family. "Not me, all of us. We can all go to the UnderRealm; the whole family." Relief driving him up onto his feet, he walked to the edge of the roof and blew smoke at the pigeons across the alley.

"Sorry, Jack, but we can't." She was standing when he turned. Still wrapped in the quilt. Looking . . . resigned? "Not for any longer than the time between rituals. We're too tied to the earth."

"But if I'm a Gale . . ."

"And a dragon. And a sorcerer. You're unique."

"So are you."

"No arguing. But unfortunately, this time, I'm not unique in a way that helps." Her thumb rubbed across a worn piece of denim, and Jack could feel the charm from across the roof. It was male. He was pretty sure it was the only one on the quilt. It was a simple protection, nothing more than a generic *stay safe*, and he wondered if her father had made it. During his visit to Ontario, Jack had met Charlie's mother but not her father, and Charlie never talked about him. Female dragons ate their mates, so Jack hadn't given his absence much thought. His mother hadn't eaten his father, but only because the sorcerer had slipped between worlds immediately after. She hadn't been able to follow until Jack himself had laid out a blood path.

Dragons and Gales were more alike than he'd thought.

"Jack?" She grinned at him, the old Charlie back. "You having an epiphany?"

"Yeah, I guess. How could you tell?"

Her grin broadened. "I can smell the smoke."

"Crap!" Ears hot, he ground out the bit of burning deck, then crouched to stroke the scorch mark out of the wood. "The Courts have sorcerers," he said slowly, remembering protections he'd heard his uncles complain about. "Maybe they'd teach me."

"Could they teach you enough in six months?"

Jack figured Charlie thought she was asking a—what did they call it?—rhetorical question because hope hadn't returned to her voice. "So put me in the car and drive me back two years," he said as he straightened. "I'll catch up."

"Jack . . ."

He spread his hands, scaled and clawed. "Dragon Prince, remember? I'm essentially immortal. What's two years? And, since I'm here, I'm obviously not there. Hang on . . ." He didn't exactly understand how it worked, but he suspected Charlie had no idea either. ". . . if you can take me back two years, then you can take me back . . ."

"You've only been here for four years," Charlie sighed. "Four from thirteen is nine. Even if twenty-one is a step up from seventeen, nine is still more than seven."

"I know that." The pale jacket he'd made from the pile of old newspapers left on the roof had no pockets, so he added some and shoved his hands in them. "Dragons ace math." He'd thought that maybe . . . "How did you know that's what I meant?"

She shrugged. "First thing *I* thought of. What does essentially immortal mean?"

"Dragons are killed, usually by other dragons, but they don't die. However, as all my uncles have pointed out, singly and collectively, there's never been a half-blood before, so there's no way of knowing for sure." Someone hit their horn, someone else yelled abuse. Jack leaned out over the edge of roof and saw a group of teenagers flipping off an SUV speeding away down 13th. He didn't get humans his age. They weren't children, they weren't adults, and they expected to be treated like both. No reason to drop a giant rock on them, though.

He turned back to Charlie to find her folding the quilt. Over the welcome return of her scent, the heavy knit sweater she wore smelled of Graham, and Jack smoked a little, unable to stop his reaction.

"If I took you back two years . . ." His teeth snapped together as he closed his mouth at her gesture. "*If.* Would the Court teach you?"

The protections around the Courts his uncles complained about had been put in place to keep the Dragon Lords out—there having been extended disagreements in the past on who the apex predators were. The Dragon Lords had been willing to fight it out, but to their surprise, the Courts had a well-honed sense of self-preservation tucked under their silken arrogance. Contact between the two races had been minimal for centuries. Minimal, and usually violent. "I don't know," Jack admitted reluctantly. "They don't like us much. Dragons," he added to be clear. "They don't like the Dragon Lords much."

"They don't like Gales much either," Charlie reminded him. "So, that's a last resort. There's plenty of the Court here, though. Wouldn't hurt to check with them and see if they can stop it."

Jack shook his head. "They won't care. They can go home."

"The full-bloods, sure, but would they be willing to open their lands to their descendants?"

"No."

"So would they be willing to let their children and grandchildren die?"

"Yes." When she looked startled, he shrugged. "They're assholes, you know that. But there's stuff about the MidRealm they like, a lot, that they won't want to give up. Maybe that'll be enough. If they do anything, if they *can* do anything," he amended, "it'll cost."

"Doesn't it always." While they'd been talking, the air had warmed enough he could no longer see her breath when she sighed before saying, "We should at least check the price."

"I'll do it."

Her eyes narrowed and for a minute he thought she was going to try and tell him he couldn't, then she smiled without much humor. "You've definitely got a better chance of actually getting the twisty buggers to listen. But again, last resort. Well, second last resort. I want to talk to Auntie Catherine again before we widen our circle. She might've seen something else."

"Wouldn't she have told you?"

"Giving her the benefit of the doubt, she might have Seen something and not have realized it was connected."

That was possible, Jack acknowledged, although Charlie sounded like she didn't entirely believe it. "And without the benefit of the doubt?"

"She's an auntie. Aunties are . . ."

"Are you two coming in for breakfast?"

Jack sucked in a lungful of his own smoke and began to cough. He could feel Auntie Gwen's regard from where she stood in the doorway of the roof access and he wondered how much she'd heard. Then Charlie was beside him, pounding on his back. "We're on our way."

"Alysha thinks you're hiding something."

"And what do you think?"

"I don't *think* you're hiding anything, Charlotte."

Wiping the snot off his upper lip on the sleeve of his jacket, Jack looked up in time to see Auntie Gwen roll her eyes.

"Neither of you are exactly subtle," she said. "Secret conversations. Bou-zoukis." Arms folded, she studied first Charlie, then Jack.

Jack squared his shoulders and met her gaze, no child to be cowed merely because he was expected to be. To his surprise, she smiled.

"Really?"

He wasn't sure what kind of answer she wanted, so he continued hold her gaze without speaking. When she finally turned her attention back to Charlie, he changed enough to blink his inner as well as his outer lid across dry eyes.

"If I ask you what you're hiding, Charlotte, will you tell me?"

"No."

"No?"

"Not yet," Charlie amended.

"Not until you've either solved the problem or discovered you can't solve the problem."

"Pretty much."

Auntie Gwen made a noise Jack couldn't quite identify. It would have sounded like she was accepting the inevitable had the aunties considered anything regarding their interactions with the family inevitable. He supposed the closest translation would be *that'll do for now*. "Then I won't ask. But don't leave it too long, Charlotte."

"Trust me, this one has a best-before date."

He wondered why Charlie'd put the emphasis on *this one* rather than *trust me*, then he remembered that once the aunties lost trust, they didn't bother to ask questions.

"Most secrets do." Auntie Gwen turned on one heel and started back down the stairs. Her voice floated up from the stairwell. "Sooner or later, it all comes out in the wash."

As the sound of her footsteps reached the bottom of the stairs, Jack opened his mouth. Charlie pressed two fingers down against his lips before he could say anything. She moved quickly across the roof, crouched in the doorway where Auntie Gwen had been standing, and brushed her palm across the wood. It looked a little like the motion he used when he fixed a scorch mark. When she straightened, she stroked the open door at hip height. As she turned slowly in place, he saw her eyes flash black, rim to rim. Scales rippled down his spine and his tail lashed once, twice in response to the power she almost never showed. It seemed Auntie Gwen had left charms behind. Two obvious charms, but clearly Charlie thought there was at least one more.

He had no idea how she'd managed to hide a charm when he hadn't taken his eyes off her.

"How," Charlie asked as though she were unconcerned about eavesdroppers, "can you choke on your own smoke?"

Unsure if the question was camouflage to hide what she was doing from Auntie Gwen, or if she really wanted to know, Jack crossed the roof and joined her. "It went down the wrong way."

Arm over her head, she patted the edge of the upper framing, grinned, and flashed him a thumbs up with the other hand. "So you blew it out and then sucked it back in?"

"You've choked on spit," he pointed out. "I've seen you."

"Fair enough." Head cocked, Charlie listened to nothing Jack could hear for a moment, then nodded. "We're good. That was the last one."

"Why would she . . ." To name the aunties was to call them. Not always, but it happened often enough Jack decided to be cautious. ". . . leave charms to overhear when she didn't want to know?"

"She didn't say she didn't want to know, she said she wasn't going to ask."

"Why . . . ?"

"You tell me."

He recognized that tone. It was the same tone his Uncle Adam had used when he'd asked why they didn't flame the lake and eat the pookah after it floated to the surface. He suspected Charlie'd turned the encounter with Auntie Gwen into a lesson on power dynamics to emphasize the difference in their ages. Jack knew Charlie was older than he was; she just couldn't seem to understand that he didn't care. And, for what it was worth, parboiled pookah tasted terrible.

"If she asked what we were hiding and you didn't tell her," he said slowly, "she couldn't let that kind of defiance stand. If she tried to force you to tell her, you'd lie and make her believe it and that would shift the power dynamic enough the other aunties would notice. Then it would be you, well, you and me, against all the aunties."

"Think we could take them?"

"All of them?" He thought about it for a moment, listening to the traffic, smelling the coffee when someone opened the door of the shop, watching

Charlie watch him. He considered what he could do and what Charlie could do. And he considered the aunties. "No. We couldn't."

"No," Charlie repeated, smiling, "we couldn't. But Auntie Gwen's reason was simpler than that. She trusts that when it comes down to it, the last note is the key the song is in. She trusts we'll put family first." Her smile changed, softened and picked up an edge at the same time. Jack fought the urge to flame in response. "You'd stand beside me against the aunties?"

"Duh."

"Well, that puts the end of the world into perspective."

"The world isn't going to end."

"It's not?"

"We're going to stop the asteroid." Because they had to stop it.

"We are?"

This new smile, Jack recognized. He wasn't sure when he'd first started seeing it, but he knew now he was the only one who saw it. "We are."

Because if the world ended, then Charlie ended—and Jack wasn't going to let that happen.

SIX

"THEY'RE DEFINITELY HIDING SOMETHING."

Allie looked up from strapping Evan into his high chair as Auntie Gwen came into the apartment. She didn't seem angry. That was good. At least Allie thought it was good. She could think of a few reasons why an auntie would be that blasé about being left in the dark and *they* weren't good.

"Charlotte not only took out the obvious charms," Auntie Gwen continued, scooping Edward up as he ran for the door, "she went to the effort of finding and removing the hidden ones. And, as we both know, Charlotte doesn't do effort. They don't call it *playing* music for nothing."

"If you're so sure they're hiding something, why didn't you ask them what it was?"

Auntie Gwen dropped Edward into the second chair. "You suspected they were hiding something, why didn't you? Never mind, I'll tell you; it'll be both faster and easier. You're afraid Charlotte won't tell you. And if she doesn't, or worse, if she lies to you, that means you're losing her. That she's on the last stage of going Wild and she's becoming like Catherine."

"Charlie is *nothing* like my grandmother."

Evan slapped at her arm. "Mama! Tight!"

"Sorry, baby." Allie loosened the belt that held him in the chair. "She didn't come to bed last night."

"And yet you weren't alone," Auntie Gwen pointed out tartly.

"That's not what I meant. She's not sleeping."

"We've already established she has something on her mind, something she has chosen to keep to herself. I'm certain Catherine Sees many things she chooses to keep from the family."

Allie only just kept her reaction from impacting the city as she repeated, "Charlie is *nothing* like my grandmother."

"Wild is Wild, Alysha, and Charlotte accepted the responsibility some time ago. As much as she loves you, and she does love you, you need to accept the fact that you'll never tame her."

Allie knew Charlie loved her. That wasn't the problem. "Jack's Uncle Adam said that to me once."

"The Dragon Lords are arrogant, overbearing, and homicidal, but they're not stupid."

"And what about Jack? He's Wild. What happens when he accepts . . ."

"He's always known." Shaking her head, Auntie Gwen handed Edward his sippy cup. "Charlotte was raised knowing she was different. She had to find out what that meant on her own. Jack was raised as a prince. He knew what being Wild meant long before Charlotte told him what we call it here."

"But he wasn't Wild there . . ."

"Oh, for pity's sake, Alysha, think about that for a moment. As a sorcerer and a half Gale, he stood separate from that family as well. Flew separate," she amended after a moment.

Allie set a bowl of oatmeal in front of Evan and another in front of Edward—the trays of their high chairs charmed to hold the bowls in place. "You didn't answer me. You didn't tell me why you didn't ask what they were hiding."

"Because, bottom line, as much as he's like no Gale that's ever been, Jack is a Gale. As much as she's a little too fond of the end justifying the means, Catherine is a Gale. And Charlotte, who could make us believe whatever was easiest for her but doesn't, is a Gale. Even for the Wild Powers, family comes first."

Allie could see that, as far as Auntie Gwen was concerned, that was that.

She wanted to believe that was enough, that the secret Charlie and Jack were hiding would come second to family, but she didn't. Not quite. How could they keep secrets and still put family first?

It didn't help when, after breakfast, Charlie announced she'd be leaving for a few hours.

"Why?"

"I've got some things to do, Allie-cat." She turned from setting a stack of dirty dishes on the counter and spread her hands. "People to see."

Allie knew that grin. It had nothing to do with humor or pleasure or anticipation and everything to do with deflection. But not this time. "Who?"

"What difference does it make?"

Allie lifted Evan out of the chair and folded her arms as he raced for his brother, already freed. "It makes a difference because I asked and you're not telling me."

"I don't tell you everything I do, Allie." The grin was gone, leaving Charlie looking both more and less like herself, the familiar caught in an overlay of other. Then Allie blinked, and she was Charlie again. Charlie, who didn't come to bed last night. Charlie, who put Jack back into his seat with a glance. Jack who was Wild like Charlie was Wild.

"I don't ask about everything you do," Allie said softly and knew Charlie heard the reason. *Please, don't lie to me.*

"If you must know," Charlie sighed, "I'm going to see Auntie Catherine. I may not have asked the right questions when I talked to her yesterday. And I wasn't going to tell you," she continued as Allie opened her mouth, "because you get all weird about your grandmother, and I didn't want to get into it with you."

"I do not get weird about my grandmother."

"Yeah, you do."

The words weren't dismissive, Allie decided watching Charlie walk to the door. Presented as inarguable fact, they were worse than dismissive. They were patronizing. "Maybe because she manipulated my life and David's life and my parents' lives and Michael and Brian—who aren't even family—to get David and me here . . ."

"To save the world." Charlie shrugged into her jacket and looked at Allie with eyes that seemed too dark for thirty. "Or at least to save Alberta. And part of Saskatchewan. Maybe a bit of Montana. You have issues, Allie, and while I'm not saying you don't have the right to issues, don't drag me into them." Her words lingered as she headed out the door. "I doubt I'll be long."

Allie probably wouldn't have seen Jack following had she not been staring after Charlie. Once she noticed him, he stopped blending with the furniture and the walls and paused, hand on the doorknob, looking sheepish. "Where are you going?" she demanded, then added before Jack could speak, "You can chase after her all you want, but she's not going to take you with her."

Jack might have been wearing a mask for all the expression his face showed. Scales glinted across the upper curves of his cheeks and across his brow. "There are those under my protection who need seeing to."

"Jack, I didn't mean . . ."

His eyes flashed gold. "Then I'm going to kill a large animal and eat it." He closed the door quietly, gently, the dragon barely contained within his skin.

When she turned, Auntie Gwen released Evan to join his brother under the coffee table and said, "That was cruel, Alysha."

"I know." Allie dropped into the closest chair. "I didn't mean to . . ."

The snort made Auntie Gwen sound terrifyingly like Auntie Jane. "Yes, you did."

"Yes, I did. I'm a horrible person. I mocked a seventeen year old who's having his heart broken."

"You don't know that."

"I do know that. I know how he feels. I know how Charlie feels. I know how Aunt Judith feels about Richard learning to ride a bike. If I extend a little, I know how the city feels about that pothole the works department still hasn't gotten around to filling in the intersection of Macleod and 11th. I know, but I can't say anything because they haven't told me, and I can't ask because I'm afraid Charlie won't tell me. You're right, I'm afraid I'm losing her."

"Of course, I'm right."

Allie lifted her head far enough to give Auntie Gwen a narrow-eyed glare. "That's what you're going with?"

Auntie Gwen smiled and set a block of shortening on the kitchen island. "It was the important point."

Two days ago, Charlie would have been out the back door and into the Wood before Jack could catch up. Today, she waited at the bottom of the stairs, keeping the promise she'd made. No leaving without saying good-bye—even if he knew where she was going and why. As her exit had prevented her from saying good-bye to him upstairs, she was sure he'd be down in a minute.

Maybe David had been right after all. There was still a hole in her heart she'd never be able to fill, but the jagged edges she'd been living with for so long had been smoothed down and the pain, that had become so much a part of her she'd nearly forgotten it was pain, had eased. Plus, she had some kick-ass emo lyrics if she wanted to get another band together.

Classic rock, this time.

When CCR's "Bad Moon Rising" started up, she laughed—it was always nice when someone got the joke—and unclenched her fists before her fingernails cut half-moons into her palms. Twenty-two months. Now *that* was a punch line.

The apartment door opened, and she moved to stand by the mirror rather than be caught waiting at the bottom of the stairs. She frowned at the emphatic thud, thud of Jack's descent. For all the comments about his size—fine, for all *her* comments about his size—Jack usually walked as though he weren't carrying around a metric shit ton of weight. He didn't throw anger at her when he turned the corner and took the last two steps down into the hall, but he definitely looked angry.

"You okay?"

He nodded, a quick up and down jerk of his head, smoke trailing from his nose. "I'm fine."

Charlie looked past him at the mirror where her reflection stood surrounded by flame. Not exactly fine. "My guess, Allie's pissed at me and took it out on you."

"She wasn't . . ." His posture suggested that if he'd had his tail he'd have been lashing it. "She wasn't entirely wrong."

And that, Charlie realized, was why Jack was angry.

"I wasn't running after you . . ." The smoke thickened. ". . . like I was begging for crumbs of your affection."

"Whoa. Allie said that?" Allie did not get to say that, not to Jack. Ignoring the fact that Jack had no need to beg for Charlie's affection, slamming Jack because she couldn't slam Charlie was a top of the charts bitchy thing for her to do. The music a low rumble, Charlie had one foot on the bottom step when Jack grabbed her arm and pulled her back.

"I don't need you to fight my battles. Anymore," he amended when Charlie raised both brows. "And stop humming, the building's shaking."

About to protest that she wasn't doing anything to the building, she realized the vibration she could feel through her feet matched the vibration she could feel in the back of her throat and swallowed the sound.

He managed a twisted smile. "I'd be flattered except I know you're not overreacting because of me. Not just because of me," he corrected before she could say anything. "And it wasn't Allie who said that." His grip on her arm tightened slightly. "My mother used to say it when I wanted to chase after my uncles."

"Nice."

"Not really. Dragon. Then she'd remind me that family is the arena where even the simplest conflicts draw blood."

Literally draw blood. And if his Gale half wasn't as consistently violent, that didn't mean Allie had the right to take an emotional swing at him, pregnancy hormones or not. "But Allie said something similar."

"If I say that she did, what are you going to do?"

He was still holding her in place. He was stronger, a lot stronger, but if she *told* him to release her, he'd have to. And she really had to do something about how stupidly overprotective he made her feel. "Not leap to your defense like a crazy woman?"

The fires in the mirror became a pillar of flame and that, in turn, became Jack's reflection—although Charlie noted that a certain amount of flame continued to flicker around his edges. "Good call," he said and let her go.

The memory of his touch a warm band around her arm, Charlie moved far enough across the hall to point out the window. The cloud cover made it look like dusk in the courtyard. A gust of wind slapped rain against the glass. "If it helps, she feels like shit."

Jack shook his head. "It's October."

"Some of it's Allie. Her touch is . . ."

"Damp."

He was grinning when she glanced over at him. Impossible not to grin back. "I was going to say unmistakable."

"Right. Oh, and cool distraction with the issues thing."

When they weren't gold, his eyes really were absurdly warm. "Issues thing?"

"That you used to distract her. So she wouldn't ask *why* you were off to see Auntie Catherine. Although . . ." Golden brows drew down. ". . . if you'd time-slipped back, you could've been and gone without saying anything."

"Allie knows when the way to the Wood is opened. It's why Auntie Catherine can't sneak back into Calgary." Not through the shrubbery. Not through the mirrors. Not without Allie knowing. "And even if I could deflect her questions, which—let's face it—I could, I don't want to time slip if I don't have to."

"Why not?"

She shrugged. Looked past him at their reflections standing side-by-side in the mirror. She was five seven, he was at least five ten and still growing. Which had nothing to do with the question, but now that she had the evidence in front of her, she couldn't stop wondering how tall he'd eventually get. Then she considered his question and thought about lying. About tossing out a smart-ass remark that meant nothing but would make Jack laugh. Didn't. Didn't have to deflect away from feelings anymore, not now they were telling each other the truth. "It makes me older. You stay out of this!" Her reflection, beginning to age, shed years so fast it ended up in grade school, front teeth missing, a plastic recorder in one pudgy hand. Jack's reflection patted her head. "Every time I slip back, I've lived more time than you have." She'd added a few more hours to the total by taking Gary to Nova Scotia.

A snort and a medium-sized puff of white smoke. "I thought after seven years, it didn't matter."

"It doesn't. I just . . ." It didn't matter. There were no qualifiers attached to *not going to happen,* but she hated feeling the distance between them widening. Although maybe if it got wide enough, it would solve the whole problem. She could complain about his music, tell him to pull up his jeans, and bake him cookies. Okay, maybe not the cookies. He'd have to really piss her off to deserve that. And she complained about his music now. Electro? Seriously? There was distance *enough* between them.

"You just?" When she shook her head, unsure of what he was asking, he gave an exaggerated sigh. "They say memory's the first to go."

It took Charlie a moment, almost long enough Jack had begun to look unsure, then she laughed and the distance between them closed again. "I can't remember what it is I like about you right now."

He shrugged, a dimple flashing. "You keep saying size matters."

"Only when trying and failing to drag your enormous dragon ass through the Wood."

"Only then?"

"Bite me."

"In a just world."

Charlie heard Truth and she was pretty sure, given Jack's senses, he could hear her heart pounding, once again, in time with his as the universe said, *you're meant to be together, except for that thirteen-year thing. Oops.* As good as the truth felt, running away, misunderstandings, and hurt feelings were a hell of a lot less dangerous than spending time with Jack without the barricade of ignorance between them. Talk to each other? After due consideration, she was going to kick David right in his white-tailed ass. She took a step back. Jack took a step forward.

The mirror showed no reflection at all. It would keep their secrets. Great. What she needed was someone shouting *this is wrong* at her, or offering pity rather than tacit acceptance.

Then Joe stuck his head out into the hallway from the store. "Jack, I need . . ." Jack spun around toward him, teeth bared. Charlie made a noise that might have been a growl although she planned on denying it later. Joe blushed so vigorously, his freckles vanished—which Charlie had to admit was fairly impressive since he'd been knocking boots with Auntie Gwen for four years. "Never mind." Gaze locked on the floor, he waved a hand in their general direction. "Later."

They took a step apart when the door to the store closed. As Charlie had already been backing up, her butt hit the window.

Jack's eyes flashed gold. "I should . . ."

"Thank Joe for his timing?" Not that he'd interrupted anything. Much. They'd been flirting with the line, not crossing it. If Jack had kept advancing, Charlie would have stopped him. She wouldn't have wanted to—she was self-aware enough to admit that—but she would have put on her big girl panties and stopped him. And possibly, putting on her big girl panties might not be the best bit of phrasing under the circumstances.

"But . . ."

"No buts," Charlie snapped, trying not to think of why she might have taken off her big girl panties. "And you probably want to go and convince Joe that he didn't see what he thought he saw."

"But," Jack repeated, folding his arms, "Joe didn't seem to care about our ages. To hear you tell it, he should have called you a hag and chased you away from me with a broom."

"Hag?"

"Crone?" His eyes twinkled. Literally twinkled.

Charlie shook her head. She could feel the condensation on the window soaking through her jeans. "He's full-blood Fey, you're a Dragon Prince, and you growled . . ."

"*You* growled."

"That wasn't me." And there was the denial, as planned. "His instincts took over and he ran. I heard it in his voice," she added. "He said *'Never mind. Later.'* but I heard, *'Don't eat me.'*"

"Oh." Jack considered that for a moment. "So I guess I should apologize to him?"

"If you're asking my advice, you guys should definitely square up before he talks to Auntie Gwen and she puts two and two together and comes up with thirteen years. Auntie math," she added when Jack rolled his eyes.

"So I guess I should apologize to him." Not a question this time. He turned to follow Joe. Turned back to the hall. "Be careful."

Her soundtrack played Hedley's "Young and Stupid."

"You'd better be referring to Jack," Charlie muttered, jerking open the back door. Six strides took her through the shrubbery. Six more took her through the Wood. The last six took her from between two Rocky Mountain junipers out onto the main drive leading up to Caesar's Palace where she answered her phone and was almost hit by a cab.

And a limo.

And an SUV.

And another cab.

Although in fairness, it wasn't entirely the second cabbie's fault as she'd become even more distracted.

"*How* many baths?" Charlie stepped in under the portico and leaned against a pillar, appreciating the warmth after the damp cold of Calgary.

On the other end of the phone, Auntie Carmen sniffed. "Seventeen. Not that we're complaining, the smell has faded significantly."

"So what's the problem?"

"He's monopolizing the bathroom. We've had to charm it to try and keep him out."

"So?"

"It's not working. Whatever tune you have playing in his head is blocking the charm."

"Really?" That was unexpected.

"Why on earth would I make that up, Charlotte? We need you to come and talk to him."

"You need me? You and Auntie Bea can't handle a man who's been naked and wet for most of the time he's been in your house?"

"Well, he's slippery, dear, we can't get him out of the bathroom."

They could. They just didn't want to. "I'm a little busy. Get hold of Jack and have him do it."

"Isn't Jack with you?"

"No, he's with Joe in the Emporium."

"But he's always with you."

"Auntie Carmen, I'm not in Calgary." Charlie watched a very hungover bridal party tetris themselves and their luggage into a van and head for the airport. "If you can't reach Jack . . ." Dragon fire had turned out to be the one thing Gale phones couldn't survive. Charlie was fully aware that this made her inability to get rid of her phone total bullshit. ". . . have Roland talk to Dan."

"I'd like to leave my grandson out of this. He's your stray, Charlotte."

"It's your bathtub, Auntie Carmen." Charlie hung up and caught a sympathetic look from one of the valet parking guys. "Family."

He nodded. "Claro que si."

Out of Town Girl led her to the 41st floor of the Augustus Tower where she found a member of the hotel staff backing out of Auntie Catherine's room with a room service trolley, a disheveled uniform, and a sappy expression. He had gorgeous dark eyes, broad shoulders, and was in shouting distance of his early twenties which explained the Rihanna now playing in the background at least. When he caught sight of Charlie, he blushed up to the roots of his sweat-damp hair.

Charlie patted him on the shoulder as she went past him into the room.

"Charlotte."

"Auntie Catherine." There might have been a plaintive *call me* from the hall as the door shut behind her. Charlie chose to ignore it. "We need to talk."

"Please, he's twenty-six and this is not the first time he's offered his services to a woman traveling alone. Although," she added thoughtfully, braiding her hair, silver bracelets chiming, "it's the first time he didn't expect to be compensated for his effort."

"We don't need to talk about that."

"Pity. It was worth commenting on." End of the braid tied off, Auntie Catherine locked a serious gaze on Charlie's face. "Go ahead, child. Talk."

"He's twenty-six?" Okay. That wasn't what she'd intended to say.

"It's not about age, Charlotte, it's about power imbalance."

"Imbalance? What power did the boy-toy have?"

"Oh, we were talking about Kevin? My mistake." She leaned in toward the mirror, licked her fingertip and ran it over her eyebrows, then turned back to Charlie. "Never underestimate the power of abs so defined you can open a Corona on them. Now then, get to the point. I'm due in the spa in forty minutes."

"You may want to cancel because that asteroid you Saw . . . NASA won't be able to stop it."

"And why would that be a reason to cancel my spa appointment?"

"Oh, I don't know . . ." Charlie picked the box of mixed nuts off the dresser and frowned at the exposed flashing lights. "Asteroid? Impact? Extinction event?"

"That seems like an excellent reason to get a massage." Auntie Catherine plucked the nuts from Charlie's hand and put them back on the sensors. "You told me they'd have years to come up with a solution. What happened?"

"It turns out that as an astrophysicist, I'm a great musician." The bathroom was definitely big enough for a tiger and she could see the Bellagio fountain from the window. Of the room. Not the bathroom. Although there was a television by the toilet. Having paced out the dimensions of the room, Charlie flipped the duvet back into place before dropping onto the rumpled bed. "There's a heavy metal asteroid blocking the rock you Saw—an asteroid heavy in metals, not a head-banging asteroid. Although there *will* be some head banging . . ."

One silver brow rose. "Charlotte."

"Right. Because the asteroid that's going to impact has been blocked from sensors and telescopes and science stuff, it's gotten too close. We've got a maximum of six months before the blocking asteroid has moved far enough out of the way that the falling asteroid is spotted and all over the news. And, news flash, no one I talked to thinks we'll get the whole six. All told, twenty-two months to impact."

"I see." Auntie Catherine tightened the belt on the hotel bathrobe, the plush fabric dipping in around her waist. "It seems we're the dinosaurs after all. I assume there's a reason you've come back to tell me this before telling the rest of the family."

"How do you know I haven't told . . . No one's called you." Obvious really. "I need to know if you've Seen anything else."

"I've Seen many things. I've seen next year's Oscars—no real surprises. I think Peter Jackson was in Armani again. I've Seen a white tiger cub born in Kiev. I've Seen a bridge fall in Chunox. Or perhaps it was Consejo. I've Seen you embarrassing yourself mooning over . . ."

"Yeah, you've seen fire and you've seen rain. Anything else that might *help?*" When both Auntie Catherine's brows rose, Charlie sighed. "Help us survive."

"No."

"That's it?" Charlie asked after a long moment. "Just no?"

"Just no." The bed dipped as she sat.

Across the road and forty-one stories down, the Bellagio fountains thumped out a few thousand gallons of water. Charlie stared at the back of Auntie Catherine's head, at the slope of her shoulders, at the bow of her spine, and realized she'd never seen an auntie look *undone* before. She sat up so that her right arm touched Auntie Catherine's left and her boots sank into the plush, cream-colored carpet beside Auntie Catherine's bare feet. It looked like she'd gotten a pedicure recently, her toenails were a bright sapphire blue. "They're pretty sure that impact'll be just south of Hudson Bay. Darsden East goes early, but the rock's big enough that the rest of us, where us means pretty much everyone, goes a little later."

"Yes, well, it is a *very* large rock." After a moment she added, "You should say dies, Charlotte. Everyone *dies*, not everyone goes. Euphemisms are for the childish and the weak, and you're neither."

"Thanks."

"It was the truth, not a compliment."

"Yeah, well, the truth and I have been a bit pitchy lately."

"I have Seen you and the young man I assume . . ."

"I don't want to talk about it, Auntie Catherine."

They sat in silence for a moment. It would be easy to give up, Charlie realized. Easy to say, *we can't stop it, we're all going to die,* and spend at least some of those twenty-two months alone with Jack. But, the truth was, she wasn't ready to die. She might be ready to trade in the so much less than it could be and slightly emotionally masochistic relationship she had with Jack for a happily ever after, but by no definition was twenty-two months ever after. She wasn't ready to give up Allie, music, the twins, pancakes, pizza and bourbon at two AM, sunrises, sunsets, pickup trucks, accents, and beer either. "You still haven't Seen the impact."

"Not yet, no."

She swept the edge of her boot sole back and forth, flattening then fluffing the nap of the carpet. Pale. Dark. Pale. "So maybe we can still stop it."

"You and I? You and I are tapped out, Charlotte. I have Seen it. You can sing of it but not at it. As you haven't brought it up, I assume Jack's as helpless as we are."

"I meant we, the family."

"It's not what *we* . . ." The emphasis was mocking. ". . . the family, do."

"No, we don't." The family didn't interfere in the concerns of the wider world. They left that up to the Wild Powers, albeit not always graciously. Or consciously. On the other hand, the concerns of the wider world didn't usually interfere quite so emphatically with the family. "We're pretty fond of eating and sleeping and fucking, so I think *we* might make an exception this time."

Auntie Catherine made a noncommittal noise Charlie chose to hear as agreement before saying, "I went back to Ontario to tell Jane."

"Auntie Jane?"

Her answering snort was entirely committal. "No, Jane Banks."

"What did she say?"

"Honestly?"

"That'd be nice."

"I don't think she believed me."

"So the aunties still haven't had a chance to weigh in." Charlie chewed at the thought. The aunties were, well, the aunties. Individually, they were like cats, but working together . . . Charlie'd always believed that the aunties could do anything. Charlie'd been taught that the aunties could do anything. By the aunties. Who didn't believe in false modesty.

"*I* am an auntie, Charlotte, and I . . ."

"So the aunties," Charlie repeated through clenched teeth, "still haven't had a chance to weigh in."

"Not as such, no."

"And *you* are Wild. That trumps auntie, or you wouldn't be staying in a hotel room in Vegas no matter how attentive room service . . ."

"Very attentive."

". . . might be. You'd be in Darsden East or Calgary complaining about the way your granddaughters never add enough tapioca to raspberry pie to soak up the juice."

"Allie?"

"Katie, but that's not my point. We need to take this to the family because me and you and Jack, we're not a part of what they are. We're more. Or less, depending on your perspective. We don't see the world the same way."

"*I* don't see the world through beer glasses."

"Don't patronize me." Charlie snapped. The champagne glass on the dresser hummed. "I'm over thirty and as Wild as you are."

"Oh, sweetheart, you have a way to go to be as Wild as I am, but, by all means, gather the family." Auntie Catherine spread her hands, the bracelets chiming with the movement, the gleaming silver fracturing the light around them. "Feel free to see if the collected power of the Gales is enough to save the world."

The Bellagio fountains thumped again as Charlie got to her feet and turned to face the bed. "You don't think it will be, do you?"

"I don't know . . ." She stopped. Shook her head. Started again. "I don't know why I told Jane. I don't know if I was telling her the world was about to end, or if I was telling her to stop it."

"Please. Like you can tell Auntie Jane to do anything."

The edged smile softened slightly. "True enough."

"Will you come if Allie calls the family together?"

"If Allie calls? Yes," she continued thoughtfully before Charlie could respond. "They'll come for her. She'll do it for you."

"Will you come?" Charlie repeated.

"No."

"Why not?"

"*I* have slipped my leash."

"Allie doesn't hold . . . Never mind." Charlie headed for the door, turned and said, "So you haven't Seen yourself actually doing something about this, then?"

And the edge returned. "Charlotte, when I was ten years younger than you are now, I began the arrangements that ensured two of my grandchildren would be who they were and what they were, not to mention where they were, in order to stop a rampage by the Dragon Queen. What makes you think I'm not doing something?"

Charlie was back in the Wood before she realized Auntie Catherine hadn't actually answered the question.

She found Joe in the store going through a box of videotapes.

"If you're looking for Jack, he just left. Carmen had a problem."

"With Dan. She called me first," Charlie added when Joe looked up.

"If he wants to leave," Joe began.

"Leave? I though he wanted to live in the bathtub?"

"As I heard it, Bea and Carmen had a fight about it, Carmen started to cry . . ."

"Auntie Carmen cries at Heritage Moments."

". . . and Dan said he wouldn't stay if he was going to be a cabbage."

"Cabbage?"

"That's what Bea said. He got out of the tub . . ."

Elbows on the counter, Charlie dropped her head into her hands. "That should've made someone happy."

". . . and he tried to leave. Bea stopped him. And Carmen says you said that Jack should sort it out."

"Jack the Dragon Prince, not Jack the Gale boy. He'll know what to say." Joe made a noise so entirely noncommittal, Charlie lifted her head and turned to stare at him. "What?"

"Wasn't it you who argued so vehemently for his acceptance as a Gale boy?"

"I don't see any reason he can't be both a Dragon Prince and a Gale boy as the need arises."

"No . . ." Joe set a stack of tapes on the counter beside her. ". . . you wouldn't."

"What's that supposed to mean?"

"It means that if Dan wants to leave, he should be allowed to leave."

Charlie watched Joe sort seasons one through six of *The Littlest Hobo* into the correct boxes and finally decided, screw it, let him change the subject. "We're keeping him within the protection of the family for his own good, but, yeah, it's a slippery slope. With great power, great responsibility, yadda yadda, and you have no idea how much I miss the days when all I had to worry about were broken strings and drunks who wanted us to play 'Freebird.'"

Joe cocked his head and frowned at her. "When was the last time you slept?"

When she closed her eyes, she saw big rocks land on people she loved while she struggled to string her guitar. "I'm pretty sure I got a couple hours on the roof this morning. Why?"

"Because you look a little rough."

"Good. Rough may get me some sympathy points." Charlie picked up a 1997 tape of *Girls Gone Wild* and frowned at the fangs and claws. Not the wild she'd been expecting. "Allie upstairs?"

"She is. Gwen took the boys to the park."

Allie was alone upstairs because the universe rearranged itself for Gales. Metaphysically speaking; geologically speaking, not so much.

"If any of the family come in, keep them down here."

After a long look at her face, Joe nodded.

Charlie tossed the tape back in the box and wondered what he'd seen.

"Auntie Bea, I need to talk to Jack."

"Of course you do. In case you're curious, although I notice you didn't ask, Dan is currently sitting at the kitchen table eating butter tarts."

"I hope he's sitting on a towel."

"Of course he is. Jack! It's Charlotte."

Jack listened without comment as Charlie leaned on the wall beside the mirror and sketched out her meeting with Auntie Catherine. "I'm about to play the whole opera for Allie, then we'll throw the aunties at the asteroid."

"If you threw enough of them, you could knock it off course."

"Catapult it is, then."

"You sure you want to tell Allie before I check with the Courts?"

"The Courts will assume the aunties already know. If we take it to the Courts before the aunties . . ."

"We'll be the first casualties."

He was smiling—Charlie could hear the smile in his voice—but he was also entirely serious. His uncles had seen to it that Jack's sense of survival was as finally tuned as any Gale boy's.

"Charlie?"

She'd been listening to him breathe for just a little too long. Twenty-two months, but he could save himself and that was . . . not exactly a comfort, but it helped. Her reflection stood on a pile of broken glass. It seemed the mirror had a sense of its own mortality. "We'll stop it," she said, and hung up.

"Allie, we have to talk."

Allie turned the mixer on low and poured the half cup of lemon juice into the bowl before looking up. "All right." Her expression suggested relief, but Charlie could hear betrayal under her words, like the snares vibrating against a drumhead. Lovers, cousins, friends, they didn't keep secrets. Hadn't kept secrets. "Pass me the flour."

Charlie slid the quarter cup of flour down the counter. "I thought this was another Wild Powers problem, like the Selkies. Keeping it from you had nothing to do with you personally."

"Okay." She tipped the flour into the bowl, then turned up the power.

"You're taking this well." Charlie pitched her voice over the roar of the machine, not bothering to mask the sarcasm. Gale girls baked when they were upset. Allie, figuring there was pie enough in the world, baked lemon squares.

"You're obvious when you have a secret, Charlie."

"In my own defense, this isn't an easy family to keep secrets in." It would certainly be easier from Vegas. She felt another wave of understanding for Auntie Catherine. "Look there's no good way to do this so I'm just going to sing out. There's a huge asteroid heading toward an impact with Earth in twenty-two months, which probably isn't enough time for NASA to stop it, so unless we, being us, being the family, although mostly I'm figuring the aunties at this point, can stop it, we're all, and when I say all I mean all, going to die."

Allie shut off the mixer and stared at Charlie while the silence vibrated through the apartment. "What?" she asked after a long moment.

Maybe a few more details wouldn't hurt. "What part did you miss?"

"The part where you're supposed to be telling me about you and Jack."

"Allie . . ." The edge of the counter creaked under Charlie's white-knuckled grip. "There is no me and Jack!"

"I know, I can do the math." Allie picked up a spatula. "We can all do the math. I understand why you don't want the whole family talking about it . . ."

"Wait." Hand wrapped around Allie's wrist, Charlie stopped her from scraping the bowl and folding her emotional state into the lemon custard. "Are you saying, the whole family knows?"

"Did you miss me saying you're obvious when you have a secret? Between you running and him scorching and all the watching you've both been doing with little pink hearts in your eyes . . ."

"Actual?"

"Metaphorical."

"Good thing."

"But the point is, I have never closed my heart to you. Why didn't you come to me?"

"Oh, for . . . Allie, focus!" Charlie released her wrist and stepped back. "Jack and I are dealing. We talked. It's cool. Well, it's actually pretty fucking lousy, but everyone in the world dying in twenty-two months kind of puts our incredibly bad timing into perspective, don't you think?"

"No, it's . . ." Allie stared down into the bowl, at the spatula, up at Charlie. "You were serious about that?" She'd finally dropped the irritating, second circle, mom-voice. Charlie hated that voice. "You were serious about the asteroid? That's . . ." She blinked, stumbled sideways, bounced off the end of the dining room table, pulled out a chair, and sat. "Everyone dies in twenty-two months."

And that was the difference between them. Allie went straight from the cause to the effect. "That's what they tell me."

"That's not . . . I mean, we can't . . ." The lights flickered, throwing the apartment into momentary late October gloom, and the mixer turned on again.

Charlie unplugged it, then just to be on the safe side, turned off the oven before moving to the dining room, pulling out a chair, and turning it to face Allie. Hands on her cousin's knees, she leaned forward. "Calm down, you're going to hyperventilate. Rosin your bow, Allie-cat. I need you to call the aunties together."

"Rosin my what?"

"Ow!"

The toddler weight lifting program had put some muscle behind Allie's swing. "How long have you known?" she demanded through gritted teeth.

"About the asteroid?" Auntie Catherine. Dan. Vermont. Gary. Charlie added it up. "Twenty-four hours. About everyone dying?" Southern California. Auntie Catherine. "Maybe ten."

"Then can I have a minute to deal!"

"Sorry."

Allie shrugged off her apology and frowned. "This is why you didn't come to bed last night."

It wasn't a question, but Charlie nodded anyway. It was most of the reason.

"Okay." Her gaze drifted around the room, settled for a moment on Evan's slightly scorched plush dragon, then returned to Charlie. "Other countries have space agencies."

"Dr. Mehta—she's the scientist I spoke to at NASA . . ."

"Wait." Allie raised her hand. "You know a scientist at NASA?"

"Yes, she's . . ."

"You have friends who aren't musicians?"

"Yes. Although technically, she's not my friend, she's the friend of Gary the bouzouki player. Yes," Charlie expanded before Allie could ask, "he's *the* bouzouki player. That's why he was important. Dr. Mehta says the other agencies have been contacted. They're trying, but . . ."

"Okay. Stop." She stared at her raised hand for a moment, waved it a couple of times, and finally cupped it around the curve of her stomach. "There's really an asteroid? A big falling rock?"

As Charlie'd already established the lack of a death wish, she figured the temptation to say, *no, just kidding* was probably the lack of sleep talking. "Yeah. NASA calls it an extinction event."

"And you can't stop it and Jack can't stop it." *Or you wouldn't have bothered telling me,* added the subtext. "All right, then." She closed her eyes for a moment and when she opened them again, Charlie could see the light of determination in them. Or possibly it was the reflection of the light over the dining room table; either way, Allie'd clearly come to a decision. One hand still curved around her belly, she tossed her braid behind her shoulder with the other and picked up the stuffed dragon. "I'll call the family together."

"Not the whole family," Charlie cautioned, "just the aunties."

"For this kind of thing, the aunties will need to pull power from ritual. Ritual needs the whole family. We might as well tell them all at once."

"We're dead in twenty-two months if we don't stop this, Allie. The fewer people who have to live with that, the better."

"The more people who know," Allie countered, "the better the chances are of finding a solution. And if it comes to it, wouldn't you rather know you'd been doing as much as you could for as long as you could?"

"That's . . . reasonable." And it wasn't like the family couldn't keep a secret. "I just . . ."

"You don't want anyone else to feel like you're feeling. Admirable, but Wild doesn't mean you have to do it alone, Charlie. It's time to stop protecting us; we're all in this together. And we'll stop it. All of us. Together."

Charlie could hear no possibility of failure in Allie's voice. "That's my girl."

The stuffed dragon bounced off her face.

"And now that's settled, didn't you used to call me stupidly masochistic for falling in love with my gay best friend?"

Given the time of year and the temperatures after dark, they held the family meeting in the house they'd inherited from Jonathon Samuel Gale or, more specifically, from Stanley Kalynchuk, the sorcerer Graham had been working for when he met Allie. Though they were one and the same, the house had been in Kalynchuk's name and therefore the will Roland had drawn up— heavily charmed by the aunties—had also been in Kalynchuk's name.

"I don't care what he was calling himself," Auntie Bea had sniffed. *"You're a lawyer, Roland Edward Gale. Fix it."*

There'd been discussion about selling the property and using the money to buy and demolish two or three smaller houses closer to the park, but four years later they still weren't positive they'd removed every trace of Kalynchuk's sorcery. Nor were they sure how to safely dispose of most of the collected artifacts in the vault, particularly those they couldn't identify.

"This one looks like a gilded pookah penis," Allie muttered, *lifting the lumpy golden cylinder off the shelf.*

"It really doesn't, dear." Auntie Carmen patted her on the arm as she passed.

It was the only property they owned large enough for the whole family, although the location meant that using it post ritual required designated drivers. They'd hung onto it mostly because of the pool. No one wanted to lose the pool, particularly not when Jack could keep the water warm enough for even a Calgary winter just by half submerging. During the later months of her first pregnancy, Allie'd spent a lot of time floating tucked up against Jack's side.

A quick glance around the room found Jack next to Cameron. They got along well, probably because Jack had never manifested horn and challenged for position—although Allie supposed *had never manifested horn* or *challenged for position* was more accurate as Jack's manifestation leaned more toward teeth and claws than the Gale norm. Charlie stood by the breakfast bar, fingertips drumming out the percussion to music only she could hear. She wasn't looking at Jack, he wasn't looking at her, they weren't acknowledging the other's presence in any way, and yet Allie barely needed to squint to see the connection between them. Second circle was all about connection. Charlie kept forgetting that.

Once we work out how to prevent an asteroid impact, I'll work on them. She couldn't erase thirteen years, but there had to be something she could do to ease their way.

Every Gale in Calgary, fifteen and older, had gathered in the kitchen or the huge family room attached. Pies already in the oven filled the space with the comforting scent of pastry and baking apples. Across the family room, at least one auntie always close at hand, David not only maintained a human seeming but was drinking a beer. The children, and they'd finally begun to have a comfortable number of them, were downstairs, charging around the basement under the supervision of the younger teens. Jennifer, Judith and Dave's oldest, had rolled her eyes with all the aplomb of a Gale twice her age, balanced Evan on her hip, and said, *"Don't worry, Allie, every adult in the city is one floor away. Wendy and I can handle it."*

Three laptops were open on the high sideboard, one linked to Ashley's apartment in Toronto, one to Sara's apartment in Ottawa, and one, on the most panoramic setting possible, to a laptop in the old farmhouse outside Darsden East where the aunties jostled for position in front of the camera. Auntie Vera was sitting with Auntie Ruby—no one needed to call it a death watch, they all knew what it was—but the rest were there. There were others, at school or working too far away to make it home, listening in. With only a few hours' warning, this was the compromise.

She'd called, they'd come.

Unable to stop herself from glancing up at the ceiling, she saw that the blades of the fan needed dusting and saw no sign at all of an asteroid large enough to wipe everything she loved and most of what she only tolerated off the face of the Earth. Of course there wasn't. It was still millions of kilometers away even if she could feel the weight settling on her shoulders.

"Charlie." Allie beckoned her out into the center of the room. "Let's do this."

". . . and that's where we stand right now." Charlie flipped up a finger. "Big rock incoming." And another. "Six months to panic stations, twenty-two to impact." And a third. "Current trajectory as far as they can tell with that big hunk of metallic rock in the way, puts impact somewhere at the upper edge of Hudson Bay . . ."

"So it won't hit us!" Auntie Carmen pried a damp, balled-up tissue out of the sleeve of her sweater.

". . . having come in on a thirty-degree angle," Charlie continued, "from the north."

"So it won't hit us," Auntie Bea repeated grimly.

"Given its size and at the speed it'll hit, if the blast wave doesn't wipe out Darsden East, the spray of debris will." Heather looked around the suddenly silent room. "What? Am I the only one who watches the Discovery Channel?"

"No," Charlie told her, "you aren't. NASA can't stop it. I can't stop it. Jack can't stop it. If we could, it'd be a Wild Power problem and we wouldn't be here tonight. So, let's pretend every possible *Armageddon*, Bruce Willis comment has been already been made . . ." She glanced over at those members of the family old enough to remember the movie, her gaze brushing past Jack on the way by because she could, "and pick it up after we've decided that Michael Bay was not providing us with an instruction manual."

"Bruce Willis would kick that asteroid's ass," Gabbie muttered. Her husband nodded.

"Not an instruction manual," Charlie repeated.

Frowning, Melissa shook her head. "I doubt we've got six months. There's one hell of a lot of telescopes pointed at the sky. A lot of the data in NASA's catalog of NEOs came from private scopes."

"NEOs—Near Earth Objects," Cameron explained as half a dozen voices called out questions. When Melissa turned to look at him, he blushed. "What? More than just muscles and a dick here."

"Cameron Edward Gale!" Even with charms adjusting the volume, the laptop speakers crackled.

His blush deepened. "Sorry, Mom."

"You're certain this isn't Catherine messing around with us?" Auntie Bea asked.

"What part of I spoke to the scientist at NASA who discovered and is tracking the asteroid did you miss, Auntie Bea?"

"The scientist you found because of an unstable telepathic street person, Charlotte?"

"Seventh son of a seventh son, sorcerer's ex-hitman." Charlie pointed at Graham. "Gale, Dragon Prince, sorcerer." Her finger moved to Jack, then she spread her hands. "I shortcut through a place that doesn't actually exist and Auntie Catherine screencaps the future. Crazy telepathic street person isn't all that out there."

"And the bouzouki?"

"The bouzouki *player,* Auntie Bea. The instrument itself wasn't much help."

"Catherine," Auntie Carmen began before Auntie Bea could answer.

"Came to me first," Auntie Jane interrupted, moving in closer to the center monitor, her tone stilling the quiet ripples of conversation.

"Of course she did," Auntie Carmen sighed into the silence.

And then, as though confirmation from an auntie had been all that was required, the silence ended in a roar of sound; muted from all three laptops, loud enough to press against the privacy charms etched into the outside walls of the house in Mount Royal.

Charlie could hear curiosity, annoyance, and speculation, but no fear. Melissa and Heather and the other members of the third circle were arguing about the strength of the ritual needed while Cameron protested there was only one of him. They were young enough to believe they were personally invincible. The second circle was old enough to know individuals might fall, but believed the family could stand against anything. None of them had seen despair curve Auntie Catherine's shoulders.

The aunties . . .

The aunties were being too quiet. Charlie'd hoped for smug superiority of the *honestly, it's just a falling rock, what's all the fuss about* variety, but she was getting nothing at all. Not here. She glanced at the laptop screens. Not from any of the aunties back east.

Was it because Auntie Jane had already known? If the aunties had gotten together and come up with a solution without bothering to tell anyone, Charlie planned to be pissed. The last seventeen hours of *knowing* she was helpless had felt more like three years. The noise dropped to background muttering as she moved to stare directly into the center camera. "So, what's the plan, Auntie Jane?"

"What makes you think I have a plan, Charlotte?"

"Auntie Catherine came to you first."

Auntie Jane snorted. "And I didn't believe her."

"Of course you didn't." Auntie Bea picked up a pair of oven mitts from the counter beside the stove and pulled them on, the lime-green silicon snapping around her wrists.

"Catherine told me the sky was falling." Auntie Jane's slate-gray brows nearly met over her nose. "She didn't mention anything as prosaic as an incoming asteroid."

Straightening from the oven, Auntie Bea set a steaming apple pie down on the cooling rack. "You probably said something to put her back up."

"Catherine's back is always up," Auntie Jane pointed out. "And you didn't pinch your edges properly, Bea. There's juice dripping onto the counter."

"First, you can't see my edges pinched or not from the angle that laptop is set at, and, second, I'm not entirely unsympathetic to Catherine's position."

"First, you never pinch your edges properly, you haven't for fifty years, and second . . ." Thirty-six-hundred kilometers to the east, Auntie Jane's frown deepened. ". . . Catherine has never grown out of the *I know something you don't know* stage. She enjoys taunting the family with it."

"She enjoys taunting *you* with it." Auntie Bea set another pie on the rack. "The rest of us are not so favored."

"I'm pretty sure she enjoys taunting me," Charlie put in.

A third pie joined the first two. "I stand corrected, Charlotte."

Auntie Gwen slid one of the big chef's knives out of Auntie Bea's reach, and the women not in the kitchen shifted so they were more definitively between Auntie Bea and the men. As the Calgary circles had grown, Auntie Bea had become less Auntie Jane's eyes and ears in the west and more her competition.

"Enough." The lights flickered and the kettle, although it hadn't been plugged in, came to a boil. Charlie glanced over at Allie who clearly had no intention of allowing the shifting power dynamics to take center stage, not when her babies were at risk. "My grandmother's part in this is done."

Auntie Bea pulled off the oven mitts. Auntie Carmen and Auntie Trisha, holding pie lifters, moved to flank her. Auntie Gwen set a stack of dessert plates on the island. All four aunties stared into the center monitor with such intensity that the two flanking laptops flickered in and out of blue screen, once, twice, three times, until they settled.

Glancing around the room, Charlie knew everyone present had come to the same conclusion—they'd skip the pie. "All right. We have an ETA, a trajectory, and an impact site. What do we do?"

"We could throw up berms to the northeast," Allie said, tucked up against Graham's chest. "Deflect the blast wave and the debris."

"*We* can," Graham agreed, glancing over at the laptops on the sideboard, "but we're a province and a half away from the impact. Southern Ontario is . . ."

"Toast."

"Toast?" Auntie Carmen turned on Roland. "This is your expensive law school vocabulary? Toast."

"If we throw a berm up to protect Darsden East, it'll only become an advance wave of the debris field." Roland spread his hands. "Superheated earth and rock, destroying everything in its path. Toast, Nana."

"We can protect Calgary with a full first circle." Auntie Gwen passed Roland a piece of pie. He passed it on.

"It's a little early to discuss shifting the family around, Gwen," Auntie Jane sniffed.

"No, it isn't." Auntie Meredith sitting in a rocking chair away from the computer, raised her voice enough to silence four rooms of ambient noise. "We can't stop the asteroid."

"Can't?" A glance at the four aunties in the kitchen showed a surprising lack of argument. Charlie's skin felt too tight. "Just like that? You haven't even discussed it!"

"We are of the earth," Auntie Bea said, and Charlie noted how at least half the people in the room turned to look at David. The other half kept their attention on the aunties, which was always wise.

"It's a rock," Charlie growled. "I can't Sing it in a vacuum, but it's a *rock*."

"Do not use that tone on me, Charlotte Marie Gale." The pie lifter left Auntie Bea's hand and hit the granite countertop with a definitive crack. "We are of *this* earth. The rock is not. It's not even in contact with the earth, and we have limited influence in the sky."

"You might remember that when the police helicopters are up," Auntie Carmen muttered.

"I said limited influence," Auntie Bea snapped. "Not grounding myself for every jackbooted thug in a uniform."

Auntie Trisha stepped between them, hands spread in a placating manner. "Not the time, ladies. Really not the time."

"Don't ladies me, you young punk," Auntie Bea growled. "My eyes didn't turn dark yesterday . . ."

David stamped his foot. Even in sneakers, it sounded like a hoof against the hardwood.

"We can't stop it," Auntie Gwen said softly. "We have to concentrate on surviving it."

Charlie took a deep breath and counted it in. *One, two, three . . .*

The family dissolved into argument again. Graham crossed the room to argue NASA with Melissa. Half a dozen of the second circle women had gathered together and Charlie could feel the power building. Their men were securing the breakables. Cameron, Heather, and Bonnie had gathered around a tablet. Lucy kept shaking her head at Roland. Rayne was on the phone. So were Sandy and Gen, two of the other third circle girls on Cameron's list. Probably talking to their mothers back in Ontario.

"We don't have time for this," she muttered. They'd had twenty-two months back when Dr. Mehta found out. Twenty-one and a half now.

"Let them have a moment," Allie said quietly behind her. "They need to process."

It wasn't the incoming asteroid that needed processing, Charlie realized. It was the aunties saying *we can't.*

"All right. Enough." Allie's voice cracked like a whip over the family, even the aunties falling silent. Apparently, when she'd said moment, she'd meant moment. "I need a list of everyone willing to move to Calgary—third, second, and first circle. Once we have numbers, we'll work on housing."

Auntie Vera leaned in close to the camera. "You can't absorb the entire family, Allie."

"She won't need to." Auntie Jane cut Allie's reply off. "We have time to branch again."

"Branch out?" Auntie Bea sniffed disdainfully. "You say that like it's so easy. If you'll recall, it took a great disturbance to root this latest branch."

"An asteroid is about to have a go at wiping out all life on the planet," Charlie muttered. "Is that a great enough disturbance for you?"

"It *might* be enough," Auntie Bea admitted reluctantly.

"Australia usually survives. I say we go south . . ."

". . . and throw a shrimp on the barbie!"

Charlie couldn't see them in the monitor, but there was no mistaking her sisters. She was a little surprised they were home, given the way they'd been bouncing around the world.

"We can help the survivors," Auntie Mary pointed out, leaning in close to the camera.

"The weather will change, there may not be many survivors."

"The family will survive." Auntie Jane's declaration moved her back to the center of the monitor. "That is our bottom line. How many non-family will also survive is still under discussion."

"There's too many people in the city now who aren't us."

Allie's head whipped around, trying to identify who'd spoken. Charlie knew who it was, but she wasn't going to say. They were right. If protecting Calgary meant protecting all the inhabitants, then after the impact they also had to keep them fed and warm. Smarter for Allie to empty the city, leaving only the family, but Charlie doubted she would.

"What about you, Jack?" Heather asked in the pause, cramming the words in as a distraction. "You fly high."

Charlie turned to where Jack was sitting in time to see him shake his head, hair flopping down over his eyes. Her fingers itched to stroke it back. Surrounded by family. Under the eyes of the aunties. Her fingers had a death wish.

"Not that high," he said.

"What about sorcery?"

To Charlie's surprise, the question came from Auntie Jane.

"You're certainly capable of turning items into things they aren't."

At least she hadn't specifically mentioned the butterflies. "I already said Jack can't stop this, Auntie Jane."

"And I believe you, Charlotte." The clear implication being that they were all fully aware Charlie could ensure belief and no one liked the idea much. Or at all. "Nevertheless, I'd prefer it if Jack spoke for himself."

Everyone, physically and digitally, looked at Charlie. Then at Jack. So Charlie looked at Jack, too.

Jack swallowed a mouthful of pie and stacked the empty plate with the others on the floor beside him. "Charlie and I already talked about this, back when we assumed the Wild Powers could stop it. I don't actually control what I do. Things don't change because I want them to; they change because I *need* them to."

"You need this rock to change, dude." Carmen reached out and punched him lightly in the shoulder.

"He's had no training," Graham reminded them.

"Training." Auntie Jane leaned in, dark eyes narrowed. "Sorcerers in this family are self-taught."

"And then killed," Graham growled.

"But if it *were* heading right for you?" Heather asked, stretching out and poking Jack in the back with her foot. "If the asteroid was overhead, over *your* head, and it was clear you'd die in the impact, would you make it disappear? Instinctively."

"I don't know. It'd disappear or I would." Jack shrugged. "I might just return myself to the UnderRealm. I wouldn't know until it happened."

"So let's drop a really big rock on him and see what happens."

"Not helping, Auntie Bea!" Allie snapped, as Jack began to smoke. "Jack, what about your uncles, the Dragon Lords?"

"My uncles?"

Charlie figured that anyone who hadn't expected the puff of smoke and had inhaled at the wrong time deserved what they got. How could they not know that Jack's relationship with his uncles was violent at best and . . . Actually, violent pretty much summed it up.

"My uncles," Jack repeated, once the coughing had died down, "might be convinced to not hunt the family to extinction should they take refuge in the UnderRealm. Although I'd probably have to kill a couple to get that much out of them," he added thoughtfully. "Besides, we can't go to the UnderRealm—Charlie already explained."

The family turned to look at Charlie. She spread her hands in the universal gesture for *well, duh.*

"All right, then . . ." Allie took a deep breath and let it out slowly. "Joe, what about the rest of the UnderRealm?"

With a room full of Gales searching for him—although Auntie Gwen looked right at him, Charlie noted—Joe slowly became visible over by one of the bookcases. "What *about* the rest of the UnderRealm?"

"The Courts. Can the Courts stop the asteroid?"

Charlie caught Jack's gaze and opened her mouth to say they'd discussed that, too, but snapped it closed again as Auntie Jane said, "The family does not deal with the Fey."

No subtext. No undertone. A bald statement of inarguable fact, it smothered every other sound in the room. In all four rooms, Charlie realized.

"We do not interfere with them, and they do not interfere with us. We deal with them if they step over the line here in this world," Auntie Jane continued, her words etched into the silence, "and that is all."

"That's clearly not all," Auntie Gwen muttered. The entire family held its breath. "Joe . . ."

"Was brought into the family by Alysha," Auntie Bea replied. It seemed that in this, at least, she supported Auntie Jane.

"Jack . . ."

"The events leading up to his conception and subsequent acceptance into this side of his birthright, were entirely unique."

Charlie saw Auntie Gwen's lip curl and braced for impact. Auntie Bea was significantly older, but that didn't necessarily mean more powerful. Only in her twenties, Allie was more powerful than any second circle Gale in memory—and that was the sort of thing the aunties never forgot.

"Gwendolyn Victoria Gale," Auntie Jane cracked the name like a whip, a third circle naming, not a first.

And all the fight went out of Auntie Gwen.

Fine. Charlie had fight to spare. "In case you've forgotten a point I made earlier," she snapped, "an asteroid is about to have a go at wiping out all life on the planet. If that's not unique enough for you to find a little . . ."

"Wildness, Charlotte?" *You are treading on very thin ice.*

"Flexibility, Auntie Jane." *I can swim.*

"And should we invite the rest of the world into our councils?"

Charlie jerked her arm free of a cautioning touch—probably Auntie Gwen's, she was the only woman close enough—and glared at the monitor. "That's not the same, and you know it."

"Yes, I do. As I know we do not deal with the Fey."

"Some of them are already leaving."

"Good. We deal with this situation as we have with others, within the family."

"Situation? Seriously? That's what you're calling this? You know what? Fine. The family deals with it. When you've figured out just how the family is going to keep from dying in less than twenty-two months, you let me know."

Allie moved toward her, but Charlie shook her head and sidestepped, slipping out the patio door as Auntie Carmen said, "I don't trust the Fey, present company excepted for the most part."

There was a single lounge chair left out by pool, the old-fashioned construction of aluminum and nylon tape that had never taken a charm well, next to it a small, round plastic table that had been white before Lyla went at it with her paints. Charlie kicked the table into the pool, gave some serious consideration to sending the chair after it, and sat down instead.

"Stubborn old women . . ."

She shoved her hands into the pockets of her jeans. The cold felt clean. Cleansing. Leaning back, she squinted up at the stars and wondered if one of them wasn't actually a star. She had no idea. She'd never cared about the stars. She cared about phosphor bronze medium strings. About pitchers of draft at Shooters in Thunderbay. About the heartbeat song of the bohdran under "Well Below the Valley." And for longer than she'd realized she'd cared about Jack. A lot more than she should.

Stars? Not so much.

"It'd serve them right if I Walked away, found a bar, got royally pissed, and picked up a distraction." Heat charmed into her clothes, Charlie settled in to wait.

"Auntie Bea wants to chain me down at the base of the tower and drop a large rock on me. Just to see what'll happen."

Nearly half an hour by her watch. She tipped her head back far enough to watch Jack cross between the house and the pool. "Missing your uncles?"

"Little bit." He shoved her over and sat beside her. The air between them warmed.

"How mad are they?"

"At you?" He shrugged. "Allie pointed out that you'd been carrying this knowledge longer than any of us and you were due for an emotional break. So they decided to cut you some slack. There's a ritual in ten days."

"I know."

"Auntie Jane's calling everyone home to take part."

"Everyone including . . . ?"

"You and me? Yeah. There was a bunch of stuff about using the power we had to hand and that before we went on, we had to know for certain ritual wouldn't work."

"Went on to what?" Charlie sighed. The aunties had been pretty definite about not being able to affect the asteroid.

Scales glistened across Jack's cheeks. "I kind of missed what they said about that."

"Thinking about ritual." Not a question. He was seventeen and he still hadn't spent a ritual in circle.

"Yeah." He huffed out a small cloud of smoke. "Charlie, I was thinking . . ."

"That explains the smoke."

"Sorry." Ears flushed, he fixed the scorch mark on her jeans and started to move away.

She sighed, grabbed his sleeve, and pulled him back beside her. "Joke. What were you thinking about?"

"Why don't we contact the rest of the family?"

"Trust me, anyone who couldn't tap in tonight will get the word." The constant sound of conversation spilling out of the house spiked suddenly. Still incomprehensible—thanks to charms etched in the glass—the emotional emphasis was impossible to ignore. Charlie waited until the volume had dropped back down to a background murmur before saying, "Hopefully not *all* the words."

"No, I don't mean . . . This circle in Calgary, it can't be the first time the family branched. I mean, Gales didn't spring up fully formed in southern Ontario and start bossing people around . . ." His voice trailed off into doubt as he shifted just far enough to be able to look into her face. "Did they?"

"No." And once again she was reminded how much family background Jack had missed learning during his first thirteen years. "As the extended dance version doesn't do much more than repeat the chorus a billion times, let's stick with the basic tune: a branch crossed the Atlantic, landed in Newfoundland, circled in, and a couple of hundred or so years later branched into Ontario."

"That's basic," Jack agreed. Golden brows drew in. "You and me, we were in Nova Scotia."

"Yeah. Your point?"

"That's pretty close. Why didn't we check if the family in Newfoundland was still . . ."

"We don't do that." When Jack's frown became a silent demand for more information, Charlie sighed. "Look, we weren't even Gales until we got to Ontario. Right up until Allie and David, when we branched we changed our name and didn't look back."

"But Allie and David wouldn't cut ties?"

"Technology won't allow us to cut ties. The world's gotten a lot smaller than it used to be and every generation, it gets smaller still. This . . ." She widened her gesture until it took in Calgary as well as the house and yard. ". . . is something new. The family's still working out the rules."

"Okay but that was before the whole asteroid thing. We could find the other branches of the family." He said *we* but Charlie heard *you and me*. He wasn't wrong. They could. Probably. They were Wild. Rules didn't apply. Most rules. All but one rule. She watched him walk to the edge of the pool and stare out over the water for a long moment before turning to face her again. "We should warn them. We should all work together to stop this thing."

Not *could* anymore. *Should.* Charlie sighed. "Jack, do you know what a group of aunties is called?"

He grinned and his eyes flashed gold. "A power struggle?"

"Got it in one."

"I was kidding."

"No, you weren't. I've met your uncles." She waited for him to nod—less actual breathing fire among the aunties, but otherwise the two groups were remarkably similar. "Because all of these aunties have known each other all their lives and Auntie Bea acknowledges deep down that she can't shove Auntie Jane off top of the charts, we manage. They're, *we're* working out new ways of dealing with each other." Leaning forward, she caught his gaze and held it. "Now think of another circle that has an auntie in the same position as Auntie Jane. That's the single point where the two circles will touch. If I had to describe it in one word, I'd say boom."

"Boom?"

"Boom. By the time the concept of working together to stop the asteroid is even mentioned, there won't be anything to work with. We can try to save the world, or we can go looking for more family and destroy it before the asteroid hits the blog-sphere."

"Two Dragon Queens can't share a territory."

Charlie spread her hands. "And there you go."

A car drove by. Two blocks down, a small dog yapped out an indignant protest Charlie almost understood. The smell of woodsmoke suggested one of the neighbors had lit a fire in their fireplace. Up in the sky, it was neither a bird nor a plane but imminent death.

"Do they know?" Jack asked. The lounge bowed as he dropped down to sit beside her again, his weight not entirely under control.

"Do the other circles know about the asteroid?" Good question. Charlie thought about it for a moment. "If they even still exist, probably not. You have to admit the chain of events that led to us finding out was . . . unique."

"But if they have a Seer . . ."

"Would they have a bouzouki player with a friend at NASA? Doubt it."

"Yeah." He blew a smoke ring and watched it drift away. "So . . . you and me in ritual. All available power in play." Another smoke ring. Another moment while they both watched it drift. "What do we do?"

Even if she survived the ritual itself without being flame broiled, Charlie didn't think she could survive afterward, knowing and not having. "We hope the horse talks."

"What?"

"Anything can happen in ten days. Maybe even the impossible." She lifted her feet up onto the lounge and stretched out, Jack radiating heat against her hip. She watched another smoke ring dissipate, a soft gray smudge against a cloudless sky. Watched the stars hide death. Just for the hell of it, she sang one long pure note up into the sky. It slid past the power lines, up over the city's rooftops, aimed at the star that wasn't. It was mostly defiance. Although the family had bent a few laws of physics in the past—they'd have bent them half an hour ago had she been in the same province with Auntie Jane—Charlie didn't expect her voice to . . .

A distant light flickered and began to descend.

"Holy crap." The lounge creaked and swayed as she jerked up. "I did it!" They weren't going to die! "It's coming down! And okay, that's not great, but if I can bring it down, I can break it up. Break it into pieces small enough they all burn up when they hit the atmosphere. Jack . . ." His arm was warm even through the sleeve of his jean jacket. ". . . look it's . . ."

"I think it's a plane."

"Shit!"

"It's okay." He sounded amused so hopefully she hadn't done anything irreparable. "It's landing at the airport."

"You can tell that from here?"

"Yeah, but I'll go check on it if you like."

Charlie reached for him as he stood, but only managed to grab the end of his tail. "We will never speak of this."

"Are you kidding me?" Jack folded his neck nearly in half, lifted a wing, and grinned down at her over his gleaming curve of shoulder. "I'm never going to let you forget it."

SEVEN

CHARLIE SLIPPED OUT FROM UNDER ALLIE'S ARM, froze as Graham shifted on her other side, and slid out of bed as he settled. Groping the floor beside the bed, she found a T-shirt and the pair of pajama pants she'd discarded the night before. Bare feet making no sound against the painted floor, clothes in one hand, she shuffled forward until her fingers touched familiar curtains, then she let herself out the French doors and into the apartment.

With early morning light pouring in through the tall windows on either side of the room, she could see well enough to cross toward the kitchen without either night-sight charms or needing to turn on a lamp. So she should've been able to see Jack sitting at the kitchen table, eating something from a mixing bowl that sounded like cold cereal, but with Jack, it was never wise to make assumptions. Should have been able to see him. Hadn't. Not until she was almost beside him and he blinked sleepily up at her. If he asked, she intended to say she'd been absorbed in plans to save the world. And that she'd meant to trip backward over the arm of the sofa, arms and legs flailing.

"You okay?"

"Fine." Rolling off the sofa onto her knees, she stood, pulled on the pajama pants and T-shirt and walked into the kitchen.

"It's just you kind of spazzed out and it looked like it might have hurt."

"I'm fine," she repeated, prying the lid off the coffee canister and spraying grounds all over the counter.

"So I can laugh." When she flipped him off, he snickered and waved his spoon at the mess. "I could clean that up for you."

"I don't . . ."

"During my last growth spurt, the one where I got taller than you . . ."

"Shut up."

". . . . I spilled stuff all over the place. I got good at cleaning up and coffee grounds go everywhere. Let me help."

"No, it's all right, I can . . ." Charlie glanced toward him as she spoke and caught the quick flicker of gold in his eyes. "What?"

"It was only an offer to help you clean up," he muttered. "Not to roll around naked with you until you smell like me instead of Allie and Graham."

She lifted her arm to her nose. "I don't . . ."

"Dragon."

"Right." Leaning against the counter, weight on one hip, Charlie yawned and ran both hands through the tangled mass of her hair. "Does it bother you?"

"A little."

"I'm not . . ."

"Did I ask you to? It's just . . ." There was suddenly a lot more scale and a lot less skin. ". . . I'm fighting instincts when you smell like them."

"I didn't know." And Charlie'd thought the whole misaligned attraction between them couldn't get any worse. Jack fighting instincts that might have even a remote chance of being dangerous to her babies would put Allie in full protection mode. The whole city would go into lockdown. "I'll go shower."

"Coffee first," he snorted, tossing his twisted spoon into the empty bowl, mostly skin again. "It's under control, and I worry about you drowning when you're less than caffeinated."

"Cute."

"Thanks."

Coffee sounded like a terrific idea.

"Does it affect the flavor?" she asked as a tiny whirlwind lifted the pile of spilled grounds back into the canister.

"Graham says it doesn't." The corners of his mouth twitched as though he wanted to smile, but wasn't sure he should. "Allie says it makes it harder to charm."

"That's not a bad thing."

"Yeah. That's what Graham says." The smile broke free and Charlie had to stop herself from taking a step back. Or forward. He didn't look seventeen when he smiled; there was too much dragon in the teeth and a hint of danger in the curve.

These were not feelings she could deal with before coffee, and she barely resisted dropping the fourth spoonful into her mouth after the first three went into the French press.

"Charlie?"

And now he sounded . . . young. Which he was.

"Yeah, Jack."

"You need to take me back four years so I can be trained."

Charlie spilled the coffee again. "What part of the family doesn't deal with the Fey did you miss?"

"This isn't dealing with the Fey, this is me keeping you and probably Katie alive."

The coffee was taking too damned long. "What?"

"Before the ritual . . ."

"The one the aunties want you and me to join." That ritual.

"Yeah, before that happens, you have to take me back in time. We'll go out to the badlands where there's room to maneuver and aim for the day my mother came through. I bet that made a mark."

"Jack . . ."

"Then we drive back to town and I use the imprint of the old gate at the Fort to drop into the UnderRealm. I mean we know I'm not in there, right? I'm in the park. And my uncles collectively got their asses kicked home, so it could be years before they even notice I'm with the Courts. And since we know they *haven't* shown up to screw things up here, they *won't* show up to screw things up here." He danced the second spill back into the canister and up into a second whirlwind; a dark roast tornado about a foot high. "I'll be back the day I left, trained. Able to control myself. Maybe able to stop the asteroid. You won't even have noticed that I was gone. And I'll be twenty-one. I know," he held up a hand before she could speak, "it's still nine years, but . . ."

"Jack! It's still thirteen years, I'll be thirty-four."

The whirlwind collapsed. "What?"

Sagging against the counter, Charlie rubbed both hands over her face. "If I take you four years into the past, I have to live those years. Avoiding myself. Waiting for the day we left."

"Why? Just go back through the Wood."

"Go forward?"

"Sure, why not? You're in the past, right? You know the future happened. Go back to where we came in when we went back."

She'd never thought about going forward, but from the past, she was going into the present, not the future and the present was obviously reachable because they were standing in it. "That might work."

"Thanks for sounding so surprised." He took the kettle from her hand and poured the hot water into the press. "I'm going to blame it on the lack of caffeine. You go back to where we came in, only at a different place so you don't end up with yourself, and I'll come back through a gate the next day."

Leaning forward, inhaling the coffee-scented steam, Charlie went over the idea and couldn't find a flaw. "Okay, smart guy, we can probably bullshit this past the aunties—safety, heritage, why no, I didn't notice anything different about Jack—but what about the Court's price?"

"Four years without you."

She straightened. "What?"

Jack slid the coffee canister to the back of the counter, eyes locked on his hands. "Four years exiled from the one who completes me. Four years longing. Four years alone. And no happily ever after once we're back together because you'll still be nine years older than me. They'll eat that kind of thing up with a spoon. A Dragon Prince caught in the one rule the Gales won't break."

"You'll pay them to teach you to be a sorcerer with emotional pain?" It was hard to hear her own voice over the roaring in her ears.

He shrugged. "That's the thing about the Courts; basically, they're dicks."

"No."

"They really are."

"No, you aren't giving them . . . that."

"You don't get to make that decision." He turned to look at her then and, if not for the slide of scales up and down his arms, he'd have looked unaffected by what they were discussing. "That's the price to keep the world from ending."

"Jack . . ."

"We can't let the world end for everyone who isn't family without doing everything we can to stop it. Right?"

Charlie palmed the top of the press and forced it down. It hadn't been

four minutes. She didn't care. At this point, she was willing to Walk back
eight minutes, beat herself out of the bedroom, and make the coffee sooner.
That Jack would offer so much of himself for those outside the family, well,
the *outside the family* was part of the freedom of being Wild, but his total lack
of awareness of how astounding it was, of how astounding he was, that was
all Jack. The Gale motto was family first. Actually, it was *Omnes Sumus nos
Postulo*, "We are all We Need"; Auntie Ruby had embroidered it on a pillow,
but family first was close enough.

"Charlie?"

She took a deep breath and met his eyes, letting everything she felt show
in hers. "I have to think about it."

"You've got nine days."

And that, that didn't sound young at all. Gods, he was complicated. And
amazing. "Oh, yay. Another deadline. You know, if I didn't already like you too
much . . ."

His smile twisted as he cut her off. "Good thing you do. If it was me feeling stuff all alone, well, plain old unrequited liking too much wouldn't be
twisty enough for the Courts. But being kept from someone who completes
me . . ."

"Completes you?"

"Totally."

"Fuck, Jack." Not the best choice of profanity, she realized.

The cloud of smoke came a heartbeat behind the sound of the apartment
door opening. Charlie tried not to think of squids and ink. It was possible she
watched a little too much Discovery Channel.

"Honestly, Jack . . ." Auntie Gwen's indignation led the way. ". . . if
I've told you once, I've told you a hundred times. You can't smoke around
the babies."

Barely able to see Jack, Charlie stepped back, a hundred thousand performances keeping her hands from shaking as she poured her coffee.

"But they're in their room." The smoke moved toward the windows.
"With the door closed."

"That's them. We're talking about you."

"Sorry."

Auntie Gwen closed the window as the smoke dispersed, invisible in the
steady rain. "Don't be sorry, stop doing it. Is that coffee?"

"It is." Charlie took a long swallow, then asked, "Would you like some?" She was a little impressed by how normal she sounded.

"No, I was inquiring for interest's sake. Of course I'd like some."

Jack passed over a *World's Greatest Auntie* mug, and Charlie resisted the urge to hum a charm in as she filled it.

"Are Alysha and Graham still in bed?" Mug in one hand, Auntie Gwen checked her watch. "It's almost nine and we need to start finding houses for sale around the park. If enough of the family is moving west, we'll need charms in place early to keep the situation under control and out of the papers."

"I thought Auntie Jane wanted us to wait until after the ritual?"

"The ritual . . ." Aunt Gwen frowned at the rain on the window for a moment. "While I agree that we need to make every attempt to ensure the family's survival, I have no idea what Jane thinks the ritual will do."

"Beyond what the ritual always does?" Charlie asked flippantly.

The look Auntie Gwen shot her almost made her regret her tone. "Yes, Charlotte. Beyond what ritual always does. However, and regardless of what Jane chooses to believe, this is no longer a world where we can do as we like, removing inconveniences after the fact." The edge on her voice made it clear she'd neither forgiven nor forgotten Auntie Jane slapping her down and there would be consequences in due time. "If we want to move a significant portion of the family to Calgary for safety, we need to deal with the Calgary real estate market and that requires Alysha's input."

As Charlie understood it, the Calgary real estate market could give an extinction event a run for its money in the *holy fucking hell* stress department. Four aunties weren't nearly enough to control it. "I'll go wake Allie."

"And Graham. He has a useful outsider's perspective." Auntie Gwen took a swallow of coffee and blinked. "Did you make this, Jack?"

"No, Charlie did."

"Really? Because it tastes like the sort of coffee people who breathe fire would drink."

Halfway to the bedroom, Charlie turned and walked backward. "I like it strong, Auntie Gwen."

"There's a difference between strong and abusive, sweetie."

About to suggest she pour it back into the carafe if it was so terrible, Charlie's back bounced off a firm barrier. Strong hands grabbed her arms and steadied her.

"Gwen." Graham sounded more resigned than thrilled to find an auntie in his kitchen on a Monday morning.

"Graham." Auntie Gwen on the other hand sounded positively perky. And she was smiling. Charlie felt Graham shudder.

"Allie'll be right out." He moved Charlie away from his chest. "I'm going to go check on the boys. Jack . . ."

"More coffee. On it."

Graham moved away and Jack got the bigger coffeepot off the top of the refrigerator. Charlie watched Auntie Gwen drink coffee she didn't like, brows drawn in, both hands wrapped around the mug, dark eyes shadowed, and had a terrible feeling she had real estate listings in her future. As though an asteroid and the whole mess with Jack wasn't enough.

By noon they'd been contacted by three second circle couples and Auntie Mary had emailed the names of four more third circle boys and their lists.

"Fortunately, there's a fair bit of overlap on the lists," Allie noted, deftly removing one of Charlie's capos from Evan's mouth. "And the eleven still in school can transfer to programs here . . ." Evan squeaked as her hold tightened. "Although I guess it's not really worth it for twenty-two months. And after that we'll have other things to worry about, won't we?"

"Mama! Squish!"

"Sorry, darling."

The twins, Charlie noted, were not on the lists. The odds were high the twins were prepping for a trip to Australia, thrilled to be heading for a continent where most of the fauna and a good chunk of the flora could kill them.

"Cha Cha?" Small hands clutched at her jeans.

"What can I do for you, Edward?"

"Up!"

We can save him, Charlie thought as she lifted the toddler onto her lap. And Evan and all five of the brothers to be named later. In spite of Auntie Jane, they were working on that now. *We can save, if not all the family—because Uncle Arthur and the oldest of the aunties wouldn't be able to leave Ontario—most of the family.* An enclave here. An enclave somewhere else. Joined this time only by her ability to Walk the Wood. Hers and Auntie Catherine's if Auntie Catherine could be convinced to help. Charlie wasn't one hundred percent positive that Auntie Catherine would bother to come home.

"Want!"

"Too bad, kidlet." She set the sharpie far enough away he couldn't reach it, although he tried. Alive was better, she wasn't arguing with that, but what kind of world would Edward and his brothers grow up in? The Gales could slide back to a more primitive existence without much difficulty, back to the land was pretty close to a religious statement, but they'd be robbed of so much.

"No, I think we should concentrate on the north side." Allie slid her tablet across the table to Auntie Gwen. "Get everything on Macewan that actually touches the park."

"That'll attract too much attention, Alysha."

"We can keep a lid on it for twenty-two months. And then it won't matter."

How, Charlie wondered, could she look any of Allie's children in the eye if she hadn't done everything possible to ensure they could grow up playing the bagpipes on their phone?

"I have to go." Leaping to her feet with Edward on her lap, probably not the best idea, but she caught him before he hit the floor, swung him into the air, shrieking with laughter, and handed him to Auntie Gwen. "I have to . . ." So easy to lie. Screw it. ". . . talk to Jack."

"You're only making it harder on both of you, Charlotte."

A little exasperation, but that was standard for Auntie Gwen. The pity in her voice, that was new. Charlie stopped at the door, and turned around. "You told her we talked about it?"

Color high on her cheeks, Allie shook her head. "Charlie, she already knew."

"Not that we'd talked about it. Not that it was suddenly all right to talk to me about it. It's no one's business but mine and Jack's, and now it's open season, isn't it? Fucking wonderful."

"Fucking!" Edward shouted as she slammed the door.

Ron Sexsmith's "Doomed" played all the way down the stairs. Charlie let it run.

Joe glanced up from the invoice books as she came into the Emporium, raised one ginger brow, and pointed his pencil toward the far end of the store. Charlie opened her mouth, then snapped it closed again. If Auntie Gwen knew, Joe knew.

Jack held up a hand as she approached. ". . . twenty-seven, twenty-eight, twenty-nine. Joe! Twenty-nine!"

"Got it!"

"Skate guards," Jack told her before she could ask.

"For when hell freezes over?" Charlie reached past him and picked up a piece of hot-pink plastic, sized to fit a child's skate. "Donated to charity sale by Jack Frost? Jutunn sandals?"

"No, just skate guards."

"Really?"

"Sometimes you lose one but you can't buy one new, so you end up with an odd number. People bring the leftovers to us." Jack shrugged. "Other people buy singles from us."

Charlie tossed the pink guard back in the box. "That's a little anticlimactic."

"Yeah, well, junk retail." He frowned. "You okay?"

"Not so much, no." She took a deep breath and lowered her voice below eavesdropping range. "Tell Joe you're leaving. We're going to find out if the Courts can help."

"But Auntie Jane said . . ."

"That we don't deal with the Fey. First, Auntie Jane's line in the sand aside, we've always interpreted *don't deal with* pretty broadly. You're Fey. Joe's Fey. The Corbae, the Loireag, Boris . . . everyone who uses this store for a mail drop or buys potions is Fey. The family dealt with your uncles right up until we sent their scaly asses home. Okay, that was mostly Allie, but Allie's kind of definitively family, so the point stands. Second, we're Wild. We do what the family doesn't."

"And we pay the cost . . ."

"No." She cut him off again. "Not for this. We tell the Courts what's happening like we figure they already know and we use their own self-interest so, if they can, they save the world for themselves, not us."

Jack grinned. "That's almost twisty enough to be dragon thinking."

"Thank you." She assumed he meant it as a compliment.

And the grin faded. "But there's nothing here they want."

"Not entirely true." Charlie picked a keychain out of a basket on the shelf beside her and dangled the miniature ball from her finger.

"Basketball?"

"Basketball. They're nuts about it. No one knows why, but it's like an addiction. Last night, while we were waiting for the kids to settle, I overheard Melissa explaining to Dave why both the men's and women's teams at UA are topping the Prairie Division."

"The Courts?"

Charlie nodded. "A full-blood on each team. The full-bloods never play in televised games—as I understand it, it has something to do with soul stealing . . ." Although *understand* might be too strong a word since the explanation twisted commonly held folklore sideways then sat on it until it cried uncle. ". . . so that explains what they're doing in Canada. Four or even five years of university ball would mean nothing to them. Melissa says they've never been benched, they play every game. As I doubt they're hanging out in the library working on their classical myth and religion assignments when they're not playing, can you find them?"

"I didn't even know they were here. They don't *want* me to find them." His eyes flared gold. "I could flush them, but I don't think Allie'd appreciate the collateral damage. However . . ." He tapped his fingers against the edge of the metal shelf. Charlie heard claws. ". . . I bet the lesser Courts will know; it's in their own best interest." Jack snorted remembering at the last instant to turn his head. "Like mice knowing where the cat is. I take it we're not waiting for sunset?"

"Good call."

"The Saddledome Brownies are the closest and the easiest to find. Fly with me?"

"It's not going to happen, Jack."

He shrugged with less grace than usual, like he was holding himself back from the movement he wanted to make, and scales slid across his cheeks, there and gone so quickly it looked as though they were moving. "I'm not going to stop asking."

The keychain went back into the basket. Charlie stared into the jumble of sports fetishes because it was safer than looking at Jack. "There's plenty of greenery around the dome. I'll meet you there."

"I'll tell Joe I'm leaving."

*   *   *

On days the parking lots were full and crowds swarmed the entrances, the Saddledome buzzed with energy, the colors of its buttresses and trim reflected back in jerseys and pennants, hats and scarves. Lit up, the skyline of the city at night cupped in its curve, it was almost art. On a rainy afternoon in late October, Charlie had trouble seeing anything more than tons of concrete surrounded by asphalt. Although, in fairness, very few buildings were at their best by the dumpsters.

Tucked in close to the building where it was more-or-less dry, she heard Jack approach—the distinctive wet laundry in a high wind sound of dragon wings—but didn't see him until he landed beside her.

"We're not going to be here long," he pointed out as she raised a brow when he didn't change, the rain steaming slightly as it rolled down the curve of his neck. "And no one can see us from the road."

"And that's the form the Brownies respond best to," Charlie guessed.

Jack looked puzzled. "The form doesn't matter. I'm still me."

"I meant, you're more threatening in scales."

"Oh. Well, yeah. Except threatening a Brownie would be like threatening a . . ."

"Girl Guide?" Charlie offered, when he paused.

He thought about it for a moment. "Not really."

"Okay." Now she thought of it, the twins had been Guides. For two years in a row, they'd sold the most cookies in Ontario; then the aunties had noticed their sales pitch and put a stop to it. "So do they just show up now you're here?"

"No, I need to call."

It wasn't so much a call as a hum. Jack dipped his head low to the ground, tail stretched out for balance and when Charlie laid her fingertips against his neck—carefully, in case the heat hadn't completely dissipated—she could feel as much as hear the sound. When a slightly higher tone layered in, she realized the dumpsters were vibrating like big, rectangular, smelly tuning forks.

"Highness?"

She couldn't quite see the Brownie. There was an awareness of a shape around a meter high, but definition kept sliding by too quickly to grab. By. And back. And by again. Temples throbbing, Charlie decided to look at a crack in the pavement.

The Brownie sounded shocked to learn the Courts were hiding from the prince. "Shocked, I tell you," Charlie murmured as it continued to be amazed at such a level of disrespect. Of course, it knew where they were.

"Why would they even think to hide from us, Highness? We are no threat. When they are not playing, they often take their ease at the Silvan Diner. Open twenty-four seven, best grilled cheese in the city. My hantri works the grill. Try the sweet potato fries."

"Hantri?" Charlie asked as the Brownie went back inside.

"Part of a kin group." The dumpster bonged as Jack shrugged and hit it with a wing, the sound wave rolling away from the building like an invisible tsunami.

Charlie charmed it flat as she dug out her phone, spreading the vibrations out into inaudible. The Saddledome was never entirely empty, and the last thing she wanted to do right now was play "dragon-what-dragon" with maintenance or security. "Okay, here it is, Silvan Diner, 4627 Bowness Rd NW."

"Why do you need an address? I thought you went into the Wood and sang your way out."

"If I could do that, we wouldn't have needed the Brownie. The Courts have no song here. You flying or sharing my cab?"

"You could fly with me."

"Still no. If you're flying, leave now." When Gales needed cabs, cabs appeared.

The Silvan Diner was one half of a single-story brick building, the other half divided into a hairdressers and a Vietnamese sandwich shop. Too far from the university to be a student hangout, it still was close enough to be a plausible retreat for the basketball teams. Although Charlie doubted the Courts worried much about plausible.

She had the cabbie drop her off in front of the small white house that separated the diner from a four-story apartment building. Her umbrella barely had time to get wet before Jack stepped out of a flare of light in gray jeans and jacket. The roof shingles, Charlie guessed, although the white T-shirt and sneakers had probably been one of the pickets from an actual white picket fence—now a picket short.

"You'd better not come in." He made an impossible leap over the fence from the lawn onto the sidewalk. At midday on a crappy Monday the road was empty, so Charlie bit back her comment on the dangers of attracting attention. Nothing like an unnecessary warning to be careful to really emphasize an age difference. "They don't trust Gales and once they know who you are, they'll assume you're trying to geis them."

"How will they know what I can do?"

He rolled his eyes, Allie's expression borrowed. "Duh. The Courts keep tabs on anyone who could challenge them, and you're Charlie Gale."

That sounded like a compliment, so Charlie accepted it as one. "I don't geis."

"You can make people do what you say; it might as well be a geis. They won't talk to you."

"I don't want you going in alone." Given the price he'd already said he was willing to pay the Courts for training, she didn't want him suddenly facing an opportunity to pay for saving the world. Not without talking it over with her first. If it came to it, they'd split the bill.

"I'll go with him." Joe ducked as Charlie spun around, and scowled up at her umbrella. "You trying to put my eye out with that thing, then?"

"How did you know we were here?"

He shrugged. "Security system in the store. Those corn husk dolls are gossips and, well, the walls have ears. Heard all about your plan to piss off the aunties and see what the Courts can do."

"But how did you know we were *here?*" Charlie repeated. "Did you follow us to the Brownie?"

"Why would I have to do that, then?"

Charlie glanced over at Jack who shrugged, and back at Joe who shoved his hands into his jacket's pockets, and sighed. Were the aunties tracking her phone? Was Allie tracking her per . . . "Oh. Leprechaun. I'm an idiot. You know where the Courts are."

"Damned right I know where they are. They're not the sort you want to be running into by accident. I'd assumed you hadn't asked because you figured I wouldn't help, given Gwen and all. Never occurred to me you'd forgotten."

"Ignoring the fact that you haven't been back to the UnderRealm since your parents swapped you out for a mortal baby over eighty years ago, we think of you as family not Fey."

He thought about that for a moment, then nodded. "All right, I'm flattered."

Although that didn't mean Allie wouldn't be tracking them. "Who's watching the store?"

"We're closed Mondays; that's why me and the prince were taking a run at the inventory. I parked across the street." He tossed Charlie the keys. "You can wait in the car unless you prefer getting wet."

Charlie waited until a panel van passed and then peered across at Joe's ancient hatchback. "That thing's watertight?"

"Cute. Only not really."

"Joe, Auntie Gwen won't be happy about this."

He met her gaze evenly, ignoring the rain dripping off his eyebrows. "Well, the way I see it, she isn't happy about the world ending before George R.R. Martin finishes *Game of Thrones* either. I'll deal with Gwen."

She had to trust he could. "Jack, you know the Courts so I'm not going to tell you what to say, but . . ."

"Appeal to their self-interest. Make it seem like their idea. I've got it, Charlie." His grin showed teeth. "Dragons are all about twisting the situation in their favor."

"I thought they were all about twisting arms off?"

"And that."

"Can't think why the Courts don't like you," Joe muttered.

"I thought I'd be going in with you." Half of her wanted to declare *if I don't go in, you don't go in*, but the other half pointed out that twenty-one and a half months until the end of the world justified a little risk. And Jack was an adult, albeit a young one. And dragons were very hard to kill. "Joe . . ."

"I'll see that he comes out again."

Jack waited until Charlie was safely inside Joe's car before he started toward the diner. Four meters of sidewalk, six meters of parking lot—he changed the color of his sneakers with every step. Gold. Black. Gold. Red. Gold. Green. Gold . . .

"Nervous?"

He shrugged and changed his sneakers to black. Uncle Adam's color. He could use a little of his oldest uncle's certainty. After a moment, he added red laces. Considering where they were heading, he could use a little of Uncle Viktor's viciousness, too.

"It's okay to be nervous. You can't let them see it, though."

Jack turned and stared at Joe in disbelief. Usually, the Leprechaun got him better than anyone in the family except for Charlie, but that was a total miss. "Dude, seriously, I'm not nervous. I'm messing around."

"These aren't Hobgoblins and Brownies we're going to be talking to, Jack; these are members of the Court. Full-bloods. Minor nobility, sure, but as arrogant a bunch as you'll ever meet. They're armed and dangerous, and you'll never know as you face them if you should expect a blade in the eye or a spell to turn your bones to jelly."

"*You're* a full-blood." Here in the MidRealm, that had weight. Joe'd flipped the finger to the Courts when the mortal changeling had died and they'd Called him home and that took guts. And he treated Jack like he treated Cameron, somehow quieting the instincts that shouted both dragon and prince. That took strength.

"I am a Leprechaun." He dropped his voice, even though the parking lot was empty of anyone who might overhear. "The Courts tolerate us because of our way with gold, but they sure as shit don't respect us and, as I have no gold, they have no reason to tolerate me."

"You have Auntie Gwen."

"That's not . . ."

"You're kidding me, right?" Jack turned to walk backward so he could look Joe in the eye. "You voluntarily lie down every night with a Gale auntie. Naked. And you get up again every morning. These guys aren't about unearthly tresses, never left their Grove, all thee and thous and sipping dew out of freaking bluebells. These guys have been living here, in the MidRealm, with the Gales. In the same city as the Gales. If they don't respect you, they've got their heads so far up their ethereal asses they've cut off all circulation to their brains."

The pointed tips of Joe's ears, barely visible through ginger hair, darkened. "Thank you."

"Not a problem." Jack had no idea what he'd said to make Joe blush, but since he had no idea why he sometimes blushed while looking at Charlie, he wasn't going to give Joe a hard time about it. "Besides," he added as they reached the diner, "At full size, I'm at least four times as big as a city bus and I breathe fire and, for all they know, given my parentage, *I* could throw a spell that would turn their bones to jelly."

"Can you?"

"Not a chance. And these guys will have been trained so they know what they're doing, and they can probably block anything I can throw by accident." He spread his hands. "But they don't know that." The heavy condensation on the inside of the diner window meant they'd be going in blind. Jack drew in a deep breath and let it out slowly. "I just, you know, don't want to let Cha . . . the family down."

Joe stared at him for a long moment. Then he smiled, lines folding around the freckles. "All right, then."

"All right what?"

"Let's be going in."

"Joe!" But Joe had pulled the door open and stepped inside. Unless he wanted to be shown up by a Leprechaun, all Jack could do was follow.

The Silvan Diner had a counter with eight stools along the left wall. The countertop held a glass case with three pies, four groupings of ketchup and napkins and salt and pepper, and the elbows of a teenage girl in a pink-striped shirt who didn't look up from her magazine as they came in. Jack's nose pinged her as Court descended, but without enough blood to need a glamour. A rectangular opening at the end of the counter led to the kitchen. Pitted blue-and-gray tiles covered the diner's floor, and four big lights dimmed by grease and dust hung from the ceiling. The two full-blood members of the Court overwhelmed a six-person booth by the window, the third full-blood sitting with them made a nonevent by their presence. Nine humans, five females and four males, filled two of the other booths along the right wall.

The diner smelled equally of food and Fey. Humans were Not Food; it was one of the first lessons Jack had learned after arriving in the MidRealm. Fey, on the other hand . . . His stomach growled, and he wished he'd eaten a second pie before leaving the house.

The full-blood at the Court's table looked up as the door closed, started, then slouched down in the seat as though that had been the intent all along— gaze skimming dismissively over Joe and locking on Jack. The Court appeared unaware that a dragon and a Leprechaun had walked into their territory although they weren't fooling anyone. One by one, even the humans fell silent and turned to stare, their expressions a mix of suspicion, aggression, and challenge—a two-legged hunting pack, Jack realized, to make up for the four-legged pack left back in the UnderRealm.

Head up, hands shoved in his jacket pockets, eyes half lidded in a way he hoped made him look dangerous and not sleepy, Jack walked toward the Court, Joe back of his left shoulder. When he stopped, about a meter and a half out, he swept a bored gaze around the booth. It was the expression Allie used when Auntie Carmen got enthusiastic about plot development on *Coronation Street*—but they didn't need to know that.

Under the University of Calgary jackets, the Court wore glamours, a shimmer of power wrapped head to toe. Their true forms had angles too sharp, eyes too large, hair too sleek. The common belief was that they had the same opinion of casual cruelty as cats. The Dragon Lords believed cats were kinder.

The third person in the booth was a Glashtin in two-legged form; under the glamour, not even as Human as the Court. Given the more common four-legged form, the leather jacket, jeans, and cowboy hat were a little weird. Jack assumed there were cowboy boots under the table, had a sudden vision of the Glashtin riding, and barely stopped a snicker.

"It ain't polite to stare, Wyrm." The Glashtin's teeth were flat and large.

Jack's were larger and sharper. He wondered if Glashtin tasted like horse.

"Yeah, yeah, you're tough. Move on, kid, no one wants to talk to you today."

Joe's foot came down on Jack's before Jack could reply. "His Highness requires a few moments of the Court's time."

A narrow-eyed gaze flicked between them. "The Court's busy, short stuff."

One of the Court ate a sweet potato fry.

"You want these guys out of here, El?" Two of the young men in the next booth stood and moved to stand behind Jack. Jack wasn't small, dragon heritage aside, none of the Gales were short, but the Court's hounds were both taller and broader. A massive hand closed on Jack's shoulder and tightened to the threat of pain. It wasn't much of a threat, but they couldn't know that.

With the scent of the Court hanging heavy over the scent of fries and grilled cheese, his change was instinctive. The Court couldn't be trusted. The Court treated weakness like opportunity. He heard a scream, smelled burning pork, and held back his strike at the last moment, his claws shredding the air in front of cloth and flesh. As his dragon form dissolved in fire, the humans stampeded out of the diner, a faint scent of urine lingering behind. The teenaged girl peered over the edge of the counter, more intrigued than afraid.

"You're kidding me." The Glashtin's heavy brows drew in to touch over his nose, attitude negated by the white-knuckled grip on the edge of the table and the faint sheen of sweat covering all exposed skin. "You did that in here?"

Jack shrugged to settle his shape and checked to make sure he'd remembered to replace all his clothing. "He shouldn't have grabbed me."

"You must be a fucking joy when it's standing room on the C. Some poor working dick loses his balance and Godzilla takes transit."

"He shouldn't have grabbed me," Jack repeated, hoping this time he sounded more defiant than defensive. He'd half expected the mass exodus to bring Charlie into the diner singing the "Ride of the Valkyries," but she clearly trusted him to get this done. "Not when you three . . ." A nod toward the only booth still occupied. ". . . smell so much like food."

"Fortunately, given who those particular humans interact with day to day, they've been spelled to ignore what they don't understand." Joe sounded calm. He didn't smell calm, but the Glashtin's nose was crap, so hopefully Jack was the only one getting the whiff of burning peat that told him Joe was grasping at straws. "By now I'm sure they've forgotten why they left so hurriedly and believe they have other things to do."

If Joe was wrong, the police were on their way, and Allie was going to kill him.

"And the burned hand?"

"We're in a restaurant." Joe shrugged. "He stupidly leaned on the grill."

"You sure that's how it'll go, Lucky Charms?"

"I am."

"Yeah, well, you may have been sure; the Wyrm didn't know." The Glashtin sounded sulky.

"Really? Have you forgotten his father's lineage? Would His Highness have changed otherwise?"

Since Jack had changed without thought for his Human audience, he was more than a little impressed by Joe's ability to bullshit. And if he hadn't changed, the Court wouldn't have dismissed their hounds. They'd have sat there, looking smug, enjoying themselves as Jack tried to talk around a

Human audience, probably taking bets on when he'd lose control. Better he lost control up front, making it clear to the Courts he wasn't to be manipulated. Given that Joe seemed to be right about the spells they'd wrapped their hounds in, no harm no foul. Probably. Unless the Courts could twist the situation to their advantage because that's what the Courts did.

"His Highness wants to discuss a situation the Court will be required to acknowledge given their presence in the MidRealm." Joe kept his voice respectful without being deferential. That came from talking to the aunties; give them an inch and they suddenly had seven million strawberries that needed stemming.

"Mutually beneficial, eh? Doubt that."

"His Highness . . ."

"Drop it, Lucky Charms. We don't recognize the Wyrm's title."

Jack heard Joe draw in a breath and held out a hand to stop a new flow of words. The Glashtin's contribution wasn't about protocol and the Court—singly, sequentially, collectively—didn't need their egos further stroked. Their belief in their innate superiority got up his nose and while he realized he'd have to deal with their more-Fey-than-thou attitude if he ended up doing the whole school house elf thing, he didn't have to deal with it now. Besides, he was still steaming about being mauled by one of their hounds, and as that bridge had already been burned . . .

A moment later, after the flames defining the change had cleared, he curved his neck until he could look the Glashtin in the eye. "Do you recognize this, then? Was I too small for you to get a good enough look the last time?"

Credit where credit was due, even though he stank of fear, the Glashtin had lost none of his attitude. "Listen, punk, you can't threaten . . ."

"MidRealm," Jack snapped, "not UnderRealm. There's never been a truce declared here." The Court might not recognize the dragons' sovereignty, but they acknowledged the threat and had negotiated terms with it.

"This is not your world, Wyrm."

"Wrong. This is *also* my world, and the powers here don't care what happens to you."

The Glashtin stood, nose a centimeter from Jack's muzzle. "The old ladies don't scare me."

"Then you're a fool." A dark, long-fingered hand, still holding a sweet potato fry, waved dismissal. "Down, Regan. And you . . . Jack, is it? . . . try to take up a little less space. Our Brownie's likely having kittens in the kitchen."

"Better not be real kittens," the Glashtin muttered as Jack collapsed in on himself, remaking his clothes from the stack of *City Light News* by the cash register. "We just found homes for the last lot."

"Alice!" The sweet potato fry beckoned.

The girl at the counter, completely unfazed by a dragon in the diner, gave a Jack a look so speculative his ears burned as she wandered over, pulling her order pad from her apron pocket.

"Pie all around, sweet Alice." After four years with the Gales, Jack recognized the smile directed at him as distinctly female. Until that point, given the shared features under the glamours and well aware that the gender of the glamours themselves meant nothing, he hadn't been able to tell. "I imagine Jack and his companion would enjoy a piece of pie made with nothing more dangerous than fat and sugar. Coconut cream for him and me, and lemon for my brother and his companion. Regan . . ." A graceful nod toward the Glashtin. ". . . will have apple. And to drink . . . ?"

Distracted by the tattoo of pale green leaves barely visible over Alice's collar, it took Jack a moment to realize the question had been directed at him. "Uh . . . coffee. Please." The please had been installed by Allie, not his uncles and it was directed at Alice's function not her bloodline.

"Stunt your growth," Regan growled.

Jack let a few scales rise over his cheekbones.

"Alice, take care of Regan and His Highness' companion at the counter . . ."

Joe reappeared.

". . . and try to keep them from killing each other."

Regan glanced over at the two Court and sighed, lips vibrating in a distinctly horselike manner. "You can't trust a Wyrm."

"We aren't going to," the male pointed out, taking a fry from the female's plate.

"You sure?"

"I'm sure we aren't going to trust him, yes."

Eyes narrowed, Regan slid from the booth. "If you need me, you know where I am."

The Glashtin slammed a shoulder into Jack's on the way to the counter.

Jack brought his tail back long enough to flick the Stetson off, exposing a set of horse ears covered in dark fur.

"Highness . . ."

When he turned toward the Leprechaun, Joe looked worried. Which would have bothered Jack more had worried not been Joe's default expression and he not been 99 percent . . . 75 percent certain he was playing to their audience.

". . . if I may remind you, we are here only to talk."

"Don't eat anyone. Got it." Jack tried to make it clear he'd also answered the advice Joe hadn't voiced—*"Don't start anything."*—but he didn't have Charlie's way with words.

Although he didn't look much happier, Joe nodded and joined Regan at the counter, a careful three seats apart, Jack noticed—not so far he seemed afraid, not so close he seemed stupid.

"Sit." The two of them tucked into the back corners, the female gestured to a place at the far end of the bench across from where Regan had been sitting.

Jack checked it out, then dropped into the space Regan had vacated instead, the gross feel of the warmed vinyl preferable to the appearance of obedience. "So . . ." He pushed Regan's empty plate away with the side of his forearm, jacket between him and whatever the Glashtin may have left behind. ". . . do you two have names or do I keep thinking of you as the male and the female?"

"Arwen." She nodded across the table. "Elessar."

"Seriously?" Allie'd made him read the books before he could watch the movies. He'd liked the movies better. He'd only just learned to read English and those books were long. Also, the first one, the easier one, had no idea about dragons. He did like the poetry, though, and the genealogical charts. "You had every name in the entire world to choose from and that's what you went with?"

"It amuses us, and we tell those who ask that our progenitors were fans."

"Progenitors?" It seemed they'd brought the stick that culturally went up their collective asses all the way from the UnderRealm. "If the names weren't enough, *that's* got to have most of the student body all up in your face."

Elessar shrugged. "Not once they've seen our long shot. After the first couple of games, they cry our names from the bleachers and disrespect is summarily dealt with."

"By others," Arwen added. "Now that the posturing is over . . ." she

sighed as though the mere thought of posturing wearied her beyond belief.
". . . let us agree that you're not going to eat us, and we aren't going to stop
your heart in your chest."

"We aren't?" Elessar asked.

"Probably not." Her eyes glittered under the glamour when she turned
to face Jack. Glittered like shards of glass, he noted, with edges that could
slice through flesh and bone. "Which brings us to the question: what could
the Dragon Prince possibly want to discuss with us? Regan, though crude,
spoke truly; the Courts do not acknowledge your title. Nor, here in the Mid-
Realm, have we interfered with the Gales. Not with the family itself or with
those they take under their protection."

"There was that young man who approached you after the game," Elessar
reminded her.

Arwen waved it off, the fluorescent lights dancing pale green highlights
across the back of her hand. "Please, the Gales would approve of my reaction
were they to learn of it. Have they learned of it?" she asked Jack, turning
toward him so suddenly he barely stopped himself from starting. "We re-
trieved and destroyed all the pieces."

"They haven't . . ." Jack began, then, as Alice set pie and coffee down on
the table, shut up so he could immediately stuff a forkful into his mouth.
Brownie-made came close to being as good as Gale pie and, as only Allie's
mother made coconut cream, it *was* nice to eat pie that didn't come with
instructions on how to take care of the twins as well as a reminder about
clean underwear he still didn't entirely understand. Brownies, on the other
hand, did not make Girl Guide cookies. His first year in the MidRealm, he'd
found that very disappointing.

With the plate cleaned, he sat back and saw Elessar had ignored his pie
completely in favor of dumping half a dozen packets of sugar into his coffee,
while Arwen had only licked a little of the whipped cream off her finger with
a pointed tongue. "You're very young," she said, speculatively.

So were they, and, for immortals, a couple of hundred years wasn't that
much older than seventeen. Which only emphasized how stupid it was to be
hung up on thirteen years. Of course here he was a dragon and with the
Gales he was a Gale no matter how uncomfortably his skin fit lately. Gale
before Wild? Definitely Gale before dragon. Thirteen years given more
weight than immortality.

"I've racked my brain," Arwen continued, jerking Jack's thoughts out of the familiar spiral that would eventually lead to seven years and from there to Charlie, "but I can't imagine what we might have to discuss. Unless you plan to betray your blood."

The flame was involuntary. It crisped Elessar's meringue.

"My point exactly." Arwen smiled.

Jack took a swallow of coffee, set the heavy porcelain mug down, and smiled back at her. He'd been all dragon in their face so they'd expect twisty. He hit them with direct. "In just over twenty-one months an asteroid is going to hit the planet. This planet. Almost everyone dies."

Elessar rolled his eyes. Given the size of the eyes under the glamour, Jack had to admit the effect was impressive. "We've seen the new light in the night sky, a careless diamond against the black."

"It's as close now as it will ever come and already beginning to curve away." Arwen licked more whipped cream off her finger. "You've been misled."

Was it weird that they knew about the masking asteroid? Probably not if it changed the patterns of the stars. Jack spread his scowl over both of them. "Our Seer has seen it."

"Catherine Gale?" Elessar snorted. "She's fucking with you."

He turned to stare. "Okay, one, way to go native with the profanity, so what's up with the whole progenitor thing? Two, not this time. Charlie's looked into it."

"Charlotte Gale? The Bard? While we'd be more likely to believe her than the Seer," Arwen pointed out, "the rock will pass. You've been misinformed."

She sounded so smug and superior that two lines of smoke curled up from Jack's nose. "The rock you can see, the careless diamond you lot are writing overwrought poetry about, yeah, that'll pass, but it's masking a rock behind it. Which won't pass. Impact in less than two years." He spread his hands and let Dan have the last word. "Bam. Bam. Bam."

"And no one knows about this but your Seer and your Bard?" Arwen snorted and somehow made it sound elegant. "Go back to your Gales, little prince, and tell them that the Courts won't play whatever game it is they're playing."

"Go back to the Dragon Lords," Elessar added, stirring one last packet of sugar into his coffee. "Their games are more honest."

"And vicious." Arwen grinned. "I rode your Uncle Ryan once."

After four years with the Gales, Jack didn't assume he knew which form. He took another swallow of coffee. "NASA knows. The American government knows. The international scientific community knows. The only people who don't know are your basic garden variety humans because they're entirely useless. Oh . . ." He waved his fork. ". . . and apparently you lot don't know either."

"Our Seers have not Seen disaster."

"Why would they? Your Seers look into the future of the UnderRealm." Jack emptied his fork and spread his hands. "Hello. The asteroid isn't going to hit the UnderRealm. It's going to hit here. Not here, the diner. Here, the MidRealm. Where you are."

The look they exchanged held conversations.

"If this is true," Elessar said at last. "Why would you tell us?"

"If it was up to me, I wouldn't, but the family wants to know if you're planning to try and stop the impact or if you're going to cut and run." Not a lie. He and Charlie and Joe were family. Filled fork halfway to his mouth, he frowned and added, "Obviously, you two won't be personally stopping anything."

"What makes you think we're incapable of stopping it?" Arwen demanded.

"You don't even believe in it," Jack pointed out.

"Belief is not a required component of ability." Elessar took a swallow of coffee hummingbirds would have found too sweet and looked up to find both Jack and his sister staring at him. "What?"

Arwen shook her head. "What my brother meant to say was that twenty-two months would give us plenty of time to leave even if it were necessary to build a new gate from the ether where Nothing hides. But it isn't necessary because there's one at . . ." She jerked and snarled, "Did you kick me?"

Elessar showed teeth. "You were about to gift the little prince with the burden of knowledge."

"My mistake." The words were almost lost under her hiss.

"Do you guys honestly think Allie doesn't know about a gate inside the city limits?" Jack sighed. "About *every* gate within the city limits?"

"It matters more, as my brother reminds me, that we are not the ones who have informed her of it." Arwen's fingernails peeled up fine lines of plastic from the tabletop. "And, as I was saying, just under two years gives us time to finish four, perhaps five seasons of the glorious game before we move leisurely home. The Gales' very nature ensures they'll be staying here." Her smile became pure malice. "If you want the rock to stop falling, you stop it."

"All we have to do is survive it," Jack shrugged, hoping the movement looked more natural than it felt. "When the dust settles, there will still be Gales. The family can save itself."

"So you want us to save the rest of world, little Wyrm?"

"No. We want to know if you're going to." He nodded toward the crests on their jackets. "Me, I kind of thought you might want a chance to save basketball. We're not going to do it. We're still arguing about saving hockey."

Elessar and Arwen locked gazes for a moment, then Elessar dumped another three packages of sugar into his coffee and said, "There's that."

"We will discuss this information among ourselves." Arwen inclined her head in what was clearly a dismissal.

"Good for you. Then let me know what you decide to do, so I can take it to the aunties and make sure there's no misunderstandings." And *she* did not dismiss *him*. Who was the prince here anyway? "Are you going to eat that?" He nodded toward her nearly untouched pie.

She pushed it to him.

"Thanks."

"It's poisoned."

Jack shrugged. "Dragon." If they were that easy to kill, he'd have fewer uncles.

They watched him eat, watched him stand, watched as Joe fell into step beside him and the two of them left the diner. It wasn't until they were across the road and nearly to Joe's car that Jack finally felt the weight of their combined gazes drop off.

"You might want a chance to save basketball?" Joe asked.

Jack opened his mouth, belched, and melted a no parking sign.

EIGHT

"**H**OW LONG DO WE WAIT?"

Charlie shifted on the chaise and lifted her face toward the sun, barely visible behind a scud of clouds. The apartment had been empty when they got back so there was no need to hide out on the roof, but given how often Jack had switched to scales lately, she figured he'd be more comfortable outside. Because it was all about Jack and not at all about how she'd started to feel trapped within the well-charmed walls. She needed to see what was coming.

They'd barely stayed inside long enough to fill bowls with sesame ginger chicken, kept warm in Allie's big crockpot, and slide biscuits into their pockets.

At least it had stopped raining.

"Charlie?"

"If they don't get back to us in the next twenty-one and a half months, I suggest we say fuck 'em."

"Not helpful. Nor funny," he added.

If the Courts couldn't help—no, if the Courts actually admitted they couldn't help, which wasn't the same thing, Charlie realized—then there was no reason for Jack to slip into the past and spend four miserable years learning sorcery. They were one step closer to not being able to stop the world from ending, but, bottom line, the world ending should be misery enough. She didn't need to look at Jack and see four unnecessary years of pain. "Ow." Rubbing her arm where he'd poked her, she turned to see him sitting on the edge of the second chaise, feet on the deck beside the empty bowls, staring down at her, expression entirely unrepentant. "What?"

Jack shrugged. "You were wearing your *I was forced to listen to Justin Bieber* face. What are you thinking about?"

"The Courts." How convenient, not a lie.

"And how if they can't help, then there's no reason for me to go learn from them."

Not a question. So Charlie asked one, "How did you get that out of a *I was forced to listen to Justin Bieber* face?"

He didn't return her smile. "If they can't, or won't stop the asteroid, it doesn't mean that I wouldn't be able to if I was trained. I'm unique, remember. Gale. Dragon Prince. Sorcerer. Wild Power. One of a kind. All bets are off."

"I'd never bet against you." The words slipped out before she could stop them.

"But you don't want me to go." Before Charlie could say anything—and since she couldn't deny it, she had no idea of what to say—he added, "Even though you go away all the time."

Unfortunately, there wasn't even a hint of sulky teenager in his voice she could respond to and use to avoid the actual issue. "I've never gone away for four years."

"It won't be four years to you."

She couldn't do this lying down. Shoulders raised against the chill that crept in the moment she moved her body away from the charms on the chaise, she sat up, tucked her knees to the right of his, and said, "Jack, if you came back before you left, I'd still know that you'd been gone for four years. Ignoring the top forty emo way I'd feel every moment of every year here . . ." She touched her chest. ". . . while it was happening and I'd see them in every way they'd changed you. Not that you were four years older," she added hurriedly before he could speak, "but the price you paid. I hate the thought of you suffering for any reason. Even to save the world."

"Yeah." He shrugged. "But it's my decision."

The urge to yell, *"You're seventeen!"* was intense. Charlie sat on it. "I know. And if it comes to it, if it's our last shot to save the world, I'll take you back." His leg jumped under her hand. His pulse matched hers. "But if it turns out that the Courts can't stop the asteroid, what exactly can they teach you besides a totally useless three point layup?"

He stared at her hand for a moment, then met her gaze, his eyes gold. "They can teach me how to be a sorcerer, and I can figure the details out myself. My father was more powerful than any of them."

The first few notes of what Charlie thought might be Leonard Cohen's "To a Teacher" started up, but she shut it down before she could be certain. "How do you figure that?"

"He slept with my mother and survived." And the subtext said, *Duh.*

"Valid point." Forcing herself to break the contact, she lifted her hand off his knee, and leaned back. "Although, you don't know that the entire Court is unable to match your father's success . . ." If Jack was going to split hairs, she'd split a few back at him. ". . . only that none of them have tried."

"And that proves they're not all hair and attitude. My mother is very beautiful and very powerful and very dangerous and she'd eat any member of the Court who tried to approach her. They'd never discover if they were powerful enough to survive actual sex."

What counted as inactual sex? Charlie wondered. "She didn't eat your father."

"Gales," he said, his tone suggesting Charlie was being deliberately dim, "are charming."

"True."

"And they have a reputation to back up the charm."

"We."

"What?"

Charlie caught his gaze and held it. "*We* have a reputation to back up the charm."

He snorted. "Your phone is ringing."

It took her a moment to realize that the snort and the statement were unconnected. "Probably Allie," she muttered digging it out of her pocket, "figuring she'd given me enough space. Or Auntie Gwen having spoken to Joe or . . ."

"I want to see my grandchildren."

"Auntie Mary?"

"Did you hear what I said, Charlotte?"

"I did. Don't you think that's a bit risky, considering there's barely a week before ritual?" With David anchoring first circle, it would be safest for all concerned if Auntie Mary stayed half a continent away from her only son until there was a lot less horn in the mix.

"Don't talk to me about risk, Charlotte. If the world's going to end . . ."

"I guarantee it's not going to end before ritual."

"And do you guarantee that I'll be able to travel after ritual? After what Jane has planned for *this* ritual?"

Charlie spent a moment wondering what Auntie Jane had planned, then decided she didn't want to know.

"Actually . . ." Auntie Mary sounded distinctly triumphant. ". . . can you guarantee *you'll* be able to travel after ritual?"

Really, really didn't want to know.

Once in the Wood, it wasn't hard for Charlie to tease Auntie Mary's song out of the aunties' chorus; it still held much of the old familiar melody and a measure or two that reminded her of Allie. Once, there'd been measures that reminded her of David, but not anymore. Any tie David still had to his mother would not be maternal.

Charlie was a little surprised to step out of the Wood into the old orchard and see Auntie Mary beckoning to her from the porch. She'd expected a quick turnaround before Auntie Jane had a chance to point out, at length, what a bad idea this was.

"Auntie Ruby's asking for you. I told her I was going," she added as Charlie reached the house, "in case she had a message to pass on to Allie or the boys."

"And she asked for me?"

"It was the most coherent she's been for about five days."

Auntie Ruby's bedroom was on the first floor, in one of the earliest additions to the old farmhouse. The walls were a yellow so bright even October couldn't dim them, rag rugs covered most of the exposed linoleum floor, and an ancient quilt did what it could to hide the entirely practical hospital bed. She had her own small bathroom and a low wide window that looked over the east flowerbeds where the asters remained untouched by frost and provided drifts of color shading from white to deep purple. When Auntie Ruby finally died, another elderly auntie would inherit both the space and the care that came with it.

Auntie Meredith and a plump tabby both looked up when Charlie entered surrounded by a cloud of allspice and cinnamon drifting in from the kitchen, but only Auntie Meredith stood. Knitting gathered up into a messy bundle, she leaned close as she passed and said softly, "See if you can convince Ruby to move on. There's a lot of work to do before impact."

"You're very calm about it."

"Don't be ridiculous, Charlotte, death is a part of all things."

"I meant about the impact."

Auntie Meredith patted her arm. "My observation stands. And I'm so sorry to hear about you and Jack. So good that there's plenty going on to distract you."

She was gone, trailing a double line of pale blue yarn, before Charlie could respond.

"That's why I didn't want them to know," she muttered at the cat. "The world's ending, and it's still going to be, 'Oh, poor Charlie.'"

The cat yawned.

Moving to Auntie Ruby's side, Charlie realized she had no idea if the skin that had collapsed around the old woman's prominent bones looked like actual parchment, but she'd seen enough cookies baked to recognize *parchment paper* just out of the oven—brittle, fragile, and stained by use. She couldn't hear a heartbeat, only a soft flutter, and each breath sounded like the last breath.

Until one of them sounded like her name.

"I'm here, Auntie Ruby."

Auntie Ruby's eyes had sunk deep. It seemed as if half the lashes were missing from the edges of pinkish purple lids, and the whites were a sort of yellow/gray. For all that, they were surprisingly aware.

"Thing left . . . to do."

"What thing, Auntie Ruby?" All things considered, Charlie wasn't really surprised when the dying woman found the strength to sneer. "Okay, none of my business. What can I do?"

"Delay . . ."

"Dying? You want me to delay your death? I'd be happy to, if only to annoy Auntie Meredith, but I don't know how. Death delaying isn't exactly a Wild Power. Death defying, yes. Delaying, not so much."

It wasn't exactly an eye roll, but it was close enough and Charlie had years of experience in eye roll interpretation.

"You're saying I do know how? I just need to figure out what I know." Telling her not to die, in a Bardic sort of way, would not end well. Although, the odds were high that zombie aunties would ensure the world welcomed an extinction event, so . . . lemons to lemonade.

"Delay . . ."

"Right. Don't stop, delay." She settled on the edge of the bed and decided it might be safer not to stroke the cat. Auntie Ruby had been old for as long as Charlie could remember—old and crazy and good for embarrassing stories about other members of the family if caught on her own. She'd cackled and not cared who heard her and, if she got her hands on a broom, she was all about reliving her glory days. It was hard to see the woman in the bed as the Auntie Ruby of memory. She'd faded until . . . "Holy crap, your fingers are cold!" The contrast between her wrist and the single finger pressed against it nearly burned.

"Hum . . ."

"I'm humming? Sorry. I do that when I think. The whole don't stop thing made me think of Fleetwood Mac and don't stop thinking about tomorrow and yesterday's gone and . . ."

Auntie Ruby found strength enough to raise the remains of both eyebrows up a centimeter.

". . . and yesterday isn't gone, is it? Not yet. It's all right here." Charlie laid her hand gently on Auntie Ruby's arm, drew in a breath of air so acidic it caught in the back of her throat, and Sang. *Remember the time you painted Surrender Dorothy on the water tower? Remember how Auntie Jane always makes the tea too strong? Remember moving with Uncle Edward in ritual? Remember sisters and nieces and cousins. Remember the sweet/tart taste of cherry pie. Remember. Remember. Remember. This isn't who you were, this is who you are.*

Auntie Jane was waiting outside the door.

"It wasn't my idea. Auntie Ruby asked me to delay her death." Given Auntie Jane's expression, it seemed smart to get the melody down fast. "All I did was redefine her life."

"All you did? *All?*"

Objectively, given that in under twenty-two months an enormous asteroid was going to slam the planet to ratshit, Auntie Jane shouldn't have been all that scary. Realistically, Charlie'd never heard of anyone able to be objective about the aunties.

"Yesterday," Auntie Jane continued, "she asked me to remind Raymond to stop at the cheese factory, and yet I didn't hold a séance to pass that on. She's dying, Charlotte. Her mind spends more time on the other side than it does here and she doesn't know what she's asking."

Charlie considered the need she'd seen in Auntie Ruby's eyes. "This time, I think she did."

"You think? You sing!"

"Not mutually exclusive, Auntie Jane." She stepped sideways, opening up a line of escape through the dining room and into the kitchen, but, for the moment, didn't take it. "Maybe Auntie Ruby wants to cross over with her cousins, a part of the final chorus." Even if they could branch the family again, Auntie Jane would be among those staying in Darsden East, tied too tightly to the place to leave. Every word Auntie Jane spoke resonated with that knowledge and not even Auntie Jane could be entirely unaffected by a countdown to death. Accept it, yes. Remain unaffected, no. The undertones were remarkably similar to Gary's. With a little less bouzouki.

"Maybe," Charlie added, "she wants to be a pain in the ass, one last time."

"That," Auntie Jane snorted, "I believe. Well, come on, then. Mary's waiting in the kitchen. We're canning some pumpkin before we start another set of pies." She turned expectantly, so Charlie fell into step beside her. "Your mother's garden had some lovely pie pumpkins this year. Stop by and see her when you bring Mary back. I'm trusting you to keep her away from David should Alysha's boy babies scramble her mind."

"Is that likely to happen?"

"Who knows? The women in this family have a complicated relationship with their boys. Scarcity adds value. An appalling number of us have the same attraction power, not to mention poor impulse control, the first of us did. That said, I assume Jack informed you that I want the two of you participating in ritual a week Wednesday. No *fourth circle* nonsense."

Air quotes from the aunties were always frighteningly definitive. Mouth primed to say no, Charlie met Auntie Jane's dark-on-dark gaze and heard herself say, "What?"

"We're not leaving either your power or his out of a possible solution."

Charlie stopped in the kitchen doorway and stepped back into the dining room, shooting an insincere smile and wave at the aunties, aunts, and cousins around the table ladling steaming pumpkin puree into jars. The asteroid had poked a stick into an anthill, and until the ritual freed them from hope, the aunties, aunts, and cousins were doing what Gales did when they had time to kill. "What's this about a solution? You and Auntie Bea actually agreed—with each other—that the aunties can't stop the asteroid."

"*Possible* solution," Auntie Jane repeated. "We don't know what the whole family working together can do until we try. When this is over, however *over* ends up being defined, I want no one able to say that we didn't try everything."

She hadn't been able to argue about that with Jack. Couldn't argue with it now. "Okay. What if Jack stays in Calgary and I come here?"

"You're staying in Calgary." Standing on the worn threshold, Auntie Jane turned her back on the kitchen and dropped her volume from commanding to *we can pretend not to hear this*. "Katie can't handle Jack. You can. I realize this will make your personal complicated relationship even more so, but we're trying to stop the world from ending and, as your sisters say, it sucks to be you."

"You talked about this with my sisters?"

"They were referring to you and Jack in general, not the upcoming ritual in particular."

"Small mercies," Charlie muttered. It wasn't pity. That was something.

"If you don't want to participate, Charlotte, you have an option."

"I do?"

"Save the world before next Wednesday."

And given that the subtext added a terrifyingly sincere, *which I'm quite sure you could do if you only put your mind to it*, Charlie had nothing to say.

"Look at how big they've gotten!" Releasing Allie, from a second or possibly third extended hug—Jack had lost count—Auntie Mary bent to lift one of the twins off the floor. "And this one's Evan . . . ?"

"Edward," Jack told her from a position of relative safety behind the sofas. He'd been hugged once, that was enough. He liked Allie's mother well enough—newly changed, she'd often intervened between him and the older aunties during the summer he spent in Ontario—but that much desperation and power mixed together was a little off-putting and he still had trouble separating hunger from, well, *hunger.*

Allie laughed as her mother peered from twin to twin. "Even Graham and I can't always tell. Jack's the only one who never gets them mixed up."

"They smell different," he explained as Auntie Mary glanced over at him.

She hefted Edward higher and pressed her mouth and nose against his hair. "They smell wonderful!"

"Sure," Jack sighed. "That end. Now."

He caught the stuffed turtle Allie threw at him as Charlie came into the apartment and tossed it from hand to hand when their attention shifted to her. From the laughing and the teasing, they didn't seem to realize what it meant when she set her guitar case down by the door. Jack knew. He saw the tight curve of Charlie's smile, the way her right thumb strummed against the outside seam of her jeans and the red boots she carried out of Allie and Graham's bedroom.

Oh, and how her gaze kept sliding past his face. He saw that, too.

During an argument about feeding the twins bananas and peanut butter . . .

"Gales don't have allergies, Mom."

"Maybe not allergies, but, if you'll recall, peas don't agree with Auntie Vera."

"No one agrees with Auntie Vera; the peas are in good company."

. . . he slipped out and waited down by the mirror. After four winters in the MidRealm, he understood what the mirror intended when he saw his reflection holding a bunch of roses and a heart-shaped box, but he kept getting distracted by the impractical design. Every time his reflection moved, chocolates spilled out of the left ventricle.

"Because I have to have a Song to follow out of the Wood, Mom, and Australia is a bit vague. No, Australia itself isn't vague, I meant that putting what I know about Australia into a Song could as easily dump me at Russell Crowe's house. Or Nicole Kidman's. I agree, Mom, neither an entirely bad situation, but not exactly useful either especially since I'm pretty sure Nicole Kidman lives outside Nashville. What?" Phone in one hand, guitar in the other, Charlie's gaze slipped past Jack once again as she came down the last few stairs. "Yes, I know most of what lives in Australia can kill you. The twins will feel right at home. Gotta go save the world. Love you, too, bye."

"You're not going to save the world," he told her as she reached the hall.

"Harsh." Frowning at the mirror, she tossed him her phone. "Hang onto that for me, will you."

Jack caught it without thinking. "I meant tonight." The silver-capped toes of her red boots were visible under the edge of her jeans. "Where are you going?"

"To find a band to sit in with."

"I know what that means." It meant the same thing the boots meant.

"Tonight it means a dark bar where your feet stick to floor, beer in plastic bottles, a couple of broken strings, and, if I'm feeling like I really need to let go, I may have a go at a banjo."

"And after the . . . banjo."

"A greasy breakfast, coffee you can stand a spoon up in, and an argument about Martins versus Taylors if I'm lucky."

"Take me with you. I know, you can't take me through the Wood. There must be a band in a crappy bar with bad beer in Calgary."

He couldn't understand her expression. It looked like pain. "This isn't something we do together, Jack."

"We have." He reached out to grab her sleeve and changed his mind, not wanting to look desperate. He wasn't desperate, he just wanted her to hear him. He just wanted to be with her. In whatever way the stupid rules allowed. "That summer in Cape Breton . . ."

"Things were a lot less complicated back then," she interrupted. "Selkie stalking aside. All I want to do tonight is get out of my head for a while. Do you understand what I'm saying? It's not Wild; it's me, not me and you."

"It could be."

"No. We're not building a life together, Jack. We can't."

If he asked her not to go, if he said, please don't go, would she stay? Probably not. But as long as he didn't ask, he could pretend she would.

When she touched his cheek, he felt her skin blister against his, but she maintained the gentle pressure, until he brought himself under control. She'd used the backs of her fingers, he realized as she blew a charm over the burn. Blisters on the tips, even with her calluses, even charmed, would have made playing painful.

"We're not a me and you," he said slowly, trying to understand, "but having a go at a banjo means you're only having a go at a banjo?"

She grinned. "If you knew banjos, Jack, you wouldn't use the word *only* in that sentence." The grin slipped. He had a feeling Charlie was keeping it on her face by willpower alone. "I'm not giving up the music, Jack. Didn't for Allie-cat, won't for you. Or, not-you, as it happens. Won't give up Allie for not-you either."

"Why would I want you to?"

"Excellent question."

He watched her reflection touch his cheek with her fingertips, scales flickering across the back of her hand. Her hand? The back door opened and without turning, he said, "We should be a me and you."

"Sucks to be us."

Up where the air had picked up a bite, he spread his wings and started a long spiral glide around the distant lights of Calgary. Charlie hadn't left the city. He could feel where she was and, with very little effort, he could track her.

He didn't.

She might have stayed in Calgary because she wanted him to track her. Because she wanted to be with him as much as he wanted to be with her. Because she didn't want it to be her decision. Given that their whole problem was all about him being so much younger, Charlie needed to stop being so fucking childish.

Allie didn't like it when he swore.

Charlie didn't mind.

As he descended, the sense of family in the city separated out into individual pockets—the houses at the north end of the park, the Emporium, the big house in Mount Royal, Katie's condo, Charlie . . .

The aunties, all four of them, were *in* the park.

Jack frowned. They took it in turns to drop in on David outside of ritual, but why all four of them. And why tonight?

Oh.

Auntie Mary was David's mother. If David's power pulled her to the park . . .

Jack didn't land. He didn't even look down. He thought he could hear David's hoofbeats.

Allie woke at five forty-eight on Tuesday morning, patted the empty space where Charlie wasn't, tugged her hair out from under her husband's arm, and stared at the ceiling for twenty-one minutes, fully aware she wouldn't be able to see the asteroid even if the ceiling were suddenly, miraculously transparent but unable to look away. Finally, she sighed and got up. She couldn't stop the asteroid or break the connection between Charlie and Jack's hearts . . .

Hand outstretched to grab her robe from the chair, she froze. She couldn't stop the asteroid, but she could break the connection between Charlie and Jack's hearts. Second circle was all about connection. With the power she held in ritual, she could remake them as two separate people, not two suffering halves of an impossible whole. Charlie would stop running. Jack would settle back into his skin. They'd stop pulling away from the family.

Of course they'd both have to be in ritual, she acknowledged, not merely skirting the edges of it, so as pleasant as it might be to think of, given how skittish they were, that wasn't likely to happen any time soon. And soon was all they had.

The great room of the apartment was quiet and the spill of streetlights around the edges of the curtains provided enough illumination for her to maneuver, illumination enough to see Jack sprawled out on one of the sofas. He'd gone flying after Charlie left; she'd heard him come in around three. Allie had no idea why he'd decided to sleep here instead of in his own room, but she certainly didn't mind. She preferred her family close. One hand curled against his cheek, he looked absurdly young. Then she moved slightly, and the shadows shifted and he looked like the man he was becoming.

Well, mostly man. His tail spilled off the edge of the cushions and curled on the floor, tip twitching slightly.

Should she talk to him about his recent changes, about how the dragon seemed to be trying to overwhelm the Gale? What would she say? Maybe this recent shifting was normal for a dragon of his age. She didn't have enough information. She wasn't actually his mother.

Her mother was in the boys' room on an air mattress on the floor, the twins piled around her like puppies, spending as much time with her grandchildren as she could. She'd have to go back today. Given how close they were to ritual and the pull of David's power, this visit had been a stupid risk. Still, if the end of the world didn't encourage stupid risks, what did?

She glanced at Jack again. Wondered where Charlie was.

With the kettle filled and plugged in for tea, she opened one of the blinds on the windows facing the road. The sun wasn't quite up, but the light promised a nice day. No rain. No snow. The sort of day they wouldn't have after the asteroid, even if the family survi . . .

Shadow.

Big shadow.

Big fast-moving shadow.

Too big. Too fast.

Familiar.

She looked at Jack.

Familiar, but clearly not Jack.

She leaned forward and looked back out the window. The pigeons weren't crammed under the newspaper box. They dipped and wove pigeon patterns on the sidewalk outside the bank, apparently unconcerned.

Allie and Jack were sitting together at one end of the big table when Charlie eased the apartment door open. They didn't look happy. On the bright side, her ears weren't burning, so at least they weren't unhappy about her. Setting down her guitar case, she shrugged out of her jacket, and headed for the kitchen. She'd already greeted the morning with four cups of coffee strong enough to neutralize the night's half bottle of whiskey, and now she needed to clear the taste of caffeinated diesel from her mouth.

Snagging the last piece of apple pie from the fridge, she grabbed a fork and dropped into the chair next to Allie. "Okay, spill."

"One of my uncles is visiting. Allie saw him fly over."

"But the only dragon I can sense in the city is Jack. And I didn't feel a gate open."

Charlie chewed and swallowed. "So he came through a gate outside the city limits, flew over to give you a thrill, and landed back outside the city limits. Gone before you thought to search for him."

"As simple as that?"

She shrugged, making a half-hearted swipe at Jack's hand with her fork as he broke off a chunk of crust. "Probably."

"Why is he here?"

"How the hell should I know, Allie-cat?"

"It was more of a rhetorical question," she muttered. "And you smell like a bar."

"Someone dumped a beer in my lap. Accidentally," Charlie added, as Jack started to growl. "I charmed it dry, but the smell lingers. And if you want to know why a Dragon Lord is visiting, you're going to have to ask him."

Allie drummed her fingernails against a mug holding—Charlie wrinkled her nose at the smell—herbal tea. "Last time they were here, they came to us . . ."

"This time, we don't wait for them." Jack shoved his chair out and surged up onto his feet. "I'll go find him."

"How?"

And there were suddenly way too many teeth for a Human mouth. "I'll pretend I have a broken wing."

"Be careful," Allie called after him. Then added as the door closed, "Aren't you worried about him."

Charlie pushed the empty plate away and sighed. "All the time; not only when he's off to attract the attention of the slightly more violent side of his family. It's pretty much a given."

"You didn't say . . ."

"He knows."

"Charlie."

Charlie waited. Gathered up the crumbs on her thumb, made a face because her skin tasted like guitar strings and bacon fat. When Allie only shook her head, unable or unwilling to continue, she stood. "I'm going to shower and change before taking Auntie Mary home."

"She's not even up yet. And she'll need breakfast first."

Bending to kiss the top of Allie's head as she passed, Charlie murmured, "Don't worry, Allie-cat. It'll be a long shower."

It was a very long shower. It was the kind of shower that, had she the time, Charlie would write songs about. The water was the perfect temperature. The pressure was exactly right. It pounded the knots out of her shoulders and sluiced the combined bar/diner patina off her skin. By the time she stepped out of the bathroom, towel snugged tight around her hair, she felt good.

As much as she'd needed that shower, she'd needed the night out more. A few hours immersed in music, not thinking about the end of the world or Jack or the upcoming ritual or Jack at the upcoming ritual had given her the strength to go on. The universe adjusted itself for Gales. There was still plenty of time for a jump to the left.

Or even a step to the right.

Her mood held through getting dry, and getting dressed, and getting back to the kitchen in time for the last blueberry pancake. Chewing, she watched Auntie Mary helping the twins eat, but stopped her on the way to the sink, hands full of dirty dishes.

"We should go."

"After I help clean up."

"We're stretching the parameters of safe, Auntie Mary. You need . . ." The theme from the *Big Bang Theory* blasting out of the drawer by her hip, cut her off.

Auntie Mary smiled. "You need to answer your phone. And turn the volume down a little."

"It's as loud as it needs to be," Charlie sighed, opening the junk drawer. "Jack dropped it in here when I gave it to him last night," she explained before anyone could ask. Well, before Auntie Mary and Allie could ask. The twins probably didn't care.

"Ring!"

"Ring, Cha Cha."

Or maybe they did. "Melissa. What can I do for you?"

"Funny thing, Charlie, I got stopped on my way to class by a really pissed-off member of the Courts in a U of C basketball jacket. She said, and I quote, Gale girl, tell the Bard the glorious game can't be saved. End quote. Do you know what she's talking about?"

The apartment door opened before Charlie could answer.

Auntie Gwen locked dark eyes on Auntie Mary, licked swollen lips, and said, "You're still here."

"We're just leaving, Auntie Gwen."

Auntie Mary snapped her mouth shut with enough force Charlie heard the impact of her teeth.

"Good." Auntie Gwen shifted her gaze to Charlie. "David's finally exhausted; get out of here now and you won't be fighting his power trying to hold her in place."

"We need more than four aunties," Allie muttered, as she lifted Evan out of his high chair.

Auntie Gwen shot her a look that said *tell me about it* so loudly even Melissa heard it on the other end of the phone.

"What was that?"

"Auntie stuff." Charlie mouthed *Melissa* at the room and turned to face the windows.

"Yeah, whatever. Did you do something to screw up the basketball season?"

"Why would I do that?" Not a statement. Not a lie.

"No idea, but we're winning and we'd like to continue winning."

"You don't play."

"What?"

"You said we. Twice. But you don't play basketball so *they* would be more accurate. They're winning. They'd like to continue winning. Words are important."

"Sure they are. You sound like an auntie."

"Ouch. Low blow, Mel."

"My point is," Melissa sighed, "she didn't look like she had her head in the game, you know?"

"No, I don't." Charlie sagged forward and rested her forehead against the glass. "But I expect someone will tell me."

Jack's uncles were old and clever and vicious, but they weren't sorcerers and they weren't Gales and they shouldn't have been able to hide from him. Not here in the MidRealm.

He swept the borders of the city, looking for the break where his uncle had crossed the border of Allie's influence. He couldn't find it. Not flying high at full size. Not flying low, shifted as small as possible, hiding his true appearance behind a hawk-shaped glamour. He crossed his own path a couple of times, but found no trace of another dragon.

Whatever his uncle was up to—and that could range from nasty to fatal depending on which of the twelve Dragon Lords had come through—he'd found a way to hide his tracks. Since that wasn't possible, he had to be getting help.

Alice was behind the counter when Jack entered the Silvan Diner, but except for Alice, the place was empty.

"Game night," she told him, glancing up from her magazine. "They're never here on game night." Her *duh* was heavily implied. She straightened and stretched her back, pushing her breasts deliberately against her uniform shirt. Without the scent of the full-bloods filling his nose, Jack could smell Nymph. He wasn't sure what kind. "You are here to talk to them, right?"

"I think they're helping to hide someone from me."

"Yeah, right." She snorted. "They don't help anyone. Although when they were in last night, they were pretty pissed about something you did."

Jack spun one of the counter stools. "I didn't do anything."

"Uh-huh. Then it was probably another big lizard they were all *fucking dragon* about."

The Courts might be hiding one of his uncles to get back at him. He didn't have the skill to break through that kind of casting. Spinning the stool in the other direction, he muttered, "Great."

"Probably not. You want something to eat? They said you guys are always hungry. Of course there's no guarantee they meant you're hungry for pie, is there?" Her smile turned speculative. After four years around Gale girls, Jack knew speculative. "So, how dangerous would it be to fuck you? Go out in a blaze of glory or just . . ." Her voice dropped to a heated purr. ". . . blaze of glory, no out?"

Great. A bored Nymph. The vinyl on the stool began to melt. Jack snatched his hand away before it stuck to his fingers. "No idea."

Her eyes widened. They were the same brilliant green as Joe's, but nothing about her said Leprechaun. "No shit? You haven't cashed in your V-card? What, are the Gales saving you for something special?"

"No. Not that I know of," he amended after a moment's consideration. "It's complicated."

Her face slid into stronger angles, the curve of her breasts diminishing as her body adapted to her belief. "You're gay?"

"Not Facebook complicated, real world complicated."

"And?"

Jack had no idea why he was still a part of this conversation. "She's older."

"So? You're a dragon."

"And a Gale. Complicated."

"Well, when you get tired of complications, macking on the elderly, and pies that tell you how to wipe your ass, come back." Visibly female again, Alice tucked her hair behind her ear, exposing the tattoo on her neck. A new leaf had budded since Jack had seen it last. "I'm not complicated at all."

Somehow, he doubted that.

Figuring anything was better than being roped into adjusting the Calgary real estate market in advance of the expected influx of Gales, Charlie'd left Auntie Mary at the farmhouse and dropped in to see her mother, remembering too late that the news of her and Jack had spread.

"Oh, sweetheart, I'm so sorry! You must be so unhappy! The world is so unfair!"

"Mom . . ." Charlie was a little taller, but her mother had arms of steel. ". . . can't breathe . . ."

"Have you looked at your list, sweetheart? I mean, really looked at it? There must be someone on there who can help."

Squirming her way to freedom, Charlie backed out of arm's reach. "It doesn't work like that, Mom."

"What about Allie?"

Carly Rae Jepsen's "Almost Said It" slid smoothly into Tommy Alto's "In Love." Charlie let it play. It gave her something to listen to other than her mother. "Allie and I are fine."

"If your father was alive . . ."

"He'd be out in the garage working on the car. Or someone's car. Is that pecan pie I smell?" she added quickly, moving further into the kitchen. "It feels like years since I've had your pecan pie."

"That's because you're never home. And now, with this unfortunate, heartbreaking Jack situation, you're not likely to ever settle down, are you? Are you sure it's not camaraderie you feel? You're Wild. He's Wild."

"I'm sure, Mom."

"So unfair. I admire how you're handling it, sweetie. So brave."

"Thanks. Now, if it comes to it . . ." *When it comes to it,* Charlie amended quietly, getting down two of the old chipped stoneware plates. ". . . are you relocating to Calgary or Australia?"

Fortunately, the potential end of the world took precedence over the heartbreak of her love life. Three hours going through her old room, deciding what to keep and what to donate to the Darsden East Volunteer Firefighters Christmas Jumble Sale was a small price to pay.

When finally she got back to Calgary with a backpack full of old band T-shirts, a ukulele, and six partial packages of phosphor bronze medium strings, she crossed to where Allie was wiping Edward's . . . no, Evan's face and let her head drop onto her shoulder. "Can your mother adopt me?"

"No, because that would be wrong."

She felt a kiss on her hair then a shrug to dislodge her. "Is Jack back yet?"

"No. He checked in a couple of hours ago—no luck—and decided to widen his search parameters."

Charlie tossed her backpack against the wall and accepted the offered toddler. "I thought he was going to play wounded bird and let his uncle come to him?"

"I guess he wants to be sure he's flopping where they'll notice."

Settling on the sofa with a noncommittal grunt, to cover the *I'll go check on him* that nearly made it out, Charlie nudged Graham until he turned Edward toward her and she could bounce the boys' fists off each other. "Wonder Twin powers activate!"

"Twin!"

"Dog!"

"You know one of the Wonder Twins was a girl, right?"

"Hey." The nudge became a poke. "Don't burden your sons with gender expectations."

Graham answered with his version of a noncommittal grunt, stretched his free arm along the top of the sofa until he could cup the back of her neck, his grip warm and comforting, then turned his attention back to the television.

If Graham was home and not busy with the babies or Allie or—in the early years—Jack, he watched the evening news, flipping between Global and CTV. The first time she'd been there when he'd settled, remote in hand, Charlie'd asked why and he'd said he liked to know what was going on in the world. When she asked why a second time, he'd sighed and reminded her that he published a newspaper. Since he published a tabloid that got less than no respect from the journalistic community—a remarkably successful tabloid even though apparently no one read newspapers anymore—Charlie didn't consider that to be much of an explanation.

She played with the boys through the local news—money released for repairs to St. Patrick's Island bridge, a small heater fire in Renfrew—wondered if the Brownies would be affected by a new restaurant opening in the Saddledome, and suddenly realized that Lisa LaFlammen, the CTV evening news anchor, had just said there was a Siren in the river in Winnipeg.

"Was she kidding?" Allie asked, leaning over the back of the sofa and absently stopping Edward from flinging himself past her to the floor.

"She thinks she was," Charlie said trying to parse out the meaning in a voice that had been broken down to ones and zeros and rebuilt again on their forty-two-inch flat-screen TV. "But she wasn't."

"She believes there's a Siren or there is a Siren?"

"Two men have drowned," Graham pointed out. "Does it matter . . ."

His voice trailed off as the three of them watched first a shaky pixilated recording of shadowed riders and flaming hoofprints crossing Salisbury Plain, pale dogs with red ears baying at their sides, then a blurry cell phone picture of a three-tailed fox in Tokyo, and finally three creatures identified as chupacabra chasing tourists along a beach at a resort in Mexico where the recording cut out seconds after the screaming started.

"That's not right," Allie muttered.

"What's not?"

Charlie tore her eyes away from LaFlamme trying to fit five deaths and a disappearance into a weird news segment without much success. She hadn't noticed that Jack had come home until he'd spoken. "There's some strange shit going down."

"Shit down," Evan repeated solemnly.

"Charlie . . ."

"Sorry." She slid over so Jack could sit on the sofa and bit off considerably more profanity when four pudgy knees dug painfully into her thighs as both Evan and Edward crawled over her lap to their more interesting cousin. "Did you find your uncle?"

"No. The only dragon track I could find was mine."

"Could he have changed and taken a cab out of the city?"

Jack turned Evan upside down. "He'd still be a dragon. Something's been hiding him since he came through."

"He's not the only thing that came through." Graham thumbed the mute off and they listened to a hysterical witness try to explain what she'd seen on the beach to a reporter who was only slightly less freaked out.

"Eviscerated, Mama!"

"Seriously?" Charlie peered at Edward, taking his turn upside down. "And yet I still get Cha Cha?"

"Cha Cha!"

"That's what I'm saying."

"We've always had the occasional Siren," Allie said thoughtfully, "but they're usually careful not to be seen."

Graham nodded. "And chupacabra are all about the backcountry. They steer clear of people. They don't chase them down a crowded beach."

"I bet it's the asteroid." Allie straightened, arms folded. "It's influencing their behavior."

"How?"

"It's unnatural."

"They're unnatural," Graham pointed out. "Or preternatural, at least."

"Pot kettle," Charlie muttered as she stood. "Salisbury, Tokyo, and conspicuous consumption on the beach are on their own, but I'm heading to Winnipeg. I've got friends there and singing in the middle of the river is something they're likely to check out."

Jack dropped the boys on the cushion she'd just vacated and stood as well. "At full size I can make Winnipeg in a little more than three hours, maybe you should go to Mexico."

"Drop me in Mexico." Graham set his sons on the floor, where they wrapped themselves around his ankles. "I've taken out chupacabras before. You go deal with Salisbury."

Allie came around the sofa to grab his arm. "You haven't shot anything in four years."

"But I don't miss, remember."

Thirteen years as a sorcerer's assassin would be tough to shake even with the seventh son of a seventh son thing adjusting his aim, Charlie allowed. "What am I supposed to do in Salisbury? Yell bad dog and sing a rousing chorus of 'The Farmer and the Cowman Should Be Friends'?"

"Would a show tune work?" Jack asked her.

"Probably not. Look . . ." Mouth open to remind them that she had friends in Winnipeg and that they couldn't go around saving the world, the world had to learn to save itself, she took a moment to do what she'd suggested and actually *look* at Jack and Graham, suddenly understanding their reaction. They couldn't stop the asteroid, but they could stop this. Stop the Siren. Stop the chupacabras. She glanced at Allie who sighed and nodded, having clearly come to the same conclusion. "All right, fine. Jack, you can leave when you're ready. Graham, you go get your penis substitute . . ."

"It really isn't," Allie muttered.

"Penis!" Edward added.

Charlie snickered through Allie's eye roll and finished with, "I'll meet you at the condo." Allie wouldn't allow Graham's weapons in the same building as the boys and had added charms to the hidden safe across town in the condo—just in case. In case of what, exactly, Charlie wasn't entirely sure. "I won't be long, but I've got some shopping to do before I head across the pond."

Charlie dropped Graham off at a golf course about three kilometers south of Puerto Juarez.

"It's the closest uninhabited area near the attacks." He swung his weapon case around into what Charlie assumed was a ready position and grinned. In spite of the total lack of euphemism in that description—on a good day she could've got serious mileage out of *weapon in a ready position*—he seemed happy. "Experience suggests this is where they'll have gone to ground."

"You going to be okay on your own?" "Johnny's Got a Gun" played not *softly* but quietly in the background.

"I did this for a long time, Charlie, it's good to be . . . useful."

And they both emphatically did not look up at a thousand and one points of light strewn across a black-velvet sky. Although, given the emphasis, they might as well have.

Seven thirty-seven leaving Calgary, eight forty-five leaving Puerto Juarez; Charlie stepped out of the Wood onto Salisbury Plain at two forty-five in the morning, the sound of the horns still ringing in her ears. Stonehenge loomed on her left, closer than she'd intended, but given the amount of pull the site exerted, she wasn't surprised. She had no more idea of what the stone circle had originally been used for than the BBC did, but with all the possibilities layered onto it over the years the original purpose no longer mattered from a metaphysical perspective. It just was.

She Sang a quick lullaby at the cluster of people silhouetted against the night on the other side of the fence, cell phones ready for the return of the Hunt, and added a charm to ease bruising—a couple of them had hit the ground hard enough to bounce. The moon was down—or maybe it hadn't come up yet—and the stars were hidden behind a layer of cloud. It felt like it might rain, but, given that it was England, she'd been expecting that. A night-sight charm sketched onto her eyelids let her walk away from the stone circle without crushing flora or fauna underfoot. If she was going to register on the Hunt's radar as more than part of the background metaphysics, she needed to put a bit of distance in.

"Not real radar," she told a toad, who shot her an extremely dirty look as she passed. "Although that would be kind of cool. Like a fish finder for people. Cool in the abstract," she amended after a moment.

She'd been walking for around forty-five minutes when she heard the hounds in the distance, baying as they caught a scent. Her scent? She stopped walking and cocked her head. One minute. Two minutes. Three. Oh, yeah. Definitely coming closer. They didn't know what she was, but they knew she didn't belong here. Her roots were an ocean and half of a very large continent away.

"I suppose it's too much to ask they lead the Hunt over the Army training range and set off a few unexploded mortars," she muttered, pulling the bag of dog treats out of a side pocket on her gig bag and opening it. The thing about the dogs that ran with the Hunt, they were dogs. Charlie had grown up with dogs.

In twenty minutes, they were close enough to see. In twenty-two, close enough to count. There were nine in the pack, large hounds with pale bodies and red ears.

Charlie planted her feet and relaxed her shoulders as the dogs swirled around her, uncertain of what to do about prey that wouldn't run. She hummed up a little power. Pulled out a treat. "All right, you lot, sit!"

Nine doggy butts hit the chalk.

"Good dogs!"

By the time the Hunt galloped up, all nine were sprawled on the dirt, chewing on barbeque pizzles and Charlie was waiting, fingers resting lightly on the strings of her guitar. She wasn't particularly worried. There was nothing like leaving flaming hoofprints in the sod to say *Hello there, I'm young and full of myself. Look at me. Look at me!*

"Why even bother to stand against us, Gale girl?" The hair toss was pure Beyoncé; only tall, dark, and silver-haired wasn't performing. "The world is ending. Why not enjoy the final days?"

"Why not, indeed. Except you don't get to enjoy them at the expense of others." If she didn't get to break the rules, they didn't get to break the rules.

The smile gifted to her defined patronizing. "The Gales do not interfere with the Fey."

"Yeah, see, do not doesn't mean cannot or, for that matter, won't." This was the Wild Hunt, albeit junior edition, so Charlie took a deep breath, opened her mouth, and Sang a piece of music so tame, so green and pleasant, so English, it was the antithesis of Wild.

By the time she started the second verse of "The White Cliffs of Dover," the riders had called their dogs and were racing for the gate, bluebirds in hot pursuit.

Charlie followed at her own pace, still Singing. And when she tossed in some early Beatles and a quick run through "I'm Henry the Eighth, I Am," to keep herself from going nuts, it made no difference to the speed at which the riders were retreating. The burning hoofprints stopped at the edge of one of the more modern chalk carvings.

"Well . . ." She ground out the last smoldering print with the toe of her boot. It looked like they'd used the carving to anchor the gate. ". . . that's convenient."

Closing the gate meant changing the carving, but it only took a slight and barely visible adjustment to lock "Land of Hope and Gory" to the site. If any variation of the Hunt tried to get back through, they'd find a full brass section locking them out.

Then she climbed to the top of the slope, slipped into the Wood between two junipers, thought about heading for Tokyo, decided the kitsune wouldn't appreciate her sticking her nose into what didn't concern her, and finally stepped out between two honey locusts in downtown Vancouver. A quick run across Granville Street later and she was heading down the stairs into The Cellar in a desperate attempt to get the damned bluebirds out of her head.

She should've gone with Blake.

Still high enough he could be seen only as moving darkness against the stars, Jack realized that the lit areas of the Forks were, if not teeming, then well populated with people trying to spot the naked woman in the river. The naked woman in the river who'd already lured two men to their death.

Humans were weird.

In the UnderRealm, people either avoided Sirens or used them as weapons against enemies who were unaware of their locations. In the MidRealm, armed with cell phone cameras and the mistaken belief that a few thousand hits on YouTube meant immortality, danger was relentlessly recorded.

If the asteroid did hit, if they couldn't stop it, Jack knew thousands of people would record right up until the flesh burned off their bones.

He gritted his teeth and circled until he managed to replace the image of Charlie burning with Charlie lying out on the roof, then, wings aching, he looked for a place to land.

The triangular park that created the actual fork between the Red and Assiniboine Rivers was unlit on the water side of the railroad tracks. It wasn't empty—given the news report that would be too much to ask—but it was dark, so Jack wrapped himself in shadow, landed unseen, and moved to stand behind three young women who had one hell of a lot of electronic equipment pointed at the water.

Given that the kindest thing he could say about most myths and legends was *close but not quite*—the Court wasn't particularly hung up on gender, their own or anyone else's—the lack of young men could only be considered a good try. Then he realized all the gesturing had a purpose and that two of the young women were deaf. The third wore wax earplugs. That got them two thumbs way up for paying attention to the important bits. Bare hands tracing words in the air, they didn't seem bothered by the temperature; although if they were locals, October weather was nothing on the winters they'd already survived.

He thought they might be scientists or folklorists or something-ists. Serious about capturing myth in a way that the cell phone holders weren't. He almost felt bad about what he was about to do to their data and wondered how they'd react if he told them about the asteroid.

Maybe if they couldn't stop the asteroid, he'd find these girls again and tell them about the Courts. And the Gales. And dragons.

Still wrapped in shadow and breathing heavily, he moved up to the left of their equipment and stared out at the river.

City lights danced across the light chop, gleaming or sparkling depending on the source, without doing a thing to make the water look less cold and nasty. Granted, a Siren wouldn't feel the cold, but if he hadn't known what he knew and he'd heard what sounded like a girl singing in that river at this time of the year, his reaction would be more *you have got to be kidding* than *oh, yeah, baby baby, I'm on my way*.

At eleven on a Tuesday night, the city had gone quiet enough he could hear the water lapping at the shore. It sounded a little like dragon wings. Like the song of the air slipping over and around and . . .

Actually, it didn't sound anything at all like dragon wings.

It sounded like water.

The girl-shape sitting on the rock-shape in the center of the river shrugged. "Can't blame me for trying."

"Yeah, I can." If he'd had pockets, he'd have shoved his hands into them. "You shouldn't be here."

She combed her fingers through her hair, the emerald-green strands falling around her in a shimmering curtain. "You're not my prince, Dragon."

"So the Court keeps saying." The three young women were frantically adjusting their equipment, hands flying in what, to his untrained eye, looked like profane gestures. Technology and sorcery didn't mix and the first thing Jack had ever learned to do with his, as he crawled out from under the shelter of his mother's wing, was hide. Even exhausted from the speed of his flight, he'd barely noticed the effort needed to extend the concealment out over the Siren. "You killed two people."

"Two die now. Billions die later." She shrugged. "All I did was sing."

Charlie Sang. As far as Jack knew, no one had ever drowned listening to her. "We're not going to let billions die."

"Really? *We* thought Gales were all about family and letting the rest of the world burn."

They weren't wrong.

"So where's the Bard?" she asked, eyes narrowed. "I was looking forward to a truncated version of *Canadian Idol*. We could keep score with the lives of the audience. She saves more than I drown, she wins. They still lose, but who cares about them."

"Go home."

"Make me. Oh, wait . . ." Her smile didn't fit on her face. ". . . you can't." One bare foot kicked a spray of water toward him. "You're fire, I'm water, and as long as I'm in the middle of the river, which is pretty much where I am all the time, you can't touch me. Everyone knows dragons can't swim."

Jack spread his wings. "Why would I swim?"

"You smell like beer."

Charlie lifted her arm and waved the damp spot at him, the darker fabric barely visible in the predawn light. "Spill on the bar. I'm wearing more beer than I'm drinking these days. Did you get them?"

"I did." Graham moved out from behind a sweet gum and into the predawn light. "And I got some information as well."

"Chupacabras talk?"

"No. I ran into a young man who works at the golf club who was also hunting . . ."

"The chupacabras?"

"Why not? It's his country," Graham pointed out. Charlie noticed he too had damp spots on his jacket and made a mental note to have him leave it in the downstairs bathroom. Pregnant, Allie had a violent reaction to the smell of blood. "Jorge was, conveniently, out on the beach this afternoon. He says he saw two people driving the chupacabras out into the crowds. After that, the running and the screaming was pretty much guaranteed."

"Did he say what the two people looked like?"

"Thin, arrogant, and tall. Real tall. He also said, they moved like dancers. Or water."

"Or water?" Charlie frowned. "Are you sure you understood him?"

"He works at a five star resort, his English is better than mine. Thin, tall, strangely graceful—any idea why the Courts would drive chupacabras out to attack people?"

She shrugged. "Who knows what the Courts think is fun?"

"Valid point. However . . ."

However trailed off into the cry of an early rising bird. After a moment Charlie realized Graham wasn't waiting for the bird to finish, he was waiting for her. Had he been Roland or Cameron, a Gale by blood not marriage, Charlie would have deflected. But, like Joe, in spite of anchoring second circle with Allie, Graham was outside the family power structure. Like Joe, there was a good chance he'd get the reasoning behind going to the Courts. "Jack and Joe and I may have mentioned the end of the world to a couple of full-bloods who play basketball at U of C. Just to see if the Courts had a way to stop the asteroid."

"The Courts don't care what happens to the MidRealm."

"They care about basketball."

"Save the world, save March Madness?" Graham thought about it for a moment. "That's shallow and superficial enough to be plausible. And?"

"They can't stop the asteroid."

"So they figure if the world's going to end, they might as well have some fun before it does."

"That's jumping to a bit of a . . ." When his brows rose, she sighed. "Yeah, probably."

"The aunties aren't going to be happy. Auntie Jane told you not to go to the Courts."

"Yeah, well, Auntie Jane's going to have to be unhappy." She scuffed the side of her boot against the ground, watching the line of darker grass emerge as she swept the dew away. "Jack and I agreed we have to try everything."

"So you and Jack are . . ."

"Frustrated, star-crossed, tediously cliché if you're not into romantic angst, and not about to break that particular rule." When Graham took a step back, both hands raised, Charlie realized she may have spit that out a bit vehemently. "Sorry."

"Not a problem." He shifted his weapon case until he could wrap his arms around it. Charlie decided not to mention the symbolism. "Allie said you two are destined? It's a Gale thing?"

"We aren't destined. I'm a free electron." With any luck, her smile looked more believable than it felt. "We just like each other too much for the age difference."

Graham hummed a thoughtful G flat. "You don't find it strange that it's all about your ages and not your species?"

Charlie shrugged. "He'd be seventeen no matter what species he was. Can we not talk about it?"

After a long moment, he nodded. "Sure. And, as it happens, I agree with your choice. About trying everything and checking with the Courts. The aunties won't."

"No shit. Remember I've known them longer than you have." She held out her hand for his. It was time they went home. "The aunties don't need to know."

Charlie was waiting on the roof, wrapped in her quilt and drinking a coffee when Jack arrived just after sunrise. She was like his own personal beacon, there to guide him home. When he saw her, he knew everything was going to be fine. And frustrating. He'd begun to find frustration comforting. Fuck his life. Eyes locked on her face, he changed, and sagged against the stairwell. "I'd have called if the aunties could make a phone that doesn't melt in dragon fire. I thought you might've Walked to me after you were done."

"I wasn't sure what would happen if you were flying."

He thought about Charlie appearing beside him and realized that at the speed he'd been maintaining, she'd have hit the ground before he got turned around. If he even noticed she was there at all. Too tired to smoke when he yawned, he muttered, "Good call. Siren's silenced."

"And the Hunt's home." She grinned at him over the edge of her mug. "Not even going to try with the chupacabras. Graham took them out *and* he made a friend." Then the grin disappeared, and Jack spent a moment worried Graham had gotten hurt before he realized that Graham hurt would mean Allie reacting would mean he'd be hearing a lot more emergency vehicles out on the streets. "I should feel like I got something accomplished last night," Charlie continued, dropping a troubled gaze down into her mug. "But if we're all going to die anyway, last night was nothing more than spitting into the wind. Tugging Superman's cape. Taking the mask . . ."

"Yeah, you and Jim Croce have made your point. But we're not all going to die." Pretty sure he'd face-plant if he moved away from the supporting wall, he put everything he had left into his voice. "We'll stop it."

"You don't know . . ."

"I know us. We stopped an old god, and it had intent. Like you said, this is nothing more than a big rock."

"That's what I said, didn't I." A deep breath later, she met his eyes and nodded. "Go us. You look like tired personified."

"You should see it from this side." It was too much effort to roll his shoulders and work the growing knots out of his back. Way too much effort to remind his body that his skin shape didn't have flight muscles. "Why don't you look tired?"

She made a grab for the quilt as she stood. "Musician. I'm used to going to bed at dawn. Also, I bleed caffeine. Come on, let's get you to bed before the traffic chopper flies over and we get another note about public nudity."

"I thought Auntie Carmen dealt with that," he said allowing Charlie to take his arm and support part of his weight.

"She did. Allie says next time she's sending Auntie Bea."

"Mean."

"Little bit."

"Are you going to tuck me in?" The humming probably meant something. Given the way he stumbled when it stopped, he suspected it was holding him up.

"As much as I admire your tenacity, no. But I will walk you to your room and see that you make it as far as the bed."

"Good." Jack bounced off the wall as they went around the hall corner, bounced off the edge of his door, bounced as he landed on his bed. "Ow. I think I found my Flames belt buckle."

"Dork."

Since he might have been imagining her kiss against his hair, he didn't open his eyes to check. Burying his face in her scent as she spread her quilt over him, he fought to stay awake long enough to ask, "Did my uncle fly past this mo . . ."

"The dragon lord flew over about half an hour before Jack landed." Allie passed Charlie a piece of toast. "I'm surprised he didn't notice."

"Winnipeg and back? He's pretty baked. Plus . . ." Charlie licked at the plum jam dripping down her wrist. ". . . I don't imagine there's much meat on a Siren." Dropping to the sofa beside Graham, she helped herself to his coffee as he channel surfed. "So, what's new this morning."

"Report of a sea serpent in Boston Harbor," he grunted, "but it's all hearsay, no actual evidence. And there's a rumor of a Spurs player with an ass' head."

"A *call me Bottom* ass' head? Or is he just an ass? Because in professional sports that's not exactly rare."

"Full midsummer night's dream team."

"Huh." Charlie ate the last of her toast and thought about it. Given that the younger members of the Court had borrowed from Tolkien, it wasn't all that surprising their elders borrowed from an older source. "I guess Oberon's a Spurs fan and he's still pissed about them losing the NBA title. Again."

"An ass head's a little harsh." Allie sat down on her other side and snuggled up against Charlie's shoulder. "And how do you know so much about basketball."

"As it happens, that's pretty much all I know about basketball," Charlie admitted. She caught Graham's hand as he was about to change the channel. "Wait. A giant beanstalk growing at a Staples?"

"At the Staples Center," Graham corrected. "It's where the Lakers play."

"Basketball again? Well, that's not obvious or anything."

"It's like the Courts know there's an asteroid on the way." Allie shifted, elbow digging into Charlie's side. "But if it's blocked, and since it's unlikely they found a scientist at NASA by way of a bouzouki player, how do they know?"

Charlie could feel Graham's gaze on the side of her head. "Truth," the

Seether version, began playing, but before Charlie could answer, or decide what exactly she was going to answer, the apartment door opened.

Auntie Gwen was no surprise. That she was followed by Auntie Bea, Auntie Carmen, and Auntie Trisha was. None of them looked happy. Although, Charlie amended silently, Auntie Carmen never looked happy before ten.

"Charlotte."

Charlie drained Graham's mug. "Auntie Bea."

"We need to talk."

NINE

SEATED TOGETHER AT ONE END of the big dining room table, the aunties looked like a tribunal. Truth in advertising, Charlie thought. Standing at the other end of the table, not entirely certain why she'd taken up the position, but fully aware that at least some of the aunties' power could be attributed to force of habit, she gripped the back of a chair hard enough the edges of the wood dug into her palms.

Auntie Bea leaned forward. "You were told not to contact the Courts."

"How did you . . ." Auntie Gwen's expression answered before Charlie could finish asking. "Of course. Joe."

"It was obvious the Courts had found out about the asteroid." Sitting a little separate from the others, Auntie Gwen's position seemed somewhere between sympathy and solidarity. "I asked if he knew how. If it helps, he tried to talk around it."

"But you kept at him." She didn't blame Joe.

"The Courts are wreaking havoc, Charlotte."

"Havoc Lake, north of Thunder Bay?" Charlie forced the fingers of one hand to release the chair and pushed her hair back off her face. "Can't see them doing much damage . . ."

"Enough." Auntie Bea's eyes flashed black. "Did it not occur to you that this reaction might be the very reason the Courts were not to be consulted? Or did you assume that being Wild negates knowledge gained by those three times your age with three times your experience?"

"Negates? There a reason you're talking like Thor? Specifically, Brannagh's Thor, because I don't remember Whedon's Thor getting to say . . ."

"Charlotte!"

She winced. Magic in a name. "There was a chance the Courts could help."

"And a certainty they'd react exactly as they did."

"If you were so certain, maybe you should have mentioned it."

"If you'd done as you were told," Auntie Carmen began.

Auntie Bea cut her off. "We don't have to explain ourselves to you."

"Oh, yeah, because blind obedience is a terrific reason to not make every possible attempt to stop that asteroid."

"Regardless of the consequences."

Charlie slapped both hands down on the table. "The end of the world is a pretty fucking big consequence! If the world ends, I want to know I did *everything!*" Auntie Carmen and Auntie Trisha inched their chairs out.

Auntie Bea did not. "The family will survive!"

"Mine won't." Graham moved to stand by Charlie's side. "I have family who aren't Gales. I may not be able to bridge the gap Jonathon Gale drove between us when he murdered my parents, my sisters, and my brothers, but I don't want my family to die."

Interesting. Breathing heavily, Charlie straightened, her shoulder brushing Graham's. He usually called his ex-employer by his alias, Stanley Kalynchuk. By using Jonathon Gale, he'd reminded the aunties that the family owed him. Charlie doubted the family would care, but it was a ballsy move.

Drying her hands on a tea towel, the normality of the action adding weight to her words, Allie stood by Charlie's other side. "My father isn't a Gale by blood."

Auntie Bea waved off Allie's father. "His only sister died childless years ago. He's the end of his line as it usually is with those who marry in." She shot an accusatory glance at Graham, willing to ignore for the moment that arriving at the seventh son of a seventh son required a lot of uncles.

"My point is," Allie told her, her voice the voice of a woman who wrangled two-year-old twins twenty-four/seven, "the family no longer exists in isolation. We have connections to the world."

"A very low percentage of the whole," Auntie Trisha pointed out, "and roughly the same percentage of the world will survive without our help."

Auntie Carmen nodded. "If we concentrate on saving the family, the family survives. If we try to save everyone, everyone dies."

Charlie would have pointed out that was a pretty fucking dismal way of looking at things, but since it was Auntie Carmen, that went without saying. "Am I asking you to try and save everyone? No. I'm telling you that you can't stop *me* from trying."

Auntie Bea straightened, shoulders squaring, chin rising. "Are you challenging me, Charlotte?"

"We haven't enough time to split our resources," Auntie Gwen said hurriedly as Allie's hand closed around Charlie's arm. "We need your power on our side, Charlie."

Oh, sure. It was Charlie when they needed her. "I'm not taking sides!"

"Because you're Wild and unconstrained?" Auntie Bea growled. "Another way of saying irresponsible."

"If you want Wild," Charlie began. Allie's grip tightened. Two years of baby lifting had made her a lot stronger than she looked.

"And speaking of Wild, Jack should be here." Auntie Bea glared around as though she could find him in the shadows. "We're well aware of who actually spoke to the Courts. Where is he?"

"He's sleeping," Allie answered before Charlie could lie. And she would have lied for Jack. "He flew to Winnipeg and back last night to take care of a Siren."

"Get him."

"He's exhausted."

"And he wouldn't be if he hadn't agreed to contact the Courts for Charlotte."

"He didn't do it for me," Charlie said. "We decided together."

"Together?" Auntie Bea rolled her eyes and the words dripped disdain. "You're thirty, he's seventeen, and he would do anything for you."

Charlie breathed in. Breathed out. Let nothing at all leak into her voice. "Are you saying I took advantage of him?"

Eyes locked on Auntie Bea, Charlie felt Allie release her and step back, reaching past her to pull Graham away, quieting his protest with a soft, "Not now."

Auntie Bea laced her fingers together, eyes beginning to darken.

"Bea." Auntie Gwen's voice barely managed to break the silence. "In this family, Jack's an adult. He's fully capable of taking responsibility for his own decisions."

"If he's an adult, he should be here," Auntie Trisha pointed out a little too emphatically.

Auntie Carmen stood. "I'll go get him."

Charlie heard Auntie Carmen's clothing rustle as she walked toward the door. Heard the soft sound of her crepe soles against the hardwood. Heard metal move against metal as the door opened. Heard the difference between hardwood and tile as she walked along the hall to Jack's bedroom.

Allie said something, but she wasn't talking to her so Charlie didn't listen. And she didn't look away from Auntie Bea.

Heard another door open. Heard the strong, slow beat of Jack's heart. Heard hers slow to match it. Slow, but pounding so hard she had to clench her fists to contain it.

"I can't wake him," Auntie Carmen said when she returned. "He's fine, I checked, but he's too deeply asleep to wake. It's a dragon sleep, not a Gale sleep."

"Wake him," Auntie Bea said.

"No." It was as definitive a no as Charlie could make it. A gauntlet of denial thrown at Auntie Bea's feet.

Are you challenging me, Charlotte.

You're fucking right I am.

Auntie Bea flinched as though she'd been struck, as though Charlie's response had physical form. Then she drew in a deep breath and snarled, "You remind me so much of Catherine right now."

"Do I?"

"She thought she was too big for the family as well."

Charlie felt Allie's fingertips brush her arm, but she'd started moving before Allie'd reached out and was halfway to the door before she heard her name.

"Let her go," Auntie Gwen advised as Charlie grabbed her gig bag in one hand, tucked her boots under her arm, and yanked her jacket off its hook. "Let them cool down a little."

"I do not need to cool down, Gwendolyn. I . . ."

Charlie slammed the door on Auntie Bea. Heard the boys start to cry and winced. Consequences. But Allie and Graham would be fine. Allie anchored second circle and she'd stood up to the aunties for Charlie's sake before. And if the aunties tried to use either Jack or Graham for leverage, they'd be reminded of who'd sent Jack's mother home. Oh, yeah, Allie could handle the aunties.

But Charlie couldn't stay. Not if she ever wanted to come back.

She paused at the bottom of the stairs to pull her boots on. Glanced at the mirror as she passed to see two golden dragons. With little experience judging the age of dragons, she assumed that the length of the mustaches meant one of the Jacks was significantly older. "If wishes were horses," she muttered. The mirror's heart was in the right place, but seeing what she couldn't have wasn't helping.

A familiar voice drew her gaze into the store. Elbows on the glass counter, Joe watched Dan do looping tricks with a pair of yoyos. Dan was definitely cleaner than he'd been and looked to be wearing about half the clothes. He glanced up at her, frowned, and said, "Remember the bears, Charlie."

When Joe turned toward her, she tried for a sympathetic smile. The look on his face suggested she was a little pitchy. "Don't go upstairs for a while."

He nodded toward the painting of Elvis on black velvet. "You're not the first to be telling me that."

Charlie stepped out of the ornamental border and dropped down on the teak lounge next to Auntie Catherine's. "You Saw this."

"Can you think of another reason I'd be sitting by a hotel pool at six in the morning? Alone," she amended after a moment. She nodded at the glass-topped table between them. "The coffee's yours."

The cardboard cup had been charmed to stay hot. Fortunately, Charlie could care less about how long ago it had been brewed. "This isn't Vegas. Where are we?"

"Los Angeles. There's a singer/songwriter I enjoy who's playing at the Hotel Cafe on Friday and I dislike changing time zones at the last minute." Her bracelets chimed softly as she twitched a fold of her batik skirt then chimed significantly louder at a *get on with it* gesture. "So, talk."

Charlie pulled off the lid and stared at her reflection in the coffee. "Auntie Bea said I was like you, too big for the family. And now I think of it . . ."

She looked up to see Auntie Catherine watching her, wearing what seemed to be an interested expression. ". . . that's a weird way of putting it. Too big?"

"Our circle is larger . . ."

"Oh, dear lord, I feel a Disney song coming on."

". . . making the family a subset of the Wild," Auntie Catherine continued, ignoring her. "Socrates is a cat. All cats are not Socrates."

Fighting her way out of a sudden flashback to grade eight math, Charlie frowned. "They're Socrates and we're the cat?"

Auntie Catherine sighed and crossed her ankles. She was wearing opalescent silver-gray nail polish the same shade as her hair. "It isn't time for you to be on your own yet," she said, avoiding the question.

"And yet you're always after me to . . . How did you put it? . . . slip Allie's leash."

"This isn't about Allie. Go home."

Because it was, by auntie standards, more of a suggestion than a command, Charlie returned a less than definitive answer. "I can't."

"You can. I Saw you there."

"I don't care." She finished the coffee and crushed the cup. "I'm not going to be tamed by Auntie Bea."

"On the one hand, good for you." Bracelets chimed again. "On the other hand, she's frightened. They all are. The asteroid is outside their circles, and they don't want the world to end any more than you do."

"I doubt that," Charlie snorted.

"Well, they don't want *their* world to end," Auntie Catherine acknowledged. "It amounts to much the same thing."

"There's a lot of people in that qualifier." She watched dawn tint the ripples in the pool pink and orange. "I'm not ready to stop trying to save them."

"You've made that quite obvious. If you'd pressed your point, Bea couldn't have stopped you. All four of them working together might have been able to, but I'm not sure they'd have realized that in time. I'm not sure Gwen wouldn't have stepped away in the end."

"I have never used my voice against the family."

"Of course you haven't. Isn't that what I just said?"

Her half smile looked entire false. "Did you challenge Auntie Jane? Is that why you left?"

"Don't be ridiculous, Charlotte. I've challenged her authority on numerous occasions, but I've never challenged *her*. I play the long game and my sister is as capable of holding a grudge as my granddaughter. Someday, when I've Seen enough, I'm going to want to go home." *To die.* For a moment, Auntie Catherine looked old. "But that's me." The moment passed. "You, however, you need to stop sitting around, watching your ass spread, and feeling sorry for yourself."

"I'm . . ."

"I still haven't Seen the impact."

The words dropped between them like pebbles dropped down a well. Charlie listened to the echoes for a while, then she said, "So there's still hope."

"There's always hope, Charlotte, that's the point of the story."

"Yeah, well my story's a little more complica . . . Oh, crap!" The lounge rocked back as she stood, scraping against the concrete tiles loudly enough to flush a pair of birds from the shrubbery. "I told Jack I wouldn't leave again without talking to him first."

One hand raised to shade her eyes, Auntie Catherine grabbed the open edge of Charlie's jacket with the other, her grip strong enough that her fingers dimpled the leather. "I find it interesting that mentioning hope leads you to Jack. And Jack, if anyone, should understand trouble with relatives."

"I'm betting Auntie Bea has the courtyard staked out, waiting for me to come back." Charlie refused to be drawn into a discussion of Jack and hope because there wasn't any. Nor was she going to mess up the fragile relationship they'd managed to balance between friendship and the happily ever after they couldn't have by talking about it with Auntie Catherine. "Can you take me through the mirror in his room?"

"Alysha has me blocked. I can't get into Calgary."

That wasn't a no. "You don't need to. Just point me in the right direction and give me a shove."

She smoothed out an imaginary wrinkle in her skirt. "Alysha will know you're back."

Still not a no. "I'm not worried about Allie."

"Given the block, it's possible that the others will feel the way open and once they've pinpointed the location . . ."

"I won't linger." Charlie took a deep breath and was very, very careful not to let anything that might possibly be considered coercion leak into her voice. "Please, Auntie Catherine."

"Why not. I have nothing planned until Friday." *I want to help, but I'll be damned if I let you see that.*

Charlie pretended she didn't hear the subtext. Safer that way.

Tossing her braid over her shoulder, Auntie Catherine stretched, slipped into the Italian leather sandals sitting beside the lounge, and walked to the edge of the pool. "I'll meet you in the Wood."

Then she stepped into the water.

And disappeared.

"Okay . . ." Charlie picked up her guitar and stepped back into the ornamental border. ". . . that was unexpected."

"It's a reflective surface, Charlotte." Auntie Catherine looked wilder in the Wood. And completely dry. "If I can be Seen, I can pass through it."

"Then you didn't need the viburnum you planted in the courtyard," Charlie realized.

"I knew that before I got to Calgary."

"Why were they . . ."

"For you, of course." The *idiot* was too obvious to qualify as subtext. "Now, let's go reassure your dragon."

His name. Charlie's voice. Jack snapped from sleep into full consciousness.

"Whoa! Flame down, kiddo."

"Sorry. I thought . . ." Actually, he didn't know what he'd thought. Suspected he hadn't. Reaching out, he repaired the sleeve of her jacket and the edge of the gig bag. "How long was I out?"

"Not very long. A couple of hours."

"Okay, that explains why I still feel like I belly flopped off a cliff. Onto gravel." He shuffled back, using his elbows to squash the pillows into shape behind him. "What's wrong?"

"The aunties are pissed we told the Courts." She shifted position on the edge of his bed, frowned, and shrugged. "Kind of understandably given the way it turned out. Anyway, Auntie Bea's on the warpath, so I'm not going to be around much for the next little while."

"If she's trying to . . ."

Hand on his chest, she pushed him back onto his pillows. "She's not. But I might if I stay. They're all on edge because of the asteroid, and since they can't push at it, Auntie Bea's pushing at me."

The Gales didn't work the way dragons did. If a dragon took out a more powerful dragon, they became the dragon to beat. If Charlie took out Auntie Bea, the Gales would close ranks against one of their own who upset the order of things and the line between Wild and too different to belong was already pretty narrow. "And your impulse control sucks."

"Yeah, well . . ."

They realized her hand was still resting on his chest at the same time. Jack grabbed for it, but Charlie pulled free.

". . . I'm using it all for other things."

"You don't have to." When her brows rose, he sighed. "Okay, whatever. If you're not going to be around, what're you doing to do?"

"Keep trying to find a way to stop the asteroid. And deal with the mess the Courts are causing."

"And what am I going to do?"

"Same thing. We'll use Winnipeg as your perimeter. You deal with everything closer than Winnipeg and I'll do damage control farther out." She cocked her head, obviously listening to something he couldn't hear, and began speaking faster. "You won't be able to reach me for a few days, but only until ritual. If I show up and join in, all will be forgiven."

Jack still couldn't hear what Charlie heard, but Auntie Bea was close enough now he could catch her scent, even through the closed door. He'd never smelled ozone so strongly. "It's that easy?" he asked. If Charlie was ignoring the threat, he could ignore it. For a while, anyway.

Her answering smile was all stage presence. It looked sincere, but he'd seen it before. "It's ritual, and I can rock the hell out of third circle."

The bed vibrated when Auntie Bea hit the door. Charlie's charm held but only just. Jack slapped up the grid he used to keep Allie out when the last thing he needed was her being mother-y all over his space. There was a lifetime between thirteen and seventeen and, as they put it in the MidRealm, he had some issues with mothering. "When did you charm my door?"

"Before I woke you up."

"Charlotte Marie Gale, open the door! Now!"

"She sounds really angry."

Her smile softened, sliding closer to truth. "I have it on good authority she's afraid but finds anger a more fulfilling emotion."

That sounded reasonable, he guessed, but worrying about Auntie Bea's anger beat worrying about ritual. Jack didn't want to think about Charlie rocking anything that didn't involve him. He stared past her at the end of the bed, found no answers in the lumps his feet made under the quilt, and finally glanced up at her face, trying to look as though it didn't matter. "Should I warn Cameron? About you being in the ritual?"

Her expression slid under his skin and burned. "No need."

And Jack remembered he was expected to participate in this ritual as well. "Charlie . . ."

Shaking her head, Charlie stood and shifted the straps of her gig bag. If it looked like she was unsure of what she was denying, he wasn't sure what he was asking so, in a way, they were even. "I've got to go."

Which was when he realized his room was a little short of greenery. "How?"

"I can tear myself away, trust me."

"No, I mean . . ." He nodded toward the door. "You can't go down the courtyard. She's waiting right outside."

"Jack Archibald Gale, you do not want to get in the middle of this, young man!" The door vibrated with the force of Auntie Bea's pronouncement. "And she is the cat's mother!"

Charlie glanced toward the mirror, took three steps sideways, and waved at her reflection. Her reflection waved back, nothing more or less than what it seemed. "Auntie Catherine can't break the surface of the mirror to pull me in. Fucking shit!"

"Allie's barred her." The quilt slid to the floor as he threw himself out of bed. "She knew that before she sent you to Calgary."

Charlie whirled to face him. He almost backed up, pushed by the intensity. Almost. "Say that again."

"She knew that before she sent you to Calgary?"

"She knew she didn't need the viburnum before she got to Calgary."

"Sure, whatever." Jack didn't see the connection, but he'd seen Charlie tap out that same complicated rhythm on her thigh lots of times over the last four years, white noise to help her put the pieces together. "Look, I could go out the window, get bigger and you could jump. We ride off into the sunset. Well, you ride. I fly."

"Shhh. Thinking."

"You are reaching the end of my patience, Jack Archibald Gale!" The grid over the door flared orange. The varnish began to bubble.

"Leave him alone, Auntie Bea!"

Allie. Stepping up to defend him. Him, but not Charlie. That was weird.

"He's using sorcery to protect her."

"Of course he is, he's hers."

That sounded like . . .

"Even if they *can't* do anything about it."

. . . the same stupid shit.

"I thought she was yours," Auntie Bea sniffed.

He'd never noticed before how completely useless his door was at blocking sound.

"She can pass through any reflective surface."

It took him a moment before he realized that totally off-topic statement had come from inside his room, then he turned to see Charlie staring at . . .

. . . a completely innocuous spot on his wall beside his second-season *Continuum* poster. "Uh . . . Charlie?"

"I can do this," she told him, her brows nearly touching over her nose. "I can. It's nothing more than reaching a bigger audience. No, the same audience, but really juicing the arrangement."

"What are you talking about?"

The argument in the hall paused; they were listening, too.

"Definitely not bigger." Charlie's left hand rose up by her shoulder, the fingers curling into familiar patterns. "It's more . . . like singing louder and rounder at the same time. No, like shaping the music with the rests. Caesurae. Fermata." She focused suddenly on Jack's face and, this time, he couldn't stop himself from stepping back when she grinned. "Birdseye!"

"Don't you mean bull's-eye?"

"Not this time. Say something to me."

"What?"

"Doesn't matter. Words off the top of your head."

"Okay, um, I still like you . . ."

The notes she Sang slipped between the words.

". . . more than I should."

Alone in his room, he sighed, and opened the door. "She's gone."

As Auntie Bea brushed past him, Allie pulled out her phone.

"Mama Mia" rang out from the floor, muffled by a fold in the duvet.

"Gone," he repeated. Then added as Auntie Bea turned, "Archibald? Since when?"

Breathing heavily, Charlie sagged against the trunk of an ash, and tried to pull in all the wandering bits of her. She felt like she'd gone through a screen. Specifically, through the holes in the screen. The screen was fine. She was . . . probably okay. "What the hell was that all about?" she snarled, having found the bit that was pissed off at being abandoned.

"Professional development." Auntie Catherine stood and twitched her skirt into place. "As Auntie Ruby would say, Charlotte, you're lazier than a pet coon. You'd have never gotten there on your own. You wander the world like a metaphysical hobo, playing your music, allowing my granddaughter to call you to heel in her bed, wallowing in the angst of a perpetually broken heart . . ."

"I am not wallowing!"

Auntie Catherine opened her mouth, closed it again, and nodded. "You're right. You're not wallowing. I apologize. The rest stands. You're capable of so much more than you attempt. You accept your boundaries without ever testing them."

She felt like she'd been playing three-chord songs her whole life. "You could have told me," Charlie muttered, stripping off the gig bag before she forgot it wasn't actually a part of her—two arms, two legs, one gig bag holding a guitar and clean underwear.

"Obviously I did tell you, or you wouldn't be here. You're welcome." And as half a dozen trumpets blew a fanfare, she stepped out of the Wood.

The really annoying thing about the fanfare, Charlie admitted, was that she'd provided it. Unintentionally. Inadvertently. Without meaning to, even, but it was all her.

"2008 NBA finals, game six, Celtics and the Lakers." Auntie Bea sat down beside Jack on the sofa, hands curled around a half-finished afghan.

The afghan was crochet, not knitting, Jack noted. He didn't relax. A crochet hook, while not as aggressive as knitting needles, could be a weapon in the right hands. Auntie Bea's hands with her square-cut nails, the small scars on her knuckles, and the smudged tattoo at the base of her thumb looked about right.

"After a rocky first quarter," she continued, "the Celtics dominated the rest of the game. Final score was 131 to 92, largest margin of victory ever in a championship winning game. I won twelve hundred dollars and replaced the transmission in the van. Three half-bloods on the Celtics that year. Damn, but they can play." Her smile grew contemplative. "And I do mean they can *play*."

Jack looked across the room at Allie, who shrugged and kept folding laundry. When Auntie Bea pointedly cleared her throat, he turned his attention back to her.

"What I'm saying is, you may have hit on the one thing they'd actually want to save. How did they react?"

"They poisoned a piece of pie. Although," Jack frowned, "she might have intended it for her brother. Am I in trouble?"

"For going along with Charlotte's plan to speak to the Courts? No. How could you be expected to say no?"

"It wasn't her plan. It was our plan."

Auntie Bea ignored him. "For shielding her? How could you know any better?"

"Charlie doesn't make my decisions for me."

"I'm sure that's what you think." She held up a hand before he could respond, the double strand of green-and-yellow yarn looped around her fingers drawing Jack's gaze. "Given the circumstances, you can't think clearly with Charlotte near."

Okay, maybe he was a little distracted every time she touched him, or was in the same room, or breathed the same air, but . . .

"And given that she's feeling everything you are and acting as the responsible party, she's not thinking clearly at all."

He supposed that was fair, but . . .

"No one ever wants to see family go through this kind of thing."

Well, duh, but . . .

"Fortunately, you're young enough you can . . ."

"Jack!"

Allie's voice seemed to come from very far away.

"Look away from her hand."

Her hand? Was there a hand behind the yellow and green?

"Now, Jack!"

Eyes watering, he jerked back.

"I can't believe you even attempted that!"

Jack had never heard Allie so angry. One of Graham's shirts had begun unweaving itself in her hands, threads wafting to the floor and reassembling into a pale blue doll with white button eyes. "Attempted what?" he demanded. That was one freaky doll.

"The yarn was a charm," Allie told him, eyes locked on Auntie Bea. "She was getting into your head. It sounded like she was trying to bury your feelings for Charlie."

"Why not? They'll never be acted on. Charlotte has her faults, we all know that, but that's a line she'd never cross. He'll be significantly better off without them. We need clear heads if we're going to survive the impact."

His head slammed into the ceiling.

"Jack!"

"Sorry." He hadn't realized he'd changed. Back in skin, he helped Allie up, frantically patting at her smoldering clothes. "Are you okay? Please be okay!"

"Hey." She grabbed his face, her hands cool against his jaw. "You haven't raised so much as a blister on me since you've been here. I'm fine. You startled me, that's all."

"I've burned Charlie."

"You and Charlie have a different relationship."

"They don't have a relationship at all and they never will. Charlotte realizes that, and he's too young to know what he wants."

"He's standing right here!" Only Allie's touch kept him from changing again. "You can't just do something like that!"

"Oh, can't I?" Auntie Bea set the afghan aside and stood. "He's a Gale and the family comes first. For the family's sake I can . . ."

"The Ride of the Valkyries" rang out from Charlie's phone where Jack had tossed it on the coffee table. From Allie's phone on the kitchen counter. From Auntie Bea's phone in her knitting bag.

"It's Auntie Jane."

"That's not my ring for Jane," Auntie Bea muttered digging through the balls of yarn.

Concentrating on fingers instead of claws, Jack picked up Charlie's phone. "Hello?"

"You had a busy night, Jack, you must be hungry."

Right on cue, his stomach growled.

"Go get something to eat."

"Jane?"

The phones did conference calls? Auntie Bea in both ears was twice as much Auntie Bea as he wanted to hear. Figuring Auntie Jane didn't need to hear from him or she wouldn't have told him to leave, he silently and carefully set Charlie's phone back on the coffee table, placed a pale blue, plush moose on top of it, and headed for the door. He'd leave from the roof, no need to bother with clothes. When he glanced back, Auntie Bea had turned away but Allie waved him on, her smile looking more like gritted teeth. Behind her, the clock on the microwave ran backward.

"The Courts chased it into the harbor."

Charlie turned away from watching the Boston skyline grow smaller in the distance and squinted at the dark-haired, middle-aged woman who'd walked over to stand beside her at the rail. Even bundled into a heavy parka, her proportions were subtly wrong. The harmonics of her voice made Charlie think of fish—and not in a beer-battered with fries kind of way.

"It doesn't mind the cold," she continued, her eyes locked on the water, "because it usually lives in the deep trenches, rising only to hunt. Yesterday, the Courts came through an undersea gate riding hippogriffs—looking, I feel obliged to point out, like the worst kind of fantasy poster cliché—and herded it here. It doesn't like the iron, or the vibration from all the engines, but every time it tries to leave, they chase it back . . . There!"

The curve barely glimpsed for a second below the waves, a lighter blue/gray against the dark water of the bay, could have been mistaken for a whale.

"It's pretty tired right now; they forced it to travel a considerable distance in a short time, but, eventually, it'll get angry enough it'll go after a boat and people will die. Nothing the Courts enjoy more than mass hysteria. We've had people out on the water since it was spotted. On the ferry . . ." She patted the metal railing with a web-fingered hand. ". . . on our own boats. We might be able to lure it away from an attack. What are you here to do, Gale girl?"

"Fucked if I know," Charlie muttered. She couldn't Sing underwater. "I don't suppose you know where I could get my hands on a waterproof sound system?"

To her surprise, the Selkie turned toward her and smiled.

"Are you sure they won't miss this stuff?" Charlie stumbled and grabbed for the edge of the cabin as the chop that had been unnoticeable on the ferry tossed the small Woods Hole Institute boat around like a cork.

"No, we're good. I do a lot of independent work, so I'm always signing acoustic equipment out. I've been working on communication among *phoca vitulina.*"

"Say what?"

"Harbor seals," Dr. Malan explained.

"Okay, then." Charlie was still having a little trouble getting her head around the whole *Selkie with a doctorate* thing. At least it was in Marine Biology not something like, oh, eighteenth century English Pastoral Poetry because that, that would be too weird.

Smiling, she handed Charlie the microphone. "I assume you know how to use this?"

"I may have hit a Karaoke bar a time or two." A heartfelt rendition of "There's No Place Like Home"—a sea serpent cried out for a classic—gave the serpent an imperative suggestion the Courts couldn't stop. Although Charlie hoped they'd try.

"He wouldn't have understood the words," Dr. Malan pointed out when she finished.

"Doesn't matter. Music's about emotion, and he understood that."

The sudden patch of rough water near the mouth of the harbor might have been a breaching minke, but Charlie preferred to believe it was a member of the Court getting his skinny ass handed to him by a giant snake.

"I was young when we left the UnderRealm." Dr. Malan paused, hands still on a half coiled cable. "You weren't singing to me, but I suddenly found myself wanting to see the great ocean again."

"Yeah. About that . . ."

"Katie . . ." Jack lifted his hands before the keys started melting. Graham had warned him he'd be taking Auntie Carmen to her yoga class if he destroyed another keyboard. ". . . how do you spell coerced?"

"Spellcheck."

He spun around to face her, the ancient chair releasing a sigh of air that smelled like the inside of an old running shoe. Graham said the furniture destroyed by the aunties while searching for Jack's father had been replaced from a secondhand store, but, as Jack had grown more used to the way the MidRealm worked, he wondered if what Graham really meant by *secondhand store* was *dumpster*. "It thinks I mean corrosion."

That drew Katie's attention off her monitor and she frowned across the office. "How can you spell coerced so badly it thinks you mean corrosion? And what are you doing?"

"Graham gave me two column inches to write up the Siren thing in Winnipeg for the paper."

"Because he feels sorry for you and Charlie?"

"Because I was there." And because he had to get away from Auntie Bea. And because if Charlie wanted him to deal with any weird happenings in the area, the office of the *Western Star* was the best place to catch an early heads up. Weird and freaky tabloids by definition kept a close eye on the weird and freaky.

"Right. Did you get a grainy out-of-focus and/or drastically pixelated photo?"

"No . . ."

"Then it doesn't count."

"So it's a pity assignment," he growled, rolling his chair back from the big metal desk.

"Jack, sweetie, it's two column inches. He doesn't feel that sorry for you. So . . ." She waved a hand in his general direction. ". . . knock off the smoke signals before the sprinkler system kicks in again."

"I can't change the way I feel."

"I know."

"Neither can Charlie."

"I know. But in seventy years, unless we all buy it in the next two . . ."

Even without Charlie's ears, Jack could hear the bitterness mixed with fear in Katie's voice. It made him feel like he was eavesdropping on something private and he wondered if Charlie felt that way all the time. Or if privacy wasn't something Gale girls worried about.

". . . either way, she'll be dead and you'll be free so I, personally, feel sorry for Charlie. It's her whole life, however long that life happens to be, it's a small fraction of yours."

"You think I'm ruining her life?" No one else had put it like that. He'd been stuck on how her constant refusal to break the rule was messing up his life. And hers.

"I think . . ." Katie sighed and stared at him for a long moment. "I don't think you're doing it on purpose," she said at last. "Now, open a window and let the smoke out. Some things in here, like me, don't react well to being sprayed with a few hundred liters of water."

Jack hauled himself up onto his feet. He was ruining Charlie's life. She'd never said he was ruining her life. She never hesitated about telling him when he pissed her off. Did she not know? Or worse, was she lying to him? Charlie could tell a lie even the aunties would believe. Would she lie if she thought she was protecting him? Sure she'd agreed that the whole situation, the liking each other too much, sucked, but there was a world of difference between sucked and ruined.

The window was stuck.

His father's protection hexes had long since been removed, but they'd warped the frame.

Claws hooked under the lower lip, he put his back into it. The window slammed open. Cracked. Before he could announce it had been an accident, a pack of Pixies slammed into his chest.

A whole pack of them hurt, moth-sized or not. Jack stumbled back, braced himself on his tail, and winced as all but one of the Pixies circled his head, shrieking. Message delivered, they swooped back outside, ignoring the Pixie who'd been stunned by the impact. Jack scooped it up off the floor, but Katie snatched it out of his hand before he could decide what to do with it.

"I'm not eating them anymore," he muttered, rubbing his chest.

She took it to the window and, as its wings started to move, first slowly then into the familiar blur, she gave it a gentle toss into the air. "Little bastard!"

"Bit you, didn't it?"

"Shut up. What did they say?" she asked around the finger in her mouth.

"There's an iceberg in Lethbridge."

"There's a mention of a freezer malfunction at a meat processing plant." Katie glanced up from the laptop. "Happened right before dawn and it's still so iced up they can't get into it. There's no report of injuries."

"Iced-up meat fridge." Jack raised one hand, palm up. "Iceberg." And the other. "Close enough."

"You think the Pixies were telling you about a freezer malfunction in Lethbridge?" she asked as he leaned forward to read over her shoulder. "I thought packs of Pixies never left their territory."

"They don't."

"And their territory's only about a square kilometer."

"If that. But news spreads fast from pack to pack. Only trouble is, there's a few hundred packs between here and Lethbridge . . ."

"One pack per kilometer makes two twelve."

For someone who worked at a freaky happenings tabloid, she was way too fixated on accuracy. "Yeah, that's what I said. Filter information through a hundred packs and the end result is about as accurate as what you'd get from preschoolers on a sugar high playing telephone."

"And you'd know," Katie muttered.

"No one told me that's what marshmallows were made of."

"Gabi said it took the girls a week to come down."

Probably an exaggeration although Jack wouldn't guarantee it. "Old news."

"I can't see why the Pixies would care about a broken freezer."

Jack shrugged. "Depends what's in it. Tell Allie I'm not going to be home for supper, okay?"

It was dark and snowing lightly by the time Jack got to Lethbridge.

"Turn left here," he muttered circling the building. "And here. And here. And here. You have reached your destination. Unless there's another freezer in Alberta where at least one Frost Giant has gone to ground." Even from a hundred meters up, he could smell the UnderRealm in the familiar white/blue ice that covered the west end of the building and spilled over the edge of the loading dock. White/blue ice that smelled of the UnderRealm? That meant Frost Giant. He assumed the building's doors were behind the ice.

All the parking lot lights were on and the crowd around the doors suggested they hadn't given up on getting in, even if nothing they'd tried so far had worked. Nothing they could get their hands on anyway. The military might have the firepower, but since all Jack knew about the military came from American movies and television, maybe not. He'd never seen a movie about the Canadian military, and he doubted the Americans would lend out either Jeremy Renner or their giant robots to get into a freezer.

If Charlie were here, she'd Sing and the men with the blowtorches and the men with the chainsaws and the men with the axes and the men with the clipboards would suddenly realize there were places they'd rather be.

But Charlie wasn't here. Even if she was, she'd be on the ground because she wouldn't have accepted a ride.

And he'd ruined her life.

His stomach growled. Allie had him so well trained he hadn't even considered eating the men in his way, but it would certainly simplify things.

If he were any kind of a sorcerer, if he were the sorcerer the family—the world—needed, he could put these men to sleep, or create an illusion so real they'd believe it, or stop time long enough to get in and out and save the day. But he wasn't that kind of a sorcerer, or any kind of a sorcerer really, so he fell back on what he knew.

A car blew up on the far side of the parking lot.

The men with the clipboards turned at the sound, and after a short discussion, one walked briskly around the corner of the building. He *ran* back.

Confused by the amount of talking—Humans were usually a lot more attached to their cars—Jack blew up an SUV and a pickup truck. Roar of sound. Pillars of flame. Full-on movie special effects.

That got everyone's attention. The area around the ice emptied of witnesses.

He landed as gently as he could, but the asphalt cracked beneath him. Wings in, head down, careful to stay behind the building, he examined the ice. The axes had etched thin lines, evidence that in a hundred years or so the men wielding iron would actually reach the doors. The chainsaws had done more damage, but from the number of broken chains tossed aside, the ice stood a good chance of winning by attrition. The blowtorches had melted deep grooves. As Jack watched, the ice filled them in.

He took a step back, drew in a deep breath, and flamed. Dragons and Frost Giants were natural enemies. The ice didn't melt, it vaporized.

As a patch of the steel door began to scorch, one of the tanks fueling the blowtorches exploded. Most of the shrapnel melted in the superheated air, but a sudden pain in his left shoulder snapped Jack's teeth together as instinct took over before he could gasp. The flame cut off.

Inhaling while flaming was fatal; his mother had told him that when he first started to smoke. Fatal, and messy.

The wound was minor; the shard had barely penetrated the scale. He touched it with his tongue, checked for poison out of habit, and ignored it to examine the building. The door was clear, so Jack hooked a claw under the handle and pulled it open.

Off was *like* open.

He changed to skin to walk into the building, stumbled, and remembered, as blood dribbled down his arm, that the injury wasn't proportional to the change and an eight-centimeter cut at twenty-meters tall was an entirely different matter at just under two meters. Plus, it hurt. A lot.

Spine twisted to try and get a better look the cut, he felt rather than saw the ice spear whistle through the space his head had recently vacated. For another heartbeat he stood silhouetted in the doorway like an idiot with a death wish, then dove to the right as the second spear passed. He froze, tucked into the deep shadow at the base of the wall, biting back an adrenaline-fueled snicker. *Seriously? Froze?*

The freezer was huge, but except for the light spilling through the door, it was also dark. It never got truly dark on the ice fields and his uncles had told him that Frost Giants had terrible night sight. Dragons, however, saw almost as well at night as they did during the day. The moment the giant stuck a snowball out from behind a hanging half of frozen cow, he'd see it. On the other hand, while his internal temperature would keep him comfortable for a while, sustained cold was not a dragon's friend. When he'd pointed that out, his first year with Allie and Graham, Graham had pointed out in turn that Alberta winters were no one's friend. The giants, however, could stay in the freezer indefinitely. Or until they needed to eat. Jack had no idea what Frost Giants ate, but if it was . . .

The water vapor in the air five centimeters above the floor froze solid. If the wave hadn't started back in the shadows and moved in a glittering curve toward the door, it would've caught him. Trapped him. Jack jumped for a tabletop, knocked a digital scale flying, and flattened as another ice spear smashed against the wall.

"Hey! Dial it back! I come in peace! I know the Courts screwed you over. You'd have never come through, here and now, had it been your choice. I'm here to help!"

"Who are you to help us, Dragon Lord?" The words cracked and groaned like ice breaking up in the spring. Sirens spoke the language seduction required, the Courts needed to be understood when they yelled, *"I'm open over here!"* But the Frost Giants refused to speak any language other than their own with such vehemence they made Quebec's language police look like mall cops. Since they never left the ice fields, that wasn't usually a problem. Fortunately, understanding language was a Dragon Lord thing.

"We talk, they listen," had been Uncle Viktor's explanation.

"Why not allow prey to try and talk their way free?" Uncle Adam had said, after Uncle Viktor had gone off to lick his wounds. *"They have no other means of defense."*

Jack sighed. His lips were already chapped from the flaming, but the Frost Giants would have no idea who Jack Archibald—turned out it was his father's father's name—Gale was when he was home. His actual name, his dragon name, involved ten minutes of lineage and a few sounds the Human mouth wasn't designed to make. It hurt, and he licked away blood when he finally finished.

"Highness?"

Something about the voice, the fear and relief combined, made Jack think of his cousin Penny. Who was twelve.

Two moving glimmers of white/blue slid between the rows of meat about halfway down the freezer. The taller was no more than four meters tall, if that, height mostly torso over short, thick legs. A teenager by Frost Giant reckoning. The second giant was half a meter shorter. Half a meter younger.

"Look, I can see you, you can't see me, so I'm going to turn the light on to even things up, okay?" Straightening, Jack patted the wall until he found a switch.

"It is true! You are a sorcerer!"

Jack looked at the light switch and squinted at the two Frost Giants who stared at him from much closer than he'd expected. As he *was* a sorcerer, and as both of them gripped three-meter shafts of ice, he decided to skip the lecture on technology. "So I'm guessing a couple of butt munches from the Courts said land of ice and snow, have a great time, something to brag about, yadda yadda, created a gate, and closed it after you went through. Am I right?"

"I do not know this yadda," said the taller.

"Not important," Jack sighed.

"The Courts told us lies," said the other, clutching the ice spear like a pointy security blanket.

"They promised adventure."

"Promised enjoyment."

"But there was only warmth until we found this shelter."

"Now we are trapped and the meat has died."

"Yeah, well, you'd love this place in February." Jack jumped off the table, skidded a bit, and slapped half a cow. "And the meat was dead when it got here."

"Not that meat." The taller straightened and gestured with one long, angular arm, fingertips drawing frost lines in the air. "That meat."

A middle-aged man stared out of a block of ice, dark eyes narrowed, brows drawn in, mouth open. He wore a puffy red parka and a toque with the name of the packing plant knit into it. He looked like he originally came from somewhere warm, and he'd died angry not afraid.

"The meat ran at us to make us leave," the taller explained.

And they'd stopped it. Him. Jack didn't blame them. He blamed the Courts.

"You are meat, Dragon Prince. Is he yours?"

"Yes. He's mine." Not when he lived, but the Courts wouldn't have sent the Frost Giants through if he hadn't told them about the asteroid.

"We are off the ice." The shorter one looked panicked. "You may claim . . ." *Water debt* was as close as the translation came although that wasn't quite what it meant.

"I don't want one of your body parts." Beginning to feel the cold through the soles of his feet, Jack moved toward the door. "If we return to the gate, to where the gate was, I can send you home."

"We go into the warmth?" The taller grabbed for the shorter one's arm and shuffled back between the swinging beef. "No."

"It's night now. Less warmth and a little snow."

"Snow." The shorter giant planted its feet and they stopped moving. From where Jack stood, it looked as if its feet were frozen to the floor. "If it is cold enough for snow, we will not be harmed."

"We will not be harmed by the warm." Jack thought the expression the taller turned his way was a frown, although given the glittering planes and angles of the Frost Giant's face, it was hard to tell for sure. "Outside this shelter you will be stronger. I do not trust you. Why should we trust you, Dragon Prince?"

"You shouldn't." Not that they'd believe him if he said they should. "But I don't want you here, and if I open the gate you came through, you'll end up where you left from."

The shorter giant's lipless mouth moved, working that through. "We will go home?"

"You will."

"The one we calved from will be angry."

"Dude, I have family problems of my own." Out over the threshold, he could hear approaching sirens. "And other problems coming in fast. Let's go. Stay unseen. I'll follow in the air."

The taller's suspicions left him unconvinced. The shorter really wanted to go home. Their argument sounded like a Zamboni drag race, and Jack had started to worry he might have to blow up another car when they pushed past him—the push was totally unnecessary, he would've moved—and raced across the parking lot to the darkness beyond. In spite of the stumpy legs, they could really boot it.

The Courts had opened the gate barely half a kilometer away from the plant within a triangle formed by two hotels and a church. They'd wanted the giants seen and that meant they wanted Jack and/or the Gales to know about it.

"Dirtbags." Snow steamed as Jack landed. Which is when he realized he had no idea of how to open a gate. He'd opened a gate to save Charlie's life, but that had been need more than sorcery and as much as he needed to get these guys home before someone with a camera left the marshmallow roast on the other side of the meat packing plant, it wouldn't be enough.

Because he was useless.

He could feel the form of the gate, but he had no idea of what sorcery the Courts had used to open it.

"This is the place. Right here. This. Is this not the place?"

The taller smacked the shorter on the back of the head. "This is the place. Dragon Prince?"

"Give me a minute." Charlie could open it. Charlie had disappeared out of his room without even a potted plant. But Charlie was a G . . . "I'm an idiot."

The shorter giggled. Seemed that had translated just fine.

"Get ready, I'm a little short on supplies so you'll only have until the smoke dissipates." Jack changed, breathed out a cloud of smoke, and formed it into the charm Allie used to open things—pickle bottles, CD cases, and the bag inside cereal boxes for the most part, but the theory was sound. Gales used the charm to open things. He was a Gale. He had a thing he needed to open. "World's most complicated smoke ring," he muttered, tugging the outer swoop into a fuller curve. When it was right—mostly right—he tossed it into the imprint of the gate. The air filled with the scent of burnt butter, and the gate opened. "Go!"

To his surprise, they went. Way too trusting. "And stop listening to the Courts," he yelled after them, "they're dicks!"

Then the giants were gone, and the smoke was gone, and only an ice slick remained on the pavement. From the blue/white gleam under the streetlights, Jack had a feeling it was permanent.

But, hey, it was Alberta. Who'd notice?

Kiren blinked up at the sky half expecting to see the asteroid dominating the stars, blazing so brightly familiar constellations had ceded their positions to the harbinger of death.

"Harbinger of death?" Apparently, when exhausted, the writers at FOX News provided her mental voice. She rummaged a half-eaten power bar out of the bottom of her tote, picked a bit of tissue off the damp end, and wondered what day it was while she chewed. Thursday? Friday? If it was actually still Wednesday, then the video conference with Houston and Washington must've created a small black hole. That was the only possible explanation for the time dilation. Too bad a few of the politicians hadn't been sucked into it.

The problem with NASA was that too many of the people who worked there were capable of putting two and two together and getting pi divided by the number of liters in a gallon minus three.

Although it sounded illogical, it turned out that the more people who put the pieces together and came to the correct conclusion, the more people there were who subsequently needed to be told.

She'd been running simulations for . . . well, it probably only felt like years. Most of them were for fellow scientists and she'd already started getting data back. One, however, had been stripped down to the "rock hits planet, planet goes boom, almost everyone dies" level, and even after that there'd been an extensive argument over both *boom* and *almost everyone*. Dr. Adeyemi had been driven to banging her head against the conference table.

Here and now, in the star-strewn sky over JPL, the asteroid was not visible.

The stars meant she'd missed the last bus to the east parking lot again—although *as usual* would be the more accurate observation. Her ass ached, her eyes burned, her skin felt like it didn't quite fit her body, but on the bright side, when . . . no, if the asteroid did finally hit, she'd welcome the chance to fall over.

The sole of her right shoe dragged against the asphalt, the rubber shrieking in protest, the sound eaten up by all the empty space around her. Even though she knew there were half a dozen engineers in the Assembly Facility . . .

"On the one hand, we might be going the way of the dinosaurs." Howard grinned at her. *"On the other hand, they're letting us play with the really cool toys."*

. . . she felt like the only person alive. Wall-E, not Will Smith, doing her job at the end of all . . .

Hoofbeats?

Kiren stopped under a lamppost and squinted in the direction of the Angeles National Forest. There were deer in the forest, there were occasionally deer in the parking lots, but as far as she knew, there'd never been deer actually inside the perimeter fence. It had been specifically built high enough to keep them out.

The sound was definitely coming from this side of the fence.

The banging two coconuts together sound of hooves on pavement.

Coming closer.

With no actual idea of how a running deer would sound, Kiren didn't think that sounded like deer. It was too . . . purposeful. This was an animal running with intent. This was . . .

A unicorn.

Large and muscular, it looked like a draft horse crossed with a narwhal, two species even Kiren—an exhausted non-biologist—knew were incompatible. It gleamed in the shadows between the streetlights, muscles moving fluidly beneath its coat. Silver-gray hooves struck sparks from the ground— impossible, but *unicorn*, so Kiren let it go—and its mane and tail both flowed and rippled so perfectly she had to remind herself it wasn't CGI.

The ivory, spiraled horn had surprisingly deep, dark grooves.

As she watched, too tired to do anything more than stand and wonder if the power bar had been a little too far past its best before date, the unicorn's nostrils flared—they were impressively red on the inside—and it pivoted on one front hoof, turning almost a full ninety degrees from its original path and heading directly toward her.

"Sweetheart, given the traditional criteria, you're way too late for . . . um . . ." Heart racing, sweat rolling down her back, her hindbrain took over and spun her behind the lamppost as the unicorn passed. She could feel the impact of each hoof with the ground. Smell salt and something sour that coated the roof of her mouth. Hear the damp snort that ended each breath. See that the shadows on the horn were stains, red-brown not black.

If this unicorn came out of a fairy tale, then it was the kind of fairy tale that featured severed feet dancing through the forest not singing mice creating haute couture.

She turned as it . . . No, he; definitely he. She turned as *he* did, keeping the lamppost between them, fighting the stupidly suicidal urge to run. Her heart pounded in time with the hoofbeats, nearly deafening her, nearly drowning out . . .

Madonna?

Someone was singing "Like a Virgin" off in the shadows between two eucalyptus trees.

The unicorn reared, screamed in rage, and charged toward the singer.

Arm draped around the post to keep her standing, Kiren thought that was a bit of an overreaction. It was a decent cover, if a tad clichéd under the circumstances.

His horn split the air between the trees—literally split the air, Kiren caught a glimpse of a sunlit wood before it closed behind him.

The silence that followed had substance, texture, and Kiren sucked tiny gulps of air past her teeth so as not to disturb it. The underbrush rustled and she stopped even that, aware she was fully visible, but convinced it would be the sound of her breathing that would give her position away.

When Charlie Gale stepped out onto the road, blue strip in her hair, jacket and jeans over red cowboy boots, Kiren drew in a deep lungful of air, choked on a bug, and went to her knees. After a moment, the coughing that had been about the bug turned into something verging on hysteria and she couldn't stop. Then strong hands gripped her shoulders and a quiet, commanding voice told her to breathe.

"Deep breath. Slowly. Okay, now let it out."

In. Out. Eyes streaming, Kiren straightened. "That was you," she said to Charlie Gale. "Singing."

"Yeah, that was me."

"And before that, that was a unicorn."

"Yes, it was."

Kiren accepted a hand up onto her feet, then waved off any other help. "What the hell is going on?"

Charlie Gale glanced toward the spot where the unicorn had disappeared, then back at her. "Dr. Mehta, do you want to go for a coffee?"

Her mouth tasted like she'd been chewing coffee filters. "I think I've had enough."

"Tea?"

Kiren adjusted her glasses, brushed the dirt off her knees, and struggled for detachment as she noted a hoofprint gouged into the road. "I could do tea."

TEN

". . . AND THEN EINEEN SAID, it's been thousands of years. Do you know how widespread our bloodline is? And I said, that's why *we* keep it in the family." Charlie let her sleeve fall to cover the bruise. "Which is when she smacked me. She's stronger than she looks."

"Eineen the Selkie?"

Nudging a pile of magazines into a configuration less likely to collapse under its own weight, Charlie set her empty mug down on top of the stack. Paper, from books to journals to equations scribbled on the backs of junk mail envelopes, covered every available bit of horizontal space in Dr. Mehta's condo. Even the studio portrait of an older couple—Parents? Grandparents?—that hung over her fireplace had a Post-it note stuck to it. "You were nearly kabobbed by a unicorn; why are Selkies so hard to believe?"

"They're just . . ." Kiren waved her hands and splashed herself with tea, having forgotten she still held her mug. After a moment spent frowning down at the glistening wet mark on the top of one bare foot, she shrugged, yawned, and said, "It's the crossbreeding. It's biologically impossible."

"But metaphysically likely."

"I guess I can't argue with that." As Charlie sagged back into the sofa cushions, Kiren finished her tea and stared into the bottom of the mug.

"What do you see?" There were no tea leaves to read, but that didn't matter much.

"Death. Destruction. Although, technically, I suppose destruction comes before death." She sighed and set the mug beside Charlie's. "Should you even be telling me all this? Selkies and aunties and the soundtrack of your life?"

Charlie considered shrugging. Decided she didn't have the energy. "Sometimes you need to talk about shit."

"I hear you."

"And I know you can keep a secret."

"And you're going to wipe my memory when you go."

Okay, that was unexpected. Although Kiren didn't look terribly upset about the prospect. "How do you figure?"

"Acknowledge the facts, consider the implications, create a hypothesis. Your family, and all the . . ." Her hands sketched unicorns and Selkies in the space between them. ". . . extras, run completely under the radar. A few random data points aren't a problem, they'll be turned into stories and we all think we know the difference between fact and fairy tale, but if someone with the ability to connect the points into an actual theorem finds out, then you're threatened with exposure. As you've never been exposed, and—excluding your monologue on the moral implications of not removing the ass head from that Spurs player on the drive from JPL—we've been talking for . . ." She blinked at her watch.

"About an hour and a half," Charlie offered.

"Magic?"

"I can see the clock in your kitchen."

"Right." Kiren waved that off. "Okay. Everything points to you and your family having a system in place to prevent exposure. As I can now expose you, you need to take care of that. Me." She frowned and seemed to think the point needed more clarifying. "My ability to expose you. I assume you're not carrying around confidentiality agreements although, traditionally, sign-ing a contract is a valid way to apply metaphysics. Applied metaphysics. Fantasy engineering, right? Besides . . ." The yawn caught her in the middle of giggling. ". . . you already told me you did Gary. Gary's memory. Not Gary."

Charlie'd always known that exhaustion and alcohol created similar symptoms. She'd never seen it proven quite so conclusively. "When was the last time you got any sleep?"

"Lying down? In a bed? My bed?" Kiren dragged both hands back through her hair. "When was the last time I saw you?"

"Come on." Charlie stood and tugged the smaller woman up onto her feet. "The sandman's waiting."

"Is he real?"

"Not as far as I know." The door after the bathroom led to a guest room/office. Also filled with paper. Shifting her grip as Kiren bounced off the wall, Charlie revised her belief that a scientist would have to be uber organized. Of course, there was always the chance this *was* organized and she wasn't smart enough to spot the system.

"Santa?"

"Jury's still out."

"Surya?"

The master bedroom was behind the door at the end of the hall. With Kiren hanging off her right arm, Charlie had to twist past her to flick on the light. "I don't even know what that is."

"Hindu sun god. One of the lesser Devatas."

"Given the family baby-daddy, I'm probably not the best person to ask about gods."

The bed hadn't been made. Charlie dropped Kiren on the edge of the mattress, then tugged the comforter free of the crap piled on it.

Kiren watched a pile of paper tabbed with multicolored Post-it notes slide to the floor, and snorted. "Paperless office, my ass." Then she snickered. "Paperless bedroom, my ass. I think you should know," she added solemnly, "I don't sleep with girls. Women. Where sleep is a commonly used euphemism for sex."

"I do sleep with girls. Women. Where sleep is a commonly used euphemism for sex. But I am perfectly willing to take no for an answer."

"You didn't ask."

"You answered anyway."

"Efficiency. Go team." She toppled sideways. "Any sufficiently advanced technology can be mistaken for magic. Arthur C. Clarke. More or less."

"Auntie Ruby was in Sri Lanka in the early sixties."

"Are you saying . . ."

"That Auntie Ruby got around. That's all. In fifty years, we'll be throwing around quotes inspired by my sisters."

"I doubt that."

"You haven't met my sisters."

"Not what I meant." Sighing, Kiren squirmed until she was lying more-or-less the right way around, her head on the pillow. "If you can't stop the Armageddon Asteroid and I can't stop the Armageddon Asteroid, then in sixty years we—where we is the whole human race including your quirkily unique subset—we will be scraping out a subsistence living in isolated pockets where incidental geography or possibly geology . . . I'm a little tired . . . provided protection. From the Armageddon Asteroid. God, I hate that name."

"None of that means we won't be talking about my sisters."

She smiled, a tired, sad smile that took a good shot at breaking Charlie's heart. "Fair enough. You know, there's speculation that after the Chicxulub asteroid the entire surface of the earth baked for over a decade."

"I didn't know that."

"Baked. We'll be cookies."

"Pie."

"What?"

"My family leans toward pie."

Kiren nodded. "I like pie. I like you. You give me hope. If there's people like you and yours in the world, anything can happen. *Anything.*"

Charlie pulled the comforter up and made a mental note to turn the air conditioning down. "Get some sleep, Kiren."

"You can sleep on the couch, it's comfortable. I've slept on it lots of times." Yawning, she rolled over onto her side. "Wipe my memory in the . . . you know, after sleeping."

The couch *was* comfortable. Between the asteroid and Jack, Charlie hadn't been sleeping much either, and it wouldn't be long until morning.

"I don't want to be pie," she sighed as she turned off the light.

Instead of heading north to Calgary, Jack detoured west into the foothills and snatched a big white-tailed buck off the side of the highway. This close to the end of October, he had a full rack of antlers and the severed head dropped like a rock. After all the flying and the flaming, a second deer would've hit the spot, but—with even a partially full belly—sleep called.

With Charlie off sorting out the Courts' crap in the wider world, he had no reason to go home. Sure, there'd be pie, but there was always pie. Sometimes, pie wasn't enough.

Since caves weren't exactly easy to spot from the air, and if he had to sleep outside, he might as well have stayed in the freezer, he broke into an isolated barn. Well, he had to squeeze through the big double doorway— with a belly full of deer he couldn't change either his size or into skin—but, *technically*, nothing broke. The barn smelled of cattle, probably rounded up and taken off the high pastures with the end of summer if *Heartland* could be trusted to have slid a few facts in under the angst. He only watched *Heartland* because Charlie watched it and Charlie only watched it because she knew one of the writers and the two of them agreed that no way Caleb should've divorced Ashley. He shoved two big round bales of hay against the walls out of his way, and curled up with his chin on a third. Protected from the wind, his body heat soon got the barn up to an almost comfortable temperature. Wrapped around the place he and Charlie overlapped, he drifted off to sleep.

"Hey, you."

Jack knew he was dreaming. Not because the Charlie facing him was his age, or, at least, well within his seven-year break, all army boots and attitude and blue/black hair, but because the connection he still felt didn't lead to her. For all she looked and sounded like Charlie, he couldn't even count it as wish fulfillment because it *wasn't* Charlie. He sat up, still in scales, putting them eye-to-eye as she walked one of the barn's beams. "Go away. I don't want you."

"Too bad." Arms out, she pivoted at the end of the beam and headed back, dust motes dancing around her like Pixies. "You can have me. You can't have her."

"You can't tell me what I can't have."

"Yeah, dude, I can."

"No, you can't."

"If you want to be a Gale, you have to follow this one rule. You can't have her."

Tail out for balance, he reared. "Yeah, well, maybe I don't want to be a Gale!"

"If you're not a Gale, you can't have her."

"Stop saying that." His wings slammed into the walls. The walls shook. "She's not something to *have*."

"Okay, fine." A dismissive flip of blue/black hair. "She can't have you. Works out the same either way. Big fucking hole in both your hearts that'll never be filled."

"Stop it!"

"You can't be together."

"Shut up!"

"No way, no how."

"Shut up!"

She burned, fat crackling, skin peeling in blackened strips. Smiling, not screaming.

She smelled like pork.

His mouth watered.

And he woke up, clutching at his connection to Charlie.

It hadn't changed.

The relief, completely illogical relief because he knew he'd been dreaming, left him feeling light-headed and he dropped his head, chin resting on the floor in the meter or so of fresh air remaining under the thick smoke that filled the barn.

The thick smoke?

Wings tight to his back in embarrassment, he put out the fire seconds before one of the beams ignited. He hadn't spontaneously flamed in his sleep in years. The third bale had been reduced to ash, but at least no one had seen; the aunties would never let him live down that kind of property destruction. And Cameron would have never let him live down the whole nocturnal emissions thing.

Pale, predawn light spilled through the grimy windows. It'd still be a few more hours before he'd be able to change into skin, but he'd digested enough he could adjust his size to fit through the door without needing to fix the frame afterward. A dump out off the main trail where weather would take care of the evidence brought him a little closer to thumbs. Not that he needed thumbs. He needed to see Charlie. He needed to hear her complain and see her smile and smell her and touch her and argue with her about how little thirteen years meant to an immortal. Eyes, ears, and nose needed to know she hadn't burned.

He'd used the blood tie to track his father from the UnderRealm, so cross-country, or countries, to find Charlie would be a piece of cake. Or, more probably, pie. Trouble was, he couldn't count on Charlie to stay put and she traveled too quickly for him to keep up. He should go home. She always came home.

The dirt rolled up behind his claws like wood shavings as he gouged four lines into the partially frozen ground. Someday, she wouldn't come home. Someday, the restrictions of family would outweigh the benefits and, like Auntie Catherine, she'd go Wild. Someday soon. He could feel her pulling away from the center of the family. Reluctantly, and not even entirely aware she was doing it, but he could feel it. He wasn't the only one. He'd watched Allie watch Charlie and knew that half the time she called her home just to prove she still could. The rest of the time, her reasons were more obvious.

Except . . . Jack frowned up at the sky. . . . the asteroid would keep Charlie home. She couldn't go Wild unless going Wild would save the world. But after the asteroid, even if only the family survived, she wouldn't stay. He didn't know what he'd do when Charlie left. She'd said they'd always have what they had, but how long would she be willing to come around and talk to him through the fence separating her from the rest of the family? He'd finally go Wild himself, driven by frustration, and spend all his time chasing her but never catching her.

"If you want to be a Gale . . ."

What did want have to do with it? Being a Gale was a matter of blood. He might not have known he was a Gale for the first thirteen years of his life, but that didn't change the fa . . .

A dragon's shadow blocked the sun.

Pines cracked as Jack snapped out to full size and were flung aside by his downdraft as he took to the air.

The other dragon flew east, the rising sun masking his color. Didn't matter. For as long as it lasted, the MidRealm was his world. Not even Uncle Adam got a free pass.

Closer. Closer. The invader was fast, but Jack burned his frustration as fuel, shredding the thirteen years that kept Charlie from him with every beat of his wings. Closer. He opened his mouth to roar and choked, coughing clouds of smoke out his nose as bands of power clamped his muzzle shut.

The other dragon dropped a wingtip and pivoted around it. Excluding Jack's mother, this was the largest dragon Jack had ever seen. As he passed, scales gleaming in the sun, he said, "I have a proposition for you, Jack. We should land and talk."

"Fucking California," Charlie muttered, dragging the blanket over her head and cutting off the beam of sunlight that had slapped her awake with sudden light and heat. It was obviously morning. She was just as obviously not getting up. Not given the time she'd gotten to sleep. Kiren had been right, the sofa was comfortable. Both long enough and wide enough and with the big, floral sofa cushions tossed to the floor, Charlie rated it in the top ten of sofas she'd spent the night on in spite of its proximity to the curtainless east window. Would've made the top five had she not been alone.

For certain values of being alone that ignored the empty place Jack should . . .

Jack!

Throwing the blanket aside, she surged up onto her feet and ran across the room to where her jacket hung on the back of one of the dining room chairs.

She couldn't feel Jack.

The connection hadn't been broken, it just *wasn't*.

He wasn't dead, but he wasn't there.

Where the hell was her phone?

Shit! She'd left it in Jack's room.

"Okay, not a problem. I'll borrow Kiren's." She spun in place trying to spot Kiren's phone, saw the backpack dangling from a doorknob and dove for it. The phone was in an outer pocket with a dead battery, but a quick run-through of Jennifer Lopez's "Charge Me Up" took care of that.

"Charlie?" Allie asked through a yawn. "What are you . . ."

"Where's Jack?" Breathe damn it! There was air. There wasn't Jack, but there was air.

"In Lethbridge, in a freezer, dealing with the Courts."

"No, he's not." Phone clamped between ear and shoulder, Charlie shimmied into her jeans. "I woke up this morning and he was gone."

"You were with him?"

"No! The connection between us was . . ."

"Broken?"

"No, not broken." She gentled her voice as much as she could. Allie loved him, too. "Gone. Like he . . . like he *wasn't*."

"Come home."

Her boots were over by the door. "Do you know . . ."

"I have no idea. Just come home."

"I'm on my way." She tossed Kiren's phone on the table by the front door, slipped out, and traced a quick charm over the lock rather than walk off with Kiren's keys. Then she paused, erased the charm and slipped back in.

Kiren was right. There was a system in place to avoid exposure and a thousand songs about forgetting. Not even for Jack could she ignore that.

Except . . .

This was different than asking Gary to carry yet another secret and keep it hidden away from those he loved. Who the hell was she to take hope away from the woman who'd given the world a chance?

Charlie couldn't hear Jack's song in the Wood. She stumbled, grabbed a branch, and hung there for a moment listening to the way the music—Allie and the aunties and her mother and her sisters and a hundred cousins and even Gary's bouzouki—didn't work without Jack. It edged around the empty places instead of filling them in and the silence shouted this was where Jack should be.

Allie'd said Lethbridge.

His Song still resonated in the walls of the meat packing plant.

"Hey, you! Yeah, you, girl! What're you doing here?"

"Piss off!" Charlie snapped and couldn't find it in herself to care when the man with the clipboard stared down in horror at the spreading damp patch on his crotch.

Asphalt and concrete both complained about the Frost Giants' passing and Charlie followed the sound of the ground cooling to the skim of ice that marked where the gate had been. Jack hadn't gone through it. He'd landed, sent the giants through, and taken flight again.

If she went to the last place he'd been heard, would she leave the Wood in midair?

Would Jack return to save her?

Would Jack return to save her? Get a fucking grip.

Could she slip between the sound of plummeting to save herself before she hit the ground? Possibly. Probably.

Maybe not.

She couldn't risk it.

"Was it the aunties? Were they on him about the ritual?"

No surprise Auntie Gwen answered instead of Allie. "Jack knew we wanted him to take part in this ritual, Charlotte. And it's the same reason we want you to take part. However painful it may be for the two of you to stay apart outside of circle once that line has been crossed, we have to be able to say that we were at our full strength when . . ."

"When we fail."

"If that's what happens, then yes." She gestured to an empty seat at the kitchen table as Allie headed toward the coffeepot. "We left any necessary encouragement up to Cameron. He's been trying to convince Jack to share the load for the last two years. The details of what happens to a Gale boy in circle are best left to another Gale boy."

"Oh, he's heard the details," Allie sighed, handing Charlie a mug of coffee. "Cameron has been quite eloquent in his pleas for Jack's help."

Charlie noted the puffy half circles under Auntie Gwen's eyes, heard the absence of Graham and the twins, realized they wouldn't be interrupted by men or children, drank half the coffee, and sat down. Allie was wearing one of Graham's shirts—which she only did when he wasn't home and she needed the comfort. Growing up, she'd worn one of Michael's football jerseys nearly threadbare, and Charlie was one of four people who knew that the faded jersey remained tucked in the back of one of Allie's drawers. Maybe five people; Michael had probably told his husband.

"If something happened at Lethbridge . . ."

"No." Charlie pulled her attention back to the current situation, no matter how little she wanted to think of Jack being gone. "I went there first. Whatever happened, happened after."

"Is he . . ."

"No!"

"Charlotte."

"Tell me you weren't going to ask me if he was dead? Tell me, and I'll apologize." When Auntie Gwen shook her head, Charlie growled, "That's what I thought. He's not dead. I'd have felt his death, and I can't feel anything. The place Jack should be is empty. The sound system has cut out in the middle of the show, and I've gotten so dependent on it I can't play acoustic any . . ." The handle of the mug snapped off. Charlie stared at the piece of broken stoneware, watched Allie's fingers pull it out of her grip and check to see that she hadn't cut herself, looked up, and said, "He's not dead."

"The dragon didn't fly over this morning." Allie shrugged when Charlie turned toward her. "If one of his uncles caught up to him . . ."

"I could still feel him if he was hurt or unconscious, Allie."

"I know, but what if he was back in the UnderRealm?"

She turned the mug until she couldn't see the broken bit, and with her guitar calluses as insulation against the heat, drained it. "The Dragon Lords can't open gates."

"Jack can," Auntie Gwen said bluntly. "And his uncle had to have arrived here through one of the gates the Courts aren't policing."

Charlie expected her to mention *why* the Courts weren't policing their gates, why the treaty was currently saggier than a rapper's jeans—the aunties were big on placing blame—but Auntie Gwen merely waited, well aware that if Charlie didn't want to listen to the silence, she'd have to fill it. Have to say something to drown out the absence of Jack. "There's a reason Jack might have gone to the UnderRealm."

"To learn to be a sorcerer from the Courts so he can stop the asteroid and save you." Auntie Gwen sighed as Charlie felt her mouth drop open. "Was it supposed to be a secret?"

"The aunties hunt and kill sorcerers."

"As both you . . ." She nodded across the table. ". . . and Alysha keep saying, Jack's different. Predictably, we're not exactly thrilled by an asteroid wiping out most life on Earth, so I think you'll find that if he can learn how to stop the asteroid, we're willing to hand wave the sorcery and call it a Wild Power."

That sounded almost believable. "Auntie Bea . . ."

Auntie Gwen smiled. It was, in the fine auntie tradition, a smug and somewhat supercilious smile. "Let Jane deal with Bea."

"Auntie Jane . . ."

"Will do what's necessary to keep the family alive, as she always has."

A little annoyed by the interruptions, Charlie muttered, "Jack wants to keep everyone alive, not only family and definitely not just me. We talked about me taking him back to spend the four years he's been here with the Courts."

"That's a great idea!"

She could hear hope in Allie's voice and hated having to extinguish it. "No, it isn't. The Courts do nothing for free and the price he'd have to pay is too high. The ritual may have forced his hand," she continued before Allie could ask what that price was, "so now he's gone to the UnderRealm to get proof that the Courts will teach him." If she was honest with herself, it was what she'd been afraid of since she'd felt him gone. "If he comes home with that proof before the ritual . . ."

"You'll be told to take him back those four years." Auntie Gwen's tone left no room for doubt. That *would* happen.

"And if you refuse," Allie said softly, "if you go Wild, you'll doom the family."

As there was nothing to gain from pointing out that she'd doom the whole world, Charlie decided not to bother. "If I take him back, Jack will pay."

"You'll both pay, Charlotte."

One hand splayed over the slight curve of her belly, dimpling Graham's shirt, Allie shook her head. "It's time travel, Auntie Gwen. Jack'll be gone for minutes her time."

But Charlie was watching the shadows in Auntie Gwen's eyes. "You'll tell me to do it after ritual."

"As much as we're willing to hand wave, we won't turn a sorcerer loose until all other possibilities have been exhausted, and—as much as you and Jack are powers separately—the two of you together in ritual are too great a power to pass up."

It wouldn't matter if they were able to raise power enough to stop the asteroid or only enough to help save the family, they'd spend the rest of their lives, of her life, living during ritual, during those few brief moments when the years between them would matter less than the power they'd raise. "Fuck you."

"Charlie!"

Halfway to the door, Charlie heard Auntie Gwen murmur, "Let her go."

Allie winced as the door slammed and paused her pursuit long enough to shout, "We can't let her go Wild!"

"Alysha."

The power of her name held her in place.

"Charlotte's voice held nothing but anger and grief. If she were breaking with the family, we'd have heard it." Auntie Gwen stood and put the mugs in the sink. "She'll do what she has to."

Holding Graham's shirt tightly around her, Allie reached out and felt Charlie's unmistakable presence heading for the roof, radiating *leave me the fuck alone*. The profanity came through loud and clear. "It sucks," she muttered, turning back toward the kitchen. "It sucks that she can't be with Jack. It sucks that ritual's going to screw up any lesser connection they might have built between them. And it sucks that there's a stupid big rock on its way to destroy the whole stupid world. The whole thing sucks!"

Allie half expected an impatient request to stop stating the obvious, but to her surprise, Auntie Gwen merely turned, leaned on the counter, and said, "I know. I was the one who spent five hours with Bea last night going over Jane's list of those in the first circle she'd be willing to send west."

"Five hours?"

"It's complicated."

"Why not the same circle that went up against the Dragon Queen? Except for Auntie Jane, of course," Allie added quickly when Auntie Gwen frowned.

"Meredith won't leave Jane. Ellen and Christie won't leave Arthur." She made a face that pulled Allie's mouth into a reluctant smile. "Five hours, Alysha. Five minutes more and we'd have needed another name on the list because I've have strangled Bea. How fond are you of this broken mug?" she added, turning back to the sink. "Throw it out or put it aside for Jack to fix?"

"Jack's gone."

"He'll be back."

"How can you be so sure?" There had been no doubt in Auntie Gwen's voice. Not that the aunties usually allowed any doubt they might be feeling to show, but . . .

"Because he'll do everything he can to save Charlotte."

"And the family."

"Probably."

"Probably?" Allie's right hand spread over the gentle swell of her belly. "He's a Gale!"

"He's a Dragon Prince and they'd laugh at the concept of noblesse oblige. Saving the family will save Charlotte. Saving the world will save Charlotte." Auntie Gwen set the last of the rinsed cups on the drainboard and faced Allie again. "I honestly don't give a rat's ass about his motivations. The family can save itself without him, but it'll be a lot easier with him. The world . . ." She spread her hands. "Well, you don't want to spend time with Bea if she misses *Top Gear*."

"How can she?" Allie sighed. "It's always on. I'm not sure even an asteroid can stop it." Before Auntie Gwen could reply, the apartment door opened and Allie spun around, Charlie's name spilling out even though she *knew* her cousin was still on the roof.

Joe shook his head and gripped her shoulder lightly as he passed. "According to a Brownie who heard it from a flock of Pixies, Jack opened a gate and went through to the UnderRealm, but he wasn't alone. There was an older dragon with him."

"The dragon that's been flying over the store!"

"It's unlikely there's two of them here so, yeah, probably."

"If Jack's gone to find out if the Courts can teach him . . ." Auntie Gwen made a face that suggested she wasn't too happy about a sentence containing more than one *if*. ". . . what part would one of his uncles be playing?"

"Maybe he contacted them to see if they could help. With the Courts," Allie added as Joe shook his head. "Not the asteroid."

"Be like taking a gun to a knife fight," Joe sighed. "Still, if it comes to threats, the illusion he has his other family behind him couldn't hurt."

"Did the Pixies say which Dragon Lord it was?"

"No, the Brownie said the Pixies had fixated on Jack, repeating the word gold like they were Pratchett dwarves three sheets to the wind."

"Pixies read Pratchett?"

"No." Joe brushed cookie crumbs off the front of his jacket. "But the Brownie's a big fan. Both the Pixies and the Brownie were surprised at the lack of bloodshed. Given Dragon Lords."

"Maybe it's Adam, then. He's usually on Jack's side."

"You should go tell Charlotte, Alysha."

She should. Now they knew for sure. "What are you going to do?"

"Since Graham has the boys . . ." Auntie Gwen crossed to the circle of Joe's arms. ". . . we're going home to spend at least an hour forgetting the world's about to end. Maybe two, if no one calls."

Allie paused at the top of the stairs to catch her breath, sagging against the doorframe, right hand absently tracing charms over her belly. She'd been exhausted for the first trimester of her last pregnancy, full of energy for the second, and had waddled through the third. So far, pregnancy number two was taking the same route. From where she stood, she could see Charlie sitting on one of the loungers, knees tucked into the narrow space between it and the other, shoulders hunched under her jacket. Her hair fell forward over her face, the sunlight making the blue streak look turquoise. She wasn't humming, or tapping, or making any kind of noise at all. She looked . . .

Not sad. Allie'd seen Charlie sad. Unhappy. Anxious. Nervous. This was something new.

Defeated.

She looked defeated.

But only until Allie started moving, then she shook her hair back and looked like Charlie again.

"You don't have to put on an act for me," Allie sighed, crossing the roof.

"I don't have to wallow in front of you either, and as I don't have to, I'd rather not." She held up her hand, the light glinting off the screen of her phone. "Did you leave this up here?"

Allie sat down on the chaise and leaned against Charlie's shoulder. "No.

But you know what they're like." It was colder on the roof than she'd expected and she wondered if Charlie was missing Jack's heat. Stupid. Of course she was.

"My mother called. She wanted to tell me that the twins love Australia."

"Of course they do. Everything's trying to kill them."

Charlie made a noise that could have meant everything was totally justified or that the twins weren't as bad as all that. Allie wasn't sure which; she wasn't as good at interpreting noises as Charlie, but on reflection decided it had to be the former.

"Do you think we can set a branch there?"

She pushed against Charlie's side until her cousin pushed back. Different skills, matched strength. "I think we have to try. But . . ." In the pause, the Dragon Queen rose above the park, Graham gave himself to her, David gave himself to the family, a heartbeat defined the difference between survival and destruction. ". . . I think we won't know until the last minute and there's as good a chance it won't work as it will. Joe says a Brownie says the Pixies say . . ."

Leaning away, Charlie stared at her. "Seriously?"

". . . that Jack opened the gate to the UnderRealm and went through with another dragon."

"Which one?"

"They didn't say. Just that he was older."

"They're all older."

"Pixies."

"Yeah, I suppose."

"The Pixies said there was no bloodshed, so it was probably Adam." Adam was the oldest of Jack's uncles and had the least to prove. "If the Dragon Lords found out about the asteroid . . ."

"How?"

"The Courts?"

Charlie shrugged in a *works for me* kind of way so Allie continued. "Maybe Adam came through to convince Jack to go home and Jack, in turn, convinced Adam to go with him to the Courts." She'd come up with that possibility during the interminable climb up the stairs.

"That's a tidy wrap-up, but a lot of assumptions." Charlie flipped her phone from hand to hand. "He didn't say good-bye."

"Probably because he knew you'd try to stop him."

"Damn right I'd try to stop him."

"If the Courts can teach him . . ."

"He'll pay in pain, Allie. And in humiliation for feeling it."

She could feel Charlie trembling and knew it wasn't from the cold.

"And I'll have to hand him over to four years of that. I don't think I can. Millions, no, billions are going to die, and I'd let it happen rather than have Jack suffer at the Courts for four years."

Allie wanted to say, *"No you wouldn't."* She didn't. There was less than no point in arguing a certainty. Instead, she shrugged and said, "Maybe they won't be able to teach him."

"And how fucked up am I that losing a chance to save the world would be good news. What kind of world are your babies going to grow up in, Allie-cat?"

"One without a diaper service is my guess."

"Allie . . ."

She tugged one of Charlie's hands away from her phone and laced their fingers together. "My boys are going to grow up in a world where they'll know that you did everything you could to make it the best possible world they could grow up in. Regardless of how many people we manage to save."

"You're sure . . ."

"I have *always* been sure of you."

Charlie's sigh sounded a little shaky, but her lips were warm and soft and, well, sure. After a moment or two, she sighed again, but more in relief, Allie thought. As if she'd set aside at least some of the burdens she carried. "I'm a little surprised the aunties aren't trying to figure out a way for you to pop the seventh son of a seventh son of a seventh son of a Gale out in time to save the day."

"They don't even know what he'll be able to do."

"They're fairly certain he's going to be something spectacular."

"How do you know they're *not* trying to figure out a way?"

"Good point." Allie could tell without looking that Charlie was staring at the other lounger and wondered how often she'd met Jack up here after a night out. Wondered what they'd talked about. Didn't wonder where Charlie'd found the strength to do the right thing because it was Charlie.

"I guess I know how he felt all those times when I left him without saying good-bye." Her voice was matter of fact.

"How do you feel?"

"Like I must have done something wrong."

Allie winced. "You haven't . . ."

"I know, sweetie, I know. Fortunately, and I recognize the irony, fortunately, I'm not seventeen. And," she added after a moment, "that asteroid is one hell of a distraction. Or it would be if every possible way of stopping it didn't involve Jack and I getting screwed. And not in a fun way."

Maybe Katie . . . except maybe meant fire. A little afraid of how much she was willing to risk Katie to save Charlie further heartache, Allie shivered.

"Are you cold?"

"A little. And I have to pee." She stood, hip pressed against Charlie's shoulder and tucked the blue strand of hair behind her cousin's ear. "You coming in?"

"No." Charlie's hand closed around hers for a second, then let her go. "I have some thinking to do."

"You used to go to crappy bars to think."

"I used to think about different things."

Charlie didn't relax until Allie reached the bottom of the stairs—ignoring the fact that Allie was not only a healthy young woman who had a perfectly normal pregnancy once before, for certain values of the word normal, but that she was a Gale and the universe didn't allow pregnant Gales to trip and fall. Although it seemed to have no trouble dropping enormous rocks on them.

Rock.

Singular.

With all they could do, she couldn't believe they couldn't stop a falling rock.

Surviving it wasn't enough, she had to save Jack, and, if truth be told, herself. Not being able to touch him outside of ritual having touched him within ritual would flay pieces off her soul every time she saw him. The only way to keep them out of ritual was to solve the problem.

Problem? Right.

A pigeon strutting back and forth on the edge of the roof froze as her laugh slid toward cackling thirty years too soon. When an auntie started cackling, the rest of the family battened down.

Solve the problem, save the world.

Save not only her family, but Gary and Kiren and Dan . . .

Dan.

"Remember the bears, Charlie."

She hadn't given the last thing she'd heard Dan say much thought at the time. Given Calgary's proximity to the mountains, it wasn't that surprising a thought for him to have overheard and some poor bastard running into bears in the wild would probably have provided the focus necessary to get through her earworm and into his head. Except . . .

It wasn't a random thought. It was a thought directed at her.

"Remember the bears, Charlie."

Charlie squinted at a pigeon strutting along the edge of the roof. His head bobbed forward into the sun, the bit of garbage dangling from his beak both blue and fuzzy.

The universe arranged things in the Gales' favor. Occasionally, it smacked them upside the head.

Smacked her upside the head.

So she remembered the bears. The bears staring out the windows. The bears freed when she broke the glass. Auntie Jane's phone call . . .

Remember the bears. Remember what had been said about them.

The pigeon sidled away as she stepped toward him, giving her an impressive hairy eyeball considering his total lack of hair. "Come on, bird, I'm not going to hurt you." He didn't look like he believed her. She could make him believe her if she wanted to stoop to compelling pigeons. She stepped closer. The pigeon spread his wings. "Stay there!"

Apparently stooping wasn't a problem.

The emphasis snapped his wings down.

"I'm not going to hurt you." She'd have told him not to be frightened, but he didn't look frightened; he looked pissed off. Bending slowly, she tugged the dangling bit of fuzz out of his beak. "Okay then. I can smell bacon from the diner on 13th. You should head over there and try to score. Or not," she added, jumping back as her field of vision filled with wings beating out an angry rhythm on the air.

Pale blue polyester fuzz. Incredibly filthy, pale blue polyester fuzz; probably home to the kind of bacteria normally found only around the toilets of the sort of bars that hung chicken wire in front of the stage. Fortunately, Charlie had a charm for that.

She dropped the fuzz, flipped off the pigeon watching her from the roof of the garage across the alley, and tried to remember what Auntie Jane had said about the bears.

Mostly they'd spoken about the creature who'd been holding them. She'd asked if she was in trouble for taking him out and Auntie Jane had told her not to be ridiculous, that he was nasty piece of work.

"Once they've started on bears, the world is a better place without them."

She fumbled her phone out of her pocket. Auntie Jane's number had moved into the top spot in her contacts list. Charlie shifted her weight from foot to foot as it rang. Four. Five. Six. Seven.

"This had better be important, Charlotte. In case you hadn't heard, the world is about to end."

"Why is the world a better place without them once they've started on bears?"

Auntie Jane sighed and turned away from the phone. "Thank you, Meredith, I'd love a tea. Christie is with Arthur again."

Auntie Meredith's voice was a quiet background rumble.

"I know the ritual is still five days away, but if she wears him out, I will charm her knees together. Bears, Charlotte, in the last hundred odd years . . ."

"And some of them were very odd." No rim shot. Charlie frowned.

". . . have come to symbolize the security of innocence. Did you know emergency services give teddy bears to children in accidents to comfort them?"

"I didn't."

"Did you know it works?"

"I didn't."

"Don't ever underestimate the power of an agreed-upon symbol, Charlotte. The only reason red lights stop cars is that we have agreed they will."

"So the old guy in Vermont, he was removing innocence and security from the world?"

"As you didn't bother to check before you blew the seals, we have no way of knowing for certain, but, given that we know he was a nasty piece of work, it's a valid assumption. Now, as thrilled as I am that you're actually asking questions, however after the fact, I need to deal with Mary and her belief that allspice will substitute for . . . Back away from the spice cabinet, Mary!"

Charlie slid the phone back into her pocket and headed downstairs.

It took her the rest of the day to find what she needed—and not only because the twins kept calling to tell her about spiders. And snakes. And Australians. So far, at least four of the Australians were as athletic as advertised. Four of the Australians, and six of the spiders.

The scent of lasagna and garlic bread rolled out over her as Charlie opened the door to the apartment. She shrugged out of her jacket and stood for a moment watching Allie and Auntie Gwen and Katie dip and weave in the movements of a familiar dance. Gale girls seldom cooked alone. By the time they could use the stovetop without a step stool, they knew how to share the space with knives and fire and sisters and cousins and aunts. Charlie could hear the music they danced to even if she'd never learned more than the basic steps herself.

Joe was still in the store. Auntie Gwen would take two plates down and they'd eat together on the glass counter, not even the most mundane of bargain hunters daring to interrupt their meal. Graham sat in one of the big armchairs, his sons curled up on his lap listening to a story of a raccoon who got on the LRT at Southland and off five stops later at Bridlewood, waddling out into the dark as though he knew where he was going. Charlie could hear the truth in the story even if the twins could only hear the funny voices their father made as he told them about the reactions of the other passengers.

She touched the empty spaces that should have been full of Jack and moved away from the door, into the twins' line of sight.

"Cha Cha!"

Dropping to one knee, Charlie waited for impact. Edward reached her first, but Evan followed close enough behind they hit essentially as one and she toppled amid shrieks of laughter. After a moment filled with sloppy kisses and four dimpled knees that seemed determined to nail her in the boob with every other movement, she grinned up at them. "I wonder if there's a present in that shopping bag."

She still wasn't sure how many words they actually understood, but *present* they knew. Sitting up, she pushed her hair back off her face and scooted back until she could lean against the sofa as Edward all but dove into the bag, passing the first plush toy back to his brother.

Evan's bear had a dark green head and body, its arms and one of its legs brown-and-white-striped. The second leg was striped pink and green. Edward held a bear with a blue head and body, its arms pink-and-purple stripes and its legs a pale lime green. Both tails—one green, one blue although not on the expected bear—sounded like a duck call when squeezed.

"These are special bears," she explained as the boys returned to her lap. "When I'm not here . . ."

"Gone."

"Yes, when I'm gone, these bears will remind you of me. When you hug these bears, you'll know I'm with you no matter where I am."

Edward cocked his head and pushed the blue bear against her chest. "Here."

"Yes." She pressed a kiss to his hair, amazed he'd made the connection. But then Graham and Allie did a stupidly cute *got my heart* when Graham left for work so maybe he'd picked it up from that. "That's right. When you hug the bear, I'm in your heart. And when you're all grown up . . ."

"Big!"

"That's right, when you're big, too big for bears, you can give them to your little brothers and . . . Ow."

Evan's remarkably pointy foot dug into her thigh as he launched himself toward his mother. "Brothers!"

Fortunately, avoiding kids was part of the kitchen dance.

"Don't take this the wrong way, Charlie . . ." Graham leaned forward, muscular forearms braced on his thighs. ". . . but you couldn't have bought uglier bears if you'd tried."

Charlie smiled and settled Edward against her heart. "I know."

Later, she danced the bears into their crib with a rousing—albeit edited—version of "Rocket Scientist" by the Teddybears. Maybe someday the boys could meet Kiren. Before Allie could come in and remind her that no one appreciated toddlers whipped into a frenzy right before bed, she segued into "To Know Him is to Love Him" by the Teddy Bears—the space between teddy and bear making all the difference.

"When you hug the bears, I'm in your heart," she repeated quietly, kissing their foreheads as they blinked sleepily up at her. "No matter what happens."

Allie and Graham both were waiting for her outside the boys' room. "Charlie . . ."

Charlie could hear tone and timbre of a complicated question behind Allie's hesitant voicing of her name. Fortunately, shared history kept it from needing to be put into words. "No, it's too weird missing Jack while I'm in bed with you."

"Weirder than wanting Jack while you're in bed with us?" Graham wondered.

"Weirdly, yes."

"We could just sleep," Allie pointed out, digging an elbow into her husband's ribs.

"No, I . . ."

"For comfort."

Graham rolled his eyes, leaned past Allie and kissed Charlie good night. "She's not looking for comfort," he said, his fingers warm on Charlie's shoulder. "Not yet."

He meant well, but Charlie walked away thinking about needing comfort later, and by the time she reached her room, she'd realized her life wasn't country music, it was Götterdämmerung. Her one true love was a seventeen-year-old half dragon she'd never be able to play naked love nest with—except for in vaguely religious scenarios under the supervision of her entire family—who'd gone missing and the best case scenario involved him arranging to be emotionally tortured for four years by basketball loving escapees from the *Silmarillion*. Meanwhile, she'd set up a third act with the leads still in diapers and the harmonies provided by someone she didn't entirely trust. Not to mention there was a good chance the finale would involve an asteroid impact large enough to shake and bake the planet.

The background music soared into Brunhilda's Immolation Scene.

"I'm not making this up, you know," Charlie muttered, opening the bedroom door.

To her surprise, Katie was sitting cross-legged on the bed wearing a black tank and orange pajama pants covered in black witches' hats.

Charlie toed off her boots and kicked them into the corner. "I'm sleeping on the roof. I came in to change."

"Really? On the roof?" Katie set her tablet on the bedside table, stretched, and stood. "It's almost the end of October. You'll know when Jack comes back regardless, so get into bed."

"Katie . . ."

"I know, it's like every other note has been silenced, right? Every other string taken off your guitar? Every other hole plugged in your piccolo?"

"Katie . . ."

"You shouldn't be alone. More alone," Katie amended before Charlie could speak.

Truth be told, she didn't want to be alone. More alone. "If you steal the covers . . ."

She slept an hour or two at a time, woke to the hollow pain of Jack's absence, and allowed Katie's even breathing to lull her back to sleep for another hour or two. Second verse, same as the first. Jack wasn't back when dawn painted the bedroom in pale grays, so she slid out of bed, grabbed her quilt, and headed for the roof. She watched the sun come up, listened to the traffic below on 9th, refused to surrender to the scent of Mexican dark that wafted up every time the door to the coffee shop opened, and she waited.

"Allie says no one's getting French toast until you come in, so get your ass down to breakfast."

Charlie shuffled around until she could peer over the edge of the quilt at Graham. As every Gale who successfully made it to adulthood knew, French toast was significantly harder to charm than pancakes. Her stomach growled as she gathered the quilt around her and stood. She could wait inside for a while.

"That was Carmen," Auntie Gwen declared, putting her phone away as Charlie followed Graham into the apartment. "The Courts have dialed back the pain-in-the-ass behavior. Nothing new since the basilisk at the Rideau Town Center. Meredith drove over and dealt with it," she added as Charlie's eyebrows went up. "She wanted to try out a new lemon pepper stuffing. Apparently, they *do* taste like chicken."

"Maybe the Courts are being more discreet. Yeah, like that's happening," Charlie snorted before anyone else could. Tossing her quilt over the end of the sofa, she dropped into her usual seat at the table. Were the Courts so distracted by Jack's pain that they'd forgotten to poke the MidRealm?

"Or they're distracted because basketball season starts tomorrow."

No surprise Auntie Gwen had followed her line of thought. A little surprise she followed basketball. "How do you know?"

"Bea's been going on about it. If it's an attempt to keep me from asking what Jane had to say to her, it's working."

The boys had brought their bears to the breakfast. The green bear fell in the syrup. "Sing, Cha Cha!" Evan demanded, handing it to her.

"Fell in the syrup, drenched from head to toes. When I tried to clean up, my paws stuck to my nose . . ." Presley's "Hound Dog": world's easiest tune to adapt, she acknowledged as she sang and danced the bears around the table while both boys shrieked with laughter.

After breakfast, after green bear, now named Grrr, had been cleaned, Charlie took her phone back to the roof.

Her mother called. Her sisters called. Uncle Richard called because he'd found an old hammered dulcimer in the attic and wanted to know if it was worth keeping. She made a quick trip to Ontario, told him it wasn't, and dropped in on Auntie Ruby long enough to hear Auntie Jane call the dying woman stubborner than a tree stump.

Back on the roof, she fed half her banana walnut muffin to the pigeons, but refused to share her coffee.

The call she expected never came.

Neither did Jack.

That evening she told the boys stories about their bears. They rode the wooden train set to protect it from bandits. They climbed the sofa mountain and planted two small socks at the summit claiming it for the twins. They cushioned Edward's fall when he threw himself off the kitchen counter although it remained unclear how he'd gotten onto the kitchen counter in the first place.

Katie stayed over another night.

Charlie woke up every hour feeling empty.

Jack was still gone the next morning.

The Courts continued to keep a low profile.

By eight, Charlie was on the roof throwing pieces of cold cereal at . . . to the pigeons, listening to the *Virgin Morning Show* on 98.5 wafting up through the air vents off the apartment over the eco store on the corner. At ten seventeen, her phone rang, the ringtone proving that the universe had a crap sense of humor. No matter how empty she felt, she'd never have used "I Can See Clearly Now." "Morning, Auntie Catherine. What did you See?"

For a moment she thought the older woman was going to play games, but she only sighed and said, "I Saw a baby playing with two worn-out and remarkably ugly teddy bears."

"Describe them."

"Excuse me?" The subtext informed her that the end of the world was no reason to indulge in bad manners.

"Could you please describe the teddy bears?"

"Better. Solid colored bodies, striped arms and legs, most of the fuzz had been chewed off them . . ."

"Wait . . ." No doubt about the bears, but . . . ". . . don't you mean babies?"

"If I'd meant babies, Charlotte, I'd have said babies. I mean baby. Singular. Now, ask me why I called to tell you."

"Okay. Why . . ."

"None of your business. Honestly, this family."

"This family what?"

"If you have to ask, Charlotte, I'm certainly not going to be the one to fill you in."

"About what?" But the connection had been terminated. Probably with extreme prejudice, if Charlie knew Auntie Catherine. "Okay. That was weird. Er. Weirder. Weirder than usual." Not that it mattered; she had what she needed.

It was Sunday. Ritual was Wednesday.

As long as she went before the ritual, it didn't really matter when she left. If Jack had gone to the Courts to get the proof he'd need to convince her to take him back four years and, therefore, keep them out of ritual, he'd return Tuesday at the latest. If all he'd discovered was that they couldn't teach him . . . Would he remain in the UnderRealm until the ritual was over? Or would he risk what the ritual would do to them in order to combine their power in the hope of stopping the asteroid? Did he even realize what it was that ritual would do to them or was he thinking like a seventeen year old and seeing it as a way around the rule? Would he wait until the last minute, when the boys had antlered up and it was too late?

"Screw it. This is like trying to play Tchaikovsky on the bagpipes, I don't have enough notes."

The pigeons gave her a collective dubious look.

"What? I like Tchaikovsky. He used cannon as percussion." She tapped out the signature measure of *The 1812 Overture* against her thigh as her background music switched to full orchestra. "Okay. Forget Jack. For all the talking we've been doing, I've got bugger all in the way of actual information. Given the given, what do *I* do?"

An argument about homework drifted up from a trio of girls down on the street. A trio of girls who weren't family and wouldn't survive if the asteroid hit. Family would. They wouldn't. One of them was thrilled that calculus had finally gotten them into applied math. Charlie's personal relationship with math ended with perfect fifths and diminished thirds, but that was no reason math geeks should die.

"I step up to the mic, that's what I do." She'd never gotten stage fright, not from her first school pageant to the last thrown beer bottle. This was no time to start.

Could she slip into the Wood between the indignant noises the pigeons made as they searched the roof for more muffin?

As one, the pigeons took to the air, circled once, and landed across the street on the roof of the bank.

Apparently not. Or at least not yet.

Probably best to head to the courtyard and out between the viburnums, avoiding questions and answers both.

It was easy enough to get her guitar from her room, and although she could hear the twins in the living room, she slipped out of the apartment without being spotted.

Unfortunately, Allie was waiting at the bottom of the stairs. "Where are you going?"

Second circle was all about connections. It was possible, Charlie realized, that Allie'd felt her decision to leave. That she'd felt all of her decisions to leave but, until now, had chosen to let her go. She remembered what she'd told Jack about Allie needing to keep people close and smoothed the edges off her response. "I'm going to the park." Not a lie. And the park was only ever and always would be Nose Hill.

"Why?"

"I want to try something."

And years of *it's a Wild thing* paid off as Allie shook her head without asking what that something was. "Charlie, we need you to help with the real estate listings. Not everyone is going to want to sell. A charm and a fair price will only go so far."

"Wait until after ritual."

"After is four days away. If it doesn't work . . ."

Charlie twitched before realizing Allie had been referring to the ritual. Allie had no idea of what she was about to attempt.

". . . or Jack doesn't come back with the solution, I want to hit the ground running. I need to know how much of the city I can protect. And if it doesn't work, you're going to be needed after to ferry family to Aus . . ." It took Charlie a moment to realize Allie was frowning at a dull patch on the guitar's headstock where the varnish had peeled off. "Is that the guitar you bought in Cape Breton? The one that helped you chase the storm?"

"Yes."

"And deal with the oil rigs?"

"Yes."

"I see."

Doubt that, Charlie thought as Allie stepped aside and she pushed past. She was not going to ask what Allie saw.

The mirror reflected a solid sheet of gold and a set of antlers—twelve point buck. If the gold represented Jack, and it always had, the mirror might be anticipating the ritual. Or warning her about the ritual. Or being deliberately obscure just for shits and giggles. She rested her hand against the glass, and a reflection of a hand rose out of the gold to meet it. It wasn't a reflection of her hand, but Charlie had too much on her plate to identify it now.

"Are you going after Jack?"

She wondered what reflection Allie saw. "Going after Jack? No."

And because it was the truth, Allie believed her. "Then you need to stay and . . ."

"Let her go, Alysha." Auntie Gwen descended the last three steps and took hold of Allie's arm. "Charlotte is clearly heading out to attempt . . . something." When their eyes met, Charlie wondered how many pieces Auntie Gwen had managed to gather up and put together behind that . . . something. "You know you can't hold her."

"Yadda yadda Wild," Allie sighed. "If you love something, let it go." Auntie Gwen met Charlie's gaze and jerked her head toward the door.

Charlie leaned in and brushed a kiss against Allie's cheek, then shifted her grip on the guitar case and headed out into the courtyard. It occurred to her that she hadn't told them how she'd left Jack's room. And they hadn't asked. Gales weren't interested in the mechanics of leaving.

"Is she going Wild?" Allie's voice slipped out around the edge of the closing door.

Charlie was gone before Auntie Gwen answered.

She stepped out of the Wood in one of the isolated, rocky areas of the park.

When she traveled into the past, she traveled through place as well as time. From Calgary back ten days to Cape Breton. From Cape Breton back three hours to Vermont. This time . . . She fought down the nearly hysterical desire to laugh and tried again. This time, no matter how far she traveled in time, she wanted to remain in the park because the park would exist as long as her family did. The trees she planned to step between would grow and die and new trees would grow, but the bones of the earth wouldn't change. This place, this specific three square meters of alluvial soil would continue to exist, as it had always existed, long enough for her to save it.

She was going to save it. All of it. All of them. She wiped damp palms on her jeans. Everyone.

If she could follow a song into the past, then she should be able to follow a song into the future.

"You know the future happened." Jack's voice in memory.

A baby and two ugly bears. The future had been Seen. It existed. Or it would exist, at least. It was real. She'd been counting on the bears.

If you go into the Woods today . . .

The seventh son of a seventh son of a seventh son of a Gale. Important, impossible . . .

Gales were adults at fifteen, admitted into ritual. Whatever Seven-seven-seven-Gale could do by virtue of what he was, he'd be able to do it then. So if Allie was eight weeks along now, it'd be thirty-two weeks to the birth of the next set of twins. Two years to the birth of the set after that if the universe continued interfering on the same schedule. Add two years more before number seven shows up. Add fifteen years for him to grow up. Charlie had a calculator on her phone but she used her fingers. Thirty-two, two, two, fifteen . . . twenty years, give or take.

The furthest she'd ever gone into the past was ten days.

The rock underfoot vibrated as David's hooves drummed out an approaching rhythm; percussion she could feel through the soles of her boots. He couldn't know what she had planned because she didn't know what she had planned, exactly, but he had to know she was going to try . . . something, and he wasn't happy about it.

In fairness, *she* wasn't overjoyed either. She took a step forward but stayed in the park. Stepping into the Wood would mean she'd committed. Which she was. Committed. Just not . . . Anyway, he was closing fast, but she still had time.

Rim shot.

"Okay. Don't think of it like twenty years. You didn't leap out of the Woods ten days in the past, you exited, stage left, during a rousing chorus." A rousing chorus was a rousing chorus. If it was rousing enough, that should be all that mattered.

As long as she didn't turn around and look at the world outside the park, as long as she didn't know for sure that she'd succeeded or failed, there was a chance.

You're in for a big surprise . . .

Schrödinger's future.

She'd be making it up as she went along.

With David a single stride away from the clearing, Charlie stepped into the Wood.

ELEVEN

THE WOOD HADN'T CHANGED. The Wood never changed.

In the perpetual late summer afternoon, the aunties' percussion threaded in and around the rustling of the leaves, a staccato *busy busy busy* touched intermittently by the certainty of pie. Allie's worried minor key supported by Graham's bass pushed through the underbrush, rising now and then amid the rowans to wind around the boys' simpler melody. Her sisters' song, sharp and edgy, ducked in and out of shadow, the sound muffled then distinct. Her mother's raced from note to note. Katie's was a base to build on. The rest of the family laid in harmonies and descants and counter rhythms. Over near where the oaks gave way to the aspens and then the willows, Gary's distinctive touch picked out "The Rain Song" on the bouzouki. A Cape Breton fiddler played "Gooden Well" by a copse of Norfolk pine.

Together the songs were a map of people and places, a way for her to get to anyone. Anywhen.

Charlie listened to the silence where Jack's song should be as she settled the guitar strap on her shoulders. No more wallowing. If the seventh son of a seventh son of a seventh son of a Gale could stop the asteroid, then Jack wouldn't have to pay the Courts in pain and the two of them could continue avoiding ritual while developing the slightly pathetic relationship the rules allowed.

"And the world won't end," she added after a minute. "That's good, too."

Allie's song first. Charlie's fingers pulled the melody from the strings, her voice adding wordless harmonies, finding the place Allie held for her. Not defining herself by that place, but anchoring herself within it. Allowing everything else to fade away. She touched the two lives wrapped in love beneath Allie's heart, careful to only Sing what she *knew* would happen. Adding only the verses that *would* occur. Music was not random—notes and chords and chord progressions were never tossed out into the universe and expected to miraculously coalesce into Song. The mathematics behind music were known, studied, explored. Art happened when head and heart sat down and jammed.

And sometimes, sometimes magic happened. Sometimes it happened in dark bars where her shoes stuck to the floor. Sometimes it happened in the secret places between worlds. Sometimes it happened as cells divided and twin parasites became people.

Still Singing, Charlie felt power flare.

Heard two new voices separate, no longer adding depth to Allie's song but beginning their own.

Charlie Sang the family gathered round—in the park, on the hill, in the circle. David on four feet, the men in full horn. Blood and pain and welcome.

There was a future. Auntie Catherine had seen it.

Charlie squared her shoulders, and stepped out of the Wood.

She stopped Singing in time to hear a baby cry. A moment later, his brother joined in, raising their voices in the indignant protest of newborns suddenly shoved from protected warmth and exposed to the great, wide world.

"Okay, then." It seemed safe to start breathing again.

The weather was no longer definitive October. The trees around her were in full leaf and the air warm enough she started to sweat under her jacket. Allie had been a day or two over eight weeks along when Charlie'd stepped into the Wood. Thirty-two weeks remaining. Eight months give or take. That meant this was June and it was still a little over a year to the impact.

She knew that if she listened, really listened, she'd be able to hear what the aunties were saying. Hear Allie and Graham rejoicing in their sons. Divide the murmur of family into individual voices and learn what was . . .

Hoofbeats.

David.

Charging.

In this place, at this time, he had to know it was her. But this wasn't her time and he knew that, too.

Charlie stepped back and froze as a familiar current lifted the hair off the back of her neck. The vantage point she'd chosen eight months ago stood immediately inside the fourth circle, the protective barrier the family raised around the park to separate their workings from the city. No one wanted a stranger to stumble into ritual, least of all the stranger—although, that said, it was the aunties who wouldn't shut up about how much harder it had become to hide a body.

Harder, not impossible. And if David felt he had to protect the circle from her, he wouldn't leave much of a body to hide.

Backing through the barrier, a barrier that she'd helped build, would announce her presence with authority. Given that she was already on the hill, it would lead to questions she—the she of this time, the her of later—shouldn't answer. The aunties heard *I can't tell you* as *I haven't told you yet. Feel free to nag incessantly.*

Of course, there was always the chance that this whole thing had gone tits up in a major way and she wasn't already on the hill because she was singing with the choir eternal, in which case hitting the barrier would evoke a completely different line of questioning and . . .

Time travel gave her a migraine.

She had a chance of succeeding only as long as she didn't know she'd already failed and while she couldn't stop David from sensing. . . .

Shit! David!

Her heart pounded in time with his approach; his hooves pounded into the sod, her heart against her ribs. Underbrush crushed or flung aside, mangled foliage marked his path.

Charlie's eyes widened as the first prongs breached the clearing. "Holy shit, that's pointy!" Horns were an accessory Gale boys sported. She'd seen the scars they left behind all her life, had acknowledged the aunties who'd died during the Hunt for Allie's grandfather, but had never internalized the danger.

She couldn't stop David with her voice, not here, not now and she couldn't step backward into the barrier.

Right hand keeping her strings from sounding, fingers on the left crossed, she stepped forward between the sound of hoofbeats as the full and deadly spread of David's rack thrust into the clearing, the massive bulk of his shoulders fading to insubstantial even as the weight of his presence tried to drag her back as she slipped into the Wood.

"Too close." She should've known David would charge to protect the family. Next time, she'd be prepared. Relaxing into the familiar sounds of the Wood, she . . .

"Crap on a cracker."

More than familiar, the songs were the songs of her time. The aunties, Allie and Graham, the twins; nothing had changed. The whole mess was even more like opera than she'd realized. She half expected to hear the Rhinemaidens singing.

"And here we are," she sighed, pushing her hair back off her face, "fifteen hours later, right back where we started from."

Anna Russell aside, the trip hadn't been a total disaster. She'd proven she could move forward in time, following the path of a Song during its creation. She hadn't yet crossed the impact point, but as long as she kept her attention on the park, on the family, the impact shouldn't matter.

Charlie snorted, snickered, and teetered on the edge of hysteria. The impact was all that mattered. Stop the impact, save Jack.

"And the world," she reminded herself. Again. "All right." Right hand. Left hand. She flexed her fingers then rested them back against the strings. Finger picks might've been a good idea, she hadn't been taking the best care of her nails, but, as she'd already played for seven months, it was way, *way* too late to think of that. "Repeat the Song to the flare of power that marked the birth of three and four, then keep going to the conception of five and six. Doubt I'll be able to miss that. Piece of Auntie Mary's blueberry pie with ice cream."

She had to force herself past the birth of the twins, force herself beyond the draw of an exit she'd already created, the emphasis of rituals flickering past as she headed for . . .

Power!

Charlie threw in a Hallelujah chorus and stepped out of the wood . . .

. . . into knee-deep snow.

Seriously? Considering how the family drew power, who the hell had thought settling in Canada was a good idea? Though the weather did make it obvious time had passed. Even in Calgary. Shivering, she noted the barrier still hummed at her heels, and bent carefully to scoop up a handful of snow, licking it off her fingers, melting it in the warmth of her mouth to ease the tightness beginning at the back of her throat. Here, in the park, it tasted clean. Cold. Purified by the family's power. And maybe, it tasted a little like Allie. Charlie grinned. But then, why wouldn't it?

Beyond the barrier, would it taste of ash? Twenty-one months less eight was thirteen. It was possible she'd emerged once again before the impact point. Possible that Allie had agreed to decrease the spacing between her pregnancies. Possible, but unlikely given Allie. If the universe insisted, she'd be more likely to dig her heels in than fling them into the air.

Still . . . Charlie bit another mouthful of snow off the clump on her palm. If she turned, what would she see? A thousand tales began or ended with doors opened that should have stayed closed and Charlie'd had her hand on the doorknob her whole life.

Except this time she *couldn't* open the door. Ask the question. Turn around . . .

"I'd have been a pillar of salt before they reached the suburbs," she told the silence.

The silence agreed.

The residue of power in the snowmelt helped relax her throat. Responding to the ritual power rising on the hill, growing damp and heated under her clothes, she reached for more. It was safe enough this time to take the time. David couldn't leave ritual. The aunties wouldn't allow him out of . . .

Slammed her to her knees, the bout of her guitar carved a crescent into the snow. She jerked it clear, found her voice, and rolled sideways into the Wood.

Metaphysical dirt still tasted like dirt. Who knew? Ass in the air, chin dimpling the ground, guitar clutched tight against her body, Charlie straightened and spat. "Fucking hell, David!" He hadn't needed to leave the circle, not with the power he commanded once ritual began. Why hadn't she warned him that she'd be in and out? Unless she had, because why the hell wouldn't she, and it hadn't mattered. Didn't matter. Wouldn't matter. David acted instinctively to protect the family against someone he knew wasn't supposed to be in the park. Because they were already in the park. Or had stepped into the Wood one day twenty-one months before an asteroid impact and had never stepped out.

"Let's go with already in the park."

Which raised the odds that he'd be waiting at the stage door every single time.

And speaking of time.

Familiar Songs rose around her.

Right back where she'd started from. Again.

The urge to leave the Wood and grab a case of beer was intense. She rubbed the dirt off her lips with the back of her hand, skin still cold and damp from the snow, and stood. Took a step forward. Heard a warning in the breeze. The leaves rustled and informed her that if she left, she'd lose as much of the Song as she'd already sung and have to begin again from scratch.

"Or," she muttered, checking her tuning, "since the foliage has never been all that chatty before, I'm afraid that's what'll happen and am refusing to take responsibility for my own decisions." The aunties would vote en masse for option two. Here and now, the aunties could go fuck themselves. Because she wasn't a total idiot, all evidence to the contrary, she didn't think that last bit too loudly.

Time as such didn't pass in the Wood. Charlie licked her lips, licked her teeth, breathed from the diaphragm, and sang her way past birth, conception, to birth again. Thirty-two weeks. Two years, give or take Allie's willingness to fight the universe's plan for her life. Forty-weeks.

She stepped out of the Wood to the baby duet of five and six and dove back in again, driven by David's hoofbeats, before the urge to turn and check on the world even came up.

"If he ever learns to run silently, I'm in trouble." Her throat felt rough and the Song had dried her mouth to the point where it took time to work up enough spit to swallow. "On the other hand, my willpower remaining untested can't be a bad thing."

She didn't chew gum during a performance, not after the first time she'd caught hell for a wad stuck to a mic stand, but she checked her pockets anyway. One used tissue. The crushed foam cover off an earbud. The expected guitar pick. A linty humbug.

Charlie didn't like humbugs and she had no idea of how the candy had ended up shoved down under the ridge of her jacket pocket's lower seam.

Lie.

Auntie Jane always carried humbugs. It helped her maintain the illusion she'd been born before Mackenzie King entered politics. She also carried scotch mints. Charlie liked scotch mints. Interesting that a humbug had shown up.

Actually, less *interesting* and more *typical*.

Having something to suck on helped, as little as she liked the flavor. "Insert dirty joke here," she muttered around the candy as she tightened her G.

She Sang past the birth of three and four. Past the conception of five and six. Past the birth of five and six. To . . .

No snow this time. No rain, but then there wouldn't be. It didn't rain while the Gales were in ritual unless the Gales wanted it to rain. It felt like spring, all damp earth and new growth, but she had no idea how much time had passed. Although this ritual was all about Allie and Graham making one final baby, *the* final baby, Charlie could feel the rest of the family laying down a harmony track. The seventh son of a seventh son of a seventh son of a Gale would grow up surrounded by cousins his age.

And not only cousins. If the world still existed—*don't look, don't look, don't look*—he'd have plenty of friends and neighbors his age. For a broad definition of neighbor that lapped against the Rockies to the west, the border to the south, the tundra to the north, and slid over Saskatchewan with nothing to stop it until Manitoba.

As the power of his conception sizzled around her, the surrounding shrubs burst into full leaf and then into flower. It tugged her forward, pooled between her legs, and spread in burning lines of need throughout her body. A distant roar pushed through the sound of her pulse pounding in her ears, and it took a moment before she realized it had to be David, challenging from within his circle of aunties. She had to leave before David fried her where she stood.

But she couldn't disentangle herself from Allie's touch. Graham's touch. Roland. Katie. Rayne. Lucy. She took another step forward.

The attack, when it came, lifted her off her feet. Airborne, she clamped her hands over the strings, forced an A past a dry tongue, and rode it back to . . .

. . . slam into the trunk of an enormous oak. Charlie grunted at the impact, breath knocked out of her lungs, head ringing. Her guitar thrummed out a sympathetic B flat. Bark crumbling behind her as she slid to the ground, she fought for air, stumbled, and finally sagged back against the tree.

At first she thought the darkness was the fault of the rising bump on the back of her head. After a moment, she realized it had nothing to do with her and everything to do with where David had thrown her. As a rule, she stayed well away from the shadows under the old oaks. From a distance, they looked fake, like blackout curtains hung to simulate shadow. Up close and personal, the shadow became very real with next to no underbrush when she looked down and no glimpse of sky through the nearly solid canopy when she looked up. It smelled like the root cellar back at the old farmhouse, a damp repository of dying vegetables. Worst of all, she could hear running water.

"And that," she grunted, straightening, "is mean. Why not offer me a pomegranate and nail the symbolism." No one had ever told her to refuse food or drink the Wood might offer, but then no one had ever told her not to sing "Sk8ter Boi" in a honky-tonk; some things anyone with the slightest sense of self-preservation knew not to do.

The music was nearly all percussion in the shadows, the aunties at their most definitive, and her blood pounded out a demanding rhythm over the lingering throb of conception. Since she had to know where she was before she could Sing herself to where she hadn't been, she teased the faintest thread of Allie's song out from under the percussive posturing and followed it.

And followed it.

And followed it.

By the time she reached a clearing she recognized, surrounded by birch and alder, her feet ached, her right calf had started to cramp, and she'd been earwormed by Shari Lewis singing "This is the Song that Never Ends." Her stomach growled. And she really wanted a lamb chop.

Step out. Eat. Sleep. Tempting, but she didn't have it in her to start over, so her only choice was to go on.

"Five more stops." Sucking the inside of her cheeks provided a small mouthful of spit. "Don't quit now."

If the conception of the seventh son of a seventh son of a seventh son of a Gale had nearly dragged her into disaster, she only survived the birth because it had driven David beyond thought. Back in the Wood, she poked a finger through the tear in the sleeve of her jacket, and licked the smear of red off the tip. Bleeding in the Wood was a bad idea.

The burst of salt and iron on her tongue made her thirstier.

The memory of Doomsday Dan's bottle of yellow *whatever* had begun to look good.

"Four more. You can do this."

Start with Allie. Sing the babies. Birth. Conception. Birth. Conception. BIRTH. Then the longest jump yet, as she Sang her way to the first ritual after Edward and Evan turned fifteen. She didn't need to fill in the details, she needed to hold the note. *Hold it. Hold it.* Her fingers rolled over the strings. It might have been a pattern from Mary Chapin Carpenter. It might have been Mississippi blues. Charlie had moved past being able to tell. All she could do was trust her fingers.

Hold it.

Hold it for years.

There was a future. Auntie Catherine had Seen it.

She'd Sung only what she knew—birth, conception, birth. Not what she wanted, what she knew; moving forward into the future that *was*.

Charlie held the note.

Then Edward and Evan entered ritual, pulling her out of the Wood and into the park.

Propped up against a rock, where she couldn't miss it, was a bottle of water and a power bar.

"Looks like the two brain cells I had remaining after this stunt have finally begun to work again." Aware of how little time she had, she snatched them up, wondered if that meant the world was safe. Could plastic bottles and power bars survive with only the infrastructure the family could protect?

She needed to look.

She needed a lot of things.

Sucked to be her.

The sound of teenage girls and predatory giggling chased her back into the Wood.

A single bottle of water was as much a tease as a solution. The empty plastic crushed in her hands, Charlie had no memory of drinking and had a suspicion it had all been absorbed by her mouth and throat before it had a chance to reach her stomach.

A power bar was a bad compromise between candy and food. Charlie ate it anyway; it had been years since she'd eaten. Metaphorically. Metaphysically. Whatever that chewy purple thing was, it hadn't come within a hundred kilometers of a blueberry and she had no trouble believing it could survive the end of the world.

Her mouth had gone dry again.

"Three more stops. You survived the Havelock Country Jamboree, you can survive this."

Allie. The babies. *Sing it* exactly *the same*. This was not the time to explore jazz. Conception. Birth. Conception. Birth. Conception. Birth. *Hold the note*. Edward and Evan.

More giggling as twins three and four joined the circle.

Another bottle of water waited, but she dropped it, flung back into the oaks by David's power.

"Asshole!" Breathing had started to hurt and her jeans were sliding off her hips, making the walk back to the familiar trees even more uncomfortable. "Two more."

Twins five and six followed their brothers into the circle.

The giggling had started to get to her. She'd never giggled. Allie'd never . . . actually, Allie had giggled. This time she hung onto the bottle. Would leaving out a fucking muffin have killed her?

Allie. The babies. Conception. Birth. Conception. Birth. Conception. Birth. Hold the note. Edward and Evan. Three and Four. Five and six. A little further.

She pushed beyond the surge of power, stretching herself past the point of pain. The ritual ended. Time passed although she had no idea how much time, could have been days, could have been hours, and she fell out of the Wood onto her knees, gasping for breath.

"Hello, Charlie." He had his father's dark hair and his mother's gray eyes. At fifteen, he was still all elbows and knees and nose, but his shoulders were broad under a T-shirt advertising a band she didn't recognize and his smile had layers she couldn't begin to parse. "We gotta boot. Mom suspects something's up."

Charlie blinked. His voice held no layers at all. It just was. The way the wind was. Deeper than she'd expected and resonant. The hair lifted off the back of her neck.

Allie's youngest shifted his grip on two worn and ugly bears and stepped forward, holding out a hand.

He didn't lift her effortlessly to her feet, but it was close—although Charlie wasn't sure if that was her or him. She felt liked she'd been cored, like she'd given so much to the final song there was nothing left of her. Certain a strong breeze would blow her away, she clung to his hand a moment longer. His palm was warm and a little damp. His fingers had familiar calluses. "Guitar?" she rasped, spat out a mouthful of blood, and ticked *gargle glass* off her bucket list.

"Bouzouki." When her brows went up, he grinned. "Who lies about a bouzouki?"

"People trying . . ." She sucked air in through her nose and expelled words with the breath. ". . . to get . . . on a plane."

"Never been on one."

Not, *never flown*, Charlie noted and closed her teeth on a question about Jack—which conveniently kept her from biting her tongue when her knees buckled.

"You don't look years younger than the you I know," he pointed out as he caught her. "You look terrible."

"Bite me."

"See, that's why you're my favorite cousin. You're never all excited and in my face about that seventh son of a seventh son of a seventh son of a Gale thing. Well, not until this morning's little talk."

"Little?"

"You need me to come back to the past with you—this you—to stop an asteroid from wiping out civilization."

That *was* little, Charlie admitted. Short and sweet. And then she processed what he'd said.

"Charlie?" Shifting his grip to accommodate the guitar, he stopped her collapse although her weight dragged the two of them around in a half circle.

"It worked."

"Duh."

He'd got that from her. Or Jack. Probably Jack, she'd mostly stopped saying it.

"But you can't bring me home again. Here again." He huffed out a laughed. "After you take me back there," he said, and Charlie could hear the care he used to choose his words, "you can't bring me back here."

"Say what?"

"You haven't tried it yet, so you wouldn't know, but my you has and she says it can't be done."

"Got here . . . once . . ." But not singing one song to cover births and conceptions and rituals while playing another to keep him with her. She—his she, future her—had a point. "I could . . . drop you."

"Yup. Anywhere." He grinned.

"You'd . . ."

"Give up the weight of family expectation about what it means to be the seventh son of a seventh son of a seventh son of a Gale for a chance to meet those expectations and actually get to live a life?" Rearranging her weight on his arm, he met her gaze. His eyes looked older, a lot older, than his fifteen years. "I'm all over that."

Charlie knew something about the weight of family expectations. Somehow, she found the strength for a smile. Given the blood she could taste on her teeth, she doubted it was reassuring.

"And it's not like I'll even have to miss the family, right? I'm going back to them."

"You grew up . . . with yourself?"

"That would be weird." He thought about it for a moment. "I never got to go to Ontario. I bet I'm there. I don't think Mom knows what happened, but now I'm gone . . ." The glee in his voice was entirely fifteen. ". . . that me can come out and keep her from killing you."

"Yay." Feeling a little stronger, Charlie staggered back a step, standing on her own. "You've been . . ."

"Trained? For world saving? I'm all about world saving." This grin reminded her of his grandmother Mary. "Just didn't know it came with time travel. That's sharp. I've been . . ." His eyes darkened and Charlie tried unsuccessfully to focus on the glimpse of horn here, there, and all over the shimmer of air above his head. "Mom just told Auntie Bea where I am and Auntie Bea's minutes from the park."

"Eavesdropping?"

"You never complained before." He frowned and she saw his father in the bend of his brows. "Or then. I guess. Anyway, we've got to be gone when Auntie Bea gets here."

Charlie was all for that. "Taking the bears?"

"No, I only brought them because you said you were aiming for them."

Not literally. Not that it mattered.

"Edward'll kill me if anything happens to them." He dropped to one knee and set them on a flat rock. For moment, he went completely still and Charlie heard good-bye in his silence.

Of course, if *she* heard good-bye . . .

Hoofbeats.

"David!"

They said it together, then his hand was in hers. "Charlie . . ."

"Okay. Hang on." One more song, that was all she needed. One more song to get them into the Wood where as long as she could maintain her grip, he'd snap back with her to where he was needed. One more . . .

Her background band, notably absent in her previous moments out of the Wood, struck up "Climb Every Mountain." Because an elderly show tune was exactly what she needed. She'd barely finished the derisive snort when the von Trapps gave way to "Everybody Say Yeah" from *Kinky Boots*.

"Better."

"Charlie?"

"Not talking . . . to you, kid." She tugged his hand up onto her shoulder and released him. She didn't need to sing them home, home was easy, she just needed to get him into the Wood and hang on. She flexed stiff fingers, dug the pick from her pocket . . . "Move with me." . . . and took them into the Wood on the opening chords of "Carry On My Wayward Son."

She expected him to be heavy. Jack was impossible. But the seventh son of a seventh son of a seventh son of a Gale was impossibly light. One hand gripping her shoulder, he walked into the Wood like he'd been waiting to step across the border all his life. No sorrow. No regret. Pure anticipation.

Classic rock for the win.

Except . . .

It seemed far too easy.

His grip tightened and in the moment before he let go, Charlie realized the power behind her was to the power in front of her as Miley Cyrus was to Janis Joplin.

She stumbled forward, stumbled *away*, and turned in time to see him change.

The antlers rising from his brow touched the sky. His shoulders grew broader. His skin a little darker. His clothing . . . gone. His eyes darkened as she watched until they were black from rim to rim.

She could see herself in his eyes. All of herself. All her strengths. All her faults. A glimmer of gold . . . He shook his head, a familiar Gale-boy motion to settle the horn, and broke the line of sight, giving Charlie a chance to jerk free. He hadn't captured her attention on purpose, not that intent would have mattered after she was lost.

She wondered for a moment why it was so quiet, then she realized it wasn't. Everything in the Wood, everything including Charlotte Marie Gale, was singing, for variable definitions of the word singing, the exact same song.

His Song.

Turned out that under the right circumstances, the seventh son of a seventh son of a seventh son of a Gale was a god.

"Get out of the Wood, Charlotte." Auntie Ruby stepped out of the shadows under the distant oaks. "Now."

Except distant seemed to be right there and . . . "You're dead." Charlie dodged the ghost's grasp, and kept staggering to the right, too exhausted to stop. "Pretty sure . . . don't have to listen to you . . . after death."

"We don't have time for this, Charlotte."

Her voice stabbed through his Song. Like drunks talking about the football game on the TV behind the bar, breaking up the color commentary. Auntie Ruby had carried auntie-knows-best into her afterlife. Auntie Ruby needed to shut up.

"Charlotte!"

"Not listening." Not to the dead. That's what they wanted, a semblance of life. For an auntie that meant being obeyed.

"You have to go!"

"*You* have to . . ." A pause while she unstuck her tongue from the roof of her mouth. ". . . go. You have to . . ." She'd spun to face him again.

He smiled. It was Allie's smile. Except more. Way more.

The Wood began to change. The perpetual late summer became fall.

Perpetual. Charlie's hands tightened on her guitar. *I don't think that means what you think it means.*

Fall became winter. Winter became spring. Summer returned for a heartbeat. The seasons passed. Years passed. Rowan berries ripened and fell. Blossomed. Ripened. Fell again. And again. Charlie locked her eyes on him because he didn't change and he had Allie's smile. She felt herself grow older and younger. Older and younger again. Felt blood on the inside of her thighs. Felt herself stretch to touch infinity. Snap back with such force she turned inside out and touched the beginning at the other end of all things.

Then it was spring again and the Wood held the familiar promise of May ritual. When he laughed, she glanced down and realized there was more than one type of wood in the Wood.

"Charlotte!" Auntie Ruby had shed the weight of age and settled somewhere between fifteen and ninety. Or on all the years between fifteen and ninety. At once. Her hair was Gale-girl blonde, her eyes both Gale-girl gray and auntie dark. Her body a double handful of dimpled curves over a core of strength. Her grip on Charlie's bicep was impressive for a dead woman.

"You shouldn't be able to do that," Charlie pointed out, sucking air through her teeth, but keeping her eyes on the prize. "Also, ow."

"And you shouldn't have been here for that. You never listen!"

"I listen." Although all she could hear was his invitation. "And, again, ow! Get your fingernails out of my arm!" He flexed his shoulders and Charlie drew her tongue over her lower lip. It no longer felt cracked and bloody. "Let go."

"No. This is why I'm here. This is why I needed the time you gave me. To keep you from doing something *stupid*."

"Something stupid?" The weight of the word actually pulled Charlie's head around.

"Fine. Something else stupid. He's not a god, Charlotte," Auntie Ruby sighed. "He's *the* god. Our god."

Charlie could hear the truth in her voice. "Our . . . the first? The walk in the woods, feeling horny god?" Who now waited for her across a very small clearing. Sliding the strap off her shoulder, she lowered her guitar carefully down onto the tender shoots of new grass. "That's impossible."

"You sang your way into a future that didn't exist until you sang your way into it. I don't think you get to say what's impossible."

She could get her jacket and shirt only as far down her left arm as Auntie Ruby's grip. Whatever. Belt buckle. Button. Although her jeans were so loose she could probably slide them off her hips without undoing them.

"I said, no!"

"And again, ow!"

"Just so we're clear on this, Charlotte," Auntie Ruby sighed, releasing her, "I'm doing this for you."

Before Charlie could force aching muscles to move, Auntie Ruby ran past, darting through the beeches, sunlight and shadow flickering over curves and dimples. Tempting enough, Charlie nearly followed.

He snorted, tossed his head, and took up the chase, bare feet striking the grass like hooves.

Hooves. David. Allie! "Wait!" At some point during the years while the Wood changed and her with it, her throat had healed. Her voice was her own again. Whether she had the power to stop him, or he felt he owed her because she'd brought him to their beginning, she neither knew nor cared. The point was, he stopped and turned. Charlie dug her boots into the soil and kept her eyes locked on his face, resisting the pull. The want. The need. "You have to stop the asteroid!"

"No, I don't." He grinned and she saw the teenage boy laid over the god. Saw Evan dunking a building block into his oatmeal. Edmund throwing a stuffed dragon across the room. Allie pushing a piece of strawberry pie across the table. Aunt Mary. Auntie Jane. Uncle Edward back before the Hunt. Saw every Gale, ever. "Think, Charlie," he said as she blinked the layers of images away. "Who trained the me that was? Who is the only sorcerer the aunties have allowed to live?"

Who had gone to the Courts to learn.

Jack. In the right kind of love story, it would have been easier now for Charlie to resist, but they'd never had the right kind of love story. "I can't move Jack through the Wood."

He winked and waved a hand. She tried not to think about how it would feel against her body. "Things have changed."

The god was back in the Wood.

Charlie'd always known the Wood was larger than the groves she passed through, the copses she lingered in, but now all boundaries had been removed and yet she could feel herself contain the whole.

"His immortal years will no longer weigh so heavily."

"I did say you shouldn't have been here," Auntie Ruby muttered, tucking herself under the god's arm and rubbing against him like a pink-and-gold cat.

"So, Jack?"

He nodded and Charlie felt her heartbeat speed up at the movement of his horns. "Jack. Take the teacher, not the pupil."

She swallowed as his fingers trailed over Auntie Ruby's shoulder. "I have no idea where I am. I can't get from nowhere to there."

"You need my help, little singer?" Allie's son had faded back into the god. "You have it. For a kiss."

Before Charlie could step forward, and she knew herself well enough to know she was definitely going to step forward, Auntie Ruby reached up and pulled the hand on her shoulder lower, over the plump curve of breast, across a pebbled pink nipple.

This was not a game Gale girls lost.

He laughed, lifted her into his arms, and, as she wrapped her legs around his waist, said, "For a song then. Something I've never heard."

He was eternal, but he was also fifteen; there had to be a billion songs he'd never heard. Which to choose? How to choose?

"*Quickly*," he growled, "while this one leaves me sense enough remaining to help."

Charlie smiled, muscles unlocking across her back. As the god himself would say, *duh*. Every new performance of any song was a song no one had ever heard because between performances, the performer changed. Neither was the audience the same audience they'd been, although Charlie couldn't think of a time that'd been quite so obvious an observation. People used to recordings believed every piece of music had a definitive sound, its emotional context trapped in amber, a butterfly pinned to a board; beautiful, but dead. Live music was just that. Alive.

Charlie sang the song she knew best. She sang herself. She wasn't the Charlie he'd known growing up. She sang the reflection she'd seen in the god's eyes. Strengths. Weaknesses. Gale. Wild. Wanting. Having. Questioning.

Even Auntie Ruby stopped writhing to listen.

Charlie stepped out of the Wood.

Time had passed. Not seasons, not years; from the surrounding sounds, Charlie guessed hours. It had been early afternoon when she'd arrived to find the seventh son of a seventh son of a seventh son of a Gale waiting for her and it was almost dusk now.

"Hello, Charlie."

He looked more Fey than she'd ever seen him look. Like he had no place in a world with engines, electronics, and light beer. And she'd seen him fifty feet long, flying, and breathing fire, so that was saying something.

Her heart, apparently under the mistaken impression she'd suddenly become the heroine in a bad romantic comedy, began to beat faster.

"Jack."

He'd made his clothes from trees and grass. Charlie'd spent enough time with him to know if they were bought or magicked and the brown jeans and pale green T-shirt were definitely magicked. And subtly wrong. The T-shirt had no bindings at collar and sleeve, the jeans had no seams or fly. He still tucked left, but then right-handed men . . . and Dragon Princes, usually did. He wore no shoes at all in spite of a distinct chill and damp grass. Although, Jack had always run warm.

Warm. She could hear hysteria bubbling up through the experiences of the last day. Year. Century. Centuries? *Time is fluid. Time spent recreating the birth of your history could easily drip.* She bit back the snicker, dried her palms on her thighs, rubbed them again, surprised by how little thigh there was, and pulled herself together to find Jack staring at her like he'd forgotten what she looked like and needed to be reminded. So she stared back. The last time she'd seen him he was "You Suffer," a song over in 1.316 seconds, and now he was Rush's "2112" and 20.33 minutes long. Relatively. He wasn't a teenager; he was a man. Tall. Large. Muscular. His hair curled against his shoulders, a paler gold than she remembered. A thin, white vertical scar split his left cheek starting below the center of his eye and ending at the angle of his jaw. Scales ran up and down his forearms like golden LEDs. His form had always slipped when he was nervous.

Golden brows dipped in. "You're too thin."

"I am?" She shifted inside the loose folds of her clothing. "Yeah, well, it took a while to get here."

The smile was familiar and not. Bigger, like everything else about him and curving around memories she hadn't shared. "Tell me about it."

She could hear echoes of another world in his voice. "You're not the Jack who taught Allie's son."

"No. I'm the Jack who will teach him."

"In the future?"

"In the past."

"Oh, for fucksake." The click as understanding dawned was nearly audible. "You stayed at the Courts, didn't you?" She wanted to pace but couldn't look away in case he disappeared again. "You lived there for all the years I sang my way through and only just emerged like a big scaly, sorcerous butterfly to be taken back to when you left to live those years again."

"What?"

"You know what I meant!" Because Jack would.

And he did. "I'm immortal, Charlie." He spread his hands, and she tried not to think about how they'd feel against her body. Remembered having the exact same thought in the Wood. Wondered if there were lingering effects of time spent with a god or if she was actually feeling it for this Jack who wasn't her Jack. This Jack, who she didn't know. "I missed you," he continued quietly. "Not every minute, most of the minutes were pretty distracting actually . . ."

Okay, now she could hear her Jack.

". . . but it was only twenty years."

"Only twenty years."

Her Jack would have shrugged. New Jack moved both shoulders in a minimal, graceful arc that mimicked the memory of a shrug. "Give or take. How many years did you live getting here?" he asked.

"Time doesn't pass in the Wood. Didn't. And that's not the point." Twenty years. No wonder he'd forgotten how to dress. And shrug. She reached up, holy crap he'd gotten big, and touched the scar.

He wrapped his hand around hers. When she flinched, a touch of cool spread over her skin and the burn faded. "I didn't pay in pain, Charlie. I'll take my younger self to the UnderRealm, to the Courts, and they'll teach me because I ask them to. I learned things while I was there that they don't want spread around."

"But you won't learn it if they don't teach you."

"But I have learned it, so they did teach me."

"So you and I, this you and I, were there when I jumped ahead to bring back the seventh son of yadda yadda and brought you instead?"

"Yes."

"We made ourselves scarce so we wouldn't run into me."

"Yes."

"But you ran into you."

"Dragon Lord. We don't mind."

"Okay." They were giant, warm-blooded lizards who flew, breathed fire, and turned into reasonable approximations of human beings; being able to look themselves in the eyes wasn't even on the list of the strangest things about them. "And if I don't take you back?"

"But you do. Because I spoke to me, remember?"

"Trying not to." She wrapped her fingers around his and tugged on his hand. "I'm feeling a bit predestined here, but let's go."

"This is the part I don't get," he began matching her stride, "because you've never been able to . . ."

Charlie hummed a D, for Dragon, and walked them both into the Wood.

". . . and I'm larger now," he finished thoughtfully. "This isn't what I expected."

It was definitively spring in the Wood, where definitively brought to mind Jonathan Coulton's "First of May." *And speaking of public sex* . . . Without thinking it through, she'd brought Jack to the beech grove where she'd left Auntie Ruby and the god. While one beech grove looked pretty much like another, she recognized it because her guitar—left behind in the heat of the moment—had taken root and grown into a small tree laden with large pendulous yellow blossoms, filling the air with the scent of spilled beer.

"There've been some recent changes."

His nostrils flared. "I smell . . ."

"That's the tree."

"I don't mean the beer. We're not alone here. Should we . . ."

Charlie tightened her grip on his hand, and tugged him back beside her when he took a step toward the trees. "No, we really shouldn't."

"Ah." Grinning, he met her gaze. "I thought it smelled like family. Not a sing-along then?"

"No." For the two years Jack had been an adult, Charlie hadn't sung along in ritual. As it were. There'd been family enough at other times that she hadn't missed it, or she hadn't thought she'd missed it, or she'd been lying to herself the entire time. When she pressed her free hand to Jack's very broad chest, his eyes flared gold and a small puff of smoke billowed out of his nose as if he hadn't been able to hold it back. "Jack?"

"It's me."

It wasn't. But it was. "It may take . . ."

"Immortal. I've got time." The smoke puffed out again, and he swallowed.

Unless his tells had changed, he was about to ask her a question he wasn't sure he wanted to know the answer to. She took a deep breath of her own. "Charlie, what happened to the seventh son of a seventh son of a seventh son of a Gale?"

Not the question she'd expected. Although not entirely surprising. "Long story."

The underbrush rustled. Auntie Ruby giggled.

"Okay, short story," Charlie amended. "I'll tell you later."

The moment they stepped out of the willows on the riverbank across from the zoo, Charlie's phone rang.

Jack flinched and muttered, "Didn't miss that."

"Auntie Jane," Charlie told him, glancing at the screen. She tossed the phone over her shoulder into the river. "Don't want to know." Didn't want to discuss it. Not until all the loose ends had been neatly tied and clipped. "So this is the day Jack . . . you, disappeared. I woke up and you were gone."

He hadn't gone yet. She could feel him . . . them . . . in the part of her heart that was his . . . theirs. It made the memory of the loss all the more painful.

"Ow."

Given the muscle sheathing his arm, no way her punch could have hurt him. "So, go." It seemed Singing them out of the Wood had roughed up her throat again. And made her eyes water. "Convince yourself to go back to the UnderRealm and learn from the Courts for twenty years."

"Charlie."

She was not going to look at him. He could wait for the rest of his immortal life. It looked like that clump of goldenrod wasn't quite dead. *Way to hang on there, goldenrod.*

"I have to go because I've already gone. *He* has to go. I don't intend to ever leave you again."

"You're leaving me right now," she muttered, actually heard herself, and winced. Heat blooming across her cheeks and up her ears, she turned to face him. "Sorry. That was self-indulgent at best and petulant at worst."

"What's the difference?"

"Only one of them rhymes with flatulent, but the point is, it's not about me." She ran her hand back through her hair and frowned at the amount the breeze gathered up and took away. A quick charm and individual hairs flared in the air like a flock of fireflies—it wasn't a good idea to leave body bits lying around. "Because if it was about me," she continued as the ash drifted to the ground, "it'd be about a grilled cheese sandwich and a plate of sweet potato fries. Go. Tell yourself what you have to in order to make this work."

"Are we okay?"

"You and me?"

He cocked his head, a dragon movement translated to skin. "I don't see another you and me standing here, do you?"

"We're . . . Jesus, Jack, don't you think *are we okay* is a little premature? We've been apart for twenty years, we're strangers."

"Look in my eyes and tell me that."

"Seriously?"

His hands completely engulfed her shoulders. Charlie wasn't used to feeling petite. It was strange although not entirely unpleasant. "Look in my eyes and tell me we're strangers."

Closer to his pupils, his eyes were a lighter amber although that might've been only the contrast between the amber and the black. His lashes were as long and thick as she remembered, tipped with gold. In them, she could see the absolute certainty that they were meant to be together. In spite of that, they were not the eyes of a seventeen year old. There were faint lines at the corners, and she could see the top point of the scar. He had history on his face they hadn't shared. "Eye-to-eye, Jack, we're strangers." Before he could speak, she pressed her palm against his chest and nearly got distracted by the muscle. The steady beat that matched her own pulled her back. "Heart-to-heart, though, we're okay."

He wrapped his hand around hers, bent his head, and kissed her finger-tips. Twenty years in the Courts, she reminded herself as he backed up and changed. What else had they taught him?

Except for the mustaches which were now a good meter and a half long and curled at the ends, his dragon form had changed less visibly than skin. He was still enormous, golden, and powerful—only more so. "While I'm there, I'll stop the petty mischief the Courts have been pulling in the MidRealm."

"It stopped when Jack, young you, disappeared."

A great many teeth flashed. "I know."

Of course he did. That was when he'd been there. In the Courts. With his younger self. "So, after . . ."

Wings spread, he paused.

". . . where do we meet?"

"I'll find you. I can *always* find you."

"That'd be kind of stalkery if you weren't a big golden dragon," she muttered, watching him fly away. Rising up over Calgary. Growing smaller in the distance. She bit her lip until it bled because if she called him back, he'd come.

Heart-to-heart, they were the kind of love song that had drunks crying into their beer.

Charlie considered making the ten-minute walk to the Emporium and grabbing some food, but couldn't remember if she was already there. Didn't matter, she had an errand of her own to run and now, or whenever she currently was, was as good a time as any.

Spring continued to bust out all over the Wood, but at least the giggling had stopped.

Jack watched his younger self rise up into the air in answer to the perceived threat of a passing dragon and remembered being that young. That intense. That certain he'd do anything, sacrifice anything to save the world. Not for the world's sake, but for Charlie. He'd been appallingly easy to manipulate.

Twenty years without her.

Twenty years meant nothing to an immortal, his younger self had told her that over and over, but he'd only lived for seventeen years when he made the choice.

Twenty years had lasted a lifetime.

He pivoted on one wing and headed into the sun, his younger self straining to keep up.

He could still feel the press of Charlie's hand against his chest, even though it had pressed skin not scales.

His younger self hadn't asked him, wouldn't think to ask him, if it would be worth it.

They both knew the answer.

"What the hell have you done to yourself?" Auntie Catherine grabbed Charlie's arm and dragged her into her hotel room.

"I haven't . . ." Charlie stumbled as she was spun around to face a full-length mirror.

"How much weight have you lost?"

It took her a moment to realize it wasn't a magic mirror. Charlie frowned and her reflection frowned with her. She looked like a bobble head, her skull out of proportion, her teeth too big for her face. Fingers shaking, she unzipped her jacket and tugged up her T-shirt. Her ribs looked like a xylophone—two, actually, one on each side—her breasts were hanging loose in the cups of her bra, and she had no idea how her jeans continued to defy gravity given the absence of anything resembling hips. Hip bones, yes. Hips, no. "Like the song says," she sighed, "no one gets to live consequence free."

"And what song might that be, Charlotte."

"Not important, and I'm paraphrasing anyway." As the T-shirt billowed down into place, she stepped out of the mirror's line of sight and dropped down into the desk chair. And swore.

"Of course it hurts." Auntie Catherine passed her a pillow. "You have no meat on your ass. You have seconds to convince me not to call Alysha."

"She's taking your calls now?"

"Charlotte."

"It's a long story. Or it will be." Charlie made grabby hands at the cup of coffee Auntie Catherine had just poured, took a long grateful swallow, and started at the beginning. Reconsidered and jumped ahead to Jack disappearing. Paused while Auntie Catherine ordered food.

"I'm not hungry."

"You've forgotten that you're hungry. Considering how you look, your brain has begun to interpret hunger as the normal way you feel. Go on."

So she continued and got through babies, ritual, and taking the seventh son of a seventh son of a seventh son of a Gale into the Wood before Auntie Catherine stopped her again.

"You nearly killed yourself to discover Allie and Graham's youngest becomes the god who begat the Gales?"

"Seriously, who says begat?"

"Charlotte."

"That's what it sounds like."

Auntie Catherine crossed her legs, studied her pedicure, and said, "I'm less surprised than I suspect I should be. Go on."

Going on meant Jack. What Jack had done. What Jack was doing. What needed to be done. Charlie got through it, set her empty mug down on the desk, and went into her big finish. "So you need to call me, the me of now and not the me that's here, and tell me, her, you've Seen two bears that look like . . ."

The knock on the door was professionally diffident, but the call of *room service* impossible to ignore.

The smell of the carrot-and-ginger soup pulled Charlie up out of the chair before the cart was entirely in the room. Unable to get around Auntie Catherine to the soup, she ducked under her arm, snatched up a warm cheese bun, and devoured half in one bite.

"If you choke, I won't save you," Auntie Catherine pointed out. "Slow down."

"Ms. Gale." He was an older man, in his forties Charlie guessed, and he held out a bulging manila envelope. "This arrived at the hotel for a Ms. Charlotte Gale in the care of Ms. Catherine Gale and your room number. Front desk had me bring it up."

"My phone." Charlie explained after he left, less well tipped than usual, she suspected, if both his and Auntie Catherine's expressions were anything to go by. "I threw it in the river back in Calgary, but it has a shot of the bears on it."

"The bears I need to call and tell you I've Seen?"

"That's right." She passed it over.

"Those are memorably ugly bears."

"Aren't they. You've Seen them after they've been worn out being held by a baby. A single baby. Not twins."

"And you're telling me this why?"

"Because you actually having that vision, the exact vision I needed, when I needed it, was too much of a coincidence. Yay, time travel."

"This will never work, Charlotte."

"It already has worked." Tongue half out to lick cheesy grease off her fingers, Charlie frowned. "It has to be the bears, doesn't it? Because if you tell me you've Seen me and older Jack, I might miss the 'hi I'll be your god tonight' part of the program."

Auntie Catherine rolled her eyes and passed her a napkin.

Charlie stepped out of the Wood about two meters from Jack's gate. She watched him emerge, watched him change, and watched reluctantly as he clothed himself in gray and purple using stone and the last wild asters of fall. She felt his heart beat faster when he spotted her and hers sped up to match.

"It's done," he said. "They'll teach me, and they'll make a few trips into the MidRealm to fix some of what they've broken."

"The ass head?"

With the temperature below freezing, the cloud Jack snorted was half smoke, half water vapor. "It took convincing, he was zero for sixteen on free throws, but, yes, the ass head goes. Once things have been put right, they'll stay home. And speaking of home, I really miss Auntie Mary's apple pie."

"It's the wear clean underwear charm, adds a certain piquant flavor."

Charlie wasn't sure if she'd moved or he had, but they were standing so close together the cool October air between them had begun to warm. If she had to trade this Jack for the Jack she sat with on the roof . . . "Damn it! I have to take you further back. Allie has to see you flying over the store."

"Why . . ."

"Doesn't matter. You've already done it."

His nostrils flared as they went through the Wood, but she kept him moving.

After dropping him off in the past, Charlie stepped back in and immediately back out again three days later to stand in front of the Emporium and think *"Remember the bears, Charlie."* at Dan. She was there, in the store, watching Dan do yoyo tricks. If she could've come up with a way to make things easier on herself, on Jack, she'd have thought that also, but she hadn't, so she couldn't. Then back in the Wood and out to pick Jack up by Drumheller where he waited, lounging on the same ridge she'd found him on once before.

Breathing heavily after the climb, she sagged against his side.

"You need to regain your strength."

"Tell me about it."

"You asked a great deal of yourself."

"I had no idea what I was asking of myself."

"You could've quit once you realized."

"Forty or four, you still do the show." She toppled over when he changed, but he caught her before she hit the ground. "Good reflexes."

"I will never let you fall."

There were a number of things she thought of replying, but after twenty years navigating the Courts, she figured he was allowed a few definitive prince-like statements. She'd have plenty of time to break him of the habit.

"Charlie?"

"Yeah?"

"That's everything, right?"

"Yeah." He hadn't bothered to dress. A patch of scales glittered in the center of his chest and he rippled when he breathed. He leaned in. She leaned in. Time to see if they had a future . . .

She jerked back. "Oh, crap!"

"And then Jack blew up the asteroid. Are you going to eat that?"

"And then Jack blew up the asteroid?" Allie glared at Charlie as Graham pushed his plate across the table. "We're going to need a little more than that."

Charlie swallowed a mouthful of pie, sighed, and dug her fork into Graham's untouched piece as she said, "It seems pretty self-explanatory to me."

"Exploded?"

"First 2007 AG5, then Armageddon."

Kiren could almost hear Dr. Grayson thinking during the lengthening pause. "Both of them?" he asked finally.

"Both of them," she confirmed. "Obliterated."

"I'm not sure obliterated is a scientifically valid observation, Dr. Mehta."

"Perhaps not, but it's accurate. We're still running the numbers . . ." Phone tucked against her shoulder, Kiren paused to accept a printout from one of the astrogeologists down the hall, both of them ignoring how her hands were shaking. ". . . but it looks like there isn't a piece left out there as big as a basketball."

"How?"

"No idea. We're showing a massive, unidentifiable energy spike, and then double booms."

"The Russians? The Japanese? China?"

"Best point of origin we've got, given that we're working around massive amounts of interference from the Aurora Borealis, is somewhere in the upper atmosphere over Alberta."

"Canada?" Kiren pretended not to hear Dr. Grayson's giggle. It was as much relief as disbelief, and it wasn't as if she hadn't made a few weird sounds herself. "The Canadians don't have that kind of tech. The Canadians are flying fifty-year-old helicopters."

And keeping them in the air, Kiren added silently. Points for both engineering and ingenuity.

"My money's on the Chinese," Dr. Grayson continued. "Or the SpaceX guys. Who knows what they're up to lately, right? Okay." He took a deep breath, entirely audible over the phone. "Okay. I'll inform the director. I want everything you've got sent to my desk ten minutes ago. Good work, Dr. Mehta, thank you."

Kiren sent the file as he hung up. Taking a deep breath of her own, she pulled her cell phone out of her desk drawer and flipped through the contact numbers, pausing to stare at one she'd never called. A number with no name, automatically added at 7:43 AM after the night Charlie Gale had spent on her couch. A night she hadn't expected to remember.

Personally, she wouldn't count the Canadians out.

Finger poised over the number, she reconsidered. There was another call she had to make first.

"Come on, really . . . What part of fully operational Dragon Prince slash sorcerer are you not understanding here?" Charlie pushed her empty plate away, angled her chair a little closer to Jack's, and glanced around the table.

As accustomed as the family was to what others might term unusual, the appearance of the new, older Jack had been unexpected. Like the Maple Leafs winning the Stanley Cup unexpected—not impossible but very, very unlikely. Joe had nearly dropped to his knees and had lost control of his glamour entirely. If Graham had been able to antler up, he would have—a random passerby on the street could've sensed the metaphysical attempt. Edward and Evan had regarded new Jack suspiciously until he changed, then they'd thrown themselves under his wings and into the loops of his tail. Their reaction had gone a long way to defining Allie's, who then considered herself free to have a terrifying freakout about Charlie's weight loss. Although she'd moved to support Joe, Auntie Gwen had been suspiciously quiet.

She'd remained quiet all the way through the severely edited version of Charlie's trip to the future—seventh sons, gods, and Auntie Ruby redacted. Allie, Graham, and even Joe had interrupted, but Auntie Gwen hadn't said a word.

"Twenty years of training in sorcery."

Until now, Charlie amended.

Hands flat on the table, Auntie Gwen turned a black-on-black gaze toward Jack. "We do not, as a family, allow sorcerers to live. The deal, when we allowed you to remain, was that the moment you stopped using sorcery and became a sorcerer, we would hunt you down like any other Gale male."

Jack's eyes remained amber, as Human seeming as they ever got. "And you, all twelve of you, meant it sincerely, but it was a justification without substance. I've been a sorcerer, albeit untrained, since I first arrived."

"True enough."

"Say what?" Charlie regarded Auntie Gwen's smile and the whites of her eyes with suspicion.

"He's a Dragon Prince and a Gale, Charlotte. That he is also a sorcerer should be the least of our concerns."

"So that whole we do not as a family allow sorcerers to live?"

"We don't. But times change and I'm very much looking forward to *discussing* the matter of him saving the world with Bea." Her emphasis suggested that by discussion she meant baked goods at twenty paces.

"Yeah, well, Auntie Bea and I need to work some things out, but I'm not so much worried about her as I am about Auntie Jane. The family response to sorcerers is not a rhetorical response, and you can say times change until you're blue in the face, but Auntie Jane . . ." Had given her a humbug. One linty candy tossed on the scale shouldn't balance Jack's safety, but Charlie suspected it did. Would.

"Jane . . ." Auntie Gwen picked Evan's shoe out of the butter and handed it to Allie, allowing the name to hang in the air much the way the asteroid had.

Interesting times ahead.

"Is there more pie in the fridge?"

"Gary, are you all right?"

He wrapped his arms around her and held her tight, murmuring "I'm fine," over and over into her hair.

"Okay." And after a minute. "You're squashing me."

"Sorry." He took a minute to breath before saying, "That was Kiren."

"Is *she* all right?"

"She's good. Everything's good."

"Okay," Sheryl said again. Gary could tell she had a million questions, and he'd never loved her more when she didn't ask any of them. "I thought you were dealing with the band's sudden lack of a guitarist."

"Right." They'd talk later. About leaving home and the world not ending and following dreams regardless. He was amazed at how steady his finger remained as he searched his contact list.

Charlie hung up the phone as Auntie Gwen came out onto the roof. She shook her head at Jack, and he went back to watching the cars pass down below on the street. "If that's a bowl of soup . . ."

"Allie's worried about you. Are you surprised?"

"No. But I'm full." Her belly curved out between the prominent bones of her hips and shifted uncomfortably as she took the bowl. "Over full." Without taking her eyes off Auntie Gwen, she held it out to the right and felt Jack take it from her.

"So, you two are together?"

Charlie thought about playing dumb as to the meaning of together, but as the entire family would have an opinion they'd happily share, she might as well get one of them out of the way. "Not yet. We thought we'd get to know each other first—all Jack knows is a memory and I don't know him, this him, at all. People change in twenty years."

Jack had turned and become a warm presence against her side. "Even dragons change," he said. "Though slowly."

"Things have changed." He'd winked when he said it.

What the hell had that meant? Not that the Wood had changed. That was an observation too obvious even for a god. Why wouldn't his immortal years weigh so heavily?

". . . old?"

"What?"

Auntie Gwen rolled her eyes as Charlie focused. "I asked, how old is he?"

"How old is Jack?"

"You say he was in the Courts for twenty years and you started out thirteen years older. Thirteen from twenty is seven. But as I doubt it's exactly seven, is it seven years minus a month or two or seven years plus a month or two."

"We saved the world." More a whine than a declaration, the pitch drove the pigeons off the edge of the roof. The last thing Charlie'd expected was to be blindsided by the one rule, the only rule she wouldn't break.

"Do the math, Charlotte."

"Oh for . . . fine. Thirty-two weeks for twins three and four . . ."

"Thirty-one and three days," Auntie Gwen corrected.

"Two years before the next conception . . ."

"Two years, three months, fourteen days."

"Hours and minutes?" Charlie snapped.

Auntie Gwen smiled. "If you want. Shall we continue?"

Fortunately, dragons were good at math.

"Happy?" Charlie muttered when they were done.

"Actually, yes." Auntie Gwen cupped the side of her face and kissed her cheek then did the same to Jack. "You two are good for each other. And I never liked it that the Wild Powers were expected to be alone. Gales need family. If Catherine had someone to run Wild with, she'd be less Machiavellian."

"You sure about that?"

"Not really, no."

Charlie took a deep breath when Auntie Gwen left the roof, turned, and beat her head against the solid mass of Jack's shoulder half a dozen times. She released him reluctantly when he moved away but smiled when she realized why he'd needed the room.

"You're magnificent, you know that, right? All gleamy gold and muscle and Wild Power barely contained by scales and I should just shut up now." She'd seen him larger out at Drumheller, but here on the roof he was the bass line that kept the song on course. The skirl of pipes at the start of every parade. A Howard Shore theme.

He spread his wings and dipped his head back under the curve so he could meet her gaze. "Fly with me?"

A dozen responses considered and discarded, Charlie settled on, "Yes."

"Yes?"

"Duh."

When dragons laughed, the world laughed with them. Or maybe, Charlie admitted, it was just her and Jack.

He adjusted his size as she straddled his neck until she felt as though she'd become a part of him and the anthem she could feel rising contained at least three verses she'd never be able to sing with children in the audience. Hidden within a glamour, Jack's wings cupped the air, the enormous muscles in his back and shoulders flexed, and they rose up over the city, circling around until their shadow raced along the road in front of the store.

The pigeons dove under the newspaper box, slowly enough Charlie suspected it was for old time's sake. She clung to the column of Jack's neck with both hands and reminded herself to breathe. In. Out. In.

It felt like . . .

It felt like flying.

He dipped one wing and circled the Calgary Tower. "Where to, Charlie?"

She sang a charm to keep her hair out of her eyes and laughed. "Everywhere! But first, let's go see a man about a bouzouki."